suicidal tendencies

THE SERIES IN CONTEMPORARY FICTION
David Milofsky, Editor

suicidal tendencies

stories by
t. alan broughton

CENTER FOR LITERARY PUBLISHING
& UNIVERSITY PRESS OF COLORADO
Fort Collins, Colorado

Copublished by the Center for Literary Publishing
and the University Press of Colorado.
Set in Garamond and Futura Light.
Jacket designed by Dan Pratt and Stephanie G'Schwind.
Printed in the United States of America by Thomson-Shore.

Library of Congress Cataloging-in-Publication Data

Broughton, T. Alan (Thomas Alan), 1936–
Suicidal tendencies : stories / by T. Alan Broughton.
    p. cm. — (The series in contemporary fiction)
    ISBN 1-885635-05-2 (hardcover : alk. paper)
    1. United States—Social life and customs—Fiction.
    2. Italy—Social life and customs—Fiction.
    3. Revolutionaries—Fiction. I. Title. II. Series.
        PS3552.R68138S85 2003
            813'.54—dc21
            2002155447

The paper used in this book meets the minimum
requirements of the American National Standard
for Information Sciences—Permanence of Paper
for Printed Library Materials, ANSI Z39.48-1984.

1   2   3   4   5   07   06   05   04   03

To Noni, Camm, and Nathaniel—
for your sustaining love and friendship

contents

acknowledgments

Stories in this collection have been published in the following places: "My Other Life," "The Wars I Missed," "Italian Autumn," and *"L' Americana"* in *Colorado Review;* "The Classicist" in *Georgia Review;* "Bill's Women" in *Green Mountains Review;* "Ashes" in *Sewanee Review* (also published in *O. Henry Prize Stories,* 1991); "The Terrorist" (as "The Masterpiece") in *Sonora Review;* "Leaving Home," "Spring Cleaning," and "The Burden of Light" in *Virginia Quarterly Review.*

"Leaving Home" and "The Wars I Missed" were both mentioned in *Best American Short Stories, 100 Distinguished Stories.*

I am grateful to David Milofsky for his generous editorial advice and support that helped these stories to reach their readers.

suicidal tendencies

ashes

When Damon White finished his second cup of coffee, he decided to go directly to his cabin rather than sit on the clubhouse porch and read his newspaper. He left the dining room without pausing to chat with any of the other members. Even though he had arrived two days earlier he had not relaxed, and often he found himself inattentive in casual conversations.

At the far end of the porch Harold Corvallis had set up his easel and was painting once again the graceful outlines of Noonmark. Damon paused with one hand on the railing of the steps. He felt his father's presence vividly. The Colonel was always present to Damon in a blurred manner, especially here where they had spent so much time and had been thrown so close together in those final years of his father's ill and querulous dependency. Damon had spent Augusts in the small cabin on the club grounds, pushing his father's wheelchair on its fixed rounds of porch or lobby, meals in the main dining room, walks along various pathways past tennis courts or bowling greens. Once when Damon's father asked Corvallis how he could bear to paint the same heap of rocks and trees so often, Harold had replied, "You wouldn't think it was wrong if I were Japanese." The Colonel had snapped, "The hell I wouldn't. We wouldn't have a Jap in this club." Damon's father had been in the Second World War and never forgave Japan. But he had not been a colonel at any time. Friends from his college days had started calling him that long before he ever donned a uniform. Augustus Hoar White had been assertive and demanding since his earliest days.

In his apartment in New York, Damon had decided that this should be his last summer at the club. The decision had seemed simple and necessary, but now that he was in his cabin again, back in the all-too-familiar surroundings, he was not certain he was emotionally ready to give the place up.

Such forms of ambivalence had always made his life difficult. "My son," his father had announced to the companion whom he had paid to accompany Damon one summer after his release from Payne-Whitney, "has always been weak when defending himself against his own feelings. The worst enemy"— and the Colonel had stared hard at the small bottle of Damon's pills—"is always the enemy within."

Colonel White's forte had been tennis, a devastating overhead smash that always raised a dust of lime on the line farthest away from his opponent, unless he chose to aim for the kneecaps. Damon had taken his childhood tennis lessons seriously, tried out for the team at Exeter, and from time to time stood on the opposite side of a net from the Colonel. But the further he advanced into adolescence, the more such contests were tainted with attempted parricide. Once he understood that, he blocked the sin with double faults and backhands soaring far beyond the baseline. "My boy," Colonel White said once to the Junior Singles champion at the end of the last August tournament Damon ever entered at the club, "has more talent than you, son. That's in his genes. But he never had the killer instinct."

Even walking through warm patches of sunlight to the cabin, Damon shuddered at the phrase, the way his father could make it sound like the last punch to the face of a defenseless Benny Paret. Was his lack derived from his mother's genes? He would never know for certain because she had disappeared before much more could be recorded in Damon's mind than gentle, thin-fingered hands, and a number of long necklaces with variegated beads that he loved to tangle his hands in. She died when he was six, leaving a vacancy that not even the most well-intentioned of his father's companions could begin to fill, and certainly not those other women who read or sang or scrubbed him into shape to face the evening meal. That was followed by brief after-dinner conversations with a father who used his hands so diligently at a place called "the office" that they could make only the most terse gestures at home—removing the stopper of a decanter, snipping the end of a cigar, ruffling the hair on the top of Damon's head before he was tucked in bed by Minnie or Evita or Peg, a gesture he felt in the roots beneath the scalp until sleep distanced him by one more night from the first six years of his life. If only he could once again hear his mother's voice, specific words, but memory was obdurate.

The maid had already tidied his bedroom, and what few books he had disarranged on the table the previous evening were neatly lined up. Damon stood in the living room, a rusticated square of stone and oak and doorways branching off to cedar-closeted bedrooms. The place was his in August by family rights. Damon's mother had been here too, introducing his memory to the resinous odors of old blankets, the chirping of tree frogs, the crickets' rasp.

He always showered after breakfast, and now he took off his clothes and folded them carefully. Habits. Rituals. When they were muddled, the mind too could become confused. Through the open window of his bedroom, he could hear the high, pulsing calls of the Morrison children taking turns swinging each other violently in the hammock. Damon sighed. He knew their play always ended in shouts and tears.

But he could not free himself from the memory of that summer after Payne-Whitney. "He's perfectly all right now," the Colonel had said to the young man across the luncheon table, a stranger to them both who had been recommended by the minister downtown to help keep an eye on Damon. "The problem never amounted to much anyway, did it, old boy?"

His father had tried not to believe in Damon's breakdown, but had relented enough subsequently to lapse into less stern expressions in his son's presence like "old boy" or once even "buddy" followed by a rough clasp on Damon's shoulder. Damon knew how extremely difficult such gestures were for the man to wrest from the grip of his ultimate belief that mental illness was merely submitting to frail tendencies any man should sternly subdue.

"It's really the pills we worry about now, eh, Damon? Tell him about the pills."

Damon turned to the young man's face, letting it remain blurred. He found it embarrassing that his father's voice carried to nearby tables.

"I take pills."

They waited. The young man stared at a triangular sandwich denuded of crusts and nestled in garnishing parsley. The Colonel's fingers drummed impatiently on the tabletop.

"For his nerves, you see. And they make him a bit groggy. Forgetful. Found him wandering up Noonmark yesterday. But on the trail at least. Do you play tennis or golf, Mr. Anthony?"

"No sir."

"Just as well. They tell me competition's not the thing for Damon right now. Well, it's up to you fellows. But I'd suggest fishing. Damon always liked that. Try the river. Do you like to fish, Mr. Anthony?"

6

"Yes sir."

"I suppose most of you fellows use worms. Can't use 'em in our stretch of the river, though."

"I tie flies, sir."

"Hell, Damon. Hear that? A real fisherman. Why don't you see who can get us the biggest brookie for dinner?"

Damon focused now on the young man's face, and for a moment he stared back. What Damon saw was pity, not merely purchased but genuine, that softening gaze a person turns on a cripple. But he was so used to seeing that expression in the past months as well as being talked about by others in his presence as if he were not there, that he merely reached up to make certain his bow tie had not twisted off line.

They began fishing below the dam at the Lower Lake, a place Damon had loved since childhood because he could stand on the high log bridge below it and look eye level along the surface of the lake's water. Today it was a calm sheet, bearing only minute glints of ripples, and the steeply wooded and rocky mountainsides seemed to be squeezing in slowly, extruding the water toward him and the frail white birches along the nearby banks. He became, in mid-bridge, the focus of the whole landscape, even of the sun directly above the cleft. As a child he had believed that one day if he touched the water it would become gold and all the evil persons would turn into stones hunched against the molten swirl.

"I caught one." The voice piped against the uneven slap of water falling over the log dam onto the boards below and the pools where fat, stocked trout nudged each other lazily to gulp at an abundance of drowning insects. Mr. Anthony was holding up a fish, finger hooked through a gill. "Come on. There's plenty."

On the bank Damon assembled his rod, gazed at the box of flies, and chose one he knew was inappropriate for the season.

By the time he had successfully crossed the slithery stones his companion had caught another and was stuffing it in his canvas creel.

"Jesus. I've always wanted to fish this river. Legally, I mean."

Damon spoke as little as possible because when he did, his tongue moved with swollen numbness. After the first few weeks in Payne-Whitney, when he had known and remembered nothing but a succession of days and nights in which the dead were alive and eager to talk, the living were sleepwalkers, beds grew straps to keep him there, and the sheets sometimes flapped ineffectually around him like the broken wings of a gull, Damon had become an expert practitioner of minimal discourse. This was a reversal for a man who had spent the previous eight years gabbing away each week on the radio as Uncle Ralph, the kindly, garrulous host of the children's program *Please Pretend*. The nod, the slight slant of head to right or left with eyes open or closed, the pursed lips of doubt, the bit lip and raised eyebrow were all he would share with Dr. Salvador for many a session of question and dumb show response.

"Would you mind," Damon said, choosing and laying down his monosyllables as if they had the ability of marbles to roll away, "if I go first down the stream to fish?"

"Suit yourself."

Until he was out of sight Damon paused to cast from time to time, making certain his fly landed on the bare backs of rocks. He did not blame the young man for his greed, in fact blessed it since that permitted his escape. Around the first bend, he took down his rod, clambered up the bank to the trail and began walking slowly downstream, through the quiet beaver meadows where he startled a solitary deer, past the falls where he paused on rocks close to the base to let spray scatter over his face and arms, walking on until the path left the brook, which cut more deeply into the gorge. On a high, slanting rock where the ancient hemlock and spruce clung to stone and shallow soil, he sat and stared down at white water and its distant thundering. When a white-throated sparrow began repeating its clear-toned intervals, he was certain he had never heard anything more perfect, and he wept.

"Well," the Colonel said when the largest trout was served up for dinner that night in a delicate sauce of butter and tarragon and parsley, its white flesh tinged toward pink, "I knew Mr. Anthony had to be a good fisherman, but I didn't expect him to skunk you, old boy," and then he laughed through a red face to show how his words were intended only as a joke.

Damon stepped out of the shower and burrowed his face in the white towel with the club monogram. His father, even in the city and ever since Damon could recall, had been in the habit of holding himself unflinchingly erect, on parade, beneath a cascade of absolutely cold water. Once as a child Damon had said admiringly, "I don't see how you can stand it." The Colonel had barked a laugh of pleasure, and henceforth Damon was permitted to watch his father take the shower. The Colonel's stern profile refused to grimace or mutter. The man did not curtail even one motion of soaping and rinsing. When he was seven Damon had tried it, held still with gritted teeth and nails cutting into his palms, until, pale and mottled with bluish patches, he had curled into his bed, admitting he would never be able to emulate his father.

A sharp cry. Silence. Then shrieks. Nate Morrison stood focusing his howls into the interior of the Morrisons' cabin. His brother Rory sat, legs crossed, a stick grasped upright—a small chieftain scowling at a cowardly subject who had ducked an assigned lashing. Mimi Morrison arrived in her bathrobe, ample figure blurred by the screen, rings on her fingers glinting in the light. Recriminations began, and Damon turned away. This could go on all morning.

Damon loved children, but with a love that contained a component of fear. A whole morning could be shattered again and again by these raucous outbreaks unless Rory and Nate were trussed up and dragged to the lake. Buckling his belt, pausing to hear the voices becoming subdued, Damon could imagine walking out into the no-man's-land between his cabin and theirs, beckoning to the boys, sitting with them under the white pine to tell them stories. Or they would join him on a walk in search of lady's slipper or toads or maybe a red fox with kits. This was a living version of *Please Pretend,* an Uncle Ralph unleashed from his microphone and script.

But the voice coming over the radio had always been more effectual than his presence. He had been permitted once to stand behind a curtain in a large room filled with children listening to a recording of one of his programs. He was accustomed to the way the voice did not sound like his own, but he had not realized what power it had over his listeners. The bodies still squirmed and talked and giggled through the theme and plug for some glutinous morning cereal, then Uncle Ralph chuckled, said, "Well, hello there, boys and girls," and the children grew still, leaned toward the loudspeakers, and were silent except for the hypnotized few who called out, "Hello, Uncle Ralph." The voice began a tale. "Once upon a time, boys and girls, in a country very, very far away, there lived an old man who had two children, a girl and a boy." A page or two later he shifted his Ralph voice and spoke for all the others—the harsh stepmother, the beguiling but evil wandering tinker, the frog who could speak.

When he was fired, Damon took the memory of that occasion with him more than any other moment during his career, although he never confronted his employers with it. For them, the simple fact was that Damon White, no matter how good the voice was, could not translate to television.

"What?" the Colonel had said, at first outraged at the network. "Fired?" But that lapsed eventually into a conversation at dinner two nights later and only a few days before Damon's breakdown. "Hell, son. We both know you don't have to work for a living, but what will you do with your life if you can't even hold onto a job telling fairy stories to kids?" Damon had said, "Nothing." His father appeared almost frightened when Damon began laughing and repeated the same word again and again in hilarious shouts.

Listeners were the children he loved—rapt faces, minds concentrated—perhaps because he identified with them then, sinking into some image he carried in himself of his own attentive being, leaning into memory, into stories that were the patterns of everything he did not and never would quite know. He longed to take Nate and Rory by the hand and lead them off through some door in the hillside where all three of them could sit and listen and understand over and over again.

But he had also watched until the end of the recording when the children's bodies began to twist and turn again. He walked away from the curtain utterly depressed. What had the storytelling been for? Again they were pinching and scratching, surreptitiously kicking. The harmony was achieved only on the surface. The shattered interior was so deep that Damon could never reach it. His chest tightened, he dreamed at night of ominous motions in the other rooms of houses too large for him to secure by completely inhabiting. Even now Nate and Rory hunched together over something on the ground between them, hands on their knees, heads turned down. Why could that picture empty him toward dread, turn them into stone figures of a sculptured group, the rest of whom, hidden by the slope, were doing something fierce and utterly forbidden?

He managed to spend most of the day by himself, walking along the river or reading in his cabin. But at dinner he saw Dede Raynes across the room, sitting with the Plimptons. She smiled and waved. He had known her sister Phyllis, and last winter Phyllis Raynes had died. No longer Raynes, actually—Phyllis Birge—since many years ago she had married, then divorced, a local man. She had died locally also, and most of her adult life was an unusual swerve away from the people he knew, as if the summer landscape they had all come to love in childhood had suddenly reached out and claimed one of them for its own, and in doing so had put a barrier between her and the rest of their set as sturdy as the steep ridges of the mountains. For the rest of his dinner Damon tried to avoid looking at Dede, but a loud, persistent tinkle of glass drew his attention to her. She was standing and hitting her wineglass with a spoon.

"Your attention please, could I . . . thank you."

Not as slim as she used to be, always chunkier in figure than the sylphlike Phyllis anyway, but still Dede was attractive in her neatly coiled black hair, the skin that always seemed slightly tanned. She held a small piece of paper that she glanced at from time to time.

"I know many of you were acquainted with my sister Phyllis, and I want to take this opportunity on behalf of the family to thank you for your lovely letters we received following her death. Many of you expressed a desire to share our grief and regretted that you could not attend her funeral service. I'm happy to tell you that there will be a service at the Congregational Church this Thursday, and I hope any of you who wish to join us will do so at three o'clock. Since this is not in the nature of a formal religious ceremony—which as you know was held here last winter—we would like to bring her to mind by sharing some music and memories, and I have also asked Dr. Blanton to say a few words. I will be singing, and I'm sure I can talk our old friend Damon White into accompanying me. Also perhaps he'll play a tune by Chopin that Phyllis always liked?" A slight turn to him, silence, everyone waiting, but Damon was staring at her, dumbstruck. "Well, I'm asking any of you who have some memories to please come and share them with us. Very informal, as I said. Thursday, three o'clock." And then into the hubbub of renewed conversation she shouted, "Thank you!"

She did not sit down but dodged through the other tables until she came to his.

"I tried to call this morning, Damon. You will be a sweetie, won't you?"

"I can't, Dede."

Her hand was on his shoulder. "Of course you will. What would the occasion be without you? And what would they think if you didn't?"

"I tell you, Dede, I don't play Chopin anymore. I never did very well."

"Try, Damon. For Phyllis."

To his dismay, the hand shifted across his shoulder to flutter on his neck, brush his ear, and withdraw, leaving a trail of some scent as it passed his face.

"There's so much more about this than you know or than I can explain now. They had a service here last winter. The daughters, their father, some of the village people. Mummy and Dad and I weren't even invited. Please. At least let me pick you up tomorrow. I'd have a drink and talk now but I'm due at the Baileys' already. Stupid little party for Doris and Bill Armitage. I'll bring my music. We can try out the Schubert, and talk. I know what I'm doing is right. For her."

The annoyance in her voice was incomprehensible, surely meant to pass beyond him to some other target. He could not stop looking into those steady eyes whose pupils were so startlingly black against a shimmering blue.

She shook a finger at him. "Remember: Dede is relentless."

The eyes, the face swooped at him, lips plucking once at his, the quick peck of a brightly plumed but predatory bird. "To-morrow. Eleven. Ta-ta."

He did not watch more than her first few paces because those hips swung against the revealing silk of her skirt as if to taunt him.

Damon tucked his hands behind his back and strode out, looking neither right nor left until he was well past all the other guests and onto the path to the cabin. There he sat on the steps in the dim light from living room windows, his head cupped in his hands. It was not Dede he thought of, but her sister, Phyllis, sitting with him by the brook, late August, where one slim maple on the opposite bank had flushed into deep scarlet well before the proper season. Damon told her the dry month and cold nights had confused the tree into thinking it was fall. He moved on to express to her the nature of confusion, of yearning, and he was lyrical and elliptical and totally uncertain of what he should do next. Although he was twenty-four and she only nineteen, he feared she had more experience. He had never made love to a woman, had hardly ever held one close until that summer.

Finally she interrupted breathlessly, not letting him talk any more about trees or seasons. "It doesn't matter whether we're certain we love each other. I want you."

She took him by the hand, and they walked to a ferned glade in the woods. Damon tumbled into a state of shocked separation from his body when he saw her unbuttoning her shirt, knew that he was doing the same to his own, and that they were stretching out beside each other on the ground. Beyond the blurred side of her face and a whorled ear, the wing of a butterfly was crushed into the matted leaves—yellow with a small orange and black circle like an unblinking eye.

When he saw her in subsequent years, at the club or down-town after her marriage to Birge, they talked only of weather, her daughters, the recent fire at the general store, how time passed. She seemed to have no idea of the intensity with which that afternoon was fixed in his mind. "Mummy," one of her children had shrilled at his knees once, "why has he got such a funny name?"

"I never would have named you Damon," the old man had muttered, that strong-featured head now looking powerless in the nest of pillows, the white hair disheveled. "Her idea. What kind of name is that, I said? Not a man's name. Foreign sound-ing. In her family, she said. Names are important. Sorry for you at school. They called you sissy. What did she expect?"

Damon leaned over the book in his lap. He had been read-ing to his father and wished to continue.

"Never could argue with her and win. Ah, Christ, Damon. She should not have died. I needed her."

And me? he wanted to call out but instead said, "The Battle of Corregidor. Chapter Three. In the fall of—"

"I don't want to die."

The face turned to him. Damon tried not to look but a glance defeated him. The eyes would not let him go. Never had his father spoken like this. The face opened out into an expression of helpless terror, mouth spread downward and trembling, voice issuing from a mask.

"I tell you I dream at night. It comes down over me. Black and heavy and I can't move. No one listens to me. You must. Don't leave me. I will not die."

The book slipped. The heavy volume of history struck the edge of the bed, then Damon's foot, and made a hollow beat on the floor as if the house were a drum set sturdily on the earth, signaling. The man was weeping, his face still stiffly immobile. Damon too could not move. They stared at each other, waiting for an answering signal, but only his father's shuddering intake of breath sounded in the room.

When the coffin was lowered, ropes straining, past the dense and cleanly sliced sides of clay soil until only its massive black top with bronze fittings showed, Damon was reminded again of the jerk of his shoulders forward to catch the book slipping away, pulled down between them, and everything about that afternoon of the burial pressed downward with crushing weight. The body in its coffin was not turning to dust but compressing, the unbreathing earth above it was weighted down by a shaft of solid air. His father did not die. He folded under.

Damon rose and went into the cabin. He turned out all the lights, undressed, paused by the door to what had always been his father's room, then rolled himself in the blanket and slept. There were no dreams that he remembered except that when he woke he believed for a moment that the day before had been a dream and that soon the voice of the Colonel would call gruffly through the flimsy paneling just as he had the day after that one evening of weakness. For the months of tenacious living left to him he returned to his unbending self. His last words, stuttered against the pressure of a stroke that left him nearly speechless for the final weeks, had been, "G-get out. I wa-want to do this alone."

While Dede drove, Damon listened, staring forward at the road because someone ought to, and from time to time he almost grabbed the wheel himself to correct her tendency to drift into the opposite lane as she talked to him.

"I want her ashes," Dede said, "that's all. That's not asking much. I don't care if they come or not, the little bitches, but I want her presence, what's left of it—not just our memories. Don't you see?"

"But why haven't they buried them, scattered them, done something?"

"'Why' is not a question I lavish on that side of the family, Damon dear. Why did Phyllis even marry that hulk Gus Birge rather than just having the twins and letting him lumber off into the woods again? Why, once she divorced him, didn't she just pick up and take the girls and go back to Connecticut instead of settling into this godforsaken place? Mummy and Dad kept begging her to move into an apartment near home. It would have been easy enough."

"Too easy?"

"She wasn't just stubborn. She was perverse."

Dede turned the car onto the driveway, stopped to shift into low gear, and began a slow ascent avoiding the worst of the exposed rocks and eroded channels. The road ended abruptly in a cluster of stunted spruce and birch, a bungalow that did not pretend to be more than a serviceable place to sleep and eat. At the farther end, the yard dropped to a sweeping view of valleys and ridges. She yanked on the brake, cut off the engine, and breathed deeply.

The girls had come out of the house and were waiting for them. They walked slowly across the lawn as Dede's voice warbled in her best mezzo-soprano, "Here he is, girls, just as I promised. Damon, these are Phyllis's daughters. Leona and Danda. Mr. Damon White."

They were not identical twins, for which Damon was grateful. Leona was smaller, built more like her aunt but even more sturdily, and after tugging Damon's hand she stuffed both of hers into back pockets and perched forward on the top step. The face tended to withhold any expression, as if wary. Danda, however, was tall and willowy like Phyllis, and if her face had been a little less narrow, the nose less aquiline, she might have been her mother's twin. He looked at her so long that she glanced away to Leona, a shy swerve of eyes, and his reaction to her beauty was almost resentment. It seemed unfair that she should have taken her mother's best features and heightened them with some other lines and colorations, the contributions of Gus Birge.

"We've heard of you." Leona kept the voice toneless, not revealing whether what they had heard was good or bad.

"We've even *heard* you." The slightest hitch of a speech impediment made some of Danda's vowels sound swallowed.

"Where, I wonder?"

The girls gave way as he advanced up the steps, preceding him onto the porch. Beyond its edge was a sheer plummet to the glinting brook below. He gripped the rail hard.

"On the radio," Leona was saying just behind his shoulder. "They had you on the Nostalgia Hour last week. Danda thought you did the princess best. But if I'd been a kid, your witch would have kept me up all night."

"It must be weird," Danda murmured over his other shoulder. "Hearing yourself like that. Would you listen if they did all the programs again?"

"No."

"I wouldn't either. I hate my voice when I hear it. And I want everything to be new."

The bitterness of his own laugh surprised him. "Lots of luck."

He turned around slowly, hesitating to put the drop behind him. He could feel it in the tightening of his thighs, the slight lean forward to pull away from it. The girls were both dressed casually in jeans and open-necked men's shirts, their feet bare, but Leona's flesh pushed and spread against her clothes, and Danda's body seemed self-contained in the slim, curved outlines of denim and cotton. Still dizzied, he could not forgive her mother for standing naked by the bank of an August brook, their lovemaking done, her shocked laughter as she plunged into the water coming back to him for months afterward.

"You make it sound impossible," she said.

"Nothing is very new after we've lived for a while."

"'Scuse," Dede murmured. "I'll just go to the bathroom a sec." And she disappeared through the glass doors into the dim living room where Damon could vaguely make out a sofa and chairs, a stone fireplace, and a sharp square of light from the side door to the driveway.

"Mother," Danda continued, "said nothing ever seemed exactly the same to her and that was one of the reasons she did not want to die. Even the pain, she said, was different."

Both the girls stared at him unblinking, as if the statement of Phyllis's death had been made to judge his reactions.

"I'm sorry about your mother. That must have been difficult for you."

"It was." Leona jerked her head toward the living room behind her. "And they didn't help. Our aunt, the grandparents. Where were they when she needed them, when she married Dad and had us and moved here?"

"We don't want to go into that, though." Danda leaned one hip onto the wooden table behind her and crossed her arms. "We don't mean to seem unreasonable, but we won't lend Aunt Dede the ashes because we don't agree with this whole second service for the summer people, and Dad doesn't either."

"It's a form of prejudice, don't you think?" Leona's tone, in spite of the words, was becoming less truculent. "I mean, if you wanted a service for her, you would have been welcome to come last winter. We didn't turn anyone away. And this kind of splitting of things into summer people and winter people is exactly what she had to take a lot of crap for all her life, you know? We won't be part of that, or let her seem to be either."

A breeze rose straight up along the cliff to the porch bearing the tang of sun-baked rock from the brook far below.

"But all this isn't your fault." Danda moved now to sit fully on the table, her bare feet off the deck. "Aunt Dede gets a bee in her bonnet and she can't be stopped. It makes Dad furious, but I told him just to let her have her service. We won't be there, and that's enough. And I know you're doing this because you care about her, so I don't want you to think we're angry at you for it. We asked Aunt Dede if we could meet you. Mother always liked you."

"How do you know?" He tried to keep the voice toneless.

Leona shrugged. "Nothing special. I remember one of those times we saw you on the street downtown. We started laughing because we thought you looked funny. I mean, it was mid-August and here was this guy in a plaid jacket and bow tie and saddle shoes and all. We'd only seen that in old movies."

"Leona."

"He asked, didn't he? Anyway, she said we shouldn't make fun of you. She said you were just eccentric and you were a nice guy who'd gone through some tough things. She said you'd always been good friends."

As if the long drop behind him were pulling his blood away, he felt slowly drained, light-headed. He stared at Danda, who was frowning, those thin, delicate features perplexed. He turned suddenly, put both hands on the railing and leaned out toward the sweep. He knew the mountains as well as his own name—Hedgehog, Wolf Jaws, Armstrong, Gothics, Saddleback, Basin, a thin peel of Haystack's ridges, then Marcy's perfect cone.

"Well, mountains don't change, do they?" he said loudly to the uprush of breeze that died before he finished speaking. "Tell me their names."

They were standing close behind him, one on each side, and he yearned to pull them closer against him. He could not change himself sufficiently to make such a gesture, but their shoulders brushed him, and he was grateful for that.

"If you start furthest left," and Leona stuck a finger decisively into the landscape, "that's Hedgehog."

Chanting together in their different voices, they named the peaks, and to slow the progress at one point, Damon said, "Which, the one with the sharp top or the rounded one?" And then, even more mercifully, Danda moved, stood directly behind him, breathing against his neck, along his cheek, and with both hands on his face from behind, she directed his gaze, moving one hand slowly forward past his eyes. He aimed along the fine hairs of the forearm, along the finger until it ended in bright, warm air, the blurred shape of a mountain. He ached, not to hold her body or the body she had been delivered from, but to hold everything they could see for only a moment before letting it go forever.

"I see," he murmured, utterly emptied by her motions as she pulled away from him. "I see."

"I hate to break this up, but I'm going to have to go to the florist's in Lake Placid."

Dede stood by the stairs with her keys dangling.

"Won't you come back sometime, Mr. White?" Danda was saying. "You should meet Dad."

"I'd like to. Thank you."

Damon waved a hand, they both lifted theirs, and then he was groping for his seat belt as Dede backed out the drive, putting a screen of trees quickly between them and the figures posed as if for a snapshot. Dede did not say anything and Damon was glad to let her concentrate on driving. She began humming softly, something she was much better at than full-voiced destruction of Schubert. As the car turned off the highway onto the drive to the club, she began chanting in a high, childlike voice.

"Ring around the roses, a pocket full of posies, ashes, ashes, we all fall down."

She laughed and repeated the verse. Damon found the tone and her nervous playfulness irritating.

"I learned it as 'A-tishoo! A-tishoo! We all fall down.'"

"Of course you did, Damon dear. That's the English version. Much more correct. You've always been very correct."

She stopped below his cabin and turned off the engine.

"You loved Phyllis, didn't you? Old flame. That sort of thing. But I've always wondered. Did you ever make love? She never would tell me that summer."

With his face turned to the side window he listened to the engine ticking as it cooled.

"I'm sorry your mission failed," he said politely.

He looked with longing at the cabin door. He could shut it and sit inside and think. Even if he had to leave suddenly that evening, he would find a way of avoiding the service tomorrow. He was glad Dede did not have the ashes, although the idea of the daughters clinging to them in their home seemed wrong as well, or dangerous for them in ways he could not yet understand.

"Not at all. The ashes are mine, and this is where you come in again, my dear."

He smiled back deliberately at her. "I think you underestimate their determination."

"I think you underestimate mine."

"I never have."

"Good. Come along."

He clambered out and came around the back, where she was opening the trunk. She stooped in, lifted an urn, thrust it into his hands, which clutched involuntarily because if he had not, she would have let it drop.

"I'll have to ask you to keep this until tomorrow. I'm afraid once they know the urn is gone, they'll be pestering me."

The smooth bulge pressing against his chest made him want to cry out sharply. She slammed the trunk lid and backed away.

"You stole it."

"See you tomorrow."

"Take it back."

Her door slammed.

"Wait," he yelled.

The car flung loose gravel against his leg, her fingers were waggling, and she swerved just in time to miss the pines. A door slapped on the neighboring cabin. Ames Morrison stared toward him from the shadow of his porch and nodded wordlessly. Damon strode into his cabin trying not to run, dropped the urn on a couch, and wiped both hands up and down against his chest, unable to stop staring at the squat object tilting back against the armrest.

The urn filled the whole room with an expanding pressure. His hands had begun to shake at his sides and he clasped them to make his fingers stop jerking. He thought he was afraid of it and that he would rush forward, seize it, run to his own car, and drive back to the twins. But then he realized he was not trembling with fear, but with excitement. The ashes were his.

Certainly he would leave before the service. He did not doubt Dede's determination, and also did not doubt his weakness if she netted him again. She was obviously most creative in arranging inescapable situations. No, distance was the only way. But he did not find that dissatisfying at all. Distance from all of this world was what he needed. The more he gazed around him, the more the room was drained of familiarity or attraction. The couch with its bamboo arms and legs deserved to be part of a decaying hotel's lobby. Everything he knew of the objects and the patina of their history was being absorbed by the urn on the mantel. Small as it was, it could contain a lifetime.

That evening, having decided to forego dinner since he was too happy with his solitude, Damon sat on the porch or in the living room and was pleased by the way the cabin and landscape, in exchange for his pledge of leaving, were giving up secrets to him that he had forgotten. The metal candle stand on the wall with the face of a dragon had been his friend and defender in his childhood fantasies. The volume of Colvin's topographical survey, squashed into a dark corner of the bookcase, was a book he had read avidly when he was ten since it turned the surrounding countryside into a place as fiercely unknown as Africa. When a breeze blew, a hole appeared between the upper limbs of the pine grove displaying the peak of Noonmark as if in an oval brooch. He thought of packing but decided there was no hurry. He knew at various times that this was merely euphoria but accepted that. He regretted he had no peanuts left for the tamed chipmunk that scampered timorously to his feet on the porch.

The evening was calm and clear. He watched the Morrisons climb into their station wagon, all of them dressed in their finest. When he stood, a faint dizziness reminded him that he had not eaten since breakfast. He pulled his chair toward the last square of sunlight and sat so that it fell onto his lap and down his legs like a quilt patterned with clustered bursts of pine needles. Nothing mattered but this utter calm, not securely his yet, but recoverable—perhaps, he even dared to think, his for longer periods and with greater intensity. He could not destroy it even when he allowed himself to look over the lawn toward the vacant tennis courts, the gray and green expanse of the clubhouse, thinking that he would never see all this again.

The light faded into dusk, the dusk lapsed into night and blinking of fireflies above the lush, dewy grass by the courts. He went back into the cabin but did not turn on the lights. As he stretched out on the couch, he held onto one fixed point of reference: that somehow to give the urn back would be bad for all of them. If he could burn the cabin down in a quick stroke of fire, he would.

"They are yours, Damon," his mother's voice was saying,

but it was muffled because between him and her face was the clear globe of a fishbowl filled with water, wavering green plants, five bright goldfish that flashed in their new home. Not just her face, his father's too—side by side—staring through water and fish and plants.

"Mine?"

"Yours," she said again.

"Feed them," his father's mouth was saying underwater. "Go on."

Damon lifted the little can above the water and dusted some food onto the surface. It floated a moment, then soaked through and began drifting down. The fish darted in and out through the particles, blotting specks with their quick mouths. He focused through the bowl on his parents, but their eyes were on the fish, not him, their faces intent. They were not breathing. Two fleeting faces. Quavering. Drowning.

"What?" her voice kept saying when he ran around to her and hid his face against her belly. "What's wrong?"

Damon rose quietly and stood in the dark room. In all those years he had not been able to hear his mother's voice, but now memory had thrown it up to him as if not even a door stood between them. He groped to the bureau, found his flashlight, and flicked it on. He lifted the urn and walked out the back door. He took the road into the reserve, aware of how loud his footsteps sounded in the silent woods. He remembered how the giant woke when his lyre cried out in alarm, how he roared in anger and Jack tumbled down the vine.

It was three miles up the road and through the woods to the dam. He held the urn tucked under one arm, flashlight in the other hand. A deer crossing the road froze, eyes bright, then it leapt away, crashing up the slope. A startled bird fluttered with a single cry from its ground nest when he turned onto the trail. The air was chill, the sky fiercely starred. To keep his own fear of the dark in check he began talking.

"Once upon a time there was a poor widow who lived in a lonely cottage . . ." And when he spoke for them he tried to make Rose Red sound like Leona, and Snow White like Danda, but in some speeches he had to pause and start again to get it right. The dwarf gave him no trouble at all and never had. The evil characters were always easiest to do. He stopped reciting when the sound of the river neared. Soon the woods thinned and he could see the wide cleft of the lake, the line of wooden bridge. The water splashed unevenly over the dam.

He walked carefully across the broad stones to the largest pool. His light shone down through clear water, the fish darting away from it, but in the deepest part two long, wide trout hung still, moving only their fins. Their backs were nearly black.

Damon knelt on the wide rock, turned off the light, and placed it beside his leg. He waited for his eyes to become accustomed to the night. At first he saw only the brightest stars, vague contours of peaks, the block of watery blackness that was the dam. Then the sky began to reveal its layers, the mountains cut clear lines in sharp descent to the lake, trees nearby took shape, and even the rocks rose out of pools of reflected stars.

His father's face drew nearer, from above, unshaven and grieving. Hands seized him under the arms and lifted him, and now his own face brushed against harsh stubble, but it did not hurt him, because he needed to feel those arms around him, and the disheveled face seemed far more soft than when it was shaved to a marble hardness. In his ear the choked voice said, "She's gone, boy, gone. It's just you and me now."

He pried at the lid, paused, then dipped his hand in and sowed ash onto the water. Most of it was too fine to grasp and so he held out the urn and turned it over. The ash and pieces of bone scattered the reflected stars into smaller fragments.

The water heaved slightly, then swirled, although the fish did not break the surface. Briefly a sinuous turmoil made disordered waves around the pool.

He looked down at the palm that had held her ashes. They had been so weightless, nearly air. There was nothing to say, but he wanted to listen, not to the voices that memory might give to him, but to the water and quick passing of wind that altered the waves falling over the dam and shook leaves with a rush. He listened and did not close his eyes, and kept listening until a faint light began to blur the stars on the edge of the eastern ridge. He hid the urn under the lip of the bank. The first high water would take it away.

The batteries died before he reached his cabin, but by then the light was strong enough for him to see tan windings of the dirt road. He would call the sisters before he left, perhaps visit them. They would still be sleeping now. He imagined them lying together in a large bed, not grown women but the children their mother might lean over in the middle of the night. Leona's face would be pressed into a pillow; Danda would have clasped her sister's arm to her, face lying back peacefully, mouth slightly open. He and Phyllis stood looking down.

He would tell them what he had done. Above all he would tell them how for a moment before they woke he was certain they were two sisters asleep in the dark woods. He had come to wake them from their dangerous enchantment.

leaving home

"Do you know how to swim?" Charlie clenched the gunwale in the stern of the rowboat.

"Yes."

The old man nodded. "I can't keep your name in mind."

"Hale."

"I don't, so bear in a little, Hale. I'm happier close to shore."

The boy glanced over his shoulder at the distant bend in the narrow lake. He would have preferred to straighten the course as much as possible, but he dragged on the port oar.

"I been up and down this lake so much I bet half this water is my sweat, and I'm still scared to get in a boat."

"I'm being careful."

"Dying doesn't scare me anymore. Not at my age. But drowning does."

Hale took a bearing on the nose of Indian Head's cliffs and pulled steadily. The late August sun was hot but dry, and the boat was piled with provisions for the camp on the second lake. The Danforths would be waiting for them—old Mrs. Danforth and her middle-aged son, Ames. Because he wanted to be rowing the other direction, back toward the valley, he tried to put them out of mind.

"What's going to happen is this: You're going to put the

dishes on the table and do all the talking while I cook and tend to whatever else needs me. I can't do that other stuff. Makes me nervous."

Charlie let one hand release its grip long enough to grope out a cigarette, but he made no attempt to light it after he put it between his lips. Hale tried not to watch the man, thinking instead of how he and Sherry had gone berrying two days ago. At first they had worked apart, picking hard as if that were what they both had intended to do. But sometimes when he was glancing at her loose halter hanging away to show the bright, white skin beyond the line of her tan, or at the lean, taut roll of her stooping hip, she would be staring at him too. They started working close together. He finally ran a hand along her arm, leaving a stain of dark juice, and she only laughed, and then they were leaning to feed each other blackberries. She held one in her lips and passed it to him. He stuck his tongue in her mouth. When the crackle of breaking sticks nearby startled them, they stood to see a black bear rooting among the bushes, and it heaved up for a moment to blink at them before barreling away into the cover of the woods. Her pail had spilled, and they carefully cupped the berries back into it before she looked at her watch and said it was time to go.

Hale shipped the oars and found the match Charlie told him to fish out of his pocket. He touched the ribs of the old man's lean chest.

"You know the Danforths much?"

"No."

"He'll talk a lot. She's all right. Tough old bird, in spite of all those manners. I guided lots for her and her husband before he died. They tip well."

"Did they say yet if it would be two weeks or one?"

"No. I'll send you down if we need more."

When they reached the bend, the wind strengthened, pushing them off course unless Hale sighted and kept compensating with the right oar.

"The boy who used to work for me broke his leg. You know Ben Mercer?"

Hale nodded.

"Strong little bugger. You don't have that kind of build, but you row good."

"He wrestles at school."

But Charlie was not listening anymore. He had a way of closing down his mind behind the mask of his face that left only the shell of his body in place.

They dragged the boat into the shed, filled the baskets, and lugged them across the mile-long carry to the next lake and the brief row to camp. In spite of his spare frame the old man slung a heavier load than Hale onto his back and walked with long, unceasing strides that the boy could barely keep up with. They unloaded in the kitchen, then went to the bunkhouse. Charlie took the upper bunk because he said he did not like anyone above him. He brought out a rifle stored in a closet and laid it across his blankets.

"In case that bear comes sniffing around at night." He did not look at Hale when he talked about the bear, one he insisted had been breaking into camps for years. "I want a shot at old Crafty. Just one."

They went down to the main house to let the Danforths know they were there. After introducing Hale, Charlie kept one hand gripped on his forearm. Although no horses were at this camp, Mrs. Danforth was dressed in riding habit, her steel gray hair drawn back in a bun. She walked with a cane. Her son's very round face was pale and glabrous. He tilted his head back when he talked so that he seemed to be looking down from some height, but he was short and stout. Even in the woods he was wearing a bow tie with his tattersall shirt.

"The Carters will be rowing up tomorrow and staying through dinner," Mrs. Danforth announced.

"The canoe seems to have a considerable leak," Ames said.

"This boy will fetch one from Porter's."

"Porter won't mind, I suppose?" Ames's lips twisted down as he spoke, his eyes widening and narrowing occasionally with a nervous snap.

"He probably dumped this one on us."

"You see, Mother? I told you Charlie would know."

As they walked back to the kitchen to start working on dinner, Charlie muttered, "You bet I know. The old lady knows. But that flit don't even know how to change his own diapers."

Charlie cleaned his kitchen and cooked and ordered Hale from task to task, sometimes forgetting he had already told him to chop kindling or set the table in the dining room. "I did that," Hale would remind him, and Charlie would only nod. "Well, do it again," he said once, and Hale went back to the rustic dining room with its stone fireplace and bark-clad chairs, the windows looking out onto the porch and the clearing that dropped away to the lake. He moved the salad forks closer to the plates.

At dinner he served the courses one by one. Charlie was sweating and muttering, pulling pans from the wood stove with his hands wrapped in his apron. When Mrs. Danforth called him to the swinging door, he came stooped and pale, and she said, "Charles Morgan, I wish I could take you to New York. You're better than any chef."

Charlie grinned, bobbed his head. "Glad you like it," he mumbled, and back in the kitchen he said to Hale, "You hear that? Christ, I'm glad she don't mean it. What in hell would I do in New York?" He stared out the window over the sink for a moment as if he could see the city rolling down the hill in the evening light.

But Hale had to stop in the dining room and talk to the Danforths when they asked him questions. Was he any relation to George Smith, the school superintendent? His son? Really, how interesting. They had heard it was an excellent school for such a small community. And wasn't he, Hale, going away to school next year? Exeter. Marvelous. The sons of so many of their friends had gone there. And so many more had wanted to but could not get in. Which led them to a brief aside about Daniel Plummington and that awful child of his who never opened his mouth without saying the wrong thing. Ames had gone to St. Paul's. Marvelous school. When Hale tried to express his reservations about going away, Ames interrupted him with a wave of his hand, again looking down at him despite the fact that Hale was standing, Ames sitting.

"Oh, I felt the same way, old man. But you'll see. After you've graduated, you'll understand how much you owe the place, and by the time you're my age you'll hardly be able to wait for the next reunion."

"Ames's father went to St. Paul's too," Mrs. Danforth said, and that led them into a shared recounting of a trip to this same camp years ago before Mr. Danforth's death from "a massive thrombosis." Hale listened as best he could but kept looking beyond their heads to the lake that had turned a dark purple in the evening light, and in the patch of yellowed sun falling on the distant shore he thought he saw two deer bending their long necks to the water. The Danforths did not seem to be talking to him anyway by the end of the story, and he was glad when Charlie's voice called him away.

"Jesus. What the hell you doing in there? Bring off them things so I can serve up this pie."

After dinner Ames asked Hale to help him and Mrs. Danforth into the canoe so they could paddle and watch the sun set behind the mountains. He was to be ready to come back to the dock when Ames called for him. Mrs. Danforth jerked her son's hand impatiently from her elbow and stepped into the canoe with the agility of a small bird. She insisted on paddling stern.

"It's one of the few things I've always done well," she said crisply to her son's back as he tottered into the bow.

Hale started by helping Charlie do the dishes, but the old man dropped a cup and it smashed between them on the floor.

"Careful, son," he said as if Hale had missed some elaborate toss. "Better sweep that up."

That was when Hale noticed the pint bottle perched behind the box of scouring pads, and after Charlie's hand dropped a small saucer he nipped from the bottle openly.

"You want some?"

"No, thanks."

"Just as well. I only brought one more this time. I'm cutting down, although they say it's good for your arteries after a certain age. But you aren't that age yet."

He pushed the shards of the saucer into a pile with one foot as he continued to wash. When he dropped the large dinner plate, he did not even look down to where it lay in two pieces. He leaned with both hands on the sink, his elbows locked straight.

"Christ," he said blankly to the dimming window.

He lifted one hand and stared at it while it trembled.

"Here." He grasped the bottle and began tugging himself free of the apron with his other hand. "You finish up and see they get settled in for the night. I'm calling it quits."

He flung the apron over a nail by the door and slammed the screen behind him. Hale watched the lean figure stalk toward the bunkhouse. Halfway there he stopped, looked at the bottle for a few seconds, then unscrewed the cap and took a long draft, his head tilted as if he were trying to gaze deep into the sky. Hale finished the dishes, banked the fire in the wood stove as carefully as he would if he were camping with his father, and then started down to the dock to wait for the Danforths. He paused in the last fringe of bushes before the water.

The sunlight only skimmed the highest peaks of the range, and then it too was gone, leaving the opaque gray of dusk. The canoe was sitting still in the middle of the unruffled lake. Neither figure in the boat moved, and Hale could hear voices as clearly as if he were in the water beside them.

"She's not the right sort for you. I told you that when I first met her."

"I think you're just jealous because she rides so well." Ames's voice was high and petulant.

"She does ride well. But at my age, jealousy over such matters would be wasted emotion."

"She likes you."

"Oh, Ames. For heaven's sake. What else can she say?"

Ames leaned back slightly to let the fingers of his hand dabble in the water. The canoe turned slightly so that Ames was speaking directly toward the shore.

"Then you're jealous for other reasons."

"Don't argue so desperately, my dear. I wish you would marry. Your father always wanted you to. But at least for his sake I won't see you make a wreck of your life with that kind of brainless piece of fluff. For God's sake, Ames, find someone substantial."

The boat continued to turn lazily in some stirring of wind so slight that nothing showed on the surface of the water.

"I'm not getting any younger," the voice said toward the opposite side of the lake, and then Ames murmured something so softly that Hale could not hear it. Suddenly his mother leaned forward over the paddle lying across her knees and stroked his face once with her hand.

The light was nearly gone. Hale walked out of the bushes as if he had just sauntered down from the clearing. He knelt on the dock, and the smell of its rotting timbers mixed strongly with the nearby resin of balsam and spruce, the smoke from the burning birch logs. He wished he had not listened. He did not understand why, but their conversation had made him lonely, almost as if he had been sent away to school already.

Even though he wanted to go, he knew he would be very homesick. Many things were beginning to make him feel that way even before he left. After he spent any time with Sherry he would find it impossible to stay inside his house. Eating with his father and mother annoyed him and he bolted his food, said as little as possible. He always shut his door when he went to his room. But when he heard their voices below, he wanted to be with them.

He tried to think of Sherry, but he could not see her face clearly. She had come so close to him that her features were blurred. He could only sense the shape of her body, as his hands moved down the shoulder blades, the inset curve of her spine. He wished she were there, on the dock with all the night shapes taking form, but he also wanted her to be more than she was, some woman he could not locate in any person he had known. He wanted to be back in the valley but knew that the woman was not there either. He had woken up sometimes from restless sleep with a sense of this woman intensely filling his mind for the rest of the day. But she was wherever he was and never accessible, as if she were a memory even though he had never known her. That seemed impossible to live with, so he wished for Sherry at least to be nearby.

"Dear me," Ames Danforth was saying as the canoe nudged the dock, "I didn't mean you had to sit and wait for us."

Mrs. Danforth's hand was wiry on Hale's forearm, and for a moment she stood still and stared back over the blackened lake before she released Hale and moved up the path with her cane on one side and Ames gripping her elbow on the other. Hale hauled the canoe onto the bank and followed them up to be certain they had all they needed for the evening. Ames looked as though he were going to keep Hale talking by the fireside, but his mother insisted on a game of double solitaire, so Hale said good night and groped his way toward the light of the bunkhouse.

Charlie's body was humped in the upper bunk, face to the wall. He did not move or speak, so Hale assumed he was sleeping and turned out the lantern. He undressed to his undershorts and rolled into the blankets. For a moment the cabin was totally blank, but gradually Hale began to distinguish the gray windows, the glint of a star between limbs of the maples and beech. When Charlie turned over, springs scraped and the whole bunk jerked. A hard object thumped against the wall.

"You tuck them in OK?"

"They're playing cards."

"Figures. Although they're beyond me, these folks. Can you imagine spending weeks with your mother up here when you're that old? Playing cards before beddy-bye? Oh, Jesus." A flare of match splashed the room into view, made the table shift into the sudden return to darkness. Charlie drew in a deep breath. "I would've jumped into bed with old Crafty before I'd sit down to cards with my mom."

He did not speak for a while. Hale listened to the slow, random dragging on the cigarette, watched the brief glow each puff signaled. He wanted to sleep now, or at least sink half-sleeping into what he had just felt on the dock. Was there really someone named Sherry? He ran his hand down his belly and thigh. Yes, there was. His body knew it. Everything was possible. Another glade, another sunny day. But again he knew he would dream and she would dissolve into the unnameable presence—generous, his own other body.

"You think we live after we die?" Charlie's voice was toneless but very clear. When he ground the butt on the bed frame a spark dropped by Hale, out before it hit the floor. "You aren't sleeping, are you?"

"No."

"I won't keep you up all night. Even if I can't sleep good. Don't pay attention if I talk some in my sleep. I'd appreciate if you'd not listen in. I don't know what I say. That Mercer boy, he'd make fun of me the next day. Thought it was funny as hell to tell me what I'd said. I don't want to know, OK? Keep it to yourself, please, if you do listen."

"I won't."

"I'm grateful." He was silent a moment. "You didn't answer."

"I don't know."

"No, I don't mean it that way. Course you don't. You haven't been there. But you're about to go to one of those high-class schools. What do they tell you in books? What are the odds?"

Hale tried to concentrate. The question made no sense to him. He was always the one who went mute when teachers asked him direct questions, even if he knew the answer. The words always flew away like a startled flock of birds.

"They don't talk about it much at school."

"I suppose not. Don't talk about it much anywhere. I guess that means the odds are near zero, right? Just get sucked up by the grass and trees but you don't even know it because you aren't there anyway. My Martha died two years ago. She was after me to talk about it. Cancer. It's not pretty at the end. She wanted to tell me about what she thought was going to happen, expected me to come up with ideas too. I couldn't. Christ, I couldn't talk about that all the time."

A door slammed on the other side of the clearing.

"Outhouse," Charlie muttered.

Hale began to feel the cabin was too small and stuffy. He should have left the door open to the crisp, August air.

"Actually, I don't sleep much at all, but sometimes better here than home. You ought to sleep easy, young as you are. A few years ago it used to bother me when I'd just lay there. Don't give a shit now. Dreams are worse. I spent my whole life in these woods, when I wasn't home, but I still hear things out there I shouldn't, things I know come from my head. They get out and swing back at me in sounds or things I see plain as if a light was shining on them. But home's worst now that Martha's dead. I'd rather hear things in the woods than in a house where I can wake and still be tricked into thinking Rusty's in his crib banging it on the wall, or Martha's closing the cellar door. Nobody has to tell me it's just my head. It happens to be the only one I've got."

When Charlie turned, Hale heard the thump against the wall again.

"If that Crafty comes sniffing around or I hear him getting into the kitchen, I want to be ready."

"You've got the gun up there?"

"Yessir. No stumbling around in the dark for me when I hear him roll down the hill. I'm gonna slither out of this bunk quiet as a snake and blast him one. You worried?"

"I guess not."

In the silence he heard the sound of a twisted bottle cap, Charlie drinking and then sighing back against the heat of the liquor.

"I got the safety on. Don't you lose sleep. Been hunting even before I was old enough to aim my pee."

Hale listened to Charlie's breath steadying, and then he too began to doze, slipping gradually into a warm, dark water where his body began to spread and extend itself like a wide cloak as it searched for someone else to touch.

But he woke with a start, sat up abruptly and hit his head on the bunk above. He could not remember where he was, and his heart pounded so hard he could not catch his breath. There had been a huge noise of some kind. Then he heard the voice outside.

"Come down from there, you buggers. Come down and I'll blast your beaks off."

Another shot was fired. Hale struggled to unwind his feet from the blanket and stumbled to the door. The next shot flashed the figure of the man firing straight up, his back arched. The shocked mountains flung back echoes. The night began to shape into a man, a star-strewn wedge, blots of trees.

"Fly off. You can't have me. Not yet."

Even more than preventing another shot, Hale wanted to stop the voice that cracked into a howl at the ends of words. He ran at the figure, threw himself against it, flinging both of them down into the high grass. Hale wrestled the gun away and tossed it, but Charlie was curled loosely under him like a puppet cut from its tangled strings.

An arc of light and a voice were coming at them. Hale could make out a flapping dressing gown, legs in greenish pajamas.

"My God, my God, what happened? What's going on?"

Ames stopped a few yards away, and his light blinded Hale so that he had to cover his eyes as he tried to stand. Charlie rolled over and stayed kneeling, staring at the ground.

"Crafty," he muttered.

"What did he say?"

"Bear. He was taking shots at this bear that breaks in."

"Taking shots? In the middle of the night? And yelling like a madman? He's drunk, isn't he? Here. Let me have a smell, Charles."

Ames stepped forward, his slipper flapping against a heel, but Charlie stood and pushed out a flat hand in warning.

"Get your nose out of here."

"My God, what if I'd been going to the toilet? You can't just go shooting in the dark like that."

Charlie turned and stalked away to the bunkhouse, scooping up the gun as he went.

"Wait! Charles Morgan, you're drunk and insolent." The man's voice lifted to a falsetto. The light was turned fully into Hale's face.

"Good night," Hale managed to say into the blinding white. He started to walk away.

"Have you been drinking too?"

Hale held still, facing the bunkhouse.

"No."

"All right. But there'll be more about all this in the morning." The man began to turn, but spoke in a voice that surprised Hale by trembling. "Oh, damn. Why does Charlie do this to me? We just can't have him when he's in one of these fits. I can't bear it. I just can't bear it."

Hale watched the light move unsteadily along the path to the main house until it became a trapped glow moving past windows, then disappeared. He shivered in his nearly naked flesh, but for a moment he held still, face turned up to stare at the patterns of branches and speckled black. He imagined himself shooting at those chips of light, the gun bucking his shoulder.

In the dark cabin he rolled tightly in the blankets.

"Sorry," the voice said finally. "It was the birds. The big black ones that sometimes fill the trees. They think because it's night and I'm getting old, they can move in close, perch up there with their beaks and shit and wait."

Hale did not answer. He heard Charlie sigh and mutter a

few times, then there was silence. He wanted to sleep but he lay and watched for dawn instead. Whenever he closed his eyes the dark behind them flapped with giant black wings that threatened to fold tightly around him.

The next morning when Ames came into the kitchen to tell Charlie he was to leave and send up another guide, Charlie put down his spatula and said, "Fired."

"Just letting you go. You know how we can't have that kind of behavior here. Next time maybe you'll keep things in order."

"No next time," Charlie said to the sputtering eggs and shoved the pan to the back of the stove. He began to untie his apron.

"I did not mean immediately."

"Well, that's what you're getting."

Charlie let the screen door slap behind him. Ames's lightly stubbled chin was thrust forward.

"You finish up here and help him down the lake. But you can come back with the next guide. Please tell the club manager I'd prefer George Eustis this time."

Hale watched the edges of the fried eggs begin to curl and brown. Without looking directly at Ames he said, "No thanks," and went out the door.

But when they were loading the boat with their duffel, Mrs. Danforth came down alone. She leaned on her cane at the far end of the dock and watched Charlie take his seat in the stern. Hale stepped in and sat but held onto the dock.

"I heard all that last night," she said flatly.

Charlie was staring at the shipped oars.

"You know Ames is a nervous sort, Charlie. He doesn't understand. He can't."

Charlie nodded.

"But I do. Or I think I do."

"I know you do, Esther."

When Mrs. Danforth waved and turned to walk away, Hale pushed off and began rowing to the carry. Halfway down the second lake Charlie broke his silence.

"She's all right, I tell you. When my Martha died, she wrote me. Told me what it was to live without her old man, how it was like not having a home anymore, even though you lived in the same place."

Hale could think of nothing to say, so he pulled harder on the oars.

"You know my house. Off River Road. You come. Tell me what they say in books. We'll talk. Come see me when you can. It gets lonely in winter."

"I will."

But he knew he would not. The summer would be over soon, and his father would drive him to the new school. He wanted to be at the end of the lake, calling to see if Sherry would be free that night. He wanted to forget about Charlie and the camp and shots echoing back from the cliffs. But to keep his course he had to sight along Charlie's face to the rocks on the distant point. He could not stop staring at the man's eyes, slate blue and fixed on some object far beyond Hale's shoulder. He could not keep himself from seeing a white field of snow, the scattered black of huge birds gliding down.

spring cleaning

May. But the snow had only just melted, new grass begun rising, and the trees were not yet risking leaves. Dick Felt stood on the porch of the rambling summer hotel with his coat buttoned tightly to his neck. He watched deer grazing in the distant hollows of the golf course. When spring came this world would be unceremoniously tumbled into summer. Leaves would burst out overnight, birds would flock in as if they had hatched with the black flies, and the heavy thunderstorms of June would flood streams not yet relieved of the winter runoff. He had seen it in other years, had learned not to come before mid-April, no matter how much earlier spring arrived in the Carolinas or how much he had to do in overseeing the opening of the place. He had been manager for thirty years and this would be the last. Then he would live with the milder shifts of seasons in South Carolina, where he had bought a small home near Charleston with most of his savings. If he were permitted to live much into retirement.

Not that he was ill or even had signs of approaching failures. He was sixty and had blood pressure that needed watching, but so did most of the people his age he knew. His father had lived until he was seventy-five, and he assumed he carried those genes rather than his mother's. She had died when she was fifty-five after an adulthood of heart problems. And anyway, they had operations now that would have added years to her life.

No, he was more afraid of the mind. He had heard too often of people who lost interest in living after they retired, whose spirits did nothing to defend the body. Dick intended to remain active. He was already on the board of directors of a winter resort near his new home; had been asked to be a financial consultant for the board of trustees at a nearby junior college; and his younger half-brother, Phil, and his wife lived not far away in Savannah. They had four children and Dick often said they more than compensated for his unmarried, unfathered state. He would not miss the peremptory treatment he could receive from wealthy, pampered guests, the cheating of suppliers, the squabbles and scandal among employees, the hazards of nurturing grass on a northern golf course easily damaged by too much or too little water.

But he would miss this: 8:30 on a May morning with a bright sun at last showing the strength to burn into the chill earth; a chipmunk scurrying along the boards of the porch nearby; distant deer occasionally lifting their heads or shying with a few high-stepping paces, white flags raised, before settling into grazing again. Or, if he let himself gaze off toward that irregular but somehow perfect shape of the nearest coned mountain, he would even admit he would miss one of those rare August nights when absolutely everything ran perfectly: all guests served the right wine, all beds made and folded down in time, the movie running without breaks in one lounge, the muted violins accompanying some discreet dancing in another. On such nights he understood that all the struggle with unbalanced accounts, pacifying Mrs. Gildersleeve's certainty that she had been slighted by the operator, having to cancel lobster night because the whole shipment came through long dead, were simply to attain the juggling feat of one perfect night when guests, hundred-year-old floorboards and staircases, pastry cook, tennis pro, a congregation of brats, and assorted fat, tiny pets all whirled in space in a circle impelled by his hands.

Deflating that morning's euphoria, the figure of the boy Seth came into sight at the bend of the driveway below Dick. The hotel was situated on a high plateau among a circle of mountain peaks, and the driveway rose steeply from the wooded valley below. The boy did not seem to be in any hurry, pausing from time to time as if he were trying to find some sign of an animal he had been stalking. He would hold still, his face turned down to the driveway, then perhaps lift a hand slowly or glance up to the sky. But he never seemed to look toward the porch where Dick waited.

The boy's hair was long and hung in a ponytail down his back. He had pale blue eyes and pale skin to match so that he reminded Dick of a white, furred animal, perhaps a malamute, who might merge with a whirl of snow and disappear. He rarely smiled and tended to speak with a slight frown as if he had to concentrate hard to make his lips move. But Dick had seen him as a child in the summers, and at that stage he had been as noisy and intractable as any of the children who had to be herded into the mountains for hikes by counselors the hotel hired as Pied Pipers. So he tried to think the boy's quiet intensity was only a stage.

"Sorry I'm late," he said when he reached Dick and stood on the edge of the porch. "Couldn't get a lift."

"Too bad you're on the other side of town. Otherwise I could pick you up on the way."

"I don't mind walking. Sometimes one of the crew picks me up, but they're still at the lake."

Dick nodded. The boy had been sent to work with the crew at the camps, but he had made the men nervous. He was so

45

quiet that they began to assume he was listening to them, and they stopped being able to gossip freely among themselves. Besides, he was a summer person and they had little to say to him. "He don't even know a two-by-four when we ask him to fetch it," the foreman had said to Dick when he called from the ranger's camp to say he was sending Seth out. "Better if you find something for him to do up your way."

"That house of yours warm enough these nights?"

Seth nodded. "I sleep on blankets in front of the fireplace. Sometimes it's too hot."

"You let me know when it gets bad. You're welcome to—"

"I'm fine."

They stood in silence for a moment. The boy almost never initiated conversation, but Dick was not certain what to talk about, and often his attempts were not encouraged by Seth's preoccupied responses.

"You're eating all right? Your age, I couldn't cook an egg. Marge does a good job down at the diner."

"I don't eat much," the voice said vaguely toward the straggling line of deer on the golf course.

"Well, let's get started. I'll show you the implements and open up the rooms in the west wing."

Dick turned to the dark oak doors of the main entrance, but Seth's voice stopped him, a monotone that nevertheless seemed taut. It made Dick jittery, and sometimes he would remember it in the silence of his own quarters, a cabin the hotel maintained in the valley for the use of the manager.

"You don't have to find something for me to do. I can get by."

"It's all stuff someone has to do. Might as well be you."

"I'm sorry I made them nervous. I like it at the lake."

"They're just not used to . . ." but he paused, uncertain if it was right to make those distinctions with the son of one of the club's prominent members. After all, he himself was probably closer in status to the working men than to Seth Raymond's family.

"Not used to people like me."

"I guess." But as he pushed open the doors and waited for the boy to enter before he let them swing back, he wondered how Seth would define those differences. There seemed to be many ways in which he was unlike most people, not just in breeding.

"You think I'm strange, don't you?"

Dick did not look at the face of the figure walking beside him through the shrouded lobby where even the moose head over the mantel was draped with a sheet.

"I've met stranger."

"I decided last night that was what I wanted people to think. I act strange, but I'm not really. I'm showing off when I do that. I want people to think I'm different."

Dick had never heard the boy talk so much without prodding. He reached the main light switches and flipped them on, a necessity since most of the windows on the ground floor were still shuttered and boarded up. But he did it also to reassure himself. Seth's voice was so slow and eerie in tone that for a moment he wondered if he ought to be alone with the boy. Was he capable of some crazed violence?

"Oh, I don't notice anything like that about you."

"But I am a stranger," Seth continued as if he had not heard Dick. "Stranger to the people I try to work with, stranger to my family, stranger to myself. Last night I set up a mirror in the living room near the fireplace and stared at my face for one hour without looking away. By the end I couldn't recognize anything. There wasn't anyone there."

Dick held still. The pale blue eyes did not blink for a long time. The boy's mouth was shut tightly.

"Here, now. Let's sit in the office awhile."

"Nothing more to say," Seth said as they moved through the lifted counter.

But Dick sat in the swiveling chair behind the desk and motioned Seth to the accountant's stool.

"It's time you quit living in that house by yourself. You come down to my camp for a few nights."

Seth's head shook. Dick never liked watching that long hair move in its rope down the boy's back. It made him uncomfortable to think of having all that hair, especially when he imagined how his own parents would have reacted if he had ever done such a thing. But he knew if Seth were his own son, he would have to endure such things. His brother, Phil, had two sons and long hair was the least of the problems they presented their father with. Besides, the boy did not flaunt it. He flaunted nothing.

"You talk like that and I worry. Staring at mirrors in an empty house. Look. It's hard enough for an old galoot like myself to be alone sometimes, but at least I'm used to it. You're young. You should be with other people."

Seth let a laugh escape. "I am. I'm lots of people. That's the problem. I don't really have a me like most people."

Dick began to feel the pressure of his own inarticulateness that the boy always brought out when he tried to talk to him. He could not understand why he wanted to explain everything to Seth, to argue him out of the odd, tortured ideas that he occasionally expressed. He had developed a genuine concern for the lad, and had wondered even on that first night when Seth had appeared at his door—a refugee from a job in Florida—why the boy could make him feel like a vexed father. Surely his own son would not have been like this, polished by a good boarding school, drop-out from an Ivy League college.

"Oh, we all feel that way sometimes. I mean, I do something strange and I wonder who I am. But you don't have to dwell on it."

"I don't. It's just that way."

"Spend too much time by yourself and all you can do is think."

"Are you afraid of thinking?"

"No, no. I don't mean 'thinking' that way. I mean thinking about yourself. All this deep stuff about who you are and so forth. Too much is bad."

"Your mind does what it wants to do. Can you stop thinking when it wants to think?"

Dick tried to lean back and look at ease with his leg crossed, but he was getting tense. He could not see the boy's eyes clearly because the desk lamp cut a shadow across the upper half of Seth's face.

"Well, I can remember when you and Jim Biddle let the air out of everyone's tires during the annual picnic. What were you thinking of then?"

"That wasn't me."

"Come, now. We knew who did it."

"No, I mean I didn't know anything then. My mind never bothered with itself then."

Dick sat forward. "It's those schools you went to, isn't it? All that learning that's going no place. You need some direction for it all, Seth, something you want to do. When I was your age I had to scramble. I read and learned a lot, but I had to figure out where I was going. You need—"

But the boy was riffling a pad of receipts on the table beside him. "Did you call my parents?"

"Yes."

"So they know I'm here."

"Well, I thought it best. That first night, I was worried."

"They don't care, really."

"That's not true. I've known your mother for years."

"So have I."

In fact, Kitty Raymond had not been very interested. "He's

turned up there? He never writes. His uncle saw him in Virginia some weeks ago."

Dick had tried to reassure her that he would give Seth a job, something to do for a while.

"That's good of you, Dick. But don't be disappointed if he walks out on you. We simply can't get him to stick to anything these days. His father's furious about the way he quit Dartmouth, after all the trouble we went to getting him in."

By the end of the conversation, Dick had been embarrassed, as if his call had been an imposition, and he was also a little annoyed that she had not recalled who he was for a few minutes in spite of the fact that he had known her when she was a teenager and her parents had begun coming to the club. Finally with relief in her voice she had said, "Oh, Dick Felt. Of course. I have you so connected with summer that I simply couldn't place you for a while."

The office was a large, high-ceilinged room, darkly paneled like the rest of the hotel and still filled with much of the furniture and fixtures from the early part of the century. The board of directors had offered to modernize the office once, thinking that Dick would want that and was probably miffed because so much had gone into the new kitchen and bathrooms without upgrading his own facilities. But Dick had refused. He liked the old wooden filecases, the slanting accountant's table and its high stool, the coat hooks made from the curved hooves and legs of deer. He and Seth sat quietly for a while, and somewhere far over them a loose shutter began thumping in the rising wind.

"I'll have you keep an eye out for that while you're cleaning. Probably needs a new clamp."

"It's going to snow." Seth stared into the lobby.

"No." Dick was genuinely shocked. He had not turned on the radio that morning, but the sky was so cloudless, the sun so mild that he saw no reason to doubt that this was spring at last.

"By afternoon."

"Not now. Not in May."

"Six to ten inches."

"I'll believe it when I see it." He stood. The idea of snow was discomforting, even ominous, but he was relieved to be talking about the weather. He could not follow much of what the boy said. The first night, Seth had come to Dick's cabin because he knew no one else in town very well. He had been drenched by an ice storm when the bus dropped him at the junction two miles north of town. At first Dick had not believed him when he said he had been working at a hotel in Florida. "You're too pale." But Seth had been a night bellman. "I slept during the day."

That evening he had taken the glass of bourbon Dick offered him, "to cut the chill," and had rambled on intensely, making leaps of association that Dick could not follow, about the nature of Spirit and Matter and whether there was a gulf between the two that made man hopelessly divided since he was part body, part soul. All this had reminded Dick of the class in philosophy he had taken just after he had retired from his winter managing job in Charleston. He had been trying to improve his mind. But now he could not remember what all the answers were that he had read, so he had nodded and listened to Seth and tried to ask questions that only puzzled Seth further. "Well, I mean . . ." Dick would begin when trying to explain the connection between what he had asked and what Seth said, but he only ended up sweating, turning down the thermostat, tossing all night in half-waking dreams where he stalked phrases that would have set the boy's mind at ease. The next morning he had made Seth some breakfast and driven him up the road to his family's summerhouse.

"You won't keep warm there, Seth. You'd better take me up on my offer."

"I need to be alone."

But Dick knew those summer homes. No insulation. No running water in winter. The boy would have to lug that from the brook below.

"If you change your mind—"

But Seth was saying his thank-yous on top of Dick's voice, and then the car door slammed. As he turned around in the narrow slot between tall pines, Dick watched the figure walk to the steps and pause. He had a way of rising on the balls of his feet with each stride that Dick recalled even from the boy's childhood. He was still standing with the knapsack slung over one shoulder, staring at the roofline as if something were perched there, when Dick began driving down through the woods. That was the first time he had felt the vacancy in himself, had put it into words by thinking, *That could be my own boy, my son.* But he also felt the figure was himself, as if only part of him were steering carefully over the narrow bridge and the other were slowly rising up the stone steps with a key in hand.

Cleaning was the only job he had been able to think up for the boy. He could not carpenter or plumb or do the finicky lawn work on the bowling green, so he had asked him to begin cleaning the hotel, room by room. There was always a residue of mouse droppings, some fallen plaster, perhaps a dead bat or two and stains from places where the melting snow had backed up against window frames and leaked in.

"I've never seen this place without people in it."

Dick laughed. "Well, you will now. All of it."

They left the office together and Dick led him to the equipment room where the brooms and dustrags and pails were kept. Then they took the stairs to the third floor, walking slowly since Dick's right knee had never fully healed after he twisted it in a fall three years before. But as they climbed the stairs that snapped from unaccustomed weight after a winter of disuse, Dick could not help seeing the place through Seth's eyes, and this was disquieting. The long corridors looked so drab and empty. Each room he opened, with its rolled mattress and draped furniture, was a blank chamber that trapped and dulled the daylight. Here the windows were not shuttered, and he could see out toward the course, the flagpole, the slopes of the mountains. But even the landscape had a disheveled, negligent look to it. What he saw was indecisive, not one season or another, waiting for something but not urgently. When he recalled Seth's weather forecast, noted that already a pewter tinge was dulling the brightness of the sky, Dick wondered if this was really the place to leave the boy—bearing dustpan and broom and cloths in a deserted beehive with chamber after chamber of neglect.

They came to the end of the corridor and the last room. Dick walked in and some fallen plaster cracked underfoot.

"Just take your time. And if it gets too chilly, come on down to the office. I've a heater there." But the words were lame. These rooms, suffused with the morning's sun, were warmer than the lobby had been.

"No one would want to stay here if they could see this. We never see things the way they really are." Seth turned away from the room to stare out the window.

The brass bedstead did look particularly drab and dilapidated when not filled with its mattress and the elegant ruffled counterpane.

"It's different in summer."

"Look."

On the roof sprawled the carcass of some large bird, reduced by the long winter and its various thaws to shreds of sinew and feathers. The skull was bare, eye sockets rimmed by delicate shelves of bone.

"Must have flown into the wall, or maybe the window. We'd better shove it off."

But Seth did not seem to hear him and was still staring. "Dead matter," he said. "That's all."

Dick was annoyed to be staring at it like that. "I said let's knock it off."

Still the boy did not move. Dick's pulse began to lift. He wanted to order the boy gruffly, even to take him by the shoulders and shake him. *Here, stop all this staring and muttering. Get on with it.*

Instead he unlatched the window and flung it up. The sash weights thumped. He reached for the broom and pushed at the carcass with the handle. A wing flapped loose and began sliding over the edge. He reversed the broom and swept at all of it with the straw end. The dead bird rolled into a confused mass over the edge and out of sight. Then he swept wildly at the remnants of bone and flesh until only a dark imprint was left on the shingles. Because the end of the broom had touched the dead bird, he was certain he had some remnant on his hands. When he came back into the room he was out of breath, and after leaning the broom against the wall he wiped his hands up and down his pants legs.

"There. Easy come, easy go," he tried to say lightly, but his heart was pounding. The boy had turned away, was lifting a dustrag from the box he had carried up. "Well, that's it, then. Need anything else?"

"No. Thanks."

Dick leaned toward the boy's back. For a moment he thought he would start yelling something or would grab the boy's arm and spin him around. But yell what? Angry for what? Instead he walked to the door, did not look back when he said, "I'll be in the office," and strode to the elevator, thinking he had better make certain it was in good repair. He stopped at each floor, and by the time he was in the lobby again he was calm. He sat at his desk and leaned back for a few moments with his eyes closed.

Suddenly he felt like calling Phil. *Boy, do I understand now what you were saying about Mikey a few years ago. They can really get under your skin, these kids.* But he would not. He thought of Phil often but rarely communicated directly. When he used the telephone he always seemed to reach his brother at the wrong moment.

He worked hard all morning on orders and on replying to various letters from members requesting reservations. In many ways this was his favorite time, the month or so when he could have the place to himself, watching it and the season slowly open up. He could see to repairs with no interruptions, could look through catalogues and arrange for a future that each year he liked to believe would go off as planned. Winter damage this year had been minimal, the crew on the lake had even reported no incursions by bears or the thieves who sometimes snowshoed in from the north on old logging roads. In another two weeks some of the staff would begin to arrive, trusted employees who had been with him for at least ten years— Beth Dee who ran the house crew, Francis Lintot the chef, and his accountant Al Moulton. They would work through the days, each knowing what to do, lunch together in the spacious main kitchen where Fran—as they called him before the season began and it was necessary to be more formal in front of guests—would have prepared some little specialty for them to eat with the lunches they had brought. Beth was widowed, the other three all single, although Al had nearly married twice and liked to joke about the occasions as "near misses."

By mid-morning Dick was not concentrating on the requisition form in front of him but reminiscing. This had been happening to him often in the past weeks. He had not been able to subdue the autumnal haze that surrounded all his acts this year. When he had turned the key to his cabin and entered to find all the small objects and mementos of his thirty-year occupation still in place with only a winter of dust to be shaken or rubbed from them, he had stepped over the threshold and paused. He had the eerie sense that he had walked through the opening in a time machine. From then on everything he did was being performed "for the last time." He emptied the hearth of fallen clinkers and the ashes of summer's final fire—for the last time; he spread the comforter and sheets on chairs in front of that evening's fire to freshen them—for the last time; he drove up the road to the hotel slowly, savoring that moment when the bend would take him through the trees and provide the first view of the rambling, turreted structure of the hotel—for the last time. He tried in subsequent days to ignore the new vision, but finally knew he could not. So he gave in and found each day was full of repetitions and yet intensely unique. *Enjoy,* he said to himself, even opening a bottle of wine with his dinner occasionally to sip a glass or two alone. He had earned this. And so he began to believe that he had put all those years into this job just for these days, these last repeated gestures that no one but he could fully appreciate.

But at times he wanted to tell all this to someone, and he looked forward to the arrival of the others. Even though they were not retiring, they would understand if he told them a few things about how the place had looked when he first arrived, or rambled through one of his stories about Old Man Angus Nicholson, the founder of the club. They would even understand those days when he felt a tugging close to pain because sometimes he did not want it to be the last time. Sometimes instead of reminding him of how often he had performed an act in the past, the act forced him to look forward into a future with no clear functions. But Dick did not believe anything could be gained by dwelling on painful matters. If you did not look into them deeply, they often withered away. Pay attention to a pain and you only feed it.

When time for lunch came, Dick left his desk, walked through the lobby, and out onto the porch. The boy had been right. The sky was covered with a heavy, seamless lid of gray and the air was decidedly chill and damp. He even suspected the haze he saw on the furthest ridges was a snow squall. Well, he would turn on the second electric heater in the office and call the boy down to eat lunch with him. He would tell Seth some of the morning's memories—about those rooms the boy was cleaning (almost all enclosed some story he could tell), or perhaps about Seth's grandfather, who had won the August golf tournament whenever he entered it. What the boy needed was some entertainment, something to get him outside himself.

At the bottom of the stairs he called out, "Seth? Seth?" His voice had a peculiar resonance there, smothered by the draped lobby and drawn upward into hollowness by the empty, spiraling stairwell.

He thought he heard a door slam on the third floor. "Hellooo. Seth?"

Still no answer. Dick took a few steps up, then paused. Maybe not. He could not help thinking of Seth's tense, uneasy manner. Better, perhaps, to leave him alone. He had told him to come down if he wanted. No need to drag the boy around. After all, he was almost a man and could look after himself. He had to learn how to tough it out. But for a little while Dick felt slightly guilty. He had to admit he was avoiding him much as the work crew had. They were right, though. Seth's presence, no matter how silent and polite, was somehow oppressive. And telling Seth about the hotel's past would be almost impossible. The boy would somehow turn any conversation around to his obsessive questions and speculations. "Too deep for me," Dick would have to say again, irritated at Seth as if the boy were only trying to show up Dick's ignorance.

Seth did not appear for lunch, and after he had thrown the empty bag in the trash basket and swept the crumbs off his desk, Dick went back to work, concentrating hard to make up for his lapses of the morning. The heater ticked off and on. A few strokes of rough wind shook the windows behind him, but by mid-afternoon he had worked his way through half of the accumulated correspondence. The season was already well booked. He would have to work hard to stay on top of things this summer.

But again he began losing his concentration. He would hear Kitty Raymond's voice, or see the shape on the roof where the bird had rotted, or see Phil when he was seven and their father had died—a boy in a dark suit rented for the occasion, his eyes wide and unblinking—an image that had made Dick, who was twenty-eight at the time, vow to remember all he could about their father over the years and tell him, tell him. He put his pen down and rubbed the tense lines above his nose. Of course, the boy had not really cared to listen, and whenever Dick had tried, the attempt always seemed so self-conscious that Phil would walk away or turn on the TV. Phil's mother certainly never even tried. Why was he thinking of Phil now? He stood and went to the window, unlatching the inner shutter.

The air was full of fine, light snow falling so thickly and through such still air that he could hardly see the long shed where the lawn equipment was kept. Snowing. In May. He had seen it before, and he knew better than to believe in its permanence. By tomorrow there could easily be as much as a foot of it, but just as easily the first clear sky would expose it to the May sun, and then everything would be bright, sparkling, and fluid. But this time he could not see that sunny day clearly any more than he could see the shed. The snow clung to everything it touched, weighting down the bows of the nearby maples. His own body felt heavy, his pulse a slow, mechanical thumping in his ears.

The sleeves of Phil's rented suit had been too small, exposing the cuffs of his shirt. But in his brother's place, Dick saw the pale, unhappy face of Seth Raymond. He imagined the boy was standing three stories above him, staring out a window at the same view. They were both watching a large, fiercely black crow flap across the space between the shed and the maple. The bird moved so slowly that the snow and landscape seemed to be shifting past the stationary crow. It clutched at the limb of the tree, shaking down white bars of snow. He thought of the boy looking at the crow and of how Phil had tugged roughly a few times at the uncustomary tie as if he were strangling. Dick imagined opening the window as he had the doors to the rooms above, turning the key with one hand, the cold knob with the other. What he saw beyond the threshold was the view of tree and crow and shed and falling snow, and superimposed on it, hanging at about the level of his eyes, were the scuffed boots, the frayed denim legs of Seth.

He turned and bumped his chair as he ran toward the stairwell. He was calling, "Seth, Seth," as he plunged upward, and even though his knee nearly buckled with pain, he kept taking the stairs two at a time. On the second floor he paused and tried to listen, but he was out of breath, his pulse beating so wildly that he could hear nothing, so he stumbled on. Down the corridor. The door was open. He stopped just inside.

Seth was standing at the window, his back turned. The room was not any different than when Dick had left him there.

"Didn't you hear me?" Dick had to catch hold of the door frame.

The head nodded.

"Well, what's going on here? You haven't done anything. This place's still a mess."

The boy did not turn or even lift his hands. Beyond him Dick could see the grainy sky.

"Answer me, damn it."

He walked toward the boy. He was going to shake him up good this time. Have it out. Enough of this. He wouldn't put up with it anymore.

His hands reached out and tugged at the boy's shoulders. He shook him hard, once. The head gave a jerk. The body seemed very lax, as if suspended.

Dick's throat constricted so tightly that any words he might have wanted to say could not come out. The figure turned but he did not let go. Seth lurched into him, and Dick found his arms circling the shoulders, his hand patting roughly against the back. The boy was weeping, shuddering in uncontrollable sobs and moanings from a face burrowed into Dick's chest.

"Help me, help me," were the words he heard, and Dick clung, uncertain if the voice were the boy's or his own.

bill's women

When the lights flickered in the bedroom, Sheila Tonson knew something awful had happened to her husband. As if she had been the one jolted by electric current, she heard her own voice say, "Bill," as the air was shoved out of her lungs.

It was a dim November afternoon, no snow on the ground yet and the light already fading by three-thirty. He had left the house with his rattling aluminum ladder to set it up against the wall of the barn where the line from the road was attached. She had not understood what he was about to do, something concerning splicing this to that in order to have a new wire to the pump house. She had only understood that he should not be doing that sort of work himself.

When she asked him not to, he said, "If I wait any longer for them to do it, I'll be without a pump in the first high wind."

She had gone upstairs to change the sheets on their bed, had turned on the light and admitted to herself that she could smell snow in the air. The first snow. She shook the flinty, clean air out of the fresh sheets, flinging them across the bed as if netting the mattress. Then she gave the top sheet an extra toss just to fill the air again with its odor. She tucked and thought of first snow, the child in her that would keep coming back to the window to watch flakes fall, hoping they would not stop until all that bare, dead ground was deeply covered, until the old year was buried and the familiar trees and fields and barn were changed to new, white shapes. For her the first snow was never an end, it was the beginning, a resurrection of sleep and dreams more powerful than spring.

She was fluffing up his pillow when the lights went out and on again, a brief gap of darkness followed by a surge of light brighter than usual. Her heart stumbled also, then beat wildly in the renewed light. She ran to the window and could see nothing but her own reflection against the blur of the yard and distant barn, so she had to go back to the bed and turn out the light. Then she could see the ladder against the wall and a heap at the bottom that had to be Bill, although at first she could not distinguish any limbs to make it seem more than a bundle of old clothes. She held perfectly still for a moment, one hand clasped on her neck. He did not move. The line from the pole by the road had sagged into the high grass. She went to the telephone and called the emergency number that rang at the firehouse. Then she went to the kitchen window.

A seam of bare sky was visible between horizon and clouds. A reddish glare seeped from it, tinting the fields. Her eyes ached from staring hard at the dark lump below the ladder. If only he would move. She could not go to him. She knew he would not want her to see him like that, but above all she could not bear the thought of having some awful image of him to carry into her dreams forever. Her hand tightened on her neck until she felt her face flushing. The ambulance was taking too long, but when it finally wailed up the road, red lights flashing, she looked at the clock. It had taken them only ten minutes.

She stood on the porch. "There," she shrieked at them, "there!"

The seam in the clouds closed, and the darkened yard was lit by headlights and a single bright spotlight they trained at the base of the barn wall. The three men knelt and worked over the ground, one moving rhythmically as if doing push-ups, another curled over as if to drink from the pool of a spring. She was bitterly cold but did not leave the porch railing. As Howard Senecal strode toward her in his drooping rubber boots and high helmet, she felt the first pinpricks of snowflakes on her bare arms.

He stopped and stood at the bottom of the stairs looking up. Because the men who unrolled the stretcher were in no haste, she knew what he would say.

"Would you like to come to town with us, Sheila?"

"He's dead."

Howard nodded. "Can I call the electric company? That downed line's alive and might start a fire."

He came the rest of the way up the stairs. "I'm sorry." He clutched one hand on her bare forearm. "Nothing we could do."

For a moment everything was unreal. The body of her husband was being carried through bright light into a red truck. The snow was beginning to glint and fog the view. Her life was utterly changed, but a man was talking about how Bill never should have been working with that line. How was she supposed to act? What was she supposed to do now? She had never felt so absurdly uncertain of herself. Only a dream could move into such an area of shocked contingencies, disconnections of fact and emotion.

Then her voice was drawn out of her once more, as it had been when the lights blinked, and again she said his name. "Bill?" She was calling his name across the long yard to the ramp of the barn as if it were any evening and she had something waiting for him inside—a phone call, a meal, a need.

The rest was motion, confusion, faces coming to comfort, Doctor Clough offering pills, a thoroughly unsoothing funeral service in an icy rain that left the fields bare again by evening but blotted with a dank fog. Within a week Sheila Tonson was alone in the house, her house now. She was forty, a widow, childless, not unhappy to be without Bill, but with nothing whatsoever to do.

She did not expect to grieve long because she thought she did not love Bill. She was very fond of him, and their four years of married life had been mostly peaceful and pleasant. Bill was twenty years older than she, had already been married, and had two grown sons who had moved to Montana and never came home. They wrote long letters once a year, a mimeographed correspondence that they sent to all their friends and relatives telling about their successes in retailing farm machinery and in various local elections. They were twins, as inseparable as if joined in the flesh.

Bill's first wife had killed herself. She had been found hanging from a rafter in the barn two weeks after the boys left for the West. No one knew what to blame her death on since she had been largely responsible for their departure, nagging them about their recent failure in running a shoe store, accusing them of being a burden to her and Bill when they should have been preparing to provide for aging parents. The Annie Tonson everyone in town knew did not seem capable of remorse.

But Sheila had hardly known Bill in those days. She had been a librarian, a legal secretary, finally a bookkeeper at Plunkett's Grain and Feeds. Here she had occasionally seen Bill Tonson come with his boys to pick up and pay for supplies. She had seen nothing extraordinary in him—one of those wide-girthed, red-complexioned, and balding men who were predominant in the gene pool of Orleans County. Only his voice set him somewhat apart, a quiet tenor, toneless but peculiarly mellow as if resonating in a mahogany box before it came out. She began to recognize it from where she sat in her cubicle near the main desk.

Whenever he came in, and even during the years of their marriage, she could close her eyes and imagine someone very different possessing that voice. This person was taller, his face thin but expressive, his hands agile and strong. From hearing Bill Tonson's voice she developed a whole theory of misplaced souls. The voice revealed the true nature, and often she closed her eyes when one of her acquaintances talked so that she could imagine the real body, not the one in which such a soul was presently trapped.

Sheila was not capable of disagreeing with people to their faces. After they were gone, she might argue or state her position in her own mind. Her parents had helped her to understand how disagreeable a place the world would be if we always stated our own thoughts in opposition to others. But sometimes when her exasperation was too great, she could not help speaking out, and the voice with which she spoke always surprised her. It seemed like someone else's. Since that voice was not consistent, she would ponder for days afterward who could have possessed her at that moment. But she kept these ideas to herself, certain there was something shameful in them.

Sheila was not passionate by nature. Her father had impressed on her the possible consequences of uncontrolled emotions. His brother had married three times, failed in numerous businesses, and finally disappeared on a trip to Mexico. She had her moments of sudden physical desire, but they seized her only rarely and never at appropriate moments. She remembered a school tour to a natural history museum in Montreal when she was in eleventh grade. She had been looking through the plate glass at a diorama of bison and a nearly naked Apache family stooped over a fire. When the other students and teacher moved on to the next case, she continued to stand there. She felt flushed and feverish, and she pressed hard against the railing post. She was certain she had been here, was that child holding a stick toward the fire. For weeks afterward she recalled with dismay how close she had come to forgetting she was in a public place.

Occasionally she would be standing at a window or in the doorway to the barn, and some wind would toss the shadows in a nearby tree or one of Bill's horses would nicker in a distant stall and she would want something to enter her body and whirl it into a dance out and away into a new life, or into one her life already contained but that she could not find. She would stand still, waiting for the moment to pass and leave her in peace again. Passion was something that seized her like a huge bird she knew only through the sudden flap of its invisible wings, an airy grappling, and it came only intermittently in her forty years. This was something to be borne and to be kept totally private.

She and Bill had been honest from the start. They had come across each other at the county fair watching a pig race. They had both bet on the black and white sow, who had lost badly. Of course they had met often at Plunkett's, but this was the first time they had not needed to discuss accounts or orders. Sheila knew about Bill's wife and the departure of the boys. Bill knew that Sheila was unmarried, into her thirties, and beginning to look more plain than ever, especially because now she took a little less care with her graying hair, letting it stray from the coils she pinned up from her bare neck. Her waist and hips were filling out against the ever-tightening skirts and slacks.

At the high rim of their fourth ride on the ferris wheel, they both admitted to loneliness, to being tired of empty rooms and a life stretching ahead of them with meals and evenings accompanied only by radio or TV. They spent a suitable two months making sure their habits were sufficiently compatible, then Sheila sold her family's house in town, where she had been living after her parents had died. They had been married in the parlor by Garth Tinker, the local JP, and had taken a four-day trip to Montreal for their honeymoon, admitting halfway through it that they would be glad to get home to the farm, which was being tended by Bill's neighbor, Jim Dyson.

Sheila did not lose weight, and Bill did not stop yearning to hear more from the boys or occasionally lapsing into an evening of too much whiskey and inarticulate attempts to thrash out the mystery of his previous wife's death. Sometimes Sheila was sorry her own life had been so unexceptional that she had no past to wave in front of him. She began to feel she knew the elusive Annie Tonson almost better than herself, or at least that Annie's past was more vivid than her own when it came to her in the snatches of scenes and conversations that Bill managed to make clear through the movements of a numbed tongue. Once she even found herself standing in the empty oat bin staring at the rafter, wondering if she would one day hear Annie Tonson's voice in someone else's body. If that were possible, then what body had Bill once inhabited?

Her own voice might be someone else's, but she could never hear it objectively enough to know if it fit her body or not. The week before she left her job at Plunkett's, she used the tape recorder in the manager's office to record her voice. She read from a book that was lying on the desk. But when she played it back, she had none of that disembodied sense that she often heard in other voices. She closed her eyes and only saw Sheila Tonson staring at herself in a mirror. She'd quit her job because Bill had enough saved up for them to get by, and the small parcel of land he had sold to developers was going to provide more income when properly invested. He could not stop farming till he "dropped in his traces," he had said, but he kept only one horse, a small herd of cattle, and let many of the fields lie fallow. The day after she quit, the indignant manager called to ask her what right she had to make fun of his reading habits by recording a page from *The Black Lace Murders*.

The marriage was, in their terms, a success. If Bill drank too much or if she suddenly could not bear the invariable snoring he lapsed into when he turned on his back in the middle of the night, she could retreat to another bedroom. He would look at her searchingly the next day, was perhaps a little gruff, but he came to accept her occasional need for solitude just as she knew the bouts with regret and anger from his past could not be avoided. What they shared was a sense of reticence. They did not probe into each other's moods or predispositions. Even if Bill flailed at a remorselessly unforgiving Annie, he did not criticize Sheila for forgetting his birthday or for walking so far into the woods on Sandler Hill for the afternoon that she did not have dinner ready at five-thirty. Both of them seemed to realize that they would have less if they did not have each other, and they could not keep each other without mutually respecting quirks and silences.

So when Sheila did not run from the house to stoop at his side when Bill fell from the ladder, she was only being consistent to the way they had lived together for four years. She had not doubted when she stood at the window that he was dead or dying. He was doing something immensely private that he might want to share with his boys or even Annie, but probably not with her. In fact, from what she knew of him, she suspected he would have chased all of them from the room had he been able to lie in a bed and struggle his way out of existence as most people did. He would have growled, "I can do this without your help," just as he would have if he were stretched under the tractor with wrenches and spare parts. His very act of trying to fix the line without the electric department's help had represented his stubborn independence.

But now Sheila had nothing to do. She was a town girl, daughter of the couple who had owned the Tom Thumb Children's Wear Store. She liked living on the farm but knew nothing about caring for cows or planting fields. She turned the livestock over to an auctioneer, and only a few days after the funeral the barn was empty, even the machinery sold to various local bidders. The money amounted to little, enough to pay the loans on the bailer and tractor, but Bill's savings were considerable and she still had the land.

At first she assumed that after she finished sorting through Bill's effects and rearranging the house sufficiently so that she would not feel his absence in the familiar objects from his life, she would apply to Plunkett's or the library or maybe see if the new Temp-o-Sec office in town would use her. She liked the idea of moving about from business to business on a temporary basis.

The attic was filled with Bill's clothes and photographs, the snow had returned and not melted, even Christmas had come and gone before Sheila had to admit she was not interested in finding a job. When she went downtown to shop and walked under the tinsel wreaths, past the loudspeakers crackling out a rendition of "God Rest Ye Merry, Gentlemen," she became confused about what she had come to buy, stood in front of store windows absentmindedly, bought a book she did not want to read, and drove home. From time to time Mable Deslauriers or Nina Farrell would drop by to gossip, or she would feel obliged to visit them because they urged it so often, but she found it very difficult to carry her side of the conversation, often responding to some comment of Mable's that had obviously been made some time before.

"You should sell the place, move into town," Nina urged. "You shouldn't be alone so much."

But instead of becoming more insistent, their visits became less frequent until they were not coming at all and Sheila spoke with them only once every few weeks on the phone.

But gradually time did not seem a problem as it had soon after Bill died. Sheila rose early, often in the dark in winter. She ate her breakfast and did the dishes while the morning news chattered at her from the television and its pictures flicked and flashed against the darkened windows. Some days she would find herself at the sink again, the same black and white images reflecting off the window, but she would be washing the dinner dishes, uncertain where the day had gone. She moved about the house, read magazines, made some curtains, walked along the road for a few miles to the bridge and back if the snow was so deep that she could not trudge into the fields or woods.

Sometimes she heaved back the barn door on its runners to stand in the darkened interior, breathing in the odor of old hay and manure, the grease of iron parts, and cracked leather straps hanging from nails. She felt at home there more than any place else, even if it was so cold that she could stay for only a few minutes. Though there were none, she sensed the presences of animals there, large and dumb and trusting, waiting patiently to be fed and watered, totally dependent on her coming and going.

On a warm day in January when the snow melted and flopped heavily from the roofs, she stood with her back against the wall of the oat bin. She closed her eyes and turned her face upward and breathed in sobs as if some huge hand were about to push her relentlessly under water. When her voice began to say, "Bill, Bill," she knew it was not her own. But only that evening, long after she had held her breath and knelt with her hands gripped between her thighs, had she known whose voice it was. Annie's. She stood in the kitchen and said his name again, but that was only her own voice speaking. Annie's voice did not come to her again all winter, even when she went to the barn, and her body remained calm.

In the spring two tall men walked through the gate and up the driveway to the house. Sheila was standing at the living room window watching the chickadees come to her feeder, so she saw their slow progress up the rutted drive. They were dressed in topcoats and city shoes and had to sidestep or leap the puddles. The fields were bare except for a few lines of white where the drifts had been deepest. She knew they were Bill's sons immediately. They dressed exactly alike, were almost the same height, and from that distance their features were identical. They stopped at the edge of the front lawn and talked together, pointing here or there, nodding, and finally walking on toward the porch.

She opened the door before they knocked.

"This is Harry," one of them said, and the other pointed to his companion, "and this, Harvey."

"I know." Sheila stood aside. "Please come in."

She had to stare hard to find distinguishing characteristics. But they *were* quite different. Harvey was heavier, not fat by any means, but he had blunted the same features his brother possessed, and his right eyelid had a droop that kept it half-closed all the time. Sheila was looking for Bill in them, but decided they must have taken after Annie.

"We're grateful for the letter you sent," Harvey said.

"And sorry we never wrote back. We thought at the time that we'd let it all be. With both of them gone, it seemed like a good time to forget."

She offered them coffee and some muffins she had just made. They accepted and said they preferred sitting at the kitchen table rather than in the living room.

"It's changed a great deal. The house." Harry's voice was

slower than Harvey's, as if he had been a stutterer in his child-hood but had overcome the handicap.

"But we're glad for that," Harvey added quickly, a hand in air. "Makes it easier."

Sheila kept staring at them. She had seen them, of course, when they were younger. But she could not connect those lanky, shy creatures, who sometimes disappeared together for hours in the stacks of the library, with these men who were nearly her age. It was odd how seven years' difference could seem so large when younger, so negligible now. Part of the trouble was that Bill always talked about them as "the boys," so she had never seen them as men in her imaginings. But she saw they were staring at her too.

"Well," Harvey said after a considerable silence, "I'll have to admit I was wrong. I don't think I knew who you were after all."

"Me neither." Harry nodded at his brother.

"You see, when you married Dad we tried to recall you and finally thought we had it figured out. But we were wrong. I don't think we knew you at all."

"You didn't. Not really." Sheila was tempted to blurt it all out, to say, *But I used to see you when you went to the movies on Saturdays and I remember the time you tricked Dan Pursell at the gas station, and what about when you came with your dad to Plunkett's—*, but she held still. It did not matter.

Perhaps the set of her lips was too stern, because Harvey said, "We've not come back to claim anything. Not to trouble you. It's just our own little voyage to say goodbye to it all before we go back for good. And we wanted to thank you."

"Not just for the letter," Harry continued. "For whatever you gave to Dad. He wrote. He always mentioned you. We're not good correspondents."

"No. You're not." She blushed, sorry she had said it, but

unable to forget some of the mid-winter bouts Bill had with the bottle or the disconsolate way he would come back from the mailbox in the weeks around holidays like Christmas.

"We could explain," Harry said, "but won't. We also didn't come back to dredge things up. It's just good to go and say goodbye, don't you think? We waited till spring."

"You're welcome to stay here."

But together they shook their heads. "No. Thanks."

"Would you show us the grave?" Harvey asked.

She offered to drive them into town and they accepted. As they walked down the porch steps, she kept her eyes on their faces intently. The barn was straight ahead, but they seemed to glance at it with indifference before stooping into the car.

"He's buried beside your mother," she said as they drove by the ramp, but neither of them replied.

The graves were in the "new plot," two acres of recently purchased land a mile from the church. She led the twins through the black iron gates, sorry she had worn her overcoat because here in town, more sheltered from the wind, the sun was warm and the ground itself gave off a green, ripe scent as if it were yeasty and bursting. The boys stood by their father's grave, hands folded in front, looking down at the inscription. Their eyes did not wander to Annie's headstone, and they positioned themselves with shoulders turned to it. *Shun* was the word that crossed Sheila's mind.

"You must be lonely." Harvey spoke toward the gravestones.

"Me? Not really. Sometimes."

Harry pushed one hand stiffly into his pocket. "It's impossible for us even to imagine being alone. We've never been without each other."

"Which doesn't mean we don't experience loneliness."

"True, Harvey. But together."

Were they talking to her? Sometimes in the car as they had

been coming to the graveyard, Sheila wondered if their conversation was more like listening to a single person divided into two bodies talk to himself.

"'William.' How strange it is to see his name like that. I never think of him as a William."

But Harvey seemed determined to continue. "Will you remarry? Sell the farm?"

"I haven't thought."

Harvey turned to stare at her, a sudden gesture as if his head had been restrained till then by a rope. In doing so his gaze slipped past her face.

"Bitch." His face was very pale, the lips trembling slightly, and the heavy lid on his right eye kept jerking.

Sheila lifted her hand to her throat. What had she done?

"Harvey. Don't."

"She drove us apart. It wouldn't have come to this, he wouldn't have died this way except for her." But his eyes shifted. "God, Sheila, I don't mean you."

"Annie," she murmured, but then she was angry. "What way? How do you know how he died?"

"I mean without us. No family, no—"

"I'm his family."

Harry had stepped forward to put a hand on her arm. "Can we go? Harvey gets emotional about it all. He didn't mean it the way it sounds."

"I didn't. That's true. I'm sorry. That sounded insulting."

The men began walking toward the car. She held still for a moment, looking down at the stained toes of her shoes, and soon she followed.

But as they drove silently back through town, over the bridge where the river roiled high and muddy against its banks, along the low-lying fields covered with sheets of grass-punctured water, her shoulders and hands began to stiffen. She wanted to yell something harsh into the quiet space the men folded around them as if they were conversing without words or even gestures. It was a language pitched outside her range of hearing. At the far end of the dirt road she could see the shape of barn and house diminished by the wide open sky, the bare fields.

"You two. What do you know about him or this place or even your mother? You ran away from all that. You left her to her own bad dreams until she hanged herself."

As she spoke she heard that voice again coming from her throat, circling out and back into her ears as if someone else who sat between her and Harvey were speaking.

"And Bill too. In all those years he ranted about her when whiskey had him, did I hear him say anything that showed he understood her or even tried? Did you? Either of you? I doubt it. Haven't you always been this way, so much yourselves that you need no one else? And Bill. Oh, he had his needs, but anyone could have done that. Cook, clean, lay out the clothes. Talk in the evening. Did he ever really need her? Did any of you?"

She stopped the car in the front yard. The porch loomed ahead. In the rearview mirror she could see the barn. Through everything she said, neither man had opened his lips. They had merely turned to gaze at her.

"Did you say that to him, too?" Harvey said. "Did you hear what I heard, Harry?"

"It follows. I guess Dad needed it, somehow."

"But we didn't."

"No. And don't."

Harvey put his hand on the door but did not open it yet. "You reminded us of our mother, Sheila. She spoke like that. *Me. Me. Me. No one needs me, no one loves me.* Self-fulfilling prophecies."

"I never talked like that to him." Sheila stared into the mirror. One of the cats that had survived all winter in the barn was stalking something at the edge of the ramp. "You made me angry just now."

Both doors opened. "We're sorry," Harry said from the rear before they slid out. "We didn't come to upset you. I think it's all been a misunderstanding."

She had to keep one hand on the car's fender when she stood outside in order to keep her balance. "Would you like some lunch?"

"I think not." Harvey was looking up at the house as if he might see someone in the windows. "We'll be going now."

"Then let me drive you back to town. I should have dropped you off there."

"No, thanks. But it's best we leave now, I think. Don't you, Harry?"

"It's a fine day. We liked the walk out."

"Isn't there something you want to take with you? His belongings, they're all in one place. You could look them over if you want. Photographs—"

"No." The voices joined again.

They both came to her side of the car. Each pumped her hand once and murmured good-bys.

"I'm sorry," she said. "I shouldn't have said those things. Only sometimes I think I understand her, I think—"

But they were already walking away, and without turning Harvey lifted a hand to wave, more a peremptory signal for silence than a farewell.

She put one hand on the warm hood of the car. The two tall figures in dark blue overcoats walked by the ramp, shoulders nudging as they strode. They were talking to each other and the sounds of their voices reached her but not the words. She watched them pass the leaning gateposts, watched them diminish in the narrowing line of the road until they were a single shape entering the tunnel of trees into the sky.

"Wait," she called out in a voice entirely her own.

But nothing held still. The grasses at her feet bobbed in a breeze, the clouds sped upward from the point where the twins had vanished. Only her own body seemed to hang still in the bright air.

the classicist

When the screen door slaps under me and I hear the shuffle of my father's feet slowly dealing out the porch stairs, I close my volume of Austen's novels and go to the window. I watch my father walk to the garage, where his car is parked and where the old rowboat is stored on sawhorses.

I do not need to put a marker in the book. I always read through it when I come home, and I know all her novels so well that I can find any scene in that old Modern Library edition immediately. And if I am wrong about where I have stopped—even so wrong that I reenter a different novel—what does it matter? Her words are a continuous river for me, and I dip in and out as I please.

I am standing in my bedroom on the second floor, my childhood room kept available for me through all the years since. I know some children don't have that kind of home. They're expected to fly out and make a nest elsewhere and write often but not return for long stays. But I am an only child, a daughter who does everything right even if it feels wrong to her. I've had plenty of wrongs, too—jobs I lost interest in or which lost interest in me, two marriages that happened so fast my parents barely had time to take sides (always mine, of course), an operation that left me with one ovary, a temporary overload of radioactivity, and a vow never to lose my hair again. At thirty-eight I came home from my mother's funeral, helped my father pack away her belongings, and went back to work. For two years I visited often, then quit my latest job as a fund-raiser for a prominent state senator and settled into the bed-room that still has faint outlines of Dumbo and Jiminy Cricket under its last coat of light blue paint.

My father needs me. For some years he has been losing touch—not Alzheimer's, they tell me, probably just arteries beginning to close down. My mother's funeral deepened the silences between him and the rest of the world. I have the clear sense that he is rowing out beyond the shoals now, into the darker water. I can't go with him, but I can be here.

He moves across the leafy lawn like a man walking through the ankle-deep backwash of waves, past my car, which has to be parked in the driveway because the boat takes up the sec-ond berth of the two-car garage. I always park it carefully in front of the door to his car since he is not allowed to drive, but I have not put him through the indignity of surrendering his keys. His license was revoked when a small encounter involv-ing his fender and a drive-up mailbox demonstrated to the police and a judge that he was not as aware of his whereabouts as he should be. He insisted on calling the mailbox "that truck parked too close to the curb." He was not mailing anything but trying to back across the lawn that he thought was the green-surfaced parking lot near the docks—and we live forty miles from the ocean.

I trust him not to row away, so the second bay to the garage is not blocked. The boat is permanently in dry-dock, as far as I am concerned, but he makes references to its position as temporary: "When we go to watch the August regatta," he will begin, or, "The crabbing should be perfect next week," or even, shaking his fist, "Oh God, if I could only be out of sight of land." At his worst moments he believes the universe began its dizzy topple and downward spin eons ago when sea creatures moved into the open air, and above all when they pushed up off all fours, incurring back problems by defying gravity. He has suffered minor back ailments all his life and has a theory that the brain functions more calmly and tolerantly when attached to a horizontal stem. But man's evolution had been permitted one cultural flourish that made all the rest worthwhile: the Greeks.

Is there any way not to love such a man? My mother and I certainly found him impossible to resist, each in our own ways. She had been one of his students and had refused to be limited to an affectionate but distant relationship. Basic Greek led to intermediate Greek, thence to advanced and an immersion in *The Iliad*. This led to Aeschylus and hints of a plunge into graduate school. But the summer after her graduation she stayed on to assist in the dean's office. The study of Aristophanes was one result. The more permanent was marriage in the fall. I followed in four years.

Every summer we went to the sea, and at the first sight of it as we crested that slight swell in the land before the salt marshes and dunes, my father would begin reciting in Greek, my mother joining him, those lines from Xenophon: "—and they heard the soldiers shouting out, 'The sea! The sea!' passing the word down the column . . . and when they had all got to the top, the soldiers, with tears in their eyes, embraced each other and their generals and captains." Then, for a few minutes as we hummed along the hot July road, my mother and father would trade that word back and forth as if it were an old, smooth stone they had long ago found when walking together—*thalassa, thalassa.*

Which is all the Greek I know. Loving my father could not prevent me from having the usual problems of resistance as a child. No school I went to offered Greek, so he tried to teach it to me at home. What child would spend an evening bent over an elementary Greek text when her usual dose of homework was done? Overt resistance would not work. He persevered, pursuing me even into the bathtub where he would recite verb forms for me to repeat as I built mountains in the suds of my bubble bath. So I enlisted in the opposing army. I threw myself diligently into the study of Latin. I excelled. I even tried to make a feeble pun, mocking my Greek word *thalassa* with the Latin *talassio.* By tenth grade I was reading Virgil in a tutorial with the Latin teacher, who could not understand where such a frenzied devotee could have come from, or how after twenty years of drilling young voices in *amo, amas, amat* someone should appear who memorized whole pages of *The Aeneid.* Poor Mr. Genovese was equally stunned when that same pupil in twelfth grade announced that she was through with Latin, that it was a dead language. He did not know it was simply a dead issue. My father had stopped trying to teach me Greek.

So now I have certain regrets, as all children must in middle age when they are past the stage of guilt and remorse and simply see the opportunities they blew. Latin slipped quietly under the rising waters of my life and now lies like a huge, intact ocean liner. Occasionally I dive into the wreck and swim through whole rooms of remembered phrases. But mostly this occurs in dreams or absentminded moments in buses or airplanes. Once, when parting from my second husband, who was anything but a successful empire builder, I silenced him by reciting Dido's lament from Book IV and almost forgave him all his minor philandering for giving me the opportunity to make Latin live. Mr. Genovese would have looked out from that rumpled, often bewhiskered face and grinned approval. He grinned rarely, and when he did, it always looked like his last.

I have come to believe that one of the worst crises of

middle-age is the way we stop fearing our parents as figures of what we might be and surrender to the comfort of being like them. After all, we never saw them as children, so childhood was all our own. They were always adults, and it is so much more economical when we become their age to wear the costumes they have left hanging for us in the closets of our memories.

So my regret is not that I cannot read Homer in the original, but that I cannot share with my father the meaning of those phrases he recites or the problems of interpretation that vex him, especially when he has been reading a new translation or some article in one of the many philological journals he subscribes to. I love the sounds. I am attentive and do not disappoint him in my willingness to listen and agree that this is great music. But that other dimension of shared appreciation, the meaning, is not there. I am still in the backseat hearing the words but not fully participating in the quiet joy shared by the two figures in the front seat as we approach the sea.

Understand, I have never wanted to take my mother's place. I think I have no confusions, or no more than the usual, concerning my father's position in my psyche. My failed marriages were not due to an ideal figure of a father superimposed upon the very real figure of a lawyer or the owner of a chain of gourmet food stores. I said my father was a lovable man, but I would not have wanted to be my mother. He was and still is an eccentric, and a child comes to an understanding of how to deal with such a man. I did not have to worry about his effect on his contemporaries as my mother did, and my friends saw just enough of him to regard him affectionately as "a character," even to envy me when they compared him to their own bland fathers. I never wanted to be any closer than I was and did not envy my mother. But perhaps I was only coming to the usual middle-aged conclusion of a sane daughter, regarding a father with the same stereotypical response I have to New York as "a nice place to visit, but . . . "

But I do live with him now, so something has not held up entirely in my life. I kept coming back to visit, but had no intention of staying. I suppose I am still thinking of it that way. But no one questions my presence. The alternative would be to put my father in a nursing home of some sort, and I have found no way even to begin to accept that. Here, his former colleagues visit from time to time, his journals come, his huge library surrounds him, and he slips in and out of the present time with no reprimands from me or the neighbors.

They are not surprised sometimes to see him resolutely striding with briefcase in hand toward the classes he stopped teaching fifteen years ago, nor to see me run after him still buttoning a blouse. He always willingly taught the eight o'clock sequence. "I'll take them waking up with egg on their faces rather than nodding off at noon with their tummies rumbling." I never force him to come home. The campus is three miles away and we have reached the classroom only once. He rarely makes these sorties in poor weather, so we walk together, and if I am slow in coming out the front door, often a neighbor will put down her gardening gloves and delay him by asking what the Greek word for *narcissus* is. He resents the use of Latin by botanists.

The one class he reached he taught very well. An advantage of teaching at a small liberal arts college is that nothing changes, especially the scheduling of classes. Professor Dinsmith had stepped into the course in introductory Greek that my father had been teaching at eight o'clock for thirty years, and he was into his fourteenth year when one Tuesday in October his former colleague beat him to the door, opened his briefcase, and began drilling the class on a verb form they had not quite reached but were willing to try. They assumed Professor Dinsmith was ill.

Fortunately I reached the doorway before Dinsmith arrived. I took him aside and explained. He himself was only three years away from retirement and already far more doddering than my father had been. He nodded. "He's welcome to them," he muttered. "Most dim-witted bunch I've ever had." So for the next forty minutes we stood discreetly against the wall and listened.

The class, a ragged chorus of early morning basses and sopranos, was chanting as if hypnotized while the tick of a pointer moved down the list on the blackboard and my father's voice, clear and firm as a priest intoning mass, led them on. Dinsmith wound his arm through mine as the class neared its conclusion, leaning into me. "God, I miss him," he said, and then his own shaky voice joined in the last five minutes of recital.

"Hello, Dinnie," my father said when we met in the hallway after Dinsmith's class had thronged by us, puzzled to see their teacher looking well. "You've got a sleepy bunch there." I knew then he must have come around again partway through the class. He can do that, popping out of his other world and into ours with the ease of a man stepping through a door frame.

"Come again," Dinsmith said. "Anytime."

But when we reached the green, my father drooped badly and we had to take a taxi home. By supper he had forgotten the whole thing. Or did he simply incorporate it into his day as he would have before retirement? For some nights I heard those students rehearsing what they did not know and forgot by mid-morning, heard Professor Dinsmith following down the blackboard of his own mind, heard my father's voice raising the dead—both the language and the moribund students. I felt like the lame boy left on the cold hillside after the Pied Piper had walked under the earth with all his charges. I had heard the music but could not join the procession.

The boat occupying half the garage had been built for my father by a class of graduate students as a secret project. One of the members of the class was the son of a boat builder and knew his father's trade. The others were willing to try. They read old texts and looked closely at diagrams of present-day coracles to be found in Greece and Ireland. At the end of the semester they presented it to my father and took turns reciting the catalogue of boats from *The Iliad*. They also served retsinated wine and some homemade mead. After the reciting was over and most of the wine consumed, they carried the boat and my father down to the college pond and launched them both into the spring evening without oars. I was ten at the time and a witness only because I had come to the pond by chance that evening to catch the bullfrogs who had begun their seasonal strummings.

At first I thought something horrible was being done to my father. A savage throng of men and women clad in tunics, raucously singing some Anacreontic poem, was pushing my father away from shore in a shiny, varnished boat unlike any I had seen before. I crouched in the reeds and waited to see if I should run for help. The boat cut neatly into the calm water, slowed, turned lazily, and stopped. My father stood and raised his hands. The students became silent. An occasional frog boomed, and the last flush of sunlight reddened the mops of the nearby willows.

I don't know, of course, what he began to chant. Occasionally he would gesture slowly with one hand, but the boat did not wobble. It turned in slow circles so that sometimes his voice was singing to the empty shore, sometimes to me, sometimes to his quiet students. They stood still, as if rehearsing for some *tableau vivant* entitled "The Listeners." On and on he chanted. The sun set, the last light faded. The glistening sides of the boat reflected the distant lamps along the campus paths. He was a dim, straight figure, and then only a voice.

Finally, silence. The water had gradually seeped up through the spongy soil and soaked my shoes. Someone called my father's name, and then they were all hollering, cheering, applauding, and one of them dove into the water, swimming to push the boat back to shore.

I went home, was scolded by my mother for worrying her so badly that she had called the police. ("Young ladies don't catch frogs." Then she added, "After dark," since both my parents were adamant feminists.) I never told my father what I had seen and heard. But I lived in awe of his memory thereafter. All that incomprehensible language and not even a book in front of him. Even now, though his memory fails him in the details of his own history, none of what he has read and studied has been lost. I am sure he will still be able to recite most of Aeschylus by heart when he is staring at my face without recognition.

So the boat took on some of the aura of that occasion for me, even though it was used mostly for crabbing at the shore thereafter, or evenings of rowing the lagoon when the tide was in. We never even considered leaving the boat for the winter in a rented space near the shore as some of our neighbors did with their whalers or sailboats. We rented a hitch and lugged his coracle home and tended to its restoration lovingly each winter. For a teacher, it must have been one of those reminders of high moments of rapport. For my father it was also a boat in which Odysseus might have sat on a calm evening, oars shipped, listening to the seabirds and plotting the last voyage.

I should mention one more confusion. I am pregnant. Furthermore, pardon the pun, I have no conception who the father is. The past year was not a stable one for me. A rush of adolescent sexual urges resulting in a confused promiscuity? Or was it another part of me who had crouched too long in the corner of my history, watching the biological clock run down? If so, that person was well disguised, because I had never wanted children consciously. In both marriages, I was the one who delayed, who had a thousand-and-one excuses. But for this pregnancy I could have implicated five potential fathers, and I would have wished none of them to rock my baby's cradle. By the time I had come home on the latest pilgrimage to tend my father, I had only a few days left in which to make up my mind. Kill it or keep it.

I am not a convincing Medea figure. But whenever I lie sleepless on my back in the bed I know best in all the world, the only bed I possess that has never groaned and squeaked to my lovemaking—a place where I can magically reassume my virginal spirit—I cannot find it easy to think of that little fish as a keeper. I have no one to talk to but myself, and myself has no words left. So I wait and listen and hear the two clocks ticking simultaneously—the timer that will ring soon announcing that beyond this point no legal ending will be available— and the heavy, slow swing of my body's pendulum reminding me, reminding me.

My father pauses by the door to the garage as if he is watching a spider web in the corner above the light. But I can see his lips moving, his head nodding to some rhythm, and I know he is reciting or trying to find his way through a passage. Sometimes now he begins a portion of a book or play and cannot recall what it is and has to keep on until he reaches a city, an identifiable headland. Then he will smile, crying out the author's name. I can't help him; I can only applaud his own childlike relief at the discovery of where he is.

He turns the knob and walks into the garage, shutting the door behind him. I wait. Already I tend to fold my hands across my belly as if there is a shelf to perch them on. It is the fall evening of a full-blown Indian summer day. The sun is setting, and as the lights on the distant water tower begin to blink, I hear nothing but crickets scraping and children howling at each other down the street. No lights go on in the garage. I time myself—a habit I have developed to calm panic when he does something I cannot understand. Far better he should find his way out of whatever strange territory he has entered now than that I should send out a rescue party. But five minutes of the gathering dusk and still yard are enough for me.

"Dad?" I lean into the garage, peering at the dark hump of his old Plymouth, beyond it to the shape of the coracle lifted on its trestles like a museum exhibit. "Hello? Dad?"

"Come aboard, Miriam."

The voice seems to descend from the rafters, certainly is floating in unlocatable space.

"Where are you?"

"I'll row to shore. Join me."

Then I hear the squeak of the oarlocks, see his figure in the boat. He has placed the stepladder against the side and sits in the bow, oars gripped but held high and still. I clamber in and sit in the stern facing him. For a moment he does not move, and then with deep, slow strokes he begins to pull at the air.

"Where are we going?"

"Only into the bay, love. Only until dark. Out of sight, out of the hearing of others."

I do not argue. I can no longer see the shapes of car or rafters, only the pale driveway glistening through the door windows, streaks of light from the distant porch. *Yes, dear father, let's row far out tonight and never come back, row down the street past all the familiar houses, past the gateway to the campus, into the fields and over the woods, into the sky filled with the smoke of burning leaves.* For ten minutes he rows with the same steady, unstrained rhythm he would have used to stroke us to the mouth of the lagoon, where he would have paused to show us the unimpeded horizon, the white-scarred plain of the open sea.

When he pauses at last to lean on the oars and we drift, I do not interrupt him. I cannot see his face, and he leans over the oars.

But finally I ask, "Did you and mother want to have me?"

At first I think he has not heard my question or is too far into his own voyage to hear.

"Always."

"No, I mean did you plan to have me?"

He laughs gently. One oar sinks deeply as he swipes a hand back through his already tufted hair. "Oh, that. No. We never made plans about the important things in our lives. When they happened, they felt planned."

I do not know if that upsets me, but I wait.

"We did not plan to meet each other. I did not plan to marry your mother, certainly not after I gave her a B in that first semester I knew her." He pauses. "I wonder how many of us are accidents, Miriam? But I gather it takes a very determined sperm to make the voyage. He probably doesn't even know where or why he is going, only that something is waiting for him there, wherever that is, and that the whole will be more than the sum of its parts. We wouldn't bother trying if we didn't sense that, would we?"

As he begins to stroke again, he recites and I listen. I am thinking—more praying rather than thinking—of all our accidents, the unknown mergings, the destinations we would reach but never know. As he rows and chants his Greek, I hum a lullaby, some quiet song my mother sang to me well past infancy but the words to which I have long since lost.

When he stops rowing I can almost feel the boat scrape the pebbled shore. He ships the oars, rises, and quietly moves to the side. In spite of his back, he is a very limber man for his age. Halfway down the ladder he pauses, lifts an oar, and takes it with him. He does not wait for me, has probably even forgotten I am there, but shuffles to the overhead door and pulls it up with a grind of chains and pulleys. The driveway, recently blacktopped, gleams like wet sand leading to the beached house. He has slung the oar over one shoulder.

"Dad?"

He turns slightly.

"Where are you going now?"

Someone's mother far down the street is calling a name over and over with weary patience.

"Inland," he says. "Far inland."

He turns and begins walking. But I do not follow. He is headed toward the house, to safety as far as I am concerned, but probably soon so far into the interior of a strange country that I will never be able to find him again. He leans the oar against the house while he opens the door, then carefully carries it in with him. I wonder where I will stumble over it.

But I am alone now in the coracle. I run my hands along the single oar and contemplate the dangers of rowing from only one side, the possible endless circle. Better to drift for a while. One oar serves well as a rudder. Maybe it is only an anticipatory twitch, but I am sure I feel that baby stirring within me.

my other life

an agony of self-realization
bound into a whole
by that which surrounds us.
                    I cannot escape
—W. C. Williams, "The Desert Music"

When I first met Polly at Swarthmore College, I hated her. She had everything I thought I wanted, and I was certain she knew that. She was a year ahead of me, not because she was a year older but because she was a year smarter. I was from Vermont, and she came from Devon, Pennsylvania, a small town on the Main Line. Polly's father was a Philadelphia lawyer. They had steers, sheep, some fields of hay and corn, pedigreed sheepdogs—a little bit of everything except money, which they had a lot of. She even owned horses, two Arabians. I had always wanted my own horse but had settled for renting a nag at the stables near my home.

Polly also had all the good looks, good grooming, fine manners, smoothly anonymous accent of a brightly polished Main Line belle. For a whole year, I never saw that veneer crack. She lived down the hall. She arrived a week late. She had missed her boat back from a summer in France. *What a character,* everyone said. *Just like her.* She always slept through alarm clocks. But Polly, as she sat like a queen among us in her diaphanous silk pajamas, let us know that she had missed the boat on purpose. She wanted more time with her French lover, Armand. One more mad, dizzy week in Paris and on the Loire.

Armand's father owned one of the country's largest chocolate factories. She would never see Armand again because he was to marry a sick little bitch in October, a family arrangement. In one of her audiences, she said, "Oh, Vermont. Didn't I read recently that in the last census there were more cows than people there?" Ho, ho. All those lovely people from New York and New Jersey and Pennsylvania and Ohio were very amused. My own laughter for a joke so hopelessly stale only made me focus scorn on myself as I lay in bed that night. Why was I in collusion? What did all of us want from her?

The next morning I woke early and went for a long walk before breakfast along the Crum, under the trestle, shivering in the chill air of late fall. I would go home. What was the use? I hated everyone around me, hated myself, hated this lush arboretum of a campus and those intense, hard-driving teachers. I did not want an education; I wanted to hear the sound of the foghorn on the jetty, to watch the lake freeze outward from shore past the bays until there was only that one black irregular hole in the widest part. In a week of still, bright, twenty-below weather, it too would close up. I wanted to put on my boots and trudge out into the middle of that lake, hearing miles of ice boom in invisible quivers, looking down through crazed layers to the ultimate dark of cold and alien water.

But I went to class—a quiz on four books of *The Iliad*. I knew it cold. I went to music history. I raised my hand and correctly identified the point at which Professor Sweeny had lifted the needle from the record as the beginning of a four-part fugue. He was ecstatic. "Someone is listening," he said. By noon I was enjoying fighting back. I went to a gym class in field hockey that I had been avoiding. "You've missed so many hours you may not pass," my boulder-kneed instructor said sternly. "We'll see," I growled and left a large bruise on the opposing forward's shin.

Although still on the same floor, Polly dropped out of my concern. I heard her voice, I saw her perfectly formed, slender body in the showers, and if I was on duty, many of the phone calls or messages were for her. But we shared no classes and no friends.

When I returned the next year, I discovered that Polly and I had both moved into the same dormitory, although not onto the same floor. But that hardly mattered because this hall was much smaller, more the size of a stone house with a cozy sense of family living space. But she was not the same Polly Brent. At first I thought she had gained weight. Her gestures were blurred; even her accent was less chiseled. She kept to her room on occasions when usually she could not have resisted joining us to sit on her imaginary dais. She was going to her classes, although she had carefully arranged to take none that started before ten in the morning. And when the phone rang for her, she often refused. "Tell him I'm out." "Tell him I'm sick." "Tell him I don't remember who he is." Finally there were no calls.

That Polly was a heavy drinker became clear to me one morning when my alarm clock did not go off and I woke at nine-thirty, having missed a class. I stumbled into the bathroom. She was on her knees in one of the stalls, vomiting. I pulled the door to her stall shut. She muttered, "Thank you," without looking back, and continued. I was drying off from my shower when she staggered out, went to the sink, and tried to get her face under the faucet.

She did not seem very steady on her feet, so I said, "Want a hand?"

"Would be helpful if you could guide me to my room."

I gripped her elbow and steered her down the hall, up one flight of stairs, and into her room. She pulled free and took a dive for the bed where she curled on her side, pale face toward me.

"Anything I can do for you?" I did not want to bag my next class, a vocabulary quiz in French. That was when I saw the bottle of vodka on the dresser, the cap beside it, a half-filled glass on the bedside table. She was watching my face.

"None of your business."

I shrugged. "Can I get you something? Do something?"

"Yes." Her mouth quivered. "Close the door on your way out." And then she was weeping, her eyes closed, fists clenched in front of her while she sobbed in great wrenchings as if her breathing were blocked. I shut the door but stayed inside.

At first, because her eyes were closed, she did not know I was still there. I stood with my back flat against the door. Her wretchedness was so extreme that I thought I had never heard real weeping before. She saw me finally but could not stop, tried to say something, probably telling me to go away, because she waved one of those fists.

I could have left or I could have smothered her with the pillow. But there was really only one thing to do, so I went over and sat on the floor in front of her and began stroking one hand across her forehead and over her hair as I vaguely recalled my mother doing to me when I was six and very ill with measles, just before she died. At first it seemed to make things worse and then she began to calm. I was surprised at how fine that lush, blond hair was. I had been right to envy it.

For a while when she was no longer crying, she merely stared past my face in dazed silence. Then she said, "I'm sorry," and tried hard to focus on my eyes.

"That stuff's not very good for breakfast."

She licked her lips as if to be certain they were in place. By now I was sitting with my hands in my lap.

"Actually it's not bad. If you're careful. This morning I woke up and started too early, or really what I mean is I never quite got to sleep so when the sun came up, I decided to stop pretending I was going to sleep and I started too soon with too much." She took a deep breath, held it a moment, then relaxed a little.

"Do you do that all the time?"

"How 'all' is 'all the time'? Lately, yes. Just a little bitty in the morning. A little bitty more in the afternoon, much more in the evening. It helps."

"Helps what?" The distant clock tolled ten. Zero on vocabulary.

"Helps me. Helps Polly Brent." She tried to smile but gave up. "Oh, shit. I'm going to be sick again."

I helped her down to the bathroom and back. This time when we entered her room, she did not dive for the bed. Instead she let her nightgown fall from her shoulders, balled it up and threw it into the corner. She walked naked to her dresser and slipped into a blue sheath of silk.

"I feel much better."

I stood with my hand on the doorknob.

"It isn't the house so much, or the divorce, or even their meanness to each other. It's the horses."

She was looking warily at the door behind me, so I closed it. She sat on her bed with her back against the wall, and I perched on the chair by her desk, still thinking that it might be best if I were on the other side of the door.

But I wasn't, so the second thing I learned was the series of unhappy events that had dislodged Miss Pauline Brent from her regal position. If she ever really had one. What I began to see was how much of Polly was our invention, all of us around her who were willing to create a world suitable for her beauty and poise and intelligence. Who was she to say no? Weren't we all making ourselves up out of the pieces others gave us?

The House of Brent was in collapse. Polly, since early childhood, had known her parents cared little for each other. They liked to say they had an "open marriage," but this meant paying close attention to various lovers in order to use their observed failings as representations of each other's poor taste ("Really, Donald, what you can see in Betsey Harding's simperings before the two of you get into bed, I don't know. She must have stuck a hatpin through her brain years ago," Ellen Brent had said one Christmas Eve while Donald and Polly and her brother, Malcolm, were decorating the tree). But knowing that, Polly had decided that she was responsible for holding them and the house together. She moved between her parents as if gripping the frazzled ends of a divided rope in each hand trying to pull those ends close enough together to tie them, or still believing that if the strands touched, some magic would splice them. She was twenty when I was sitting in her room and both ropes had gone slack. No one was attached to them anymore. Her parents were divorcing each other viciously, although to Polly each one claimed to have found true happiness at last. All of her conscious life Polly had held on tightly. Suddenly she had nothing left to do but live her own life. She could not find it.

"But the horses." Her voice quivered. "They're selling my horses."

I asked if I could see them. She shook her head. The house in Devon? No, again. Then abruptly she leaned at me. "Yes. Let's go. Now."

She owned a little MG her father had tired of and not traded in when he went on to Ferraris and Maseratis. She took a long, cold shower first, was waiting for me in the parking lot, her wet hair loose to dry in the October sunshine. But her hands were steady. She tossed her hair in the breeze and drove with deft assurance. She was doing something she liked to do. I slumped down, let my head rest against the back of the seat, let the landscape rush over me.

Months later, under the influence of a second bottle of wine for lunch at some inn she drove us to, I told her that my mother had killed herself when I was nine, slicing her wrists on a summer afternoon when I was away at camp and too young to understand much of what had happened except to feel an unending absence. Polly looked at me without speaking after I had finished as if listening to a very distant sound.

"Do you remember that day I took you out to Devon? When I had been so drunk and you listened to me?"

"Yes."

"I wish you'd told me then."

"Why?"

"I needed something from you. I had told you everything and I wanted to be given something in return. No, I mean I wanted to give something to you by listening also. I owed it to you."

"But there's nothing to tell. I was much too young when she died."

Polly and I rarely spoke of my mother again. I told her I wasn't avoiding the subject. It simply was not part of my own consciousness anyway. My mother was a woman I never knew.

A discreet sign outside the unoccupied house announced For Sale, but there was no look of neglect or absence about the trimmed hedges, clipped lawns, carefully plucked beds of marigolds and chrysanthemums. She had a key, and before we stepped in she turned, shielded her eyes with one hand, and looked down across the nearest field toward a very large, solitary, and spreading oak with a fence surrounding its trunk.

"There they are." She pointed.

In the shadow of the oak, two horses grazed, necks sloped down, tails twitching lazily. I had the sense of a framed painting, lovely but nothing one could walk into, as if its wide, panoramic spread were suitable only for a museum.

She took me on a tour, and her voice was so unemotional that I might have been a prospective buyer in the presence of a real estate agent—until we reached the room she called hers. It was on the third floor. Compared to all the other rooms— high-ceilinged, windows almost full length to the floor, letting in broad swatches of light and making the fields, the trees, and the distant river seem only a step away—hers was cramped. But the sky dominated her room. The slow, fall clouds of the quiet day were shifting across a hazy blue.

"We moved here when I was seven. They didn't want me to have this room. They put all my stuff in the room downstairs, but I spent my time here, and one morning they found me asleep on the floor with my blanket and pillow. They had to give in. It was weird. For almost a year after, they still called the room downstairs 'Polly's bedroom,' and Mother kept it decorated as if I lived there. That was all show for her friends or the time in spring when the house was part of the historical tour. It's a very old house, you know."

She was sitting on one of the window seats and I on the footboard of the bed, still watching the sky over her head.

"The main reason I liked it was I couldn't hear them arguing. Up here, I only heard cars coming or going, maybe a door slamming, mostly wind or, best of all, that sort of quiet ticking snow makes. I would imagine I was an Egyptian princess in a tomb waiting to be kissed awake, listening to the sand blow against the stones. Look!"

She waved me over. The horses were racing across the field in long strides, necks extending, manes and tails blown back by the wind of their motion. They wheeled and stopped suddenly, tossing their heads a few times, then grazed again as if nothing had happened.

"Do you ride?" she asked.

"A little."

"I can't bear to touch them now. But at least you understand."

We both kept looking at the field and the horses. I was remembering my own nights when I might wake and hear my father coming home late after he had abandoned the house to me and the wind after my mother died—how slowly his footsteps came up the stairs to the room she had left him to, how I hated him for that because I wanted him to forget her for what she had done, to shut her out of his mind, to move to another room in the house.

Polly and I became roommates. One night, lying in the beds in our disheveled space, I began rambling on about boyfriends. When I paused in some anecdote, she said, "Hannah, you ought to know something. I'm still a virgin."

I waited. For a moment I wondered if I had stumbled onto a strange twist in someone I thought I knew. I had read in my psych course about women who were eternal virgins, who never acknowledged the physical penetration as a reality, only the giving up of some spiritual chamber that they had preserved intact in spite of any visits by lovers in the antechamber of the mere body.

"How do you mean that?"

"Seriously." Her voice maintained its even tone, something I had come to see meant she was in a highly emotional state. "I've lied about that." She started talking faster then. "Not recently, Hannah, not since we've really known each other. Oh, I let you think what you did, but there never seemed to be a place for me to tell you otherwise. You'd made up your mind. Don't be angry."

For a moment I did feel betrayed.

"Armand?" I asked tentatively.

"Who?"

"Your trip to France. You don't remember Armand?"

"Oh, that. I made that up. Of course there wasn't anyone like that. Do you think my father would have let me out of his sight anywhere in France, or that school I went to for the summer would let me out alone? God, they all but manacled us together when we went on tours to museums or little towns. The fall you remember, I didn't miss any boat. I was in Devon and I didn't think I'd come back to college."

"No Armand at all?"

"None. I wanted much more than an Armand so badly. When I started talking about it, to all of you, I made it cheap, just an echo of everything you all wanted. Not that I would have minded an Armand. But what I really wanted was so much more complicated."

"Wait. You *can* do that, then?"

"What?"

"Sit in a room with a lot of other people and start talking and know what they want you to say? Or be?"

The white column slumped into a half-moon curve, and one hand stirred, twisting the rope of her hair. "Sort of. I mean, I know when I start to tell something whether it matches what you want to hear, and then it becomes a kind of game. Can I stay on the beam? How far can I go with the fantasy before it isn't yours anymore? It's a form of lying, but sometimes I'm lucky and it's not too far away from the truth."

My silence was not intended to be cruel. I just did not know what to say.

"I've done that since I was a child, Hannah. My parents punished me for the lies they uncovered. But that didn't stop me; it only made me more clever, a little like training a dog to walk a tightrope on its hind legs. When I fell off, I was punished, but I assumed it was not for the act but for performing it poorly. They never caught half of the lies from the beginning, and even wanted them. Right away I knew it was the best way to keep my own world away from them. I found out their tolerances, how far they could believe, then gave them what they wanted to hear."

"Wasn't there anyone to share things with?"

She did not answer. A car moved slowly by; the lights washed from the ceiling down the wall to show her sitting cross-legged on her bed, hands in her lap, her head down and long hair hanging, spread out on each side of her face.

"Polly, are you telling me the truth now or telling me something you think I want to hear?"

She did not answer.

"Please tell me. How can I know you at all if you're doing that?"

"I'm very careful with you, Hannah. I don't think I've lied to you."

I leaned back against the wall. She did not move. I don't remember if we said anything else or just fell asleep.

In February of her senior year, Polly met a man named Dave Warnock, who was a graduate student in economics at Penn. Dave and Polly were married late that summer. I was maid of honor. The wedding took place in Haverford, a compromise location that her mother and father accepted after extended negotiations by her uncle. I found them both so pleasantly vapid at first that I began to doubt her stories of a bitter childhood. But late into the champagne and after I had not caught the bouquet and refused to sow rice on my friend, her parents began to throw words at each other across a depleted table with the vicious accuracy of experienced dart players.

I did not graduate from Swarthmore. My father died that summer. Not unexpectedly. He had a history of heart trouble, and doctors had cautioned him to exercise more, to avoid overtly stressful situations. But his work for GE was everything to him, and a contract with the Defense Department for a new gun they were developing had sent him into a few months of intense traveling, planning, persuading. I can't hear the guns rattling off at the practice range in Underhill without thinking of his death. I suppose I might have used what came from his insurance policy to finish at Swarthmore, and they offered me a generous scholarship, but I decided to take courses at the University of Vermont instead and to get my teaching certificate as quickly as possible. It was time to be practical.

Polly came to my father's funeral and helped me through those first days afterward when sorting belongings in a house too big for a single person seemed so torturous a job that I could have burned the place down rather than sell it. But she had her own life with Dave that she could not leave for long, and when I thought of Swarthmore without her, I had even less desire to return.

I did my student teaching at Burlington High well enough to find a job there when I graduated. I had expected it to be a beginning only. Perhaps I would not teach forever. Perhaps I would find a job at a school in another state. Perhaps I would stumble across a whole new interest. But I was busy. I did not dislike the teaching, and on occasion I was praised so I continued. I found myself living in a city that was changing fast, in a country that stumbled through assassinations, a hopeless war, a presidential resignation.

Polly and I saw each other occasionally. Sometimes she would telephone. We wrote. But soon the letters were only once a year or so, and I admit I was not a good correspondent. Dave had his degree. He was rocketing through the academic ranks. He received grants. They spent a year in England. What could I offer for news in return? "This year the lake did not freeze over." "They say the flora on top of Camel's Hump is threatened by the boots of hikers." My father too was reduced to memory. From time to time, I returned to that vague sense of some presence, some connection called Mother. I decided the presence was too vague to forgive.

Polly called one evening to tell me that Dave had accepted a position at UVM. They arrived so close to the beginning of the school year that I was too busy. We spent some evenings together, I toured them around to various sites on warm fall weekends, and then we had our flood of duties. I had a friend named Don, and he tried to be a friend to Dave, but they had little in common except for a love of fishing. But Dave did his with flies on mountain brooks, and Don waited eagerly for the lake to freeze so he could trundle his shanty across the ice and sit over the hole, pulling up perch. When I went to some occasion at their house to which their university friends were invited, I found myself immersed in an academic world I could not enter with grace—economists earnestly comparing statistics (and oh, the shaking of heads, the comfortable tone from some shared sense of betrayal in departmental politics), circuitously in-joking conversations about tennis games, or to one side the dulcet voices of the chorus chanting their fascinated horror at the president's wife's taste in wallpaper. I wasn't married, and the women did not know what to do with me.

One Saturday morning Polly made a grisly but humorous mistake. She saw in the newspaper that a Donald Mahoney had died, and not reading the article carefully, she ran to the phone.

"Hannah? Are you all right? What happened to Don?"

I told her Don was sleeping comfortably enough in his apartment and that we didn't share any space now. I could hear her breathing deeply a few times.

"You can't imagine the fright that gave me."

She paused, then a voice that might have been the Polly I had come to know in a dormitory room years ago said, "Hannah, I'm so sorry. I'm sorry for this wasted time. It's over, though. I'm through with all that. I can't stand it; it wasn't me. If I knew I had to do that forever, I'd just leave Dave."

She wanted to talk. Later that morning? Take a drive, maybe. It looked as though our usual two days of spring were here. For the rest of the morning and into the afternoon over a long, luxurious lunch in Weybridge, we babbled at each other, and midway through our second bottle of wine, we recalled another inn so many years before where we had stopped for lunch after our first drive together into her landscape in Pennsylvania.

But that summer Polly was hurled violently into a new life where it was hard for me to follow her. She insisted that she had died. For a few seconds. She and Dave had been driving through Ohio on their way to visit his parents in Chicago. He had been driving. He was angry because the next gas station on the turnpike was fifty miles ahead and he would not have enough gas to make it. A truck went out of control but he should have seen it. She was in critical condition. *No. Don't come.* Just had to have someone to talk to and knew Polly would have wanted him to call.

She had not been wearing her seat belt. Twisting away from the truck, she had been thrown against her side into the collapsing dashboard, her head snapping hard against the frame. It was that reflex of turning that probably saved her life, since her shoulder struck first, then her head. But Dave was certain she was dead. Her face was only inches away from his, turned to him, her eyes wide although she was unconscious. For a moment she was not breathing. His legs were pinned although only bruised, one arm broken, but he could not move away from the staring, blank mask, that transformation of her face. It took two hours to extricate them, while he kept yelling furiously, "Hurry, hurry, she's still alive!" and her breath, uneven and slight, foamed red at her lips.

Polly woke with her broken ribs strapped in place, her lung reinflated, a wide bruise for some time immobilizing expression on one side of her face. But all that would heal, and soon the tubes of the tracheotomy were removed, the opening closed up, plans made for some plastic surgery that she did not pursue because later she decided that was vain. But I think she really wanted to keep the scar.

What she said as soon as she could speak was, "I died."

Dave reassured her that she was alive. Impatiently she explained that she knew that, but what she meant was that briefly she had died. He was sympathetic. How? Why? What did she mean? She tried to tell him. She wept in frustration. No words, no words.

She insisted that what she was describing was impossible to tell because the only words we had for it were loaded with emotions of fear or desire and that what she had felt, seen, was intensely beyond all that. She became silent. Months later, when they were home again, she began reading about death wherever she could. She discovered a woman who for most of her professional life had studied and written about dying, and without mentioning her to many people at first, Polly became a sort of disciple, writing long letters to her, sending money for her research, even making a trip to California to visit her institute.

She gave me books to read. We discussed them. I was fascinated, even if skeptical of the evangelistic fervor with which the woman insisted that our ignorance was willed, a form of dementia. It all reminded me of certain moments I had read of in history when whole cultures became obsessed with cults of dying, staring at skulls, dancing in graveyards, expending enormous vitality on the celebration of death. But even when I agreed with Polly, I lacked a last dimension and failed her in some way. I had only the imagination, had not been there.

She yearned for that ultimate communication that would not need words, the shared silence of survivors. Her attitude seemed bound to arouse our resentment.

When she returned from California the first time, we were afraid she would move there immediately. Dave was frantic. "But how can I hope to find a position midyear when there are so few openings anyway?" He wrote to anyone he knew in economics in various California universities, even junior colleges. She looked at us as if from a great distance.

"Hannah," she said, her eyes on the snow blowing in swirls around the bare willow, "I can't tell you. A room full of us, and we did not have to say a word. We sat in a large circle, and she said, 'No one speak now for a while,' and we were silent and *we knew, we knew.*"

That niggling voice in me would not be any more still than Dave's. Was I merely being defensive, was it just the part of me that abhorred the idea of holding hands in a group and chanting, or repeating together the Pledge of Allegiance, or leaping to my feet with everyone else when a ball cleared a fence? From Swarthmore days I knew Polly's yearning for inner and esoteric knowledge, her brief forays into palmistry, astrology, Jungian mystagogy. I was ashamed of that voice in me. Like her, I could not forget the reality of her scar, and it reminded me of my own sense that the world was about to be hopelessly diminished when we thought she would die. But again and again I heard those words: *"We knew, we knew."* They were full of pride, the superiority of the chosen few. I wanted to snap back, "You're not the only one who can die."

She settled, however, for occasional trips. She became a Northeastern rep, contacting other members, recruiting some, setting up discussion groups, talking to local newspapers. Then abruptly she withdrew. "I've decided I don't need them," she said, and I did not press. But a month or so later, I read a UPI story about how her "leader's" organization was being investigated for various forms of fraud. Apparently the woman's eloquence concerning death did not limit her capacity to enjoy a lively bank account.

Polly announced to me that she and Dave had decided on a divorce. But what they had chosen to do was live together in a divorced state—that is, become legally separate again to see whether the institution of marriage itself was preventing them from seeing each other and their situation clearly. Polly would fly to Mexico for a divorce. They had instituted proceedings in Vermont. In the interval between the two legal actions they would decide whether to continue living together or not.

For Dave it was a clear, reasonable contract, none of the indefinable spume of plans and designs that had been dashed up and over them during the past years of Polly's "discovery of her true life." As for Polly, she thought of it as a stripping away of masks. They would be two naked, separate human beings living each day with the risk that it might be their last together, waking each morning to pause and confirm their decision to continue for another handful of hours in each other's presence. But I foresaw two persons a year hence found slumped in a room of their house, staring blankly at each other's feet in a state of total spiritual inanition.

Polly asked me to come with her to Mexico. She would cover all expenses. She did not want to be alone. I agreed to come, but only if she let me pay my own way. She began to argue but knew me well enough to stop, put a hand on mine, say, "Dear Hannah." That hand did not tremble, but only because of the determined grip.

We stepped out of the plane in El Paso, and I was squashed by heat. I did not recover during the next days. Even when we wandered through chunks of air-conditioned space, I was stunned, and much of what I recall now comes to me through the rippled haze of a shimmering curtain. A limousine was waiting for us—a van from the Camino Real, our hotel. The driver flung our baggage into the back with the belongings of others like us, held open the door long enough for us to stoop and slide into our seats. Strangers, some familiar from our own flight, but all of us wearing the immobile faces of the herd. Most were women, but a man across from us blinked with a nervous tic that exaggerated the pinched angles of his face. We drove into a flat landscape, a perfect grid of streets, unmarred white glare of sky. No one spoke. As we crossed the bridge that arched over the muddy Rio Grande between El Paso and Ciudad Juárez, the traffic moved sluggishly. I longed for a breeze, but when the air stirred, it was only friction of heated layers. A figure was slumped in the middle of the bridge, a bundle of rags, faceless because his head hunched forward under a wide sombrero. The driver was talking to himself in Spanish. The others were staring ahead or sideways. Mannequins.

"Do you think they're all getting divorced?" Polly whispered.

"No. I think they're all dead."

My hair was glued to my neck. The city on the other side was denser and more crowded. Walls hemmed us in. People on foot, on bicycles, pushing carts, in carts, swerving in and out on sputtering three-wheeled vehicles. The sun spun over the top of a plaza with a truncated brown tower. We plunged under an arch, entered a small devastated area filled with blocks of demolished adobe and garbage. At the far end of a ragged lot was a new structure built like a fort. Camino Real. I staggered with Polly through the hissing door, and glacial air fell on us. Dark wood was carved to excess, brazen objects on the walls, serapes and paraphernalia looking as ostentatiously Mexican as a movie set. The carpets tried to pull me down like sand while I trudged behind our burdened porter and Polly, watching the heels of her sandals flop forever ahead of me. I waited until the door closed and threw myself on the bed. Water running in the sink. I closed my eyes.

When I woke I leaned up on both elbows, breathless, heart pounding. I had one shoe on, and I could not focus my eyes on anything in the room, dim because evening had come already. She was sitting in the studded Naugahyde chair, drinking clear liquid from a small glass. On the floor beside her was an ornate bottle with a sombrero-shaped cap.

"I poured you a glass too." She pointed to the bureau where it waited. "Tequila. Almost dinnertime. You don't want me to drink alone, do you?"

I lifted the glass; she raised hers.

"We're off." I winced.

"The second's not as bad. Let's eat. This is my last night as a married woman."

In the restaurant, everything was carefully arranged to have no character—dim lights, heavily darkened chairs that appeared to be solid and handcarved. But when I pulled in to the table, I could feel the flimsiness of it all. An electric candle flickered in the goblet between us, the menus were as huge as folding screens, the waiters smoothly obsequious. From nowhere a vapid medley of Mexican songs arranged for a thousand violins was oiling the air. Other diners were scattered about the room, but we could hear no voices. Polly asked the waiter for drinks, something typical, native, for both of us. He looked puzzled, brought Manhattans.

I stared at the woman two tables away. She was small, round-shouldered, her gray hair carefully curled. She tilted forward slightly to meet each spoonful of soup. Perhaps she was fifty, fifty-five. When she had finished her soup, she placed the spoon delicately on the plate and gazed straight ahead, folding her hands in her lap. The waiter bowed, drew away the bowl. As if she sensed me, her head turned slowly, unfocused eyes swept over me, then back. But she retreated to her own space, snapping her head into the slot of her forward stare, and the only sign of disturbance was one quick touch at her hair with a hand. Could she really be about to be divorced? But surely no one would come to this place for a vacation.

Suddenly I imagined I was there for a purpose, not Polly. I was there because I could not touch or speak or even lie with anyone in that unconscious but secure space of sleeping in the same bed. What violence inside us could make us puppets over our soup, strings tangling far inside but attached to invisible hands? Had there ever been any hope for Polly and Dave, for me and my men? Or for my mother?

We ate, drank two bottles of wine in an attempt to compensate for the tasteless food, and staggered away from our table and that room. Later I sat on the edge of the pool, the wax jungle behind me, parrots screaming at their cages, my feet fading into a robin's egg rinse. At the far end of the kidney, the huge face of an Aztec god was sticking out a tongue of water. Overhead was a black sky studded with real stars, and I tried hard to watch them without falling backward. Only three or four other swimmers were there, stroking on backs or sides or bellies through the bright splotches of underwater lights. None of them seemed to know each other. They moved in slow circles or treaded water in silence, not touching, always averting eyes toward the sky or water. The god kept vomiting.

I recall floating on my back with Polly's voice somewhere nearby, coming in snatches as the water rose and fell over my ears. The stars were swimming too. I stared and stared until they blurred. A watery sky, chips of light, all of us on our backs washing and rolling with the waves, surrounded by stars, planets, dying lights, floating wide ellipses of tug and push.

When I climbed out, she was standing poolside, mopping

her hair with a towel large enough to be a bedsheet, talking with one of the few men who had been in the van. He was smaller than she, slight and trim, a bikini enunciating clearly the outlines of a *putto*-like prick. He had the pointed ears, curled hair, somewhat raised small lips of a faun.

"I was hoping we could go out for a drink," he said when I reached them.

I pulled the blurred images of Polly together until they were almost superimposed, then shook my head.

She smiled. "Sleep?"

"Sleep."

She braced her arm around my waist. "Perhaps tomorrow evening? You'll be here still?" she was saying to the man.

I was lucky the next morning. I had escaped the punishment I deserved. No headache, no queasiness. I opened my eyes to see Polly by the side of her bed, wriggling into a silky, cool sheath of a dress printed with gay poppies and daffodils and pansies. She was Flora preparing for some woodland prance.

"Welcome to the first day of my divorce."

We tried to find a place to sit in the lobby. All the chairs were filled with people doing their best to appear casual, but the pages of the newspapers were never turned, and fast breathing belied their bored faces. So we stood tensely near the desk, turned toward each other with nothing to say.

We tucked ourselves into the back of the limo. I sat by the window. We left the rubble of the square and twisted back through streets of a city fully in motion. What day was it? Burlington was on another planet. Again, too many people were going too many places at the same time. The van moved through them in peristaltic spasms that had nothing to do with traffic lights or the occasional ineffectual policeman. Conflicting waves of people on foot or battered vehicles washed by in crosscurrents at intersections. From time to time we passed a store where a group would be watching the flickering purple of TV. We slowed to pass a swirl of people craning to see a white-smocked attendant spread canvas over a sprawled body. The boy pedaling his cart had paused to gawk, his knobby, barefooted legs straight down to hold his balance on the pavement. Suddenly from our right, a heavy iron cross advanced, held high by two old men, and behind them came three girls dressed all in black, faces veiled, their feet bare. They clenched hands stiffly by their sides, but no one was watching or following them. We passed a car turned on its side, the blackened hull of a burned store, a storefront mosaic of ten television sets all playing the same face at once, a square with a dry fountain, a sitting donkey being tugged and beaten at the neck, its face impassive. I closed my eyes.

The voice told us to watch the curb, please this way, ladies not to leave purses in the van, please, and then we were rammed through revolving doors, and like a stranded fish, I gasped in a bronze-lined lobby, shivering in cold air.

A cubicle among cubicles under fluorescent lights. A man in a dark suit did not look up from Polly's folder. "And this is all to the best of your knowing true?"

"Yes."

"And agreed to by your spouse?"

"Yes."

"And this is his signature?"

"Yes."

"And now yours here and here." Scribble. "And you have the validated receipt?" Crumple.

"Here will be your copy. Observe, please, the seal and that all else is in order. We will retain these for taking now with you to the courthouse. Thank you. Please proceeding into hall two."

He never looked at us. The papers were not handed to Polly

but pushed delicately forward by the tips of the fingers that retreated before she grasped.

"To the left," he said.

The elevators opened again as we passed the main desk. Another herd milled forward. None of ours. A different hotel. I tried to count quickly. Two, three dozen? Every fifteen minutes? All day. Five days a week. In how many other buildings? Our own people stepped out of their cubicles, eyes searching for the number. I held onto Polly's elbow, fearful of being washed away. We were in the wide, stinking *cloaca maxima* of American marriage.

This is not my story, I kept telling myself, *this is not my story. I am not married, I never have been married, I never will be married,* I chanted in a tense conjugation. An arrow and the number two. We slowed to the jam of emptying cubicles. I turned, panicked. Polly was not there. We were being pushed forward toward the open doors. I whirled. She was behind me, her face pale. I wound my arm around hers. In the elevator she said something.

"What?"

She shook her head.

The wall opened. The rope across the lobby kept us in the preferred chute, out the rotating blades where Polly and I stayed together, hopping forward like birds to keep our heels from being mashed. Then we were in the van, driving through the streets again.

We lurched to the courthouse, were ushered into a high-ceilinged room where other groups were waiting. The walls were painted with gaudy murals of allegorical figures holding scales and swords and books and severed heads, conical breasts bared and draped, horses rearing, infants impaled and radiant with light, the country's savior trampling over the armies of the mangled. Clerks wheeled stacked documents through; a clock struck the hour; we were steered into a larger room with a kingly dais, a judge in robes that bulked him up on the squat spread of his throne. Here a God of mammoth thighs and arms stared with swollen eyes at us from the ceiling, flanked by a Christ who gnashed his teeth in suffering, a Virgin Mary whose overripe face oozed with tears of sentiment. Staffs beat the floor. We were hushed. The judge tottered up in his robes, swayed, his tiny voice issued some benediction or curse, a sleeve flapped at us, he collapsed and stamped once with a seal. We were divorced.

"That's all?" Polly said blankly as we looked for our van, found it by the dent in its backside, and climbed in just before the driver pulled away.

By mid-afternoon I was focusing the shower on my face again. Polly was asleep when I came out, a body sprawled on its back, mouth open. I was the white attendant throwing a huge fishnet over her. I stood at the window and watched a maid making the bed in the opposite room. She turned on the TV and sat on the edge of the stripped mattress. A rocket was separating into pieces very slowly. Cartoon jets made spurts against the stars and pod-like feet unfolded. I put on fresh underwear and stretched onto my bed, turned to watch when Polly whimpered and rolled onto her side.

An old drunk woman had plucked at my sleeve in one of the basket shops. Her irises were as milky white as a blind dog's. The lines in her face had been carved and smoothed and carved again. Were all those urchins pulling at our sleeves hers? Who could ever fill so many hands, so much need? I stared at the space above Polly's head. I could not see them, but I pushed against whatever demons milled over her, tearing each other in their eagerness to stab and flail. I slept.

I woke to a sharp rapping on the door, groped into a bathrobe, helped a groggy Polly cover herself with a sheet. A cart, a tub with ice and a protruding bottle, a droop-eyed bellman.

"You want open?"

"No, thanks."

He handed me the card, waited while I fumbled in Polly's purse for a tip. He stuffed it in his pocket and was gone. Five o'clock. Polly was still half-awake.

"Auguri," the note read. "At six? Your friend, Claudio."

"Claudio who?"

Polly blinked. "Oh, Lord. Last night I promised we'd go drinking with him. I think."

"Should I open the champagne?"

"Wait. I can't think yet."

She swung off the bed, tangled her legs in the sheet, almost fell trying to stand, cursed, and freed herself. While she showered, I made up my mind. I had no intention of leaving the room that evening, not even until we left for our plane the next afternoon. I had two books. Ciudad Juárez did not exist, off my map forever, and I also had no intention of screwing up my thermostat again with violent alternations of temperature. Polly was singing in the shower. Polly never sang when she was happy, only when she had excess nervous energy.

I told her I wasn't joining her and Claudio.

"Sorry, Hannah. I can't sit still tonight. I don't want to think."

I sat on the edge of the bed for a moment, then went to the bathroom and the cold water. My father had told me how he learned from my mother to hold an ice cube wrapped in a washcloth against the inside of a wrist when the weather was too hot. She would say, "It cools the blood," chilling her delicate wrists, the corded bluish veins. And sometimes on lazy summer afternoons, she would reach to rest that damp wrist against his forehead.

Polly left in a whirl of silky layers, hair flowing free, crosscurrents of fine powders and perfumes and a quick, cool kiss on my forehead. For a while I lolled. The luxury of solitude. I lay very still, looking vaguely at the ceiling. Then I slept and found myself in my apartment. The wind was stirring slightly, a thunderstorm flashing and grumbling distantly over the northern spread of the lake. But the storm rolled toward me with slow and crushing weight. Everything behind it was covered forever with suffocating darkness. The trees began to bend, my mother was kneeling on a dusky lawn, her back to me. "Don't, don't."' My voice would not leave my throat. She held her hands out, urging the storm onto us.

Polly's hand was on my shoulder, her disheveled form leaning at me in the dark.

"Was I talking?"

"Unhappy sounds."

I could smell the stale residue of tobacco, booze, recognize the minor slurring of words.

"Happy drunk? Or nasty drunk?"

"I'm back from there, whe'ver that was." Her arm waved toward the door and she lurched as if she had thrown her body with it by mistake.

Very drunk.

"What time?" I asked.

"We recently entered a next day. It is the eighteenth of whatever."

She stood, lurched, sat, stood again, and began fumbling with the buttons of her dress.

"Need help?"

"No." She let the dress fall, trod it down, made her way to the bathroom, and kept talking to me through the open door.

"I thought you were seeing the town."

"Saw many bars. Saw streets with colorful local scenes. Listened to soulful songs and paid the piper. Cried a little together about the untuning of love and the sadness of life and how sadly the beautiful woman in red made music." The toilet flushed, and she clung for a moment to the doorjamb, then plunged forward, toppling onto the bed. She crawled up it, leaned her back against the headboard, knees drawn up. "Saw that living forms are all continuous. Burlington, Ciudad Juárez, the cactus and the eucalyptus and *Pinus strobus.*"

She turned out the light. We breathed quietly now, and our faces were turned toward each other in the dim glow from the courtyard.

"You're all right?" I asked.

"What was his name?"

"Claudio."

"Thank you. My turn never seems to have come."

"For what?"

"To hold your hand. You've never needed me like I've needed you."

After a while I said quietly in case she might have fallen asleep, "What did *he* need?"

"A momentary stay against confusion."

After a silence in which I thought she had fallen asleep, her voice, very much awake said, "Every thought I have is another lie."

I reached across the space between our beds, and she took my hand in hers. I remembered the oldest Polly I knew, sitting in a queenly barge of lies, watching our rapt gazes as we floated slowly with her down the river of our fantasies.

We let go, and I lay on my back, surprised at the spasm of frustration that I did not want to express to her now. After so much time, where were we? Had nothing happened in all those years, or was it that we had already known years before that this was where we would eventually be? I clung to whatever I could. I was Hannah of Burlington, she was Polly. I was a teacher. I lived as best I could.

"Don't be angry," she was saying quietly. "I'm divorced. I do not love Dave Warnock and there's no point in trying. I died once and was resurrected. A dubious gift."

I could almost feel the doorknob clutched in my hand as I had stood on the threshold that morning in Swarthmore. What if I had said a casual word and gone to my quiz, gently closing the door behind me?

"Good night, Polly."

"You *are* angry. Angry friend Hannah. Don't be afraid. Dying is not nearly as bad as it's cracked up to be."

"Good night, Polly."

No alternative but silence. In that silence I would try to think, away from all this roiling frustration her muddled words roused in me.

"Good night, Hannah."

Had we gone on, I would only have pressed her again about what she had seen on the other side of that dark, thick wall she called her "death," would have asked how it could have made much difference in her life if she was still the person she always had been. But I was wearier than I had expected, and as if this were only a lovers' quarrel, I drifted eventually into the silence of sleep.

When I woke her bed was empty. She had often been able to rise early from a night of drinking, then shower and show few aftereffects. For a while I lay on my back, wondering why I had taken her words so personally the night before. What did it matter what she told me or kept to herself? The truth was simply that our friendship had endured.

I found her where such things often happen. She was lying naked in the bathtub, water up to her neck, her head lolling back against the wall. The water was her own blood diluted.

I had heard nothing.

The plane that took me home carried me and her body. On the way to the airport, we crossed the bridge from Ciudad Juárez to El Paso. Again, the figure of a man sat slumped near the highest point of the bridge's curve. He lifted his head as we passed, and for a moment our eyes met, or at least I traveled through the line of his gaze. I wanted to stop our bus, wanted to leap onto that sidewalk and run to him. I would have shaken him by the shoulders hunched in his tattered serape. I would have asked him to tell me, tell me what we can do about the lives of others when we so insufficiently understand our own. Once I lay nine months in the belly of a woman, and then, because at least I still can see them shining in their pasts, she became more distant than the stars.

the wars i missed

For instance. I am standing on the platform of the railroad station in Bryn Mawr, Pennsylvania. I am twelve years old and on my way to school. It is a day of October contrasts— cool and damp in the frosted shade but warm where the sun cuts out its sharp-angled blocks. I suppose this is Indian summer, although now that I am much older and live in a less hospitable climate, I recall nothing in Pennsylvania so stark with contrast as the reprieve of Indian summer in New England.

I am trying to say something about The Present, about being witness in the flesh, and I want to call up this morning as proof of what that is and what it is not. The air is musty with dying leaves, horse chestnuts rotting on the sidewalks, drying clinkers in the rail bed. My canvas book bag leans against my leg. My ticket is in my pocket. I look down the straight lines of rails to where they curve out of sight toward Rosemont and listen for the hiss of steel on steel I will hear even before I see the blunt first car of the Paoli Local. Each day I walk a mile to the station, take the train three stops to Wynnewood, then climb on the school bus driven by a large, patient man named Napoleon. He drives us to the rambling brick mansion that houses my small private school. In the afternoon I am often taken home with other students in a school van.

The Paoli Local continues on from Wynnewood to Philadelphia, so I am in the company of very composed lawyers and executives with briefcases from which they will take letters, papers, and reports to read in preparation for their day. If I am lucky I will find a whole empty seat and keep a place for Peter Staples or for Charlie Morris, who may get on the same car at Haverford. Otherwise I sit next to one of those silent, pin-striped eminences whom I cannot imagine as fathers or husbands.

This is the main line, but my family is not living here for the reasons these people are. In my family, I am the only commuter. My parents live and work on a campus. They rent faculty housing. Philadelphia is a place we visit to gawk at William Penn high above us or throw peanuts to the elephants.

I want to pluck out this single day, even though it is many years distant from me now. But in doing so, I make it bear a burden of representation, standing for more than its single self. The maze we meander through has no fixed center, or at least I have abandoned the idea that a center waits for us. The maze has so many centers that what we choose on any given day is what we believe in. And any single day is wrapped in its past and future. I choose this day and warn that I am no philosopher. No compelling logic forms what follows. Shapes, perhaps. A pattern I think or want to perceive. Instances. For instance.

This is 1948, so obviously I have missed one war, except for the ways Peter and I played it out. As we learned how to listen to the radio or pay attention to the newsreels, that play became more specific, laced with German words, names of cities, types of aircraft. We took our turns being Good or Evil, sharing the *Luftwaffe* wings one of Peter's uncles had taken from a POW and given his nephew for Christmas. On a snowy hockey field we invaded Russia. Terrifying the frogs and soaking our Keds in summer we crossed the Rhine, trampling my mother's favorite patch of watercress.

But the real war did touch us. Peter's cousin was a ball turret gunner. His plane made it back, but the turret was shattered by ack-ack, and whatever was left of Carl Hinson fell somewhere in the Ruhr. My parents did their war duty by inviting soldiers from the Valley Forge Hospital to visit us for some home cooking. One of them—I only recall his nickname, "Buckles" which he insisted we call him—was so concerned at the dullness of my father's carving knife that he pulled his own Army issue from a pocket, flipped it open, and offered it. "Killed two Japs with that," he said matter-of-factly when Dad was slicing the breast for second helpings.

By 1948 and that October day, most of the surviving heroes have come home. Our history teacher, Alfie Hardy, to whom we sent gang-written letters when he was stationed in London, has come back to instruct us in the dynasties of ancient Egypt and the dimensions of pyramids. The stars of loss have been scraped off the windows and the blackout shades replaced with more translucent fabrics. No, not my war. But I can still be swept backward if I hear a snippet of dialogue from some black-and-white version of that world when I flick through the channels on a sleepless night or when I hear the somber tones of Edward R. Murrow describing the blitz.

In order to reach the platform where I am waiting, I have had to cross under the tracks. Since my earliest memories I have always loved and dreaded that tunnel. Before I could speak and tell her otherwise, my mother thought my joy at being taken to the station was because I liked the huge steam engines, and on days when she was not being a dean in her office she would push me in the perambulator, tilt me high enough to see over the edge, and wait for the chug and clang and earth-shaking clatter to pull in, my hand pointing, eyes wide and unblinking. But finally she came to understand that was small pleasure for me compared to being wheeled down the steps and into the damp darkness of the tunnel. I would howl with anger if she pushed through to the other end and began the ascent without pausing.

What I wanted was to stop in the middle, under those tiny stalactites of ooze, waiting for a train to cross above us. Then, in the thunder and clatter as I stared straight up, as if in a dream I would scream as loudly as I could but never hear my own voice. I was under the train and in the train, I was in a dream and wide-awake, I was the train and was myself—and even now cannot explain what ecstasy that was.

I wish I could say I am merely standing on the platform waiting, absorbing that October day. But if this moment is to stand for many others, its depiction must contain the same confusion of restless consciousness. I did not grow up to be one of those adults around me. After college I left Pennsylvania—my parents left too—and I have never been tempted to return. I do not mean that bitterly. I say that only because the place I live now is the only place I want to be. Like my father, I am a teacher, probably no more embedded in a community than he was–other than that floating world of academia. Just as he did, I walk to my office and classroom, albeit through more snow in certain seasons. I do not commute. But as I walk up the hill, kicking the leaves, my mind wanders as much as that boy's in Bryn Mawr—backward over some recent conversation, ahead to the day's possible events.

The train is late on that October morning. But I am distracted by a number of anxieties. I will have to face Miss Alley's anger because I have not memorized the Latin vocabulary for that day, and she has an infallible ability to nose out such lapses. I suspect I have not drawn a clear enough diagram of the final battle of Actium to satisfy Alfie Hardy. And I am wondering if Chum Deal will be driving us home again, drop-ping off Peter, then Charlie, then Anne Margolis, finally Brad Cummings even though my house should be next in order. Chum and I will be alone, and instead of driving straight up Gulf Road he will take some twists and turns until we are parked in the field on the bluff overlooking Conshohocken. Then we will make love.

I am too young to understand what we are doing. "Love" is something I hear about in the songs my sister listens to. It has to do with men and women who can't stand being without each other but more often than not have to suffer some awful pain because of willed or accidental absence. From time to time my friends and I have taken a crack at using that emo-tion in the presence of some older schoolmate or even a young woman teacher. But it doesn't work for long.

Peter, Charlie, and I would not have used the word because only girls did, but no doubt we all had a "crush" on Chalmers Deal. He was young (what does that mean to a twelve-year-old? I try now to imagine what his real age was—late twenties?), a fine athlete, newly married to the school's one secretary, Amy Ball. He had made it into uniform but not into battle. All of us on the six-man football team (he was the coach) had been to his house and seen the picture of his square-jawed, smiling face under its dark curls handsomely set off by the brilliant white of a Navy jacket and cap. I never lost that childlike wor-ship of him, even after he had pulled me into his own lunar landscape. I seemed to accept the irony that his choice of me for those moments of intense privacy made me special, more chosen than any of my peers—and yet I could not boast of this to anyone. He was my way of cutting loose from a family, especially a father, who I thought did not care enough for me. But I could not flaunt this in my father's face.

I was special because he was special. The two spinster ladies who ran the school, Misses Alley and Ratcliffe, doted on him as if he were an adopted son, and although he taught a different subject each year, they had unshakable faith in him. I overheard Miss Ratcliffe say to my mother once after a parent-teacher conference in which, to my dismay, Mother had complained that I was not receiving enough homework in French, "Oh, well, we must give Chum a little time. He's not taught French before. He'll settle down. The war did such terrible things to all of them, you know."

From the bluff we could see the steel mills below, the glint of river here and there, the dingy town made to look picturesquely spread along the valley by distance and the haze of autumn. We were also parked in the open field in such a way that we would not find ourselves surprised by other persons as we had been once when he drove us to a seemingly secluded lane near Villanova. A woman had drifted by on a bicycle, a bag of groceries in the basket up front. By the way she turned her face back to us and nearly lost control as the handlebars wobbled, we knew she was curious why a man and boy would be sitting so close together in the front seat of a parked school van.

Chum's face drained white. He pushed me away, zipped his fly, started the engine, and made a quick U-turn. For the next mile or two he drove with his eyes more on the rearview mirror than the road ahead as if she might pursue us on the airborne bicycle of the witch in *The Wizard of Oz*. My own pulse pounded. I had no fears for myself. But I knew from our conversations about secrecy that his life would be ruined—he'd lose his job, his marriage, his friendships. What we were doing was as dangerous as being on an unarmed freighter surrounded by subs. But I would escape and he would be blown to bits, and I could not bear that idea.

Even if I could not have named what I felt for Chum, the emotion was no less intense than what I called love in future years as I blundered through a number of marriages, a series of failures that finally left me standing naked and alone in a hotel room confessing groggily to the night clerk below that I had just swallowed the contents of an aspirin bottle. But my feelings for Chum did not remain fixed in the forms they had when we were alone in the school van or glanced at each other during practice or in geometry class. Once I was old enough to understand the forms of betrayal his actions represented, I found anger, bitterness, even resorted at some periods to a kind of homophobia.

But gradually I began to believe that I could look back to him and those years with some purity of memory, the emotions purged of all the ways of looking at them that I had invented since. I think that began when I was sending my last son off to school for the first time. He was born when I was nearly fifty, and each of his steps into his life took on for me a ceremonial and often elegiac tone. I was keenly aware that in his rites of passage I was being given a last chance to re-experience my own. He was only going to first grade when it all came back to me, although the age of six might seem to have little to do with myself at twelve.

But the beginning of school is the start of the parent's true ignorance about what his child is doing, thinking, living. When I walked back upstairs after buckling him into a neighbor's car that would take him away, my own most secret life came back to me so strongly that I could not prepare for that morning's class. When my wife, Kay, paused at the doorway to my study, then came in to put her hand on my shoulder because my eyes were filled with tears, she assumed that the separation trauma of the first school day was proving harder for me than for her or our child. I could not tell her that I was being affected by a union—or perhaps simply a reunion of present self with an undiluted past self. I had not yet told her about Chum and that year of my own childhood. I had no intention of doing so.

The emotion was both a tangle of all I had experienced then

and also something I need to call—for lack of a better term—
gratitude. Gratitude for what age and distance can bring, an
ability to recall without that fog of the intervening years and
all I had been taught about abuse and betrayal since then,
gratitude for the facts of my own specific life, no matter how
painful at times. At a dinner party only a few weeks later, my
euphoria was shattered. But I will come to that.

I am aware as I stand on the platform in 1948 that in the
small railyard behind a nearby shed, a place where coal cars
and a few tankers can be shunted for unloading, a crew is
working on the bed with pickaxes and crowbars. This is nothing unusual, and often I see them either from the train window as we flash by or as I wait in one of the stations—usually
four or five men with a leader whose job it is to stand at some
distance staring along the track in the direction of the next
possible train.

He will have a whistle and a sign on a pole that he can ro-
tate, red on one side, green on the other. The workers will
look up when he whistles and move to a vacant track to wait
while a train passes. It is more hazardous than one might think
since express trains can come by on the two middle lines with
considerable speed, and occasionally someone will step aside
in the wrong direction. This morning, however, the workers
are on a shunt line.

I saw them as I approached the station, but now I can only
hear them—pickaxes striking into the loose rock, someone
pounding at a spike, a voice yelling up the line, laughter. The
man standing next to me folds another page of his *Wall Street
Journal*. I am wondering if it is worth cramming some Latin
into my head. But I am too full of yesterday's meeting with
Chum.

"You won't ever, ever tell?" he says quietly to the ceiling of
the van.

He is sitting in the driver's seat, his head back, one arm

around my shoulder. I am tucked against him, the side of my face resting on his chest. His heart pounds dully in one ear, his voice comes both from his chest and from the air above. My arm is tucked behind him, around his waist, and is growing numb from the pressure of his lean against it. My other hand lies loosely on one thigh.

His belt is unbuckled, the pants spread in an open V down the zipper of his fly. I have finished helping him to the relief he needs. He moans at the end, pushing my hand away to cover his spurting with the handkerchief he always holds ready. It is afterward that I like best, when that crazed nervousness, the too-quick laughter, eyes looking around and never directly at me, leave him, and after a few moments of silence in which he closes his eyes and seems to have gone very far away, he comes back to sit like this, his own body relaxed, a hand gently ruffling my hair as I lie against him.

He smokes cigarettes so much that even when he is not lighting one, I can smell the acrid nicotine on his stained fingers or in his jacket. Sometimes he will touch me too, but usually he asks me and I say, "No, I'd rather not." But I can feel no shame in those moments of peacefulness afterward, when all the bewilderment of his frenzy, of the blank and breathless look that seizes him as he moans and thrusts my hand away, departs and he begins to breathe slowly, to fold me into his life by telling me things I can only vaguely understand. Those moments are why I come with him, would never betray him, think I could face anything but the end of what we have together.

"I know you wouldn't tell, but sometimes I wake up at night in a sweat and think of what that would do. Amy wouldn't understand. I do love her."

I am not at all jealous. Amy has brown hair that hangs in thick bangs, falls straight, and then curls under just above her shoulders. She is short, a little plump, but unfailingly pert and friendly when we bring her our milk money or pay for the subscription to the *Weekly Reader* or just find ourselves being talked into a relaxed state when we are sitting in the chair beside her desk, waiting in the antechamber before being called in to be lectured by Alley or Ratcliffe on our latest sin. If one of my friends had taken my place in the van, I would have been inconsolable, but I could share Chum with Amy.

"Remember I told you we were going to have a baby? How last week she thought she was pregnant? All week I was happy, really happy, and she just danced around for days. But it didn't work. Yesterday she started bleeding again. False alarm. We've been trying so hard."

I don't say anything. I want to imagine it all: the bleeding, the way you might know you are going to have a baby, how weird it must be to have something going on in your belly, something growing there that you can't even see. Chum had been the first to explain the arcana of monthly bleeding, of bewildering moods surrounding it, of invisible connections to the phases of the moon. At home my mother and sister were no longer familiar. At first I thought they had kept a secret from me, but the more I thought of it, the more I was certain that the fault was with my father and his usual absences. He never knew how to be intimate, and all of his life when we met or parted, I have had to be the one who insists on something more than a formal handshake. Perhaps his silence about all things physical was mere reticence, but that silence surrounded sex with a dense, attractive gravity.

"I didn't really like it when we did this for each other in the navy, Hank. We did it there just to get it over with, that horniness that made it impossible to sleep, and you got so tired of beating off. Christ, we could be out there on the boat for months. You just did it and got it over with and went to sleep. I'd never done anything with a man before the navy."

He gropes in his shirt pocket just above my head for a cigarette, and soon I hear the scrape of a match, breathe in the smoke as it drifts toward the open window.

"Christ, it was boring—the navy." He blows smoke through his nose, then turns his face to me. "You ought to be careful about Alley's class, you know."

I lift my head slightly so I can hear better. We rarely talk about school, and when we do it is usually to give me a warning of some sort. He worries about how well I am doing, wants to make sure I keep my mind on the work. I can take it from him. It isn't scolding like I might get from my parents.

"Why?"

"She was saying in the staff meeting yesterday that you don't seem to be 'bearing down.' You know how she says that: 'Old man, you'd better just bear down a little more or you may find yourself in hot water.'"

I laugh. He has her voice and intonations down so well that only the pitch is wrong. But it is not mockery. What is clear even to me is that he cares for those two old ladies just as much as they do for him.

"Don't be surprised if she calls you into the office soon. Why don't you just memorize that vocabulary?"

"I hate it."

"Why?"

"Latin. Everyone knows it's useless."

He does not answer for a while. I am hoping he'll start talking about something else, maybe the football game we have coming up with the Springfield School for the Deaf and Dumb.

"Don't start thinking that way, buddy. If you do, you're going to have a hell of a bad time because big chunks of your life are going to feel useless."

He sits up with a jerk and pushes me away.

A battered blue Chevy with some boy and girl looking for their own privacy turns along the dirt tracks away from us, nosing to the edge of the bluff. Even as Chum is buckling his belt and leaning forward to turn the key, the silhouettes of the couple's heads merge into one. We usually drive the few miles back to the edge of my parents' campus in silence. This day is no different. As I pull on the door handle he reaches and puts a gentle circle of thumb and forefinger around my other wrist.

"Alfie's going to be driving the rest of the week. No more of this for a little while."

I try to shrug casually, then wave and walk through the pseudo-Gothic gateway toward dinner, homework, my taciturn responses to "What did you do at school today, Hank?"

I was the one who found the bluff overlooking Conshohocken. Or I should say I rediscovered it and then led Chum there. One Saturday afternoon I took a bike ride well beyond the limits my parents had proscribed. I did that often during the summer I was twelve, not knowing where I was going or why. But it was a long summer while I waited to go back to school and to Chum.

Beyond lay the twisting, hilly roads that could take me to Valley Forge—past estates with their duck ponds, fields where well-curried horses grazed. I remember the first time when, heart beating, I edged the wheel across the imaginary line I had honored for so many years. I leaned over the handlebars, one foot still on the ground that represented obedience. I pushed off, pedaled, made a big circle back to safety, then swung out toward the west in a straight line, taking all the speed I could from the downhill slope to help me up the next ridge and into outer space. I pumped all the way to Valley Forge that afternoon, flinging myself down in the grass near an embankment of cannon, staring dazed at a blue and unchanged sky.

At first I transgressed only once or twice a week. On clear, hot days I might circle the campus, touching all the borders, wheeling out a few yards then back. I never quite knew when my orbit would be broken by the tug of the larger body of the world any more than I was certain when I might lie in my bed, body naked, on one of those thick and humid nights and close my eyes and let myself imagine that the hand stroking me was really the touch and need of someone I had seen that day in pictures or in the drug store where I bought my comic books and ice cream cones. In either case I did not know where I was going or why the moment seized me, tearing me away into a life I could not recognize as my own.

On one journey, turning along a road I thought I had never traveled, I came to a long ridge with fields dropping away on each side, an occasional apple orchard. The road began to climb, I had to stand and pump, and near the top I veered onto a small dirt road that passed through some briars. When the bluff opened out beyond them, the site seemed familiar, as if I had dreamed it very recently. I laid my bike in the long grass and walked to the edge.

The memory was on the edge of memory, so not entirely lost, and that night at dinner I interrupted my father's usual preoccupation with some article he had been working on.

"How old was Tammy when she had her eyes operated on?"

My sister frowned. She did not like referring to those thick lenses she had to wear.

"Eight," my mother answered.

"Seven," Dad said without looking up from the careful incision he was making along the bone of his pork chop. Then he stared at me sternly as if recalling how he should be treating me. "Don't disappear after dinner, young man. We have something to talk about."

The significant glance he and my mother exchanged made the situation look grave, or at least bad enough for her to turn it over to him.

"Both seven and eight," she said. "It took two years."

"Does he have to always say ugly things when we're eating?" Tammy made a phony shiver.

I said nothing for a few minutes, but put extra ketchup on my mashed potatoes, a mixture my sister thought revolting even when done subtly.

"What's the name of that place we used to drive to sometimes at night when I was little—to look at the stars or watch the sun go down?"

My father's knife stopped moving.

"You remember that?" he said slowly, then went back to his operation.

"Sure. It was always in the summer and you'd say the house was too hot. I know it was when Tammy was having her operations because we always went alone and Mom was at the hospital keeping her company."

"Quite right." Dad nodded, and after all his careful labor he ignored the pork and turned his attention to piling some potatoes and peas onto his fork. "So hot the second summer that you couldn't sleep and I hated sitting around in the apartment listening to you complain."

My mother was watching. "I didn't know you two were gallivanting around."

"You didn't need to, dear. It worked. You'd walk home later and find Hank sleeping and me sitting in the living room reading and you thought I was something of a magician to get him to sleep like that. I never told you how we did it. You had enough on your mind."

"You mean I would have worried about the two of you driving around and Hank not getting to sleep till nine or ten."

"Well?"

She laughed. "I might even try worrying now."

My father forked his perfectly prepared meat.

"Great pork chops. What brought all that to mind, Hank?"

"You didn't answer my question."

"Conshohocken. Or at least that's what you can see from there. The steel mills. You used to like the place when it was dark because if they were pouring ore into the vats the fires would make everything glow, right up into the sky like northern lights. It was a great place to see the stars too. I tried to learn some of the constellations and show them to you. Anyway, there was almost always a breeze, and lots of times you'd go to sleep even before we started back and then all I had to do was carry you upstairs and plop you in bed."

I had not expected that long an answer from him. I had not expected such warmth of tone nor a memory filled with so much closeness. Surely that was not my father he was describing, and I wanted him to know that.

"I don't remember any of that," I said as flatly as I could, the closest I could come to saying, *You're lying.*

"You were very young." He reached for more mashed potatoes and began an extended discussion with my mother of a recent faculty meeting. That my father had changed somewhat since those days was not a distortion coming from my own shifts. But what can a child know of the struggle for tenure and failed promotion and lack of recognition in one's field? I would know something of that later and find it easier to forgive the man who had achieved tenure but never rose above assistant professor.

My sister was late for her cheerleading practice and excused herself from the table with an impatient flounce. When she left she slammed the door hard enough to let us know she was going to some place better, but not so hard that my mother felt required to call her back and make her close it gently. I tried to escape after dessert, but my father followed me into the hall. My mother was clearing the dishes.

"Let's go into your room," he said, and I knew that she was not to be part of it.

I waited for him, sitting in the window seat. When he came from their bedroom, he walked over with an envelope in his hand and placed it on the desk nearby.

"Where did you get these?"

"What?" I did not recognize the envelope.

He handed it to me and I looked inside. They were the pictures I kept deep under my sweaters in the bottom drawer. Women in every pose without a stitch of clothing. Sometimes accompanied by men. In color. Billy Gilbert had sold them to me at school. He had sent away for them.

"They're disgusting, Hank. Your mother found them. She was shocked."

For those first moments, I was too. I entered a blank space, without shame or anger. My chest was strapped tight, my hands cold.

"Listen, son, I want to know where you would get such revolting stuff, and then I want some promises from you. But first I want to know if you'd like to talk about any of this. Do you really know what this is all about?"

"What?" I said again.

"Matters of sex. What happens with men and women. Why this sort of thing gets sold or why it appeals to some warped people."

"I know about all that."

What did I know? All I was sure of then was that I wanted him out of my room, wanted both his disapproval and his mawkish concern for my knowledge to be on the other side of my closed door. I wanted my privacy back, which had been lost the moment my mother's hand touched something unfamiliar under my sweaters.

"Then if you know all that, you should know better. You

know that the good part of what happens between men and women is not like this. This is just preying on our weakness, the appetite that's necessary but which isn't like this when it's expressed through love. This isn't love, Hank. This is just rutting."

I did not answer. I would not have answered even if he were holding a whip in his hand, something he never could have done but that, at that moment, I would have preferred.

"I just want to tell you that this has got to stop. I want you to promise that. You see, this sort of thing shows no respect for your mother or your sister. Living around someone who has this sort of material, or even who thinks like this, isn't right. It isn't even safe."

I did look at him now, out of a surprise that opened beyond my anger. My mother? My sister? What did they have to do with those women who puckered their lips and held up their pink-tipped breasts to the camera and to me? He left me with that, taking the envelope.

"Think it over," he said from the doorway. "We'll talk some more about this." We didn't. For his own reasons, he must have wanted to avoid that conversation as much as I did.

The next day I rode out to the bluff again, and this time I sat on the edge, my knees tucked to my chest, looking over the wide, sunny valley with my eyes half-closed, trying to imagine the sky pocked with stars, the red light shimmering up from the line of low, gray buildings and their stacks. For a moment I could actually feel my father's hand on my shoulder, then the way it would ruffle through my hair before I dozed, and the sky began to die down to a simple, impenetrable black.

On the morning I am trying to keep in mind, the train is late. Even some of the preoccupied travelers have begun to lower their newspapers impatiently and lean forward to look down the track. But I can hear the steely hum in the rails even before the train comes into sight.

A strange howl, then from somewhere beyond the screen of buildings near the shunt, voices yelling—not quite anger, but the words are lost in the rattle and shriek of the oncoming train.

Again and again over the next days, sometimes in my dreams, I try to slow down those next few minutes in which my concentration is shattered. Impatient men and women are nudging me forward toward the steps up into the maroon carriage; the conductor is making sure we all know this is local to Narberth, then express to Penn Station; a woman is running from her car and yelling a name until a man nearby turns to take the briefcase he has nearly forgotten; and from the corner of a shed the foreman appears, sign still clutched in his hand, his mouth open and yelling something toward the station house that I can't make out.

Years later I will see a print of Edvard Munch's "The Scream," and I will put the whole scene together into that one image, as if I see only the open mouth of the foreman and everything around it is concentric circles of some terror that speaks through him. But my hand is on the railing, I look ahead to prevent myself from treading on anyone's heels, and then I am in the quiet space of velour seats, the smoky air of pipes and cigarettes. A whistle. Jerk. The world is gliding. I stoop toward the window as I slide into a seat. Through it, for only the briefest moment, I see the freight car on the shunt line, a group of men gathered by the wheels at the nearest end. One of them is standing straight, his hands to his ears as if some unbearable noise is issuing from the ground their presences conceal from me.

Many years later Peter and I tried to recall everything about that morning, but finally had to admit we were lying, that all we were really doing was picking out the pieces from a collage of many similar mornings. But that afternoon was etched in my mind with considerable detail. I had been moving through the day toward a conversation with Chum at recess, toward an event as brute as being run down by a freight car.

Peter and I were enjoying our dinner and letting our reminiscences loose. We thought we were both heading out into new lives—I into graduate school at the University of Pennsylvania, he as a commissioned officer to Korea. We brought back the names of friends and teachers, recited what snippets we could recall from memorized rituals ("This, the pomegranate, juicy and ripe with seeds," I had intoned at the Thanksgiving pageant, holding up the fall fruits one by one, reciting some Greek translation while dressed in a very Roman toga). We were still too young to believe in anything but continuity, so we were certain that one day soon we would repeat this dinner at Bookbinders with even more memories to share or narrate. We did not know this was the last time we would speak to each other except in my memory. The struggle to hold a bald peak in Korea ended Peter's life and our friendship.

Again, not my war. I clung to my student deferment through all those years, dragging it out until none of us were needed. Peter and I did not argue, but my reluctance to join him was clear and even selfish. I wanted no part of a world that would make me march in unison, learn how to load and clean a gun, take me away from the books and the sounds of music I had come to love.

Gap-toothed, pug-nosed, always freckled, Peter had the kind of flesh that always looked a little soft, pudgy, but I had learned through childhood how hard and strong the muscles were beneath. In our few outbursts of anger I had never won a wrestling match, and he was the only member of our little football team who seemed to have no fear when we had our yearly demolition derby with the Springfield School for the Deaf and Dumb.

"Whatever happened to Napoleon?" I asked. "And Stella?"

We usually had a round or two of the "What Happened To" game on an evening like this. Sometimes the point was to find someone from the old school that the other person might not recall, a kind of one-upmanship of memory. I rarely won.

"You remember the little house on the edge of the property? Used to be some sort of gatehouse when the place was an estate. We'd sneak down there sometimes at recess, but we never figured out how to get in."

I nodded. I *had* been inside. With Chum. There were two deadbolts on the door and he had found both keys on a chain in Miss Alley's desk. The place was bare, uncleaned for years, pebbles of mortar fallen around the fireplace, the smell of mildew and rot in one corner of the living room where the roof leaked. That was an afternoon of risk, some desperation on Chum's part that he did not explain, and in fact he hardly spoke at all in the brief time we were there.

"Well, last time I visited I asked about Napoleon, and Ratcliffe said he'd retired. But she told me to stop at the gatehouse on the way out because he'd like to see me. They'd fixed it up for him and Stella. Thought you had me, didn't you?" Peter pushed aside the carcass of his lobster, unsnapped the cord of his bib. "Well, try this one. Chalmers Deal."

So I paused. I took my time and drained my third glass of beer, caught the waiter and asked for another. I was telling myself to play dumb. But I was angry at Peter. How could we have been such close friends and he had not guessed? How could I have been through all that with no one to help me? Only later that night, lying sleepless in bed, did I realize the anger was against my own paralysis. How could I have been so good at concealing all that even when I was a child? Was it an image of how deeply deceptive I could be, or did it mean even Peter had a life totally unknown to me—and if so, what the hell was the illusion of intimacy that friendship gave? And if I'd told it all to someone, wouldn't Chum Deal have gotten the treatment he deserved?

"Give up?" he asked as our plates were being removed.

So I told him about Chum and me, but I kept it as brief as possible. I did not want to see his reaction as I spoke, and I stared at his hand that slowly turned a knife around and around on the stained tablecloth.

"You win that one," he murmured shaking his head. "Son of a bitch. You too."

"Who else? You?"

"No, no. You know how I never liked the guy. Always thought he was a phony."

"What did you mean 'you too'?"

"Charlie Morris. He told me and made me promise never to tell anyone. I wasn't sure Charlie was telling the truth. He said that he and Deal would stop in the school van when Chum was driving. He tried to make fun of it, but it was almost like he was boasting. It made me sick, even if he was just making it up."

I was as glad as Peter must have been to change the topic as soon as possible. We went back to talking about the football games, drank too much, and then concentrated on foretelling our futures. I spent time afterward trying to find a place to put that information about Charlie. Mostly I was angry that Chum had made me feel so special when I wasn't. Finally, it cheapened the dignity of the pain I had carried with me for all those years. The currency of my own experience had been devalued.

I still dream about the games we played with Springfield D

and D. If ever there was a time when I felt myself in touch with pure Anglo-Saxon energy, a monosyllabic world of rocks and sod and roots, it was when I had centered the ball to Peter and heaved my body against my immovable opposite, or when I ducked him, took three steps, turned to receive a short pass and clenched against the inevitable crush. We never won. We considered it an accomplishment even to hold on to the ball for four downs at a time. All we hoped to do was use up time and thereby keep the score from getting past fifty.

They were not mean. In fact they were models of gentility after the play ended. Always one of them was there to offer me a hand up, grinning, nodding, sometimes looking with concern to be certain there were signs of life. But once the ball moved, they threw themselves into the game as if all the needs thwarted by silence were at last finding a way to explode. They fell on us, popped up, and fell on us. They could not hear the whistle and could only know the play was over by our rag-doll postures and the windmill signals of the referees. No penalties could be assessed them for late blocks or piling on. It was a game played with blurred outlines, and I have waked years later from a dream in which some undefined, headless force of hulking shoulder pads and stony knees is crushing me against a wall while I try to signal that the play is over.

But glory was waiting in Springfield too. In the last game we played with them before I left that school and was sent away to mope through four years in New England, I scored the only touchdown our team had made in all the games we had played with them. I can remember my surprised gratitude for the way not only my own teammates but our opponents treated me—mobbing me in the end zone, laughing in those high moans and shrieks, lifting me on their shoulders. Were they simply relieved that at last we had broken through so that they did not have to suffer from the guilt of their infinite superiority? After the game was over we gathered in their dining room for our usual send-off of lemonade and chocolate graham crackers, and they stood close around me, clapping my shoulders, demanding their interpreter speak their signs to me that said again and again, "Great play" or "That's the fastest fifty-yard dash ever."

"How does it feel to be a hero?" Chum said to me, pausing by my bus seat, grinning, his voice loud enough so that everyone turned and peered to see what I would say. In the weeks since he had put an end to our meetings he would treat me with that kind of forced joviality.

I froze against the stagy bravado of his voice, and when he ruffled my hair, I drew back.

Chum shrank away in mock fear. "We get tetchy when we're important."

I had not let myself weep for our breakup and would not have then except that it came on me so unexpectedly, like one of those tackles after the whistle had blown. I did not sob or turn away. The bus and faces and the figure of Chalmers Deal simply blurred, and I sat there. The motor started and the figure turned and walked to the front of the bus. No one said anything to me for a few moments, then Peter leaned over the back of my seat, gripped my shoulder and hissed, "That asshole!"

I don't think it is morbid of me to try to imagine the worker who died on the tracks that October morning just before I climbed onto my train, heading toward my own worst day. I had to take the train home again that afternoon because the school van was being repaired. I did not want to go home, did not want ever to go back to that school where I knew I would still see Chum day after day, and wished the train could rattle on until I reached places with names I had never heard and could not even have pronounced. I picked up the afternoon newspaper from the seat beside me after its owner got off at Ardmore. The picture showed the same freight car I had glimpsed from the window that morning, but beside it was a stretcher bearing the form of a man muffled in a sheet, two attendants stooping to lift, three other workers standing by, hands hanging like sash weights along their thighs. The story had his name, which I have long since forgotten, said he was thirty-five, had a wife and two children, had been working with his back to the car when it came uncoupled and rolled silently toward him. He had turned at the last moment when someone yelled, lost his footing, and his shirt was snagged by one wheel. He tried to roll away, but the car drove over his midsection, crushing his spine and killing him immediately.

I climbed off at Bryn Mawr and did not look across the tracks, glancing over my shoulder only once after I had turned the corner into the path through the estates near home. That night in brief intervals of sleep, I tossed in my bed, waking startled by my attempts to roll away from the dark wall of hissing wheels that bore down on me.

After I had read the "human interest" stories in subsequent editions of the papers that let me hear the nature of loss in the words of his wife, see the fatherless children hanging by their legs from the bars of the playground, I moved into that quiet and more frightening gap at the center of my own experience on that day—the fact that I had been there but not been there at all. Only a matter of yards away from me a life was finished. My hand was on the railing and I heaved myself up the first step. The whistle blew and my train began to move even before I sat down. All around me were invisible lines in air, the confines of each mind. Peter was waiting on his platform in Haverford for this same train. Chum was waiting to seek me out at recess. In an infinity of events, what witness do we bear?

Chum walks up to me at recess with a football in his hand.

He is grinning, but the smile is too fixed, the "Hi, buddy" too stagy.

"Go out for a pass."

I take a long run past the fallen tree where the second graders always play "King of the Castle." I am near the edge of the woods when I hook, hold out my hands, and the ball is there. He walks the route I have run and stands a few yards away. The others are well to one side.

"We're going to practice our laterals now. Don't come any closer. Can you hear me?"

"Sure." I spiral the ball to him.

"Stay there." He backs up a few paces. "Still hear OK?"

I nod. The ball returns in a gentle arc.

"Now listen. Carefully. And please don't do anything silly when you react. Just keep the ball going."

I cannot understand his fixed grin, the words that have a tone entirely at variance with his postures.

"We can't see each other anymore. It's got to be over."

The ball slips through my hands and hits me on the chest. I stoop and pick it up. "Why?"

"She knows. Amy. About us."

I swallow, flip the ball in an awkward wobble that he barely catches.

"How? Who told her?"

For a moment he says nothing. The ball goes back and forth a few times.

"She might even be watching us now, from the office windows. I don't want you to talk to me about this ever again. Or to tell anyone. I promised her."

"How?" I say again. I do not really understand yet, although the last words have a clear finality that is battering down any of the walls I have built in the past seconds.

"I told her."

"Why?"

"I had to. I don't know." For the first time the smile is gone. The eyes blink. The ball streaks at me hard and I take it against my gut, have to catch my breath.

"I don't know, Hank. I had to tell her, and I did, and we had a terrible time. But she loves me and she's worried what might happen. So she wanted me to promise we wouldn't meet again. I did. Now I need your promise."

The whistle ends recess. Miss Ratcliffe stands by the side door, her hand to her mouth. The sun glints against the silver in her lips.

"What promise? Promise what?" My voice is shaking.

"Not to tell. Not to try to talk to me about it. Never to show in any way what we've done."

I hug the ball with both arms. I cannot speak.

"Toss it. Keep it going as we walk up the field. Say it, Hank. Please."

"I promise."

His mouth is drawn tight. "I'm sorry. Do you understand that? I care. I do. I'm just"—and after he bends to pick up the ball he has bobbled, he looks hard at me, shrugs—"just sorry."

My mouth is dry. I taste the air as if I have been jamming my mouth full of the fallen leaves around us. Still, we walk parallel, tossing the ball.

"Someone will explain it to you. Someday. It was wrong, buddy. Don't hate me, but it was wrong."

I am afraid I will cry. Ahead is the door, the last group of kids moving past Miss Ratcliffe.

"Hurry, old man," she calls out to me.

"Go out for one," he says with that fixed grin and pumps toward the door.

I run. I do not look back. I see the wall, the long windows of the two stories above, Miss Ratcliffe and her whistle dangling from its chain against her purple sweater. I can tell by the widening of her eyes that the ball is coming. I do not turn but flash by her, brushing one elbow. The ball flies past my neck, into the building, splats against the newel post, bounces along the floor, but I take the steps up two or three at a time. I straight-arm the door to the bathroom on the second floor. I lock myself in one of the johns, but the tears I expect do not come. I perch on the toilet lid and stare and catch my breath before I go to Miss Chapin's class in current events.

Perhaps Amy was not watching us. That may have been Chum's invention, just like the idea that one day someone would explain it all to me. He never did, and who else could have? Amy? I hoped so. For the rest of that year I watched her. Whenever possible I walked past the open door to her office. I began to have problems with my schoolwork, problems in my attitudes toward teachers, and I became inordinately fond of fighting, especially with boys older and stronger than I was. I licked some of them, but more often than not bore home bruises, torn clothes, and once a lip that required stitches. I took no pleasure in those long lectures from Ratcliffe that often ended in a sympathy I had to struggle to resist. She would interrupt her scolding to say simply, "Now come on, old man. You tell me. What's the problem?" But I could resist because the point of my bad behavior had been to land me in the antechamber, and once I was with Ratcliffe, I had failed. On the other side of the door was Amy Deal. I wanted her to be sitting across that desk from me. I wanted her to walk around it and kneel and take my face in both her hands. *Tell me, tell me. What's the problem?*

She did not treat me any differently. I saw no hitch in her smile, no tendency for her preoccupation with forms and figures or secretarial duties to falter when I sat in her office waiting for Ratcliffe to call me in. I would stare at her and she would look up, focus on me, smile, and return to her work. I will never know if she knew and was so terrified of my knowledge that she gave no sign, or if she knew nothing and Chum had invented her knowledge as a device to end our relationship. Worst of all, when he showed how easily he could begin treating me like anyone else in his class or in the hallway, I began to doubt all of it. I gave my father a fierce silence as retribution for the way the adult world had betrayed me. I gave my friends just enough of whatever they were used to so that they would not ask questions. I gave myself dreams in which I fell from room to room in a building so old that its floors were cracker thin, only strong enough to hold me for a moment before giving way. I would call out my own name as if I were looking for myself, but there were no lights in the rooms. Each floor saved me from the full plunge that I knew would be my death, but no floor was strong enough to hold me up for long.

I have a good friend who is a veteran of the war in Vietnam. We teach together and share an office, an arrangement that works because most of his classes are in the morning and mine are in the afternoon. But we often meet for lunch and our rivalry on the squash court is a source of lifelong pleasure for both of us. He was in intelligence and can tell stories about interrogations of women and even children that are harrowing enough to enter my nightmares. He rarely talks about the year he spent there, especially to me, since once again I was not there. His specialty is in the literature of that war, and I do my best to read the poems, stories, novels he thinks are worthwhile because then we can share that part of his life I witnessed only on the evening news or through the *New York Times*. Once again, not my war. They have all gone by me at a distance. Few men my age have not been on or near some battleground. I was always sailing away from Troy, and when stories are told late at night over the campfire, I have very little to share with the men.

At times in the office when Larry and I are working, he will rise suddenly from his desk, a book he has been reading still clutched in his hand, and walk slowly to the window that looks over the roofs and green to the lake below—and while he stares toward the distant shore beyond the water, the book slanting away in his tight hand, I will know something in it has nudged him into a world he can never forget and where I cannot join him. Then I feel like that lame boy in the "Pied Piper" who has been left behind:

> *The music stopped and I stood still,*
> *And found myself outside the hill,*
> *Left alone against my will,*
> *To go now limping as before,*
> *And never hear of that country more!*

Or is Larry like the lame boy excluded from our world by what he has seen, and the books he reads are the echoes of the music he has heard? At least he has witnesses—those books, those authors and friends who have shared that terrible experience—even if it can never be fully explained to Larry's satisfaction.

He has cornered some funds each year to invite some of those writers to campus to read their work or to discuss it with students. He always invites me to whatever social functions surround the events, and my wife and I have spent some lively, boozy evenings at his house with his wife, the interruptions of their three kids who never seem to sleep, and the honored guest. We talk mostly about other things, but always during the evening Larry and the guest will hunch over their beers (wine for me, and Larry always has some bottles around, although he hates the stuff), start laying out dates or the names of places and persons, and the rest of us will carry on those parallel conversations that pick and peck, flare up and die because all of us are really listening with the other ear to the conversation we cannot join.

One evening, very recently, more guests than usual had been invited. The honored writer was so famous that Larry found himself pressured to invite more than just the usual friend or two. Even the dean had read the man's recent novel. But the table was large enough to hold all ten of us if we were careful not to flourish our elbows when talking. This was hard for the writer, a short, broad-shouldered and florid man who was very active in his chair. He talked loudly, drank beer as if his plate were piled with salt rather than the aromatic boeuf bourguignon that Delia, Larry's wife, had cooked for us, and did not hesitate to attempt a conversation with someone at the other end of the table.

The women had been taking potshots at him all evening, and he loved it. No one had even made him flinch. His soldiers and terrorists and their wars or acts of violence were steeped in a macho tone of the old dispensation, so much that they could rouse a weird sense of nostalgia. He knew that, though, and critics would point out how all that superstructure was used for self-conscious purposes unlike his predecessors. Even in conversation he had proven himself to be paradoxical—he could lapse suddenly into very quiet, watchful moments, and then respond in such a way to show that he had been listening and reacting quite sensitively to the conversation around him. Frankly, I was not sure if I liked him or not. I could not help feeling he manipulated our reactions to him in some way for his amusement.

I sat beside Kay, and she had been talking with him while I attempted to say something to the dean across the table. But I gave up trying not to listen when the man said to her, "Fine, sweetheart. Change it, if you like. But after all, men are the ones who go off together and don't come back or come back blasted in one way or another. Someone needs to describe it. We need to talk about it with each other."

"Men, you mean."

"Yes. But you're welcome to tune in anytime."

Larry looked a little uneasy. I knew he liked the man's work, and he had talked me into reading a great deal of it, but Larry had been warned that the man in the flesh was often more blunt than the subtle consciousness to be found in the books. Kay, however, has a sense of humor that carries her through most things gracefully. I've rarely seen her show anger in public, although I've taken my share of it at home for various lapses. I saw her turn her head to one side, that slight smile on her face that in someone else might have been a frown of irritation.

"I've always wondered, though. When they're not fighting, they all seem to be making love, those warriors in your books. Always to very lovely and tractable women. Are there ever any homosexuals in the armies in your books, Howard?"

I heard the conversations quiet nearby. Howard put down his glass of beer. He was grinning broadly. Then he threw back his head and laughed and slapped Larry on the shoulder when he came out of it.

"Is that what's missing?" He looked at her archly, lifting his napkin to wipe his lips. "By God, that's what I'll have to put in the next one."

"I think I'm serious," she said, and I could have warned Howard McCann that when Kay is smiling her small smile and says she's serious, she has taken umbrage at something and will not be put off easily. "I've always thought that letting loose a homosexual in a room full of certain kinds of men would be like releasing a mouse in a drawing room full of women with long skirts and hoops. Watch them shriek and run."

We had all had too much to drink. I swear none of this would have happened if it had been Larry and Delia and the usual group. It was the presence of deans and chairpersons and bookstore owners from downtown that changed the tone. On the usual evening we would have long ago come to accept each of us for whatever we were and found some way to enjoy it. Bad tone from incompatible company leads to allegorizing. Howard was no more super-macho than his books. But he was drunk and becoming insecure enough to be whatever he sensed would be inconvenient to others. He turned his glass slowly on the table in front of him, frowning slightly at it.

"I'm not sure what you mean by homosexuality, sweetheart. How committed do you have to be to be labeled? Put men together with men for a long period of time, with no women in sight except what's locked up in a man's mind, and you'll find plenty of homosexuality, if that's your definition. Men fondling men. Yes, men loving men. Isn't your question itself a form of labeling, a form of fear?"

We still live in the penumbra of the sixties. Under the cover of its long shadow we have no fear of revealing intimate matters to strangers if it seems to serve the attitude of truth telling. I could see Howard moving that way. I put my hand on Kay's thigh under the table. It was tense, like a small creature readying to pounce or run.

Afterward I thought through the next few moments and realized I was touching her for reassurance. I was uneasy. I was warning myself. She did not glance at me.

"Look, sister. When I was stuffed into a compound for half a year, until that bomb dropped nearby and most of us scrambled out into the jungle and some of us made it back to base, I was lonely, and I needed it, and I found it. He was a kid who'd just come in, a good fifteen years younger than me. What can you say? We did what we did, and we got relief from it, and we were even damn fond of each other." He looked up, chin out, but this time no grin, and the thrust seemed to be holding back against some internal pressure rather than the usual strut. "And I was pissed as hell when he tripped a mine on the way back and left most of his guts strung across the branch of a tree."

Kay began to say something but Howard held up a hand.

"I'm sorry. I didn't mean to lay it on so heavy."

I have never seen such a sudden transformation. He seemed to be smaller in his chair when he leaned back, looking out at us with his hands folded across his chest.

"I don't think the definitions do much," he said quietly. "Men. Women. That's fine. But sex? Men are beautiful, women are beautiful. We're androgynous, aren't we?"

I felt that thigh relax. She picked up her fork. I could tell that not only was she relaxed, she was no longer interested.

But I was. My pulse had lifted with his own tone of defensiveness, and oddly enough his sudden lack of tension did not lower mine. I did not like the way he had thrown experience at us and then retreated behind it. What did his anecdote really explain?

"Kay's right. Why *don't* you write about it?" I said. "If you think that's the truth of the world you present, where is it in your books?"

He tilted his head as he stared at me. My voice had begun to tremble as I finished. Kay had turned to look at me, but I would not take my eyes off Howard.

"If I had to write about everything, I'd get nothing done."

"But if you only write half-truths, what kind of world are you presenting? Is it worth it? Don't the best writers take on the toughest things and help us to find out what it is to be a full human being? Aren't you taking the easy way out?"

This time Howard shrugged. He lifted his glass, saw it was empty, and held it out to Larry.

"I need more of this, buddy. And I think your friend—Hank is it?—needs more wine."

Larry was pouring, and I was swallowing hard, trying to understand why I wanted to go on but could not find words even vaguely related to what I'd begun, when Howard said, "You write that book, Hank. You tell that truth. But you might find it tough to do. Experience counts, you know. Larry tells me you haven't been in a war, haven't been in anyone's army."

When I stood, shooting up from my chair, catching the edge of the plate with my belt so that it clattered down and nearly upset my empty glass, I had no idea why. But staring at the head of the table where Howard was leaning on his elbows and Larry still held a pitcher of beer, I knew I had to get out of there. I turned, shoved my chair away, and strode through the living room and onto the deck.

It was a cool night, clear enough for some layers of stars to shine through the town's lights. I leaned on the railing as if on the stern of a huge ship. A cat streaked across the dim lawn. I was thinking of Chum Deal and his troop carrier, of the rank odor of cigarettes in the tweed of his jacket, of the football we passed back and forth up the lawn to the schoolhouse, and I was angry—not at him, but at myself. Hadn't I left all that behind? I thought I had accepted it and gone on.

I heard the footfall on the boards behind me, but for a few moments she did not touch me.

"I'm sorry," I said.

"He's obnoxious."

"A little. Not that much."

"Come back in. McCann apologized, said he wasn't insulted because he likes a good argument, likes things better when they're—"

"I know. I can hear it."

"And then Larry told a really funny story. Delia's about to serve dessert."

"I'm going home now."

"Hank?" He came out to the railing where we were both standing but not touching.

"Sorry, Larry."

"Don't be. That was a stupid thing to say. About not being in a war or in the army. I haven't heard that since they used to say, 'America, love it or leave it.' But I don't think he meant it that way."

"It wasn't that."

"Look, I didn't tell that to Howard because I feel that way either. We were talking about you and I was telling him how sometimes I hate the way I've backed myself into thinking that only people who went through 'Nam are the ones who really understand. Not just the war, but everything. That's when I mentioned how you—"

"No, Larry. It doesn't bother me."

He sighed. "C'mon, buddy. Delia made this thing called tiramisu. You'll love it."

But I wouldn't go back, and he had to accept that, and even though she could have hitched a ride, Kay insisted on coming home with me.

We were hardly on the road when she asked, "Then what was it?"

"I don't understand how, I don't understand why. I can try to tell you the what, though."

We drove out Spear Street and she didn't even ask why we were going the opposite way from our house, the babysitter, the ritual chatter about how wonderfully the kids behaved. I parked on the little overlook where the lands fell away to the lake, the black silhouettes of the mountains, the starry sky. I began talking right away, but I did it slowly. I wanted to get it right. Peter was the only person I'd ever told it to, and even with him I had hardly done more than tell the fact. In some places it was hard going, but most of it was not as hard to tell as I thought it would be.

I quit and we were silent. At the other end of the lot a car parked and turned out its lights. I thought I saw a shooting star and was turning to tell her when I saw her face turned up and put mine down and kissed her. Her cheeks were wet.

"That bastard," she said. "That fucking bastard."

What had I expected? I don't know. I'd lived with all of it so long that I wasn't sure it had any sense anymore. I hadn't told it angrily, although God knows, I had learned that night that somewhere deep in places I will never reach, far beyond any chance of ultimate healing, there is an unforgiving pain.

"Thank you," I said.

"I'm not sure who I'm crying for, or why. For you, I know, but really for that boy, the one I never knew. For that boy." And she was weeping again.

For instance. I am sitting in that seat as the train continues toward Haverford. Already the puzzling image of men stooping around the freight car and the body they conceal is fading into the imagined landscape where I am in the front seat of the van as it noses slowly over the last bumps in the field before Chum pulls on the brake and we stare out through the autumn haze toward the smoking stacks of the steelworks. For instance. I am grabbing the bill the waiter sets between us in Bookbinders, holding it away from Peter as he tries to snatch it back. *No—I will pay.* It's a form of bon voyage. Let him pay when he comes back. Let him come back to tell me all the stories of that far-off place called Korea. For instance. The boy who has been my opponent for four years, the center who has brushed me away when I try to block him and has stolen pass after pass from my reaching hands, grabs my arm as I am about to climb onto the bus after that final game. He is blinking, grinning, shrill moans exhaled with each breath. He throws his arms around my neck, clutches me so tightly I am choked. He runs beside the moving bus, staring at me and waving, waving. For instance. I am the boy so young that I have only a few words in my vocabulary, but I do not need them to express my mingled fear and joy as I stare at the ceiling of the tunnel and the world thunders around me.

For instance. I am the boy held tight against the chest of a man who is weeping. He is not my father and not my brother. Probably he weeps for himself. Perhaps he is not even weeping. It is the first time we have made love, and I do not dare to look up at him. All I know is that sometimes in the middle of the night, I am that boy—I am that man.

italian autumn

The slight, elderly gentleman seated in the railway station at Montecatini was wearing a thin and tightly knotted bow tie that accentuated his pointed nose and chin. His granddaughter, who stood nearby reading the framed timetables, had not inherited his physique. Her ankles were thick, her brow wide and heavy, and her shoulders were slightly rolled. She kept both hands in the side pockets of her jacket or behind her back as if she did not want to be reminded how thick and short-fingered they were.

Although they did not speak to each other as the waiting room gradually filled, from time to time their glances would meet, they would smile, and once her hand rested casually on his shoulder. Even when they had settled in their seats and the train had begun its journey down the valley to Florence, he watched the landscape in silence as she leafed through the Blue Guide she had taken from her purse. They were so at ease with each other's company that they might have been a couple long married. They had the calm aura of trust in an invisible shield around them, even in such places as a rattling train carriage.

Anne and her grandfather had come to Italy for a vacation. Although they traveled together once each year, planning the trip for months ahead, this one had a special significance. It was the first time Enrico Donato had returned to his homeland. As they descended from the slopes near Montecatini and clacked along the dusty green plain toward Florence, Anne wondered when her grandfather would begin to tell her his memories of the landscape. He had been born and brought up in Florence, had left the country when he was twenty-two and his bride, Nina, was twenty.

Because he had suffered a mild stroke the year before, the trip also had an elegiac quality to it that Anne tried to ignore. Often before they left he insisted that he did not expect to find relatives or friends since he had not kept up with them over the years. But sometimes her grandfather would become preoccupied as if rushes of memory were welling up between them. She would ask, "What are you thinking, Nonno?" and he would stare past her shoulder until she felt like a stick figure standing at the vanishing point of a very geometrical piazza.

Their taxi ride through Florence was tantalizing to Anne, who was impatient to stop at all the sites she had studied. But for Enrico Donato the Duomo and its tower were not the revered objects of photographs and lectures. He laughed and told how he and Martino, known as *La Mosca*, had tried to climb over the iron gate to retrieve their straying soccer ball and been chased by carabinieri. The soccer ball had been abandoned.

"No! Punto. A destra, non a sinistra," he insisted, leaning forward to the driver, and here began the first confusion and argument. Anne could only listen. She understood some Italian but could not speak it.

Polite at first, pausing at the curb, the driver said the street to the right was named otherwise than the one requested, and this had been so since he could remember. Nonno sternly announced that his own memory was longer and he did not care if they had changed the name, he knew where he was. Old age, the driver said through a tight jaw, deserved to be honored, but with all due respect, he could not drive there since the street was one way. But if the signore insisted, they would circle to come down it, and what did the gentleman expect to find there?

"Ah." The cabbie shrugged victoriously. "Then you're in for a disappointment. This street has only shops and restaurants with storage above."

Nonno paid the driver and climbed out of the taxi without saying goodbye. They turned the corner, searched out a number, and suffered their first defeat in front of a dilapidated awning announcing *Carne di Suina* and *Salsicce Tedesche*. The proprietor, who leaned in the doorway with hands in pockets of a bloody apron, shrugged. To his memory, there had never been a residence here, but he admitted his business had been there only for ten years.

But in the twisted streets that finally did have apartments over whatever small business struggled below, fragments caught Nonno's attention. *There. Look.* The little archway with the steps beneath it into that next alley. Surely here he and Daniello had waited every evening for his friend's father, who often traveled all the way to Pisa for the cloth Daniello's mother turned into handkerchiefs and scarves. Anne stooped again and again to read the faded script above doorbells, once roused a puzzled matron who blinked, then eyed them calculatingly as if they might be shaken loose from some coins. No, she had not heard of Donatos living here or nearby. A Donato lived over there, but, she said with a sneer, "He is only from Sardinia and recently arrived."

To the clacking of printing machines an aproned man at least as old as Nonno shook his head decisively. He had been here forever. He had seen floods and bombs and the sun rising and the sun setting and years when he was told the world would end, but no Donatos had lived here. They would be welcome to, he added, if they worked and were honest and not like these present bums who expected everything to be given to them. Regarding Nonno with a fierce sympathy, he crooked an arthritic hand on his shoulder and said, "They don't understand what it is to be our age, the young ones, but we'll outlive most of them. We have already." To nail down his vow, he spat sideways into the sawdust.

They stood by the Arno. Nonno looked down at the barely moving water, its surface blotched with the falling leaves of nearby plane trees. Here the sun beat directly on them, and she grasped his arm to urge him back to the shady side of the street.

"All right," he answered when she suggested the attractive restaurant with its inner garden.

He looked at the menu and shrugged. But a glass of wine helped. The cannelloni was fresh and delicately flavored. She was relieved when he lifted his second glass of wine and said, "It's been so much longer than I let myself admit." They laughed when she reminded him that, after all, it had been over fifty years.

When he had nearly finished his cannelloni and a third glass of wine, he paused to sit back for a moment, "to digest before I finish," he said. His head nodded forward, and he dozed with hands folded in his lap, the sun dappling his shoulders through the wide grape leaves. Neither she nor the waiter could bear to disturb him, so she ordered some figs for herself and then a cappuccino. Finally he lifted his head slowly, blinked, licked his lips and said, "Nina always refused to return to Florence, you know. Too bad. What fun we would have had, eh?"

He promised to walk back to the station by the most direct route, but his pace began to slow. She was suggesting a taxi when he leaned forward with both hands on his cane and said,

"Ah," as if the wind had been knocked from him. She clutched his elbow. He raised his cane with both hands to point it forward like a divining rod.

"That's where Nina's cousin Carla lived. Look. Even the same lion's head."

They crossed the alley. He lifted and dropped the knocker twice against its metal base.

A series of bolts slipped back and tumblers began a slow revolving in two locks. Anne tried to read the nameplate but it was too corroded. The door cracked open as far as a heavy chain would let it, and slowly, first one eye in a very wrinkled brow, then the other appeared at about the height of Nonno's chest. The person said nothing.

"Carla?"

Her toothless lips sucked in, then puffed out.

"I'm sure you don't recognize me either." He laughed. "It's me. Enrico Donato."

The old face swayed slowly back and forth.

"Can you hear me?" Nonno leaned closer.

The curved hump of the woman's back thrust her neck forward.

"I'm Nina's husband—Enrico." He began speaking in a high, insistent tone as if she were walking away from him, his Italian so rapid that Anne wondered if she were understanding all that he said. "At Cousin Carmine's wedding you made me dance with you almost all night because you said you were jealous of Nina and me and would never have a husband. Were you right?"

But the face only narrowed its eyes.

"This is my granddaughter. We've come all the way from America." He put a hand on the jamb, tips of his fingers traveling the links of chain. "Can you tell me about the others? Where have they gone?"

Out of her mouth came a slight hissing of alarm.

"Please. Don't you remember me? Nina died. But she never stopped speaking of you."

When the voice began to issue from her puckered lips, both he and Anne leaned forward.

"I don't remember you or anyone. I lock my doors because once people came and stole things from me. I tell you I don't know who I am or who you are and I don't care."

The door began to close. Nonno called, "Wait," but the seam shut tightly, and even before he could lift the knocker, bolts were slipping back into place. He let the lion's head fall with a single hollow rap, reached as if to knock again but spread his flat palm on the door and leaned. Then he began to walk with such determination for the first few minutes that she had trouble steering him into the correct turns. In the train, Nonno lolled his head against the side cushion, his eyes closed.

They had adjoining rooms in the Hotel Croce di Malta, each with its balcony overlooking the umbrella pines and paths leading toward the entrance to a spa. They had been assigned to table six and a very lively old waiter who took an immediate liking to Nonno, leaning close to him to say, "These other people, so many French and Germans"—he pinched his fingers together—"they understand nothing, have no sense of how to live. Look, signore, how much more infirm they are than you and I. It is not just the blood, it is understanding the ways to live," and the hand tapped twice emphatically, once on his temple, once at his heart.

Almost everyone in the hotel was elderly or ill, and at certain times of day wheelchairs and crutches and aluminum walkers clogged the elevators. But their waiter had more concern for the decay in beliefs that had once made Montecatini important.

"Years ago in this season there would be no rooms available in town. Anywhere. But now it's all pills and cutting people up to put in new parts."

Nonno had insisted they stay in Montecatini since he remembered from his childhood that this town was a resort of great beauty, a place where his profligate uncle had squandered his wealth, much to his family's dismay, in pursuit of a cure for a life-long melancholy that a later age would have called "manic-depressive." In the gaps where people should be, in the wide empty porticoes and the ornate gateways to the baths, Anne sensed invisible presences hovering, generations who had come not just to recover but to display the exuberant good health of their bank accounts. That laden vacancy was disturbing, as if she were surrounded by all the lives she could never quite know.

The next day Nonno complained of a headache and stayed in his room. Late that afternoon he tapped on Anne's door and suggested they take a walk. But he moved slowly, pausing often to stare up the sloping path to the one spa that was still functioning, and for a long time he sat on a bench by an open field, watching the distant figure of a man walking his dog on a long rope. When Anne put her arm through his, he started as if he had forgotten she was there.

"Was Carla someone you hoped to see again, Nonno? Can you tell me what you're looking for?"

"Looking for? I'm not looking for anything."

On the third day Nonno sat in his room facing the balcony, his shoulders slumped forward. Anne knelt by the arm of the chair.

"Would you like to have a doctor come see you?"

He shook his head slowly. "I'm not sleeping well, that's all. I dream. But sometimes I think I'm not dreaming."

That evening when she ate alone, their waiter said, "The winds, signorina. It will rain tomorrow. We're like barometers, us old people, and our bodies know things before other people's do. Look around you." And she did, finding many tables empty or half-occupied. "Tonight many eat in their rooms or not at all. This will pass quickly, though. At this time of year, good weather prevails." His rheumy eyes regarded her with affectionate concern.

Her relationship to Nonno was longer than some marriages, and for Anne it was deeper because he was part of her life even before memory had begun to function with clarity. For her, time had never existed without him. In her childhood they had invented a separate world. He could call her to come down from her room and join him on the porch divan to swing and read together. She would say, "I'm coming, Nonno," prolonging her arrival, making him call out again if only to coax her, anticipating the joy of a lazy summer afternoon in which the slow shuttling and squeak of the divan would accompany his voice in the chest beneath her ear until the story rocked her into waves of sleep. Sometimes she would wake to find Nonno's head tilting away into the cushions. She would tuck her face close to the rumpled vest where his heart was the clock that measured her nap time.

Ever since the death of her grandmother five years before, Anne and her grandfather had been living together in a condominium near Saratoga. At first she had been unable to sleep at night because she did not know how to interpret the sounds an old man made in his sleepless nights. His room was next to hers, the door between often kept ajar, and she would hear the pacing of slippered heels, sighs as deep as breathing exercises, and occasional mutterings of conversation. She had to learn how much of even his best nights was spent waking and which sounds showed distress that could be comforted. Once she knew this she could either roll over into sleep again or rise to tie her bathrobe around her, knock gently on his door and say, "Nonno, are you awake? I can't seem to sleep. Shall we read to each other for a while?"

She had decided when she was thirty that she would never marry, and that was a relief. Her good friends married, had children, sometimes divorced, and usually were happy to have her aunt-like presence in their homes. She became a godmother so often that she began to find it hard to remember all the birthdays. Although she had tried to form intense relationships with men in college and then at work, she could not find out what enabled a person to go beyond the first stages of intimacy. The more known some man became, the less she could open up to him. If she began to understand him, she realized he must be beginning to understand her also. But shouldn't there always be something mysterious and unknown between people? After all, she had never really understood her parents. Or had they known her better than she had ever had a chance to know them? They had died too soon, in an automobile accident when she was nineteen. Her grandparents had tried to give her a new home, but she was already very independent by then.

On the other hand maybe she did not want to live so close to someone for all the years of a marriage only to find she had shared her life with a stranger. When she began to brood on such matters, she would take herself out to dinner, enjoy a good half-bottle of wine, eat a sinfully rich dessert, and savor a measure of Grand Marnier as she read in bed.

The rain began falling straight and hard. After three days Nonno was eating little, rarely left his room, spoke to her only intermittently, and when he did, his voice was either peremptory or querulous. She had never experienced weather like this, an oppressive constancy of water whether it was actually raining or not, as if they lived in the dense source of all rainfall. The air remained warm but so laden that everything had a fine slick on it, and clothes blotted up the wet air. The rain fell and slackened and fell again in almost indiscernible alternations of downpour and drizzle and mist. Even the branches slumped toward the drenched earth.

Anne found herself avoiding windows. She turned up the

sound on the TV that always produced revolving pictures. She struggled not to be influenced by Nonno's mood or the weather, but even the staff behind the main desk spoke abruptly. She opened her door a crack to see one maid in the hallway pushing a cart of dirty bed linen at another while calling her a lazy bitch. She watched tensely, her own pulse rising to their angry voices.

Their waiter, his normally starched, clean jacket rumpled and face bristled in patches where his razor had skipped, gestured at the nearly empty dining hall as if his hand had grown very heavy.

"They blame us. But how can we control the weather? We do everything to make comfort and then they blame us. Is that fair?"

Nonno became petulant. The food Anne ordered up was not cooked well enough. He pushed aside the broth because he said it was mere dishwater used to drown a few noodles, or he glanced at his soup, stared at her angrily, then asked, "Why minestrone when I asked for the broth? Do you think you can trick me like this?" No use to remind him gently that he had agreed to minestrone after she had argued that he must have more food.

Once he shoved a plate of chicken livers from his tray onto the floor. His voice rose into a high whine and his eyes filled with tears. "This isn't liver, this is gizzard and hearts. Do you think I'm too old to tell the difference?"

She stared at the livers and gravy splattered on the rug. She clenched her fists. Around them the rain fell, her dress clung to her thighs and calves as if she stood in the downpour itself, and she would have walked away to beat her fist against a wall if he had not slapped his cane down hard against the nearby chair. When she lurched to him, he only writhed and pushed her away, saying, "Leave me alone."

They had argued before in their life at home, but never in

such a sustained and petty manner. In a numb moment of calm the next day, she sat at the little desk in her room with a blank piece of paper in front of her. Everything was a sodden jumble—damp paper, mind as blurred as the ink. For two days she had wanted to write to friends. But the words would not come. She tossed the pen aside.

He stood looking at her fiercely from the doorway. "Why did we ever come back to this country?"

"You wanted to."

"You must have known how painful it would be for me."

"I did not."

"All your life I've told you things from here." The free hand struck his chest. "And you only listened and waited for me to make a fool of myself."

She stood. "That's not true. And anyway, I don't think you've told me much at all."

He slammed the door behind him and slipped the bolt.

"Nonno." She put her ear to the door. She could hear nothing through the rain. "Open this door."

For an hour she waited, sitting on the edge of her bed. What purpose did any of this have if all that was left for her to do was drag a demented grandfather home? Anne began to brood. She was old enough to know that was one of her more disagreeable characteristics, and had she been at home she would have sought out one of her godchildren as a reminder of how unimportant her concerns were. But here she had only Nonno, and he *was* the problem.

She knocked again but the rain drowned out any response. She telephoned his room. She listened to the ringing until the operator asked if she would like to leave a message. *No, thank you.* "Silly old man," she said aloud to the dead receiver before she jammed it back on its cradle. Then she was afraid—how would she know if something was wrong? A stroke. Helpless on the floor, trying to reach the phone. She should have the manager come from the main desk with a key. But the door would open, she and the manager would stare in at Nonno who would be sitting in his desk chair, arms sternly folded, ready to rave about her evil intentions, to enlist strangers in his sense of injury. How could she watch him destroy his dignity in front of them?

She cupped one ear to the door, trying to blank out the steady hiss of rain. She heard a drawer opening with a reluctant squeak. His cane struck down on the floor as he paced close to the balcony. She drew up her chair and waited near the door so she could be ready if he relented. She held her book open, reading the same paragraph six times with stubborn determination. At last she slipped into its world.

The rain blew against the windows, then fell in a gush as if someone on the roof had heaved the contents of a pail, and at last it gave way to a wan but insistent sunlight. A block of clear light and shadow across her lap caught her attention. She turned to the window, held for a moment between the world of her book and the urgent surprise of sunlight. She could hear the water running in his bath. He would be cleaning up for dinner. She made herself ready also and waited. Exactly at the usual time the bolt slipped, but he did not open the door. She had to do that, and he was waiting, bow tie neatly pointing under his clean-shaven chin. She smiled, took his arm, began to turn with him to the door.

"Do you forgive me, Nonno? We were tired. The rain."

But he did not answer. At the dinner table he stared past her, his face impassive. Most irritating of all was the way that face became its usual mobile self when he chatted with their waiter. Yes, he was feeling much better, and such oppressive rains were insufferable. If it was certain the sole had been caught that morning, he would try it. But light on the butter. By dessert she was frantic, nearly in tears.

She pushed the cake aside. "This is childish. I said I'm sorry."

He refused to look at her eyes. "We should go home. When we get there, I'm moving. Into Greenmount Manor."

The mask of his face became as firm as the marble bust of an emperor.

"*Caffè, signori?*" Their waiter leaned close.

"*No, grazie.*" Nonno rose slowly. The waiter pulled back the chair. "*Ma per la signorina, caffè e sambuca, per favore.*"

Let him have his dramatic departure. With cold determination she drank the coffee and sambuca, and she listened with a perverse pleasure to the shrill fluctuations of the French woman's voice at the neighboring table as she berated her gray-fleshed husband, the food, the waiter, anything she could nag.

Upstairs, Anne listened to his preparations for bed. She did not try the door. Only one way left to bring him around. Like a child who has stamped his foot in the doorway and shouted that he will run away from home, he must be allowed to play out his actions until they collapsed on him. But in the darkness, eerily silent now that the rain had ceased and the rest of the world listened for a brief period before throwing up the usual racket of traffic, dogs, and loud conversations, she wanted to weep. Somewhere behind this monumental statue her own Nonno was trapped. What was the spell to bring him back?

He did not answer her knock in the morning, yet he had to be up since she had slept late. She pushed the door open. Bed unmade. Some clothes here and there in neat piles, but no suitcase. A sheet of hotel stationery on the pillow.

> Dear Anne,
> Please go home. I do not blame you. We tried. But I want to be alone now. What is to be gained by bitterness and anger? No one can help in the end. I'm going to Florence.

Only as she pushed around the slow and conflicting currents of travelers in the Florence station did she clearly understand how impossible her task had become. Where in this unknown, crowded city would she find one old man? Even here in the small area of quay and concourse she would not be able to see him. What disturbed her more was to think that she might not recognize him, might be looking so hard that he would be invisible. She sat for a moment on a stone bench. Where would he go? She closed her eyes. She tried to recall all of his anecdotes about Nina and himself, any mention of particular places or areas.

The day was unusually hot, a reversion to mid-August. She went to the Boboli Gardens, walked in the midday heat along paths by walls where only lizards could bear to be exposed, past dead fountains of flaking concrete and headless putti, through sudden dark tunnels in the overgrown hedges where once she disturbed a sprawled cat suckling four blind kittens. She tried to follow a map of the gardens but she could not figure out how to read it, and she kept imagining that Nonno was in some special enclosure of privet, the hidden center of the maze.

Thirst drove her to a bar for mineral water, then she walked through all the settings of movies and books—the Ponte Vecchio, the Uffizi, Palazzo della Signoria, the Duomo and Baptistry—and she was neither native nor tourist but obsessed wanderer, impatient with the people who were doing what they should. The straps of her sandals rubbed her flesh raw, her dress clung wetly, her sweat turned sour through the long, hot day.

All the time she felt an urgency that would not let her stop to think, as if a large, firm hand were shoving her forward. Her eyes began to sting and ache with staring, and all she saw were old men stooping or sitting or gesticulating. Their faces passed her in windows of buses. She nearly ran directly into a swerving taxi in order to catch up to a figure ducking furtively into an alley, but the man turned a startled, unknown face to her, his urine jetting against the wall. By late afternoon her heels were bleeding, she knew her own body would not tolerate much more, and she tried once again to trace a few paths in the Boboli. Clutching an *aranciata* she bought from a cart near the entrance, she sat on the shady side of the amphitheater.

Her flesh was covered with a fine layer of grit and sweat. Her head ached. Should she give it up, hope that he would be at the hotel when she returned to Montecatini, or that he would come back soon? What difference would that make? Even if she found him and he were as he always had been, hadn't something been changed by all this? She closed her eyes tightly. Nothing was the same, but she could not locate what had changed. All she knew now was that this day of panic was beginning to feel more like running away than a pursuit.

She was dizzy and doubled forward to place her head between her knees. If only she could curl up on the stone and close her eyes for a few moments. But she did not trust the world to leave her alone: those men lurking everywhere, jackets slung over their shoulders and dark glasses perched on their brows—watchful, smiling, and eager to talk if her gaze lingered for more than a casual flicker.

Anne breathed deeply and slowly. The bowl of the amphitheater caught and magnified all the small sounds—birds fluttering in the nearby bushes, two boys chasing lizards on the other side, a tour group making their way toward the upper terraces of the gardens.

She sat up and leaned back on her elbows, still keeping her eyes closed. A small breeze fluttered around her ankles, shifting the hem of her skirt. She opened her eyes and stared at the pale blue sky with its fluff of clouds. She might have been gazing at a baroque church ceiling. She expected angels with trumpets and swirling robes to coalesce and dangle at her from the fleece. She looked down to the obelisk.

A man and woman were standing in front of it with their backs to her. He was reading the guidebook as she listened with her face turned to the same sky Anne had been watching. He ran his finger carefully down the page as if the print were very small. His hair was gray and slightly disheveled. The woman lifted her hand to shade her eyes, perhaps to see more deeply into the sky.

Anne stared, hardly even blinking. How often she had seen her father stand like that with a book in his hand, glasses resting on his nose, as he read and glanced over the rims to see what he was reading about. How often her mother would listen but let her gaze wander, happy to have her husband educate his own focused attention while she took in the fringes that interested her more.

Someone behind Anne yelled a name, and the couple turned. The man called back, "Peter, my God. What a coincidence."

A figure jogged past her, down the steps. They greeted each other effusively, all three talking at once, and then they sauntered toward the upper slopes. Anne watched them until they had turned the path behind some hedges. She found herself imagining she was the one who had died and her parents had lived to stroll like this in Florence without her, and she was both sad and immensely relieved.

She limped from the Boboli toward the river, hobbled by the soreness of her feet. All she could do was return to the hotel. Perhaps a message would be waiting for her. Rather than crossing the Ponte Vecchio, she wandered along the river to the next bridge. The water was slow and brown. Ahead of her she glimpsed a flash of white hair as an old man disappeared down the steps to the river bank. She leaned over the parapet.

Could it be Nonno? Where had he found such a costume—a black jacket and gray pants, the cloth faded and threadbare but elegant in cut? He stopped by the edge of the water and stared down at it.

She looked across the river and saw another white-haired figure also staring at the man. Surely this one was Nonno. When he shifted his gaze to her, she waved. For a moment he did not move, then his hand rose and opened its palm toward her almost as if firmly closing an invisible door between them. Then he lowered his hand to the stone.

The sun was beginning to set. It cast a rosy wash over the parapet and houses beyond. The man by the river had taken off his jacket, and he was folding it very precisely as if about to pack it in a suitcase. He placed it beside him on the bank. Then he sat on it and removed both of his shoes which he placed neatly beside the coat, toes pointing at the river. In his stocking feet he stepped in and waded forward until he was in as deep as his waist. The man stood still for a long time, his hands in the water. The scene was making even less sense to Anne than one of her dreams. He lifted a hand and stared at the palm. He turned it slowly and looked at the other side. Then he walked out of the water but did not stop for his shoes or coat. He came up the stairs, still in just his socks. The trousers were soaked and muddied. As he passed Anne he stared through her, his lips moving as they whispered, *"Son' morto, son' morto."*

She turned. Nonno was leaning toward her and pointing toward the Ponte Vecchio. They began walking. For a while he continued to point and nod, and then he only stared at her with one hand shielding his eyes from the sun as they strode downstream on the opposite banks of the river.

the terrorist

Dante Scariotto woke, sat up, and clutched the cot's wooden frame. In the still, dark room, the cot was the only furniture, and sounds of motion were amplified by the empty space. A dream still surrounded him, the one he had known since childhood. A huge bird was wheeling and plunging downward through darkness, its feathers on fire, eyes wide and beak thrust open, but it made no cry. Even though Dante was only watching the bird, its pain was his, each nerve end burning in a flame but never consumed. He flattened his palms on his thighs and breathed deeply.

But he was perched above Via Fani, not lost in some nameless sky, and this was the day of his masterpiece. He pushed the button on his wristwatch, lighting up the face. Six. Raising the thick shade on the window would reveal a sky already pale at its edges. He buttoned his shirt collar and tightened his tie, then groped for a jacket that lay on the floor beside the cot. He put it on and held his hand flatly across his breastbone. The dream always left him hollow in his chest, and in the dark he could imagine his own body stretched out like the curved staves of a boat long ago beached. The staves would rot until only an impression of a keel remained, and soon not even the sand would record that he had been there.

He yanked the shade, and it rattled up. At the intersection of Via Fani and Via Stresa the stoplight was cycling through its signals for an empty street. His view from the top floor of the partially abandoned building allowed him to see along Via Fani in both directions for some distance, but he could follow Via Stresa only west. He closed his eyes. He needed a cup of coffee.

The others would be awake by now also, driving cars from various places in the city where they had been stashed. Moretti would be calling Morucci to be certain no one had been arrested that night. If Morucci did not answer, the whole thing would be off. Seghetti should have been checking the Fiat 132 carefully. Only last week the ignition had failed and was replaced. Watching buildings nearby take shape from the brightening sky, Dante held his hands behind his back and imagined everyone as if creating them—eleven men, one woman. His little army. The actors in his play.

He trusted them. They had rehearsed this so often that only quirks beyond their control could change things now. What was more disturbing was the possibility that various characters in the drama who were not under his direction might fail to play their parts as they should. What if Ricci, Moro's driver for eighteen years, ate clams that disagreed with him, and he woke unable to bring the usual Fiat sedan? Judo Leonardi, the chief guard, would find another driver, but a borrowed car might be bullet-proof. And the three men in the escort Alfa Romeo? To have to count on five people to perform their routines to perfection on any given day might be expecting too much.

But Dante was certain of Moro himself. Through months of surveillance he had never wavered from his workday routine. Leaving the penthouse apartment at 79 Via Forte Trionfale, only one third of a mile away, driving down Via

Fani to the intersection with Via Stresa to reach Via Camilluccia in order to stop for a few moments at the church of Santa Chiara was as necessary to the man's ability to function as a regular heartbeat. Dante had discovered in his research that even twelve years earlier a right-wing newspaper had written a satirical article on Moro's methodical nature and called attention to the ease with which he could be assassinated since he never failed to go to the Santa Chiara church each morning on his way to work.

Rivera in the Alfa Romeo would be driving too close to the Fiat's tail, fearful some car might come between his and Moro's. Leonardi would be relaxed, chatting with his boss, who could almost be called a friend. His previous behavior as chief guard indicated he felt Moro was in jeopardy only when he went to public occasions. Perhaps he knew his boss too well, a disadvantage to someone who should have been guarding a figurehead rather than a friend. Perhaps he had come to think Moro was too amiable a person to be a target. Even though the escort car carried an arsenal of M-12 rifles capable of firing five hundred rounds per minute, they would be, as usual, locked in the trunk of the car.

Dante was sure he knew the five men as well as anyone could except those who lived with them intimately. For months they had been watched, their phones tapped, their conversations in bars or waiting rooms overheard, their daily habits monitored so closely that sometimes Dante had been forced to warn an overzealous tail to back off for a day or two. The three police officers in the following squad cars were young: Giulio Rivera, twenty-four; Raffaele Jozzino, twenty-five; and Francesco Zizzi, thirty. He was proud that Zizzi was known to him as well as the others even though the man was a substitute driver and only three days ago he had been assigned to the job. "Find out about him," Dante snapped to Morucci when he brought him the news. "We can't have any wild cards in the game." But he was no more threat than the others, and, in fact, his eagerness to keep this prized job made him even more vulnerable.

Rivera had his own theories about how to drive the escort car and was stubbornly unwilling to take the advice of the anti-terrorist unit to drive further behind the Moro car. The unit had warned that driving close gave the escort too little time to react if the main car was attacked or its progress interrupted, that there was less risk in having a car come between the escort and main car than in being in tandem. Already Rivera had given the Moro car a few taps on the bumper and even a scratch on one fender while tailgating in heavy traffic. "Specialists, specialists," he had been overheard complaining in the corridor of the substation, "they give plenty of advice but who does the driving? Eh?"

Then there was Ricci, Moro's driver. When Dante had received the report that Ricci, on a family trip to the beach, had been seen leaning from his car window, hand puckered and waggling in air at a car that had tried to shift into his lane, his high, thin voice howling, "You crazy cow of a woman driver," Dante asked which woman Morucci trusted most. To Dante's surprise he had not said Adriana, but suggested Barbara Balzerani, the one they all knew as "Sara."

"She should be the one to drive the station wagon," Dante had said. "Ricci will only think she's a crazy woman driver. It should give us a few more seconds."

Oreste Leonardi he knew best. Old Judo, the warrant officer from the carabinieri. Only two days ago he had stood and chatted with Leonardi over coffee and some pastries at the small bar near the headquarters of the Christian Democratic Party. When he had asked Judo politely if the man ever feared for his life in these dangerous times of terrorist raids, Leonardi had shrugged and waved a hand in dismissal, repeating the old peasant saying that no one ever touches the ones at the top. He was fifty-two, and like his boss Moro, he could be suddenly quiet and watchful, even if his mannerisms overall were much more bluff and energetic. But his weakness was too much affection for his family. Dante thought it was a form of sentimentality for that tough, old soldier exterior to be so flimsy that the man could become watery-eyed when discussing the attainments of a child, producing a worn photograph as if that were the final proof that such a paragon could exist.

All five men, of course, were trained to protect, even at the expense of their own lives, but Dante was certain that only Judo's need to protect Moro had reached the dangerous instinctual level because he genuinely loved his boss. So he had insisted Moretti take weeks of intensive target practice. They had to take out Judo in the first few seconds. Wounds would not be enough. The man would crawl over coals in order to save Moro. For that part of the man, Dante had a deep respect.

A man walked down the street at a brisk pace, telescoped umbrella swinging from his wrist. He paused to let the light change, as if obeying were so ingrained that even in a street without traffic he had to wait for green. Dante nodded approval. This kind of conditioned behavior was exactly what he was counting on. He wanted the patterns learned by his disciples to be so automatic that fear and tension would not interrupt their timing, wanted the daily routine of the five with Moro to surround them with a falsely secure sense of the casual.

Dante left the window to take a few turns around the room. The plaster was badly cracked and chunks had fallen from the ceiling. They powdered under his tasseled, black shoes. The cot was bare, and he had only spent the one night there, not really expecting to sleep. He had stood at the window three other days in the past two weeks, watching rehearsals carefully. They had never used all of the cars and motorcycle at the same time. So much activity might have caused suspicion, and the crucial maneuver—the backing of the white Fiat 128 through the corner at the intersection—was illegal and could be rehearsed only at night on an empty intersection. Dante put his hand to the knot in his tie again to be certain that it was tight and centered, then combed his fingers through his thinning hair. He turned his back to the window as if ignoring the sun would make it rise more quickly.

He had treated Sara gently after the last rehearsal even though her timing had been off. She was too crucial, as driver of the Fiat, to risk putting additional stress on her. Besides, she had criticized herself for walking around the corner, imagining herself to be driving backward, nearly ten seconds too late to intercept Mario, who had been pretending to be Moro's car. That would have been more than enough time for Ricci to have made it through the intersection or at least sufficiently around the parked Mini Cooper to be able to evade Sara. The whole plan depended on halting the blue Fiat. It was, Dante knew, the weakest link in the events that would inexorably follow. If the Fiat kept moving, or only paused too briefly and could continue on, the job was botched. Dante, from his perch in the window, had often wished he could drop some metal plate from his height so that it would land precisely in front of the blue Fiat. If only he could push a button that would halt the flow of the world for those few seconds necessary to do the shooting and to grab Moro. But then the beauty of it all was in the risk, this complicated dance in which only a small number of the performers had studied the choreography. If it worked, surely his genius would be recognized.

Dante had put his hand on Sara's shoulder and taken her aside when they were back at Via Gradoli.

You know, don't you?

She had nodded. *I was counting carefully and then lost it for a few moments. I think it was the flower man. He was arguing with someone.*

Don't worry. The flower man won't be there, and you'll be in the car, and you know it all so well you could do it in your dreams.

She had laughed, her young face full of the kind of energy and toughness he had chosen her for, even if most of the time it seemed much more tired and worn than it should be at her age.

I do, Dante. I dream it every night.

What pleased him above all was the way in which they had treated him, as if they recognized his superior talents, could ignore all the ways in which, when some of them had known him before, they had not valued him enough. When the committee had accepted his plan and chosen him to carry it out, they immediately gave him a dignity he had not experienced with them before. So many of them were young, students or drop-outs from universities, and rarely from the working classes as he had been. If all went well, he would have their respect permanently.

He glanced at his watch again but continued to make himself stand facing the wall. He closed his eyes. Antonio Spiriticchio would have wakened already, left his apartment near the Piazza del Popolo to make the long drive across town to pick up his flowers for the day, and discovered all four tires of his small truck slashed. His day would be wasted, but surely the expense of buying new tires would seem less to him than death in cross-fire. His presence on that corner would have introduced a dangerously unpredictable element. Dante stiffened when the coruscated shield of a newsstand on the street was flung up with a harsh rattle. The day on Via Fani had begun. He looked at the ceiling, then walked back to the window, counting his paces.

The light was full now. He could see everything. No more conjecturing, imagining, tinkering with plans, thinking, *What if, what if.* Reality. But as his pulse lifted with excitement, he sensed a slight letdown. The dream was always more exciting than the reality. He had created what he was about to witness, but surely some of it would go differently from what he had planned, and his plan was so exquisite that he could almost wish it might have remained intact as a possibility rather than the blundering event that it would have to be, even if it was successful. Below him was a peaceful crossroad, sidewalks, the façade of Olivetti's Bar—recently closed down—a newsstand up the street run by a proprietor unaware of the news he would be selling by that evening. All this would explode, twisting lives into new directions because he, Dante Scariotto, had made a plan. But he could not prevent the backwash—that somehow all this was chance, a fragile design pasted onto randomness. What meaning did any of this have? How could he make himself believe these few minutes meant anything when time itself stretched forward and backward so incomprehensibly? What difference did it make if Moro were kidnapped? What if he and his mother and father had never come to Rome? What if there had been no war in Europe when he was a child? What if he had never been born? What if, what if?

His father, Vincente, interned in England during the Second World War, had developed a tolerance for the English that Dante had not inherited. He blamed them for his lonely childhood, a time when he and his mother stayed with relatives in L'Aquila, hoping for letters from his father or information as to whether he had been randomly killed by a German bombing raid. But when his father returned, he came to hate the man.

His aunt's house was perched on the hillside. His childhood took place in cold fogs, narrow alleys where sun did not seem to reach the street level until spring and where cobblestones were dank under the thin soles of his shoes, and in rooms they did not enter except for sleeping because only one charcoal stove was humped in the kitchen. Here they huddled, arguing loudly with each other or bickering and sniping. His mother did not have the patience to wait out the war and attached herself to a cousin, Alberto, and in the stark room next to Dante's own that was furnished only with its one brass bedstead and a cracked mirror, they would moan and tussle close to the wall where he lay. He hated those animal grunts and groans, and later in his own life when he made love he choked back his voice, ejaculating into a furious silence.

When his father had returned one August, Dante saw no violent scene or even an argument. Alberto packed and left and sent them one postcard four years later from Brazil. That winter, he and his father and mother, who was pregnant by then, moved to Rome. Just before he left the apartment, Dante went into his aunt's room. She was downstairs berating his mother for walking out on her. Dante took the volume of recordings she listened to every Saturday on her wind-up machine. He slipped each record out of its sleeve, broke it gently over his knee, and slid it back into the cover. *Is that Alberto's child?* he said when his father brought him to stand by the bed to see his sister for the first time. *Kiss your sister,* his father said flatly, but he could tell that if he came that close his mother would slap him hard across the mouth. He felt no sorrow when the baby died a year later, although his sobbing mother had to be held up on each side as she was leaving the funeral service.

He never understood what kind of work his father did, except that it was illegal. Once he went with him when Vincente was paid off. He walked just ahead of Dante but kept a firm grip on his hand. It was a warm evening in late June, and

Dante could feel the sweat that slicked his father's wrist when it rubbed against his own. They had stepped down from the bus that had brought them from the apartment in the Magliana and into the wide square of Piazza Venezia where the Vittorio Emmanuele Monument was looming behind them. Dante knew Vincente held his hand not because his father was afraid he would get lost in the press of people around them on a Saturday night but because he did not want him to dawdle. He hated the hard grip, the way it squeezed the joints of his fingers together until they ached. But he had no intention of showing pain or asking for release. He had learned never to let the man know when his actions caused discomfort, whether physical or emotional, because then his father would only repeat them.

He's just trying to make a man of you, his mother had said once when she found Dante holding a rag with ice cubes to his bruised arm, but Dante kicked the bathroom door shut, yelling, *Leave me alone,* in only a slightly higher-voiced version of what his father would say to her when she asked for money to pay their debt to the butcher in the market.

Vincente moved down the smaller streets away from Piazza Venezia in strides that did not break their pattern to make way for other pedestrians, and Dante had to duck and weave like a dinghy towed in the wake of a larger craft. Occasionally someone cursed when Vincente's shoulder brushed him, but the man did not respond. In a small alley near Via Pastina, Vincente let go of Dante and groped in his pocket for a crumpled piece of paper.

Read it. He thrust it at Dante, who smoothed and held it toward the last glow of daylight in the sky above them. One of the few powers Dante had over his father was the ability to read.

Number 76.

Vincente lifted the knocker, letting it drop heavily four or five times. The man who opened it did not stand aside.

Your name.

Vincente Scariotto.

He checked a list he held.

Who's he?

My son. I had to bring him with me.

Upstairs, then left. You're late, but not the only one who is.

Vincente had assumed a humbly slumped posture, shoulders rolled forward, and now he lifted his hands, palms up, as if asking for absolution. The other man shrugged. Dante could not bear the way his father would shift his demeanor whenever he sensed he was in the presence of someone more powerful than he. As they climbed the stairs, he rubbed his hands together and muttered as if still making excuses to the man below. At the end of a long corridor on the third floor, two men were sitting and talking together at a table. A wide box in front of them was stacked with white envelopes. For a few moments the men kept up their gentle argument about the virtues of gnocchi and whether they were truly of benefit to an inflamed bowel. Finally one of them turned slightly and put on his glasses that he had been gesturing with as he spoke.

Yes?

Vincente Scariotto. I was told to . . .

Yes, yes. You all were. You were also told to be here by eight. It's nearly nine, and look at this. He jabbed at the remaining row of envelopes. *I suppose you think that we've nothing better to do on a Saturday night than wait till you feel ready to come.*

Very sorry, very sorry. Vincente rolled forward on the balls of his feet as if he would willingly drop to his knees, rubbing the knuckles of his two fists together. *We're from the Magliana, you see, and the buses . . .*

Never mind, the other one said testily. He leaned forward to file through the envelopes. *It's always the buses. But when you need to take a shit, you know how to get to the can in time. Maybe money means nothing to you.*

He held still, his face not looking up at Vincente, his thumb and forefinger pinning one of the envelopes as if hesitating about whether to lift it out of the box.

No. I assure you, sir, the money means a great deal to us. You see my boy here? Nine years old already, but look at him, please. He's as small as a five-year-old, weighs less than some of the dogs in the neighborhood. We never have enough on the table. Times are very hard.

The two men nodded as if Vincente had passed some necessary test. They stared at Dante, making him want to do something outrageous like biting his thumb at them or lifting the horns of his fingers.

Ours are older now. But it was worse during the war, Scariotto. Where were you?

Vincente drew out a battered pack of cigarettes, one that Dante knew the man had been carrying with him for a week, smoking a few puffs from a cigarette, then pinching off the spark and putting the stub back in the pack to savor again later. He offered the pack expansively, and the men each took one cigarette. Vincente lit all three and breathed in deeply.

England. I was caught there. Working for intelligence.

Excellent. Better interned than on the field, eh?

Other than the basic fact that his father had been a prisoner in England, Dante knew very little about his reasons for being there in the first place. He invented new versions frequently, depending on what the man thought suitable for the occasion, so Dante did not listen as the three continued their conversation. At last the envelope was handed to Vincente, the two behind the table remained seated but shook his father's hand when he reached over the table, and as he and Dante walked down the stairs, Vincente tore open the flap and pulled out the flattened bills.

Bastards, he said quietly.

In the first few bars Vincente went to, Dante was told to sit in a corner on a chair and wait, but later his father, who had begun to sing in a toneless, loud barking as they wandered to the next lit entryway, made him sit with him at the bar or the same table and bought him Coke or an aranciata. The man talked to anyone who would listen and respond—men beside him, women behind the counter—always about the hard times, about how the idiots running the country did not understand what it was like to be "one of us," about the ways he and the other person he was talking to had risked their lives for this fine freedom they all had (sometimes as a soldier, sometimes as a partisan, occasionally as a spy for the Allies, once as a loyal defender of Mussolini, who had been the only one to really understand the greatness of Italy), and a few times he would buy a drink for the other person if he sensed the man was better off than he was. Dante did not answer when he was spoken to. He hated the maudlin ways all of them would recognize his presence, especially the women, who wanted to say how handsome he would be, how intelligent his eyes were, how hard it all was on the children especially.

Finally they knocked on the door of a darkened apartment house and were ushered up the stairs by a bored young woman in a housecoat and into a room draped in red velvet, furnished with leather chairs and couches, where more women in various costumes were lounging and smoking or standing in front of mirrors and plumping their hair.

Ah, it's Vincente, girls, someone called, and they all turned. *Payday, payday.*

An old woman, bent nearly double by her curled backbone stood from behind a table and lifted her hand to point a bony finger at him.

Wait. Can you really pay or are you tricking us like last time?
Vincente dug into his pocket and pulled out a wad of the
remaining bills.

OK, the woman croaked. *Ladies, I want to see those lire in my
hand at the end of the evening. Your kid?*

Vincente pushed Dante forward and introduced him. The
woman peered, her eyes squinched.

Doesn't look like you, Vincente. Are you sure?

Is a man ever sure?

Who'd blame the wife of a lout like you? the woman behind
them said.

But Vincente only laughed, and the laugh surprised Dante
because it was so relaxed, so unlike the tense bleat he always
heard the man give when listening to the radio at home or
talking with a friend in the street.

No one's perfect.

Dante sat on a couch in the corner of the room. His father
came in and out, drinking sometimes with a group of the
women, sometimes disappearing into other rooms with one
or two of them. Some other men came in from time to time
also and talked to the old woman before going off with one of
the women. When any of the girls came to sit with Dante, he
did not answer their questions, and usually they would shrug
and go away or merely sit there filing their nails or lolling
back to doze for a few moments. Dante worked furiously to
keep his eyes open. He detested the smell of the place—overly
sweet perfumes, the punky sweat of various men who came
and went, the layered and absorbed odor of cigars and cheap
cigarettes and some sour disinfectant. But he too must have
dozed because he woke to the sound of accordion music, and
in the center of the room on a wooden chair, a blind player
was sitting, the same that he and his father had passed on the
street below when Vincente had tossed a few coins into the
hat beside him. Now he leaned back and yanked his accor-

dion open and shut, wheezing out chords and wavering melodies as Vincente and a few of the girls danced around him, laughing and stumbling as if they were in a hummocky field.

One of the women broke loose from his father and came to Dante. She was huge, her hips broad and buttocks spilling out of the tight panties she wore, her breasts wobbling and straining against the thin strip of cloth that crossed them. She dropped herself onto the couch beside Dante and suddenly heaved him onto her lap with a strength that Dante was not prepared for, and off balance he could not resist her. In a moment she had reached in front and unzipped his fly, pulling out his penis and waving it toward the others in time to the music.

Look at the conductor, Giuseppe. How can you keep the tempo unless you watch the conductor? The blind man grinned in the direction of his shouted name.

But Dante was off her lap in a moment, his back to the others. She was laughing, facing him, and she pulled roughly on his arms.

Come on, sweetheart. I've seen the goods. You could do a man's job with a tool like that.

Dante held still. He waited until he had enough saliva, and then he thrust his face forward and spat at her. She shrieked and began swabbing her nose and cheek with the pink boa she wore around her neck.

The little bastard, the little bastard! she howled, and Vincente yanked him by the arm and shoved him into a chair nearby.

Party's over, the old woman's shrill voice called from the desk, and the music stopped abruptly.

What d'you mean, over? Vincente stood in the middle of the room on his splayed legs, chin thrust forward.

It's all gone, Vincente. You got what you paid for.

The man reached into his pocket and pulled out a few coins, looking at them distractedly.

See? Now run along quietly, friend. Show the young man some dignity, eh? We don't want to have to get rough like the last time. Besides, we all want to stay friends.

The little bastard! the woman shrilled once more.

Vincente turned but almost lost his balance. *All friends, aren't we? Silvia. He's only a kid. He didn't mean it. Say you didn't mean it, Dante.* But he was looking at the wrong corner of the room, frowning as if trying to see Dante in the distance.

Go home, old friend, the old woman called again. *Don't worry about Silvia. She's used to taking what comes out of a man.*

Then they were on the street where the quiet was so sudden that Dante's ears rang. His father began staggering out the alley, motioning with his hand for Dante to follow. After a while he said over his shoulder, *Shouldn't have done that. She was only joking around.*

But Dante did not answer. He was so weary that his father's weaving pace, taking up most of the narrow street, made him feel he must be on the deck of a ship and that he would fall soon, perhaps into a deep slumber. In a narrow alley off the Via Corso, Vincente paused and slipped his head under the stream of a small fountain in the wall. When Dante came closer he noticed it was the statue of a man holding a barrel, his face leaning forward with the effort of bearing it, his hands splayed across the staves. He was wearing a strange cap, and most of his face had been eaten away, but the eyes were still there, deep sockets that expressed a quiet, friendly mind.

Vincente withdrew his head, then threw handfuls of water against his face.

You know this man? He gestured to the face.

Dante did not answer.

Of course you don't. You'll never learn anything going to school.

Vincente's hand shot out and grabbed Dante by the shirt collar, pulling him forward. But instead of cuffing him he held him tightly, one hand on each shoulder.

Dante, Dante. You are my son, you know. You are. My only son. Don't think badly of your father. I can't help it. The women. I never had money like this, and sometimes now I do. I love to spend it, Dante. I need to. All those years waiting to come home. To what? To all this? One of the hands let go for a moment, just long enough to sweep the air above Dante's head as if visions of everything the man feared and detested were flitting around them. But he gripped Dante again, harder. *You've got to understand. I didn't mean what I said. Many times I don't. I'm a hard man to live with. What I meant was go to school. Do well. Don't let them get you like they did me. I'm ruined, Dante. Ruined.*

He said the last words with a choking voice, and Dante was afraid his trembling face would begin weeping. The man's gaze focused on the fountain over Dante's shoulder, and he let go of him.

The Porter. That's what they call him. He was a real person. They made a statue of him.

For a moment Dante considered with cold precision that he could gather enough spit, just as he had with Silvia, and he could lean forward and let go in his father's face. Perhaps the man saw something in Dante's expression because his lip curled slightly and he nodded.

Why give you good advice, you wimp? You'll never be a man. Not like your father. You'll always run. Look. Come here.

He yanked Dante close to the fountain.

See that face? Do you know what the man has?

Dante shook his head.

He has syphilis. Do you know what that is?

Something you catch from whores.

'*Something you catch from whores,*' Vincente whined in a prissy voice. *Do you know what whores are?*

The women you were with tonight.

No. He knocked Dante in the back of the head so that his forehead beat lightly against the wall beside the fountain. *Those were friends. Whores are people like your mother. Whores are women who live off men because they can't make their own honest living, who suck them dry with their nagging and their whining for more prick up the ass. Now listen. This is true, Dante. They say that if you touch the Porter's face, you'll get syphilis. Do you know what it does? It eats out your brain. Your nose drops off, like his. You die with sores all over your body. If you have any guts, touch his face.*

Dante did not move.

Touch it. Vincente reached and grabbed Dante's hand. He tried to pull free, but the man was still much stronger than he was. *Touch it.*

His hand was dragged forward toward the battered face. He did not believe his father, but he did not want to touch the face. The expression on it now did not seem kindly. It was leering, the face of his father when he was leaning over the limp form of his mother. But his hand was rubbed harshly against the stone. The worn and broken features scraped his palm. When his hand was free, he pulled it back, wiping it against his thigh. His father was laughing.

Oh, my God. You really believed me, eh? Look at you. He imitated his son, wiping his hand along his thigh.

When they walked out onto the street again, Vincente groped with his sleeve and looked at his watch.

Shit. Missed the last bus.

He led them to the small park at the foot of the Capitoline.

You take that bench, he said, gesturing Dante further along.

Just before dawn he could hear his father vomiting and saw his dim figure hunched over the curb. In daylight Vincente discovered he did not have enough change left to pay for the bus so they walked back to the Magliana, and when his mother met them at the door, Vincente shoved her aside and staggered to the bedroom after pausing to vomit on the kitchen floor.

Even in his most excited moments, as now when he stood ready to witness his masterpiece take place on the street below him, Dante could be overcome by a feeling of suffocation, as if he were permanently locked forever in a confessional, the heavy, dark wood and oppressive sense of the priest's presence just beyond the screen. He had never been to confession after the time his mother had made him go. It had happened after his father disappeared, probably beaten and dumped in the Tiber by any one of the competing families he worked for in the city. Dante was roving the streets with a small gang of teenage boys his own age who lived in the Magliana. The oldest of them had made arrangements with a front in the neighborhood who was especially interested in bicycles and small appliances that could be stolen from the streets or apartments anywhere in the city. When three of them were caught and jailed, his mother heard from one of the boys' mothers that Dante had been part of the group and that she was angry her boy had to suffer and not the others. His mother kept pounding on the door to his bedroom until he had to unlock it, and then she stood just inside the room, her face blotched red as it became when she was too angry to control herself, and she raged at Dante for fifteen minutes. Then, as she often would, she broke into racking sobs, lifted her hands to the ceiling as if God were just beyond it, and implored Him to put her immediately out of her misery. Because, she pointed out between gasps, her life had been nothing but pain and disappointment and now she was cursed with a son who hated her so much that he would not refrain from disgracing her in the sight of her friends and neighbors.

Dante kept the bed between her and himself, knowing that

at this point she would try to throw her arms around him, to pull him against her body with its increasingly sagging breasts and belly that disgusted him when he looked at her and made him dizzy with nausea when he felt them pressed against him. *I want you to come to Father Bernardi, that's all. All I ask is that you confess to him, Dante, confess all this business and your sins and be absolved. Is that too much? All I'm asking for is some peace of mind. I've tried so hard, Dante. I've tried so hard for you. Please.*

He did not say no. For the next two days she never left him alone when he was in the house, trying to extort that promise from him, until he finally said, *Yes, if you'll fucking leave me alone.* He did not like Father Bernardi, not only because he was the parish priest and always trying to ingratiate himself with the young men in the neighborhood, but because Dante knew why he did it—in order to please the boys' mothers and make himself more amenable to them. Evidently it had paid off as far as his own mother was concerned. Sometimes he would come home and find them together in the kitchen talking quietly over coffee and biscotti, and once, when he came home unexpectedly early, he glimpsed the priest's cassock lying disheveled on the couch, and he turned quickly and descended the stairs, not wanting ever again to hear the sounds his mother could make when she was being laid.

He confessed to minimal knowledge of the thefts, spoke with anxiety that he should become associated with such people. But as the confession droned on, the voice of the bored priest running through the expected questions, responses, platitudinous advice about Dante's soul, he felt his shoulders tightening, the veins in his neck beginning to pound with the pressure of his anger. What could he say to the fatuous imposter that would sufficiently insult him? He knew the man was beyond his reach, but he could not simply leave the booth.

One thing more, Father. I have a terrible wish to confess to.

What, my son? Remember, though, that wishes are not sins until they become acts.

Do you have wishes that never become acts, Father? Or when your wishes become acts, are you in a state of mortal sin?

If they were evil enough, I would be, Dante. The man answered so blandly that Dante could tell he had no suspicion of what Dante might know.

I wish to kill my mother.

He saw the shadowy outline of the priest's head turn to face the screen.

Kill your own mother?

Yes, Father. I hate my mother.

Dante, Dante, what are you saying? Think carefully. Your anger is one thing, but I'm sure you don't mean what you are saying. Why would you think such a thing?

Because she fornicates, Father. She commits a terrible sin when she does so.

Dante. How do you know this? Remember, your father is dead. The flesh is weak. Perhaps she's made an occasional lapse, but carnal desire is very potent. Surely you can forgive and understand.

I could, but I know she's fucking a priest, Father. She's helping someone else be damned forever.

The man did not answer for a moment. Dante held his breath.

When the voice resumed it was quiet but tense. *I think you've finished your confession, son. Would you step out for a few moments?*

When the man came around the other side of the booth, they stood quietly facing each other for a few seconds. The church was empty except for the two of them. Before Dante could lift his hands, Father Bernardi had lashed across his face with his palm so harshly that for a few moments Dante could hear only his ear ringing. The priest leaned close to him as if daring Dante to try to hit back, but the man was taller and far stronger.

Now listen, you punk. I've been in the streets with scum like you. I came out of this city and grew up in worse times than you'll ever know. What you see, you forget, right? If you keep your eyes open, you keep what you see to yourself. Otherwise, you might lose those pretty eyes. Clear?

Dante said nothing.

About your soul, I can't give advice that you'll heed. But your body you understand better, I think. Now make your feet work and don't come here again with your phony confessions.

Dante was walking away when he turned at the doorway. Father Bernardi was still watching him as if he wanted to make certain he did not sit in one of the pews.

I have something else to confess, Father, he said loudly so that the dark interior echoed with his voice. *Now I have two people I want to kill—my mother and you.*

Two months later his mother announced glumly that a notice had been posted saying Father Bernardi had taken a new calling in the north of Italy.

Good news for them, Dante said without looking up from his plate of spaghetti with vongole, and his mother only gave one of her long-suffering sighs.

Dante's wife and daughter lived in Verona, but he had not seen them for three years. Marriage had been a mistake. He mistook as interest Lucia's initial willingness to listen to his various theories concerning the political system, mistook for pride in him her silence when he outlined his own ambitions, even mistook her insistent coaxing when he was in bed with her as a deep need for his passionate attention. What else could all that have been but a mistake given the fact that five years into their marriage he had found a note on the table when he returned from a trip to Sicily, her bureau empty, Carla's bed stripped of its stuffed animals, the checkbook indicating she had taken half of their account's contents with her? To Verona. To her sister's house.

The note was lucid and dispassionate. She had been trying to tell him, she said, for more than a year that his life bored her, but his life was the only thing he wished to talk about. His concerns did not concern her. She expected society would continue as it always had, no matter what theories he had or how many meetings of this or that he went to. She did not care what his vision of the universe was, except that increasingly it seemed to give him an excuse to treat her with coldness and indifference. She reminded him that they had not made love for two years. She wanted Carla to grow up in a world where suffering could neither be explained nor condoned, where she might even have a chance to experience joy, an emotion all too absent from her present surroundings. Yes, he might visit them if he wished, but only if he notified her sister well in advance. She ended by saying that if she knew him at all, she expected she would not have to worry about seeing much of him anyway.

He had been annoyed that she had left him before he could leave her. Now he would never have a chance to dramatize his indifference for her. Only once was he seized by a fierce anger. The heat in the apartment failed on a particularly cold and drizzly day in January. He stood in the middle of the kitchen. He was wearing his overcoat but still shivered. The dishes and pans from numerous meals were stacked and unwashed on counters and the table. A strange lethargy had infected him in the past week and he would simply take a dish and rinse it when needed. He had not carried down the garbage for weeks.

In the cold that made his fingertips turn white, he was swept back to that dingy, frozen flat in L'Aquila where the acrid smell of charcoal seeped into every room and their clothes so that he could not escape it even if he left the house. He had sworn he would never live like that again, but Lucia had reduced him to this. She had returned him to L'Aquila, to the hoarse voice of his aunt calling out in the middle of the night, *For God's sake, you animals, can't you stuff your mouths when you fuck?*

That afternoon when the heat came on again, he washed all the dishes, scrubbed the floors, took his clothes to the cleaners, and never ate at his apartment again. When he brought a whore back to the apartment that night, he made her stand naked in the middle of the bedroom, her back to him. She faced the wall while he sat in a chair asking her to lift and lower her arms slowly as if she were some heavy, featherless bird trying unsuccessfully to leave the ground.

8:20. His masterpiece would be performed only once. The Mini Cooper came slowly down the street and parked in the right-hand lane near the flower vendor's corner. Dante drew in a deep breath and became calm, even serene. He had done all that he could. From his vantage point he probably had the best seat in the house. Time to watch.

The driver of the Mini Cooper locked the car door and strolled casually down Via Fani toward the Mobil station until he was out of sight. He was unessential to the rest, not part of the basic crew. The blue Fiat 128 and Fiat 132 drew up to the curb outside Olivetti's. The occupants sat low in their seats, motionless. If they were there, then the other blue Fiat 128, around the corner on Via Stresa, must have arrived too, although that was the one location that Dante could not see. Then the white Fiat 128 edged up and stopped just beyond the newsstand on the upper end of Via Fani. All the various cover cars and the car that would escape with Moro were in place.

But nothing would seem unreasonable about cars in these positions at this hour. Like any other street in Rome, the usual disorderly sprawl of traffic was beginning.

Finally the white Fiat 128 station wagon drove into its place along the curb just around the corner from the Mini Cooper. It would be well-shielded from the view of Ricci driving Moro's Fiat because of the flower vendor's empty stand and the parked Cooper. Dante did not need to look at his watch to know the time because of the four men in uniform sauntering down the street. They carried Alitalia flight bags, their caps set back jauntily. They were wearing what appeared to be the standard short blue rain coats of flight personnel. But the hats were phony, bought by Adriana at a costume shop. The men stood near the junction, putting down their bags, talking casually as if waiting for transportation to the airport.

A man and a woman with a leashed dog were walking slowly down the Via Fani. Dante clenched his fist. The dog lagged, wanting to sniff the curb or mark posts, and the couple did not seem to be in a hurry. The man nodded to the proprietor of the newsstand and said something to him from across the street. They began a conversation, the woman smiling as she listened, the man hunching his shoulders and laughing at whatever he heard from the vendor. Dante gave a small shrug. So be it. Innocent bystanders. In great historical events, they took their chances. Either the dog hurried them along or they found themselves entangled. That was fate.

Dante leaned again to look up Via Fani past the intersection with Via San Gemini where the hill became steep. Nine o'clock. Moro would take only two or three minutes to come out, sit in the back seat, perhaps wave to his daughter or son if they were leaving too. Dante counted out the seconds. Two minutes. The Honda motorcycle driven by a man in a woolen ski cap coasted slowly down the hill and made a looping U-turn just beyond the intersection, the signal that Moro's car and the escort had started out.

"The comedy begins," Dante said aloud.

As he had through all rehearsals, Dante began snapping his fingers as he once had seen a famous director of plays command his actors during a scene, indicating the timing of their motions on stage. He counted slowly and snapped when the next event should begin. Snap. The dark blue Fiat appeared, and the Alfa Romeo was close behind. Snap. The white Fiat by the newsstand that the cars had just passed pulled slowly away from the curb, made a U-turn, and stopped in the middle of Via Fani, the driver ready to jump out and halt all oncoming traffic as soon as the shooting began.

Snap. The four flight attendants leaned down to their bags and began to unzip them, careful not to reveal the AK-47s and Skorpions. Snap. The station wagon eased back slightly but did not yet make its move around the corner. The two cars approached. Sara jammed the wagon into reverse, backed through the intersection as if she had changed her mind and decided to take Via Fani rather than Via Stresa. Snap. Ricci, who still had room to stop and avoid her, put on his brakes, but Sara took another quick jerk backward as if her clutch had accidentally engaged. Snap. Steel against steel. Snap. Rivera could not stop quickly enough. Again, the squeal of brakes, clash of a slight impact.

Snap. The doors of the station wagon were flung open. Sara leaped out, gun in hand, with Moretti on the other side as the flight attendants drew out their weapons.

Then Dante could not hear his own fingers snapping. The gunfire shook the window panes. Sara and Moretti were pouring bullets into the front of the blue sedan, a deadly cross fire angled to exclude the passenger in the back seat. Glass fragments splattered into bright sunshine like spray from a fountain. The flight attendants were firing rounds into the escort car. But what had happened? Two of them fired nothing from their rifles, then slung them aside and grabbed their pistols. Dante recognized the motions of frustration—jammed guns. He ground his teeth.

Ricci and Judo slumped motionless. Rivera jerked in his seat as if someone were pulling strings attached to his legs. *Watch out*, Dante wanted to yell. Jozzino had opened the right rear door. He was crawling out, pistol in hand. He lifted it, fired twice. Morucci ran up behind him and shot a few times into his neck. Jozzino flung his hands out and lay on his back, legs twisted under him.

The men from the Fiat 132 were pulling Moro from the back seat, dragging him across the street to their car. Moro dropped his briefcase, and papers spilled out of it. They shoved him into the car. With the new escort the car pulled out, phony police sirens wailing. Sara turned, glanced up to Dante, waved her arm in a large circle, and ducked into the station wagon. The others ran to various cars. They drove away. Snap.

Silence. Dante held still. Nothing moved in the scene below him. Fragments of glass strewn along the paving and roadway glinted in the sun. Dark splashes of blood stained the shattered windshields and made seams down the car doors. The figures in the cars lay still in the awkward positions of men who were so weary that they had slumped against the hard surfaces and fallen asleep. Even from his distance Dante could see Jozzino's mouth wide open, the eyes staring in disbelief at the sky. A sheet of glass in one of the windshields buckled and smashed on the street.

As if that single sound in the enormous silence gave permission to move, a man who had been driving his motorcycle up from the Mobil Station and dropped it to take cover, walked stiffly, hands held to his neck in a protective gesture, into the crossroad and up to Jozzino's body. He picked up a newspaper that had fallen from Moro's car and began placing sheets of it over Jozzino's face as if one piece could not sufficiently cover what he saw. Somewhere directly below Dante a woman was screaming, pausing only to take in breath. In the distance the first sirens began to wail.

Dante closed his eyes. His shoulders relaxed and then his knees. He put out a hand to steady himself. He opened his eyes. One more look. People were running along the streets toward the crossroads. Cars stopped and the drivers stepped out cautiously. A crowd was gathering. He would merge with it and then slip away to Via Gradoli where he would wait for Moretti and word that Moro was safely imprisoned wherever the committee had chosen to take him, a place even he did not know. But he should not be seen standing in the window. He turned away, walked toward the door, and paused.

He stared at the empty cot. The sagging canvas still showed the indent of his body—concave impression of his head, torso, the sharp heels like talons. He stooped to push the canvas up from beneath and wipe away his shadowy presence. He could not stand the idea that his body would leave such a common, anonymous shape.

l'americana

Fall 1969

Olivia sat near the doors to the patio. A hot sea breeze gusted across the boards, sometimes billowing the gauze curtains against her bare hip and shoulder. The sea was a distant rustle of waves, and the eddy of breeze from nearby trees smelled of fallen leaves. Sometimes she heard the high call of a child on the beach. When the patch of sunlight reached her legs, she moved the chair further into the room.

She kept staring at the disheveled bed, and occasionally she leaned forward, elbows on her thighs and face propped in hands. She was watching the corpse of her stepfather, Arturo. He lay on his side, facing her, eyes wide and unblinking. The fist that he had clasped in pain against his chest had relaxed slightly, but the twist of his mouth, even the small creases around his eyes, still expressed puzzlement. *Sono morto,* he had called out as if surprised by an astounding fact. She had been lying on her back beside him, his sperm still slick on her thighs, and at first, because his back was to her, she had not understood. She saw his legs jerk upward so that he assumed a fetal position. When she lifted herself on one elbow to peer over his shoulder, he gave a choked breath and held still.

Arturo? Her breasts brushed his back as she leaned, then she pulled away, disentangled her legs from the sheets, and walked around to his side of the bed. One leg twitched, and then he was still again. The eyes stared through her. His belly hung loosely distended under the chest that did not move. Only the head of his penis showed from the hollow formed by his drawn-up legs.

For a moment she stood, her arms at her side, and then she moved one hand across her belly, along the soft hair of her crotch, and the breeze blew coolly on the places where she was still wet. She reached forward slowly and touched the rough hair on his arm, then his chest, with her fingertips only. She wanted to accustom herself to being in the presence of death, to be able to think of the lifeless human body as indifferently as if it were a lightbulb turned off. She glanced at the clock by the bed. In an hour her mother would be home, if the plane had landed in Rome on time. She calculated the journey from Da Vinci to Ostia. She had time to sit and think. For a while she stood naked at the door, staring down the sloping sand to the beach and sparkling water that could be seen from their bungalow. But she did not like having the body behind her, his wide eyes staring at her, at nothing. She brought the chair to the doorway and sat there, facing him.

She was not surprised he was dead. Two years earlier he had been advised to change his habits. *What do they know?* he had said to her mother when she argued with him in the hospital after his first heart attack. *It's my body.* He had glanced over Norma's shoulder to Olivia, who knew the words were meant for her more than her mother because he had said toward the end of the year when she was sixteen, *My body is yours now, Olivia, even more than it belongs to your mother. But she'll never know this.* Olivia listened but kept her own body safely re-tracted beyond the surfaces he touched or openings he entered. She still did not fully understand why she had let him slip into her bed in the apartment on Monte Parioli that first night, his voice in her ear saying, *Quiet, Olivia, quiet. She's sleeping from the pills, but we must be quiet.* And as he moved his hands all over her body, then his tongue, he kept saying, *I won't hurt you, kitten. I will never hurt you.* This was true. He never gave pain. When it happened during the day, she tried not to look at the folds and wrinkles of his face, and when she did come, finding it impossible to hold back because he knew what to do and was so persistent, she swallowed her voice, only showing where she was by her choked breathing. But when he made love to her, he always kept his eyes shut, and even though she never forgot who he was, his motions took on a strange impersonality, a force that was blind but very deft.

Really, Olivia, her mother would say at least once every month, *it's been long enough now, don't you think? You don't have to be so relentless. Try to be more kind to Arturo.*

The man would give her another present—gold chains, an ancient cameo, rings with delicately colored gems—and Norma would approve.

He's so sweet to you, she would say. *You're so relentless.*

When Olivia turned nineteen, Arturo had given her an Alfa Romeo convertible. Norma did not like cars, and she was not jealous.

Unfortunately, Arturo had said to Olivia this week when her mother had flown back to America to be at her own father's funeral, *your mother is not watching her weight. You must never do that, Olivia. You must never let your belly grow fat.*

Olivia stared; the body did not move. She wondered if something like rigor mortis would set in and if that would mean the position of the body might clench. She did not want to see that happen, but she could not leave the room yet either. She was waiting to see if she would feel anything more than the vague aversion to staring at a body that no longer had life in it. Piero, her boyfriend in the Movement, had described how he had been part of an action in which he and his friends had killed a bank teller. He described clinically the bullets hitting the man, how the blood pooled on the marble while they filled their bags and warned the other tellers and patrons to lie down and hold still. Her training was almost complete, and she knew soon she would be involved. She expected to leave her mother and Arturo forever—disappearing to work for some cell in the north. Forever, if it took that long to remake society; less time if she ever wanted to see them again.

Arturo had always smelled good, not only because he was a man who loved cleanliness and the aroma of various body conditioners that he used, but also he had skin that had a slightly almondy odor in itself, so clear to her that once when they lay in bed afterward she had said to him, *You don't need those lotions and things. Your skin smells good without them.*

He had turned on his side to stare at the wall beyond her without speaking for a long time. Then he had lifted one hand and stroked it slowly along the curve of her hip.

Why didn't we meet when I was your age? Why couldn't you have been born when I was? Now I can only have your body from time to time. Then, I would have wanted your soul also. I would have believed in souls.

You don't have either part of me, she had said simply, and he had laughed because he liked sharp answers.

Then please to give me your nonbody again, he tried to say in English, moving his hand slowly up the inside of her thigh.

She did, as she had every few months since that first night, always telling herself after each occasion that she never would again. But the weeks would pass, and she would be intensely aware of his presence somewhere in the house—clattering a pan in the kitchen, walking slowly up the stairs, or she might come home and hear the water running in the shower and know he was at home and her mother wasn't. She would wait for him in her bedroom. Sometimes he would not come, as if he sensed that she would not be able to say no if he waited another day or two. For the first year she thought she hated him and was only waiting to find a way to hurt him deeply— by something she might say, or by leaving so many clues that her mother would no longer be able to conceal their relationship from herself. But soon she discovered that the person she really hated was herself for her inability to resist the gradual descent toward his waiting hands, the slow thrust of his hips when he would sink so far into his own sensuous enjoyment that she knew she had become an impersonal presence. She could not even deny him access to her dreams. She never told Piero. She wanted to, but that confession was too valuable, something she would hold in reserve in case she needed a final proof of his love — and since she was not certain yet whether she could say she loved Piero, she did not yet want to put him to such a test.

The phone was ringing. She looked at the clock, considered not answering, but picked up the receiver.

"*Pronto?*"

"Olivia, dear? Is that you? Put Arturo on."

"I think he's sleeping."

"Never mind then. Mustn't interrupt the siesta. I'm calling to let you know that I'm through customs. I won't be long."

"I may be gone when you get here. I've a meeting in Rome."

"Not another. Olivia. Can't you stay home this evening? It's so dangerous now. I just don't like those people you see. We could all go to Bernardi's for dinner. I've brought you a wonderful dress from New York that you'll look quite stunning in."

"I won't know until they call me. I'm only saying I might not be here."

"If Arturo wakes, tell him I'm on my way."

"*Certo.*"

But her mother did not hang up. "Are you still there, Olivia?"

"Yes."

"I had a terrible time, love. Almost no one would talk to me at the funeral. Also, I went to your father's grave. Silly of me. I haven't thought of him for years. Can we talk about your father soon, Olivia? Would you mind? Could I talk with you about him sometime?"

"I didn't really know him."

"Of course not, dearest. Maybe I didn't either. But so many things have come back to me. I mean, just you and me talking about him. Arturo might not understand and all. We could meet in Rome some morning for lunch. Maybe at Vecchia Roma. Your classes will be over at the university soon, won't they?"

"I'm not taking them anymore."

She heard her mother drop another *gettone* into the slot.

"Then what do you do there? You're there all the time."

"I have friends."

"I've told you I don't like your friends."

"You don't have to."

"I'm only saying what I'm thinking, dear. I say what I think, especially to you."

"Can you tell what I'm thinking when you can't see my eyes?"

"I love your eyes, darling. I think they're even more beautiful than when you were a baby. I like seeing them be happy. I'd do almost anything to make them be happy."

She could hear her mother breathing. She suspected she had been drinking heavily all during the flight. She was standing behind Arturo now, his broad back flecked with patches of dark hair stretching down to the crease in his narrow butt, the testicles showing tucked between his thighs.

"Well, never mind. We'll have lunch anyway. You're right. I don't have to like your friends. I don't have to have lunch with your friends."

Again she paused, and Olivia waited.

"Olivia, dear, it's fall. Is there anything nicer than fall in Italy? Remember Vivaldi? He does fall so nicely. It's all sweet and sad at the same time. It's been a long year, don't you think? I mean, you've just not been very nice. I think you can relax a little, Olivia. I think you don't have to show me year after year how much you wish your father was alive or that I'd become a nun after he died or that you still don't like Arturo. And I get so sick of your politics, your friends. Never mind. We'll talk."

A voice interrupted asking for more money, and Norma did not even say good-bye before she hung up. The phone lapsed into a dead hum. Olivia listened to it. The sound was soothing because it was so steady and meaningless. When she talked to her mother now, she felt as she had three years before when she, Norma, and Arturo had climbed Vesuvius together. They stood at the top of the crater, where the slope ahead dropped steeply and fumes filled the air with the odor of sulphur. She could not see the bottom because the sun was down and the horizon only a band of pale light. As if she were standing on a beach facing a dark sea and the wave that had broken over her legs was sliding back down the sand, she could feel the pit pulling at her. All she had to do was stop leaning away from it and she could slip, rolling deep into the middle of the earth. One of their guides began singing—something about Naples and coming home and how beautiful the women were—in a quiet, clear-toned tenor. Arturo joined him. Olivia looked at his shadowy form standing beside her, and the voice seemed to come as much from the star-specked sky beyond him as from his body. When he rested one hand lightly on her shoulder, she did not move away from it. The hand was warm and held very still.

Olivia put the phone back on its cradle. The sun would soon be shining on Arturo's body. It had already crossed the rug to the bed table. She would have to decide whether to wait for her mother to arrive. She was not sure she wanted to be present when Norma found Arturo. But she was also curious. She was never quite sure if Arturo and Norma loved each other. Once Arturo had said that he loved her, Olivia, and had said it over and over in her ear as he thrust at her from behind, but she had not believed it, and he had never said it again. Sometimes she would catch him staring at her when he did not think she would notice, and she had never seen someone look at her quite like that. It was not like the lust when they came to bed together after a long absence; not even the half-lidded way he would look at her when they were finished and he finally opened his eyes, face close to hers. Her mother always looked to either side of her eyes, but she thought at times that her mother did love her, especially lately when Olivia seemed more aware of how old Norma was getting, how she was no longer as lovely no matter how often she went to all the places she paid to help her be so. Perhaps what Arturo had been doing was looking at her with love. If so, it was too late to ask, and even if he had answered yes, she would not have believed him.

When the phone rang again, she picked it up immediately and did not say anything.

"Who's there?" the voice said in Italian.

"Olivia."

"Piero here."

She laughed. He always spoke so abruptly. He did everything in sudden, fierce gestures—swiping a match in a wide arc across the box, dragging in the first smoke harshly, pulling doors closed behind him as if trying to tear off the knob.

"It's tonight," he said. "It's time."

"And then we'll go where we planned?"

"Yes. Be where you should be at six."

He hung up. Taking no chances, probably. She would be in Piazza Venezia at six, and if she were not met punctually, she would keep walking and not come back. Whenever she left Piero, she was not certain she would ever see him again. But she liked that. It focussed her attention and made him stand out—even if only when she glanced back at his retreating figure—from buildings and streets and other people, as if he were surrounded by a bright line. And she was increasingly respected by the group, even had her own code name, *L'Americana.* If all went well, the next day they would go to the home of the judge on Via Nomentana and wait for him to go to work. After the kneecapping they would leave Rome immediately and stay in some small town in the Abruzzi for a week before proceeding to Milan. She would be free, so meshed in subsequent events that no one would be able to separate her from everything else that happened—free of all this.

When she first knew Piero, he had tried to shock her with the things he said, but she knew it was a test and learned quickly not to flinch. *Do you want me to tell you how it is to kill someone? There's a high level of abstraction. One must become abstracted the closer one comes to the event. But there's passion too. A mixture of the two extremes. One floats over the act, and the act is both understood abstractly and felt passionately. At the moment you go to attack another person, there's a part of you that you have to silence. To mutilate. A part of you rebels and says, "No!" You defeat that person, the weaker one. That's where the satisfaction comes, not in the actual killing, the moment of blood when the person falls, although that's where the passion expresses itself. It's afterward, the knowledge that you've done it, can do it, can give yourself to something larger than yourself even though part of you wants to be fearful and selfish.*

Once after making love, he lay on his back beside her and said, *I'm going to tell you about my first mission. About the difficult moment, the one that comes in some form whenever I'm involved in these things. We followed the judge in our van. He had a driver. They stopped at a* tavola calda *on the way to his office. The man went in himself and we decided to shoot him when he came out. One has to be flexible, ready to change plans if a better opportunity comes. We had intended only to kneecap him. He was leaving the place when we jumped out of the car. He had a container of some food, perhaps lasagna, and he had lifted the lid, was holding the container in one hand and taking a forkful of the food to his mouth. He was leaning forward, the fork almost there. It was only a second—less, probably—but I could have retreated. He was eating, you see. He was just a man, hungry, lifting some food to his mouth. But luckily I remembered what he'd done— those decisions in his court, the ways he patched up the corrupt system with his reasonings. He was only a cog. A cog that eats.*

She calculated her mother's distance and began checking the room carefully, gathering all her own articles of clothing, any signs of her presence. She swept her hands over the side of the bed where she had been, looking carefully to see that they had left no stains. She turned when she reached the doorway. No. It did not look right.

Stooping over the bed again, she lifted the covers gently along Arturo's body until they draped over his shoulder. She looked down at the profile of his face, the eyes that were still wide but unnaturally dry and dull. For a moment she remembered the first time he had entered her, first time any man had done so. *Piano, piano,* he had whispered, and she stared past the wisps of his hair, the sharp point of an ear. She had wanted to call out to her mother, *You have done this to me, you have done this to me,* but instead she felt as if she were her mother and that for a moment her mother was sleeping quietly in her daughter's body and this man had no name or nationality but had simply arrived to deliver a message so simple that she would never understand it.

She had time to shower, finish putting a few articles in one of the duffel bags she had long ago packed, never knowing when the message might come, here or elsewhere. When her mother's car cracked over the pebbles and stopped, she waited in a closet, the door partly open.

"Olivia, dear? Still here?"

She did not answer. She could hear Norma dropping her keys in the tray by the door, walking across the marble floor to the living room.

"Arturo?"

She would not hesitate to wake him now, having given him his siesta. The footsteps returned and moved toward the other end of the bungalow. Olivia slipped to the front door, picked up the keys, and paused. When her mother began screaming, she moved quickly to the car, started it, and spun out of the drive. She would leave it at the train station, where the police could find it later if her mother called them. All the way into Rome, swaying gently over the uneven tracks, Olivia tried to remember what her mother's scream had reminded her of. Then she recalled the student production she had seen recently, but she could not be certain whether the scream had been Clytemnestra's or Cassandra's.

Winter 1978

Olivia followed the three figures through the gardens—the man and woman she had come to know as Bruno and Anna, and the slim young girl who was her daughter, Cara, but now named Caterina. It was a warm Saturday, and even by midmorning enough people were strolling along the paths to make it easy for her to lag behind and not be recognized by Cara. The child had been with her for only a few hours on two different occasions in the past six years, so Olivia thought it was unlikely that she could pick her out. Mainly she did not want Bruno or Anna to see her until she was certain a brief meeting might be safe. The couple looked much older than they had in their first meeting, when she had given Cara to them, Bruno walking with a slight limp in one leg as if his increased weight was harming his knee, Anna's hair streaked with a dull gray. Cara was becoming recognizable as Olivia's child —a lithe body on long, thin legs, her light brown hair pulled tightly into a ponytail that hung down her back. She held her arms tight to her sides and stayed close to the couple. Olivia wondered if the child ever skipped or ran like some of the children her age who were dashing off the paths, chasing each other, or holding up the plastic windmills they had bought from a vendor at the entrance to the Villa Borghese. The bright oranges and reds glimmered in patches of opaque sunlight.

A time had come when she and Piero were becoming too well known to the authorities, and they had spent two months moving from town to town in the Abruzzi, never staying at any of the small hotels or rooming houses for more than two nights at a time. Piero did everything less abruptly now, as if he had been worn smooth by the friction of their lives. He began singing to her when they walked the roads at night, spent less time telling her his theories. Sometimes she would ask him to read part of the newspaper to her and then tell her what he thought. That was when she began to listen less carefully, letting the voice remind her of the days when he could take her into a place where she felt the wide expanse of hope.

If the world did not have to be the way it was, then her life did not have to be what it had been either.

In Milan she discovered she was pregnant. *We'll name her Cara,* she said to Piero, but could not tell him why because she was not certain herself. Even now, if she closed her eyes, she could see Piero wearing a medical smock like the obstetrician. Nurses were moving busily nearby. He was holding a baby swaddled in a white towel, its dark hair still glistening with mucus and blood. She could feel nothing from her waist down. Piero was staring with half-closed eyes at the baby he held, as if she shone with a strong light.

She had never been able to decide if the confused and inarticulate feelings she had for Piero could be called *love*. But with Cara she felt defenseless. She could not protect herself from the rush of images the child always evoked in her—even the smells of the infant's body when she had held her close and naked after a bath, the sharp and bitter odor of her urine-soaked diapers, the nights of listening carefully to her breathing or the first cries of hunger. She could not hold back the longing that would make her want simply to pick her up and hear that breathing close to her cheek, something that even her long discussions with Piero in the evenings, when both of them constructed versions of the world they were helping to create for Cara, would not mute. Whenever she considered letting Piero into that room in the house of her emotions, she would find the door locked and did not search for the key. Sometimes she resented or mistrusted Cara, as if the simple fact that she had been part of her own body, had emerged from it with such definable needs, enabled her to take advantage of her mother, entering her emotions on unfair terms. But in brief moments, before she would turn away quickly from her own thoughts, she would feel elated, even victorious, as if she had glimpsed some light so brilliant that she could not bear to look into it for long. If this was love, then at least she had known it once or twice.

With the Moro affair coming to its conclusion, she and Piero had to be ready for anything. Like most of the people in their Roman cell, each moved to different rooms around the city every night—a cot set up by some sympathizer, apartments rented in the names of various international companies with the understanding that they were for traveling executives. She had stood looking in the mirror of a bathroom in an apartment not far from the house on Monte Parioli where she and Norma and Arturo had lived. An old woman whose husband had been in the partisans in World War II lived there and had said almost nothing to Olivia as she quietly came and went for three days. She looked at the lines forming around her eyes, the way her lips in repose tended to turn down slightly at the corners now. Deceptions. Even the eyes she stared at seemed without identity to her. They looked at her looking at herself and cast back an image of eyes performing the act of looking at eyes. *If you are my mother,* Cara/Caterina had said two years ago when they stood side by side in the Piazzale del Gianicolo after having watched Punch be beaten into submission by a shrill Judy, *why don't you take me to an island where no one can find us and we'll be safe? Aunt Anna tells me you love me so much that you gave me away. I think that's a lie, don't you? I think maybe you're someone pretending to be my mother so that Aunt Anna won't seem to be a liar.*

When the three stopped by an ice-cream stand, bought cones, and sat down nearby, Olivia sat on the rim of a nearby fountain with her back half turned. She knew they were on their way across the park to the zoo, where they went many Saturday mornings if the weather permitted. Anna had promised, when Olivia had handed Cara to her and Bruno, to keep talking English to the child, a language Anna had learned from her English mother. Olivia had been surprised that the woman had kept her promise, as if she expected it was given only as a way of easing the pain of separation. Olivia tilted her face so that the sun fell on it fully. Spring.

Olivia stood so quickly that for a moment she was dizzy. They were gone, no longer sitting on the bench with their ice-cream cones. Could Bruno or Anna have seen her and decided to take Cara back to their apartment? Olivia strode along the path, peering ahead into the shade, through the groups of women with children in strollers and carriages, the men in sweats carrying soccer balls, holding the hands of their sons. She broke into a run.

They were at the entrance to the zoo, where Bruno was buying tickets. She waited on the other side of the street, catching her breath, and when they passed through the turnstile she crossed and bought her ticket. She knew where they would go eventually because Cara had told her two years before what her favorite animal was, so she did not try to follow them but circled to the scuffed earth of the pens where the elephants were standing, each with one leg chained to keep it from rubbing against the single tree in their small compound. She sat on the bench at some distance where the untended trees cast thick shade and she could watch without being noticed.

Cara came first, well ahead of Anna and Bruno, who were talking intently. Bruno held his hands behind his back but occasionally released one of them to wave it emphatically. Anna kept shaking her head. With her back to Olivia, Cara stood still, arms folded, her thighs against the iron rail that kept her from the moat around the elephant yard. She did not even seem to be breathing. Olivia stood, and when Bruno stopped walking, his hand frozen in midgesture, she knew he had seen her. He said something to Anna, who moved to stand behind Cara as if trying to keep her from seeing Olivia if she turned.

"You shouldn't have. No, you really should not be here," Bruno said in a low growl.

"No one followed."

"How can you know that? Everyone is following everyone now. This Moro thing only gets worse every day. The police come by the park near our house each hour. Sometimes I think I see people watching Cara. She says she keeps seeing the same man standing outside her school. Probably it's her story to worry us, but this is too much risk."

"I had to see her."

He closed his eyes, pressing his lips together. Olivia expected him to say something about his heart, the stress, but instead he only sighed.

"Yes. I understand." He stood beside her and turned, making a quick gesture with one hand toward the two watching a huge, old bull douse himself with dust, his wide ears flapping. "Beautiful, isn't she? Would you know her if you saw her on the street? Without us?"

Olivia did not tell him how often she had stood at a distance and watched her daughter. In the past year she had not been able to resist, drawn to the places she knew Cara would pass like some of the people she had known at the university who were hopelessly in need of one drug or another, haunting Piazza Navona with their guitars and pretending to be there for singing and socializing with other students.

"I want to talk to her."

When Anna looked toward them, Bruno motioned to her. She put a hand on Cara's shoulder and leaned close to her ear. The child turned slowly, frowning as she peered up the slope.

"She might say no, you see." Bruno clasped his hands behind his back.

Olivia wondered if he almost wanted that to happen, some final sign that the girl did not need her real parents anymore.

But Cara began walking up the scruffy grass of the slope. She stopped a few yards away, staring at Olivia, her face without expression.

"Why are you here?"

"I needed to see you."

"You didn't need to see me for a long time. Did Bruno send for you?"

"She's told me sometimes that she didn't think you really wanted to see her," he said quietly to Olivia, still watching Cara. "No, Caterina, I didn't. This is a surprise."

"Will you sit with me for a while?"

Cara did not move. She glanced at the bench as if trying to decide whether it was too far away. When she reached it she sat, staring down toward the elephants.

"Is it all right if we're alone for a few minutes?"

Bruno went to join his wife. Olivia left some space between herself and Cara on the bench. She was afraid the girl, perched on the edge, eyes flitting nervously from side to side, might run down to Bruno and Anna.

"Do you like the name Caterina?"

She pursed her lips but did not look at her mother. "That's what everyone calls me. I don't believe in the other name. Bruno says it would be dangerous for me to get used to it because someone might trick me by calling out to me. I mustn't pay attention if anyone says it to me."

"I think of you as Cara."

"That's because you named me, isn't it? Or did my father?"

Olivia did not answer. The elephant had begun to rock back and forth as if hearing music far inside itself, an adagio perhaps.

"I've seen you," Cara said softly, her eyes turning down to stare at the tips of her sandaled feet. "I've seen you watching me sometimes. Especially near the Piazza Repubblica where I change buses in the afternoon. You try to hide. You wear dark glasses, or you sit at a table with a newspaper and pretend you aren't there."

"I shouldn't," she said quietly. "It's dangerous. I ought to stop doing it, especially now."

"I'm told it's dangerous. Ever since I can remember, I've been told everything is dangerous." Cara gave her head a toss, making the ponytail whip behind her. "No one's ever hurt me or threatened to hurt me. How can I believe any of you? Why do I never see my father?"

She frowned toward the elephants.

"Why do they chain the elephants like that? They can't get out. The moat is too deep. The fence is very high. They don't look well enough fed to be strong or dangerous. Do you like elephants?"

"It's important that you believe us. Maybe this is almost over, Cara. Maybe we will all go somewhere—you, your father, and I."

"If I don't know my father or you, how can I know if I want to go?"

"He loves you." But Olivia knew how lame that sounded.

"Do you love him?"

For the first time her daughter was staring at her directly. Olivia wanted to tell the truth. So many lies surrounded them.

"I think so. I've been with Piero for many years now. If I don't love Piero, maybe I don't love anyone."

"Me?"

"We don't know each other well, do we?"

"Did you have a mother?"

"Yes."

"When did she die?"

"She's alive, but I haven't seen her for some time."

"Why do you do everything like this?" For a moment Cara

looked as if she were going to stand, but she only leaned forward on her straightened arms. "You're a mother, but you left me. Did you leave your mother or did she leave you?"

"We had very little in common."

"What is 'having something in common'? I'm not sure I believe anything you are telling me. I believe Bruno when he talks, and usually Anna. Bruno tries to tell the truth, and when he doesn't he gets embarrassed, so I know. Anna lies better, but they are only lies trying to keep me happy. I'm not sure you love me at all, or my father. Is Piero his real name? Did your mother love you?"

Olivia turned to watch Bruno, who was becoming nervous. She tried to answer Cara, but her voice locked far back in her throat. She raised her hand as if to hold its palm in the small patch of sunlight that was striking the bench between them. Then she moved it slowly toward Cara. She knew the child could see her motions, but she did not pull back. When her hand touched Cara's head, she brushed it lightly across the hair, down her neck, onto the long spread of the ponytail.

"Anna brushes my hair every night. Then I go to bed and try to sleep. Look."

She pointed at the elephants and stood quickly. Olivia could see nothing new that the animals were doing, but when Cara began walking away, she knew the child had only diverted her attention so she could leave the bench. She stood. Cara took Anna's hand and began walking, tugging the woman along. Only when they were nearly out of sight did she glance back, her eyes wide and unfocused, and then she was gone. Bruno was still there, as if waiting for Olivia to come down, but she turned and walked the other way, stumbling occasionally because she was looking only at that image of Cara's face she always carried inside her—her infant gaze.

Tuesday, May 9, 1978

Her mother was praying. Olivia sat in the second pew behind her in Santa Maria del Popolo and stared at the back of Norma's head. For a while her mother sat perfectly straight, staring forward to the altar where some flowers were dimly lit by the votive candles. An image of the virgin, a framed mosaic, shimmered in the trembling light. Then she dipped forward, her form shrinking and head lowered against the back of the bench in front of her. She must have been kneeling on the floor. Olivia leaned not to pray but because she could not believe that this was her mother or that the woman could be praying like any of the older women she might see whenever she stepped into one of the churches in Rome to retreat from the oppressive heat or to believe that here, at least, she might not be followed or observed.

She had followed Norma. Wandering away from the room where she and Piero had stayed the night before, violating everything they had been told not to do, she had walked aimlessly down the Via Giulia to Piazza del Popolo, a place she liked because of the lions with their spouting mouths and a wide enough space so that she felt she could not be cornered. She would meet Piero at the apartment again at noon, then they would move on to the next place, if he had been told where that might be. Communications were breaking down.

She had spoken to her mother only once, three years after Arturo's death. She did not know how Norma had traced her, but she called the apartment in Rome where Olivia and Piero were staying and they arranged to meet in Campo dei Fiori. She could tell that her mother did not recognize her—hair cropped, wide dark glasses concealing her eyes. They walked along the bank of the Tiber, where Olivia would be able to tell quickly whether she was being watched or followed.

It was cruel of you to not tell me that day I came home. You must have known Arturo was dead.

Olivia did not answer.

We won't talk about that. I've been very unhappy. You never understood. I loved Arturo. I know how much he played around, the other women. I even knew some of their names. But he always came back to me. He needed me to forgive him.

Why do you stay in Italy?

I haven't anywhere else to go, dear. I like Rome. You like Rome too, don't you? Or do you do everything, you and your friends, because you hate Rome, hate Italy?

Why did you want to see me? It's dangerous, you know. For me.

They paused for a moment and turned to the sluggish river and dull brick walls of the Castel Sant' Angelo.

Come back with me, Olivia. We could go somewhere else. Anywhere you want. Even the States. I wouldn't make the same mistakes again. I need you.

She looked hard at her mother, at the way her last face-lift had not worked well, leaving the skin looking much too taut so that it had become even less expressive than it had been. For a moment she saw her as one of those curved but petrified figures of Pompeii, someone caught and held forever in solidifying ashes.

I have other things I need to do.

Need? What do you know about need? You've never been hungry or cold in your life. Please. Take off those dark glasses, love. I can't see your eyes. You only use your mouth for talking now.

I haven't anything else to say.

Please.

I don't love you. I don't know if I ever did love you.

Norma's eyes narrowed, not in anger but as if she had been slapped hard and she was determined not to let the other person have the satisfaction of seeing her react.

You did. Before your father died. Someday you will again, even if you choose not to tell me.

Don't get in touch with me again. Unless you want to be responsible for killing me.

She ducked quickly across the street and did not look back. She thought she heard her mother's voice calling once shrilly above the noise of the passing cars, but it might have been a gull.

As she sat by the fountain, one hand dabbling in the water, the traffic circling on its way toward the Via del Corso, she had seen the woman step out of a cab near the ramp to the Pincian Hill, pay the driver, then stand irresolutely as cars swerved around her. She was very fashionably dressed but much too fleshy for the clothes she was trying to wear. She looked toward the fountain and then down the trident of streets leading out of the piazza. To numb her anxiety for Piero, who had been so depressed lately, for her own blank mood, for the gray but tension-filled day, she studied the woman and conjectured. What would happen if she moved suddenly? Surely she would become another statistic in traffic mortality. None of the drivers even bothered to honk. She had a certain stillness about her pose, though, that was not like a tourist wondering where the restaurant or church or boutique might be. She stood and stared and did not even move her hands, which had smoothed the dress over her hips and now rested there.

My God, the voice in Olivia's head said, *that is my mother.* She did not move her hand from the water or attempt to hide herself. But the distance was too great. She knew her mother well enough to know how poor her eyesight was. She concentrated on Norma's posture. Everything about her was not what she remembered but what she could imagine her mother would look like if she did not care anymore about how she looked. Her shoulders were rounded forward, her figure was blurred by flesh that drooped and sagged—belly that pressed against a dress made for a smaller woman, a slightly splayed posture to her legs as if they were unwilling to accept the neglected body. Norma had turned quickly, moving toward the entrance to the church.

Olivia did not hesitate. The interior was cool and dark. She pressed her back against the nearest pillar and let her eyes adjust. When she was certain she had found Norma, she moved carefully down the side aisle and sat behind her. The woman did not move for a long time. She was staring forward and did not pay any attention to figures who crossed in front of the altar or left adjacent pews. When she kneeled, she buckled as if someone behind her had shoved the heel of one hand against her head. She was making small motions somewhere that made the shape of her head and shoulders tremble from time to time. Olivia wanted to move forward, to sit close to her in order to know if she really was praying. Surely if she were, Norma would be merely leaning into a deep well and listening to hear if the pebble she dropped struck water or stone or never stopped falling.

Norma rose and stood for a moment facing the altar. She did not make any motions with her hands or bow her head before she walked to the end of the pew and began moving toward Olivia, who did not turn away. The woman kept coming through the dim air, looking neither right nor left, her steps firm and face without expression. Just as she was passing Olivia, her eyes glanced over her, but they did not pause or show any recognition. Then she was gone.

The eyes had taken her in, scanning the small space she lived in, then moved on. Someone else passed close by. Olivia walked slowly to the entrance and out into the square again. She did not see anyone she recognized. The woman was gone. Perhaps she had not been Norma. But when Olivia closed her eyes for a moment, taking into her mind the image of the lions spewing water, the blur of traffic, she knew it did not matter whether the woman was Norma or not. She had been presented with a truth just as firm as the lions that she had insisted on being taken to see when she and her mother had first come with Arturo to Rome. *Back there,* he had said, *is a church built over a place where our peoples thought demons lived. This is something they thought because of Nero, who was buried there.* She had asked who Nero was, but her mother and Arturo were splashing each other with the band of water from the lion's mouth.

For a while she walked down the Corso aimlessly. Traffic was lighter than usual, but because she was not concentrating, she was often bumped or nudged by other pedestrians. The distant wailing of a siren grew louder until it was painful and close, and then the police car sped past and continued down the Corso. At the newsstand in Piazza Venezia she stopped, her heart suddenly beating hard. MORO DEAD. A picture of a man in the trunk of a white car. Bystanders. MORO DEAD.

She moved quickly. As she walked, occasionally breaking into a run, she unzipped the lining to the pocket in her jacket, and without drawing out the documents, she checked them with her fingers—her American passport, a phony one for Piero, and the one for Cara that she had made Bruno obtain that winter. Everything depended on timing now. Reach Piero. Remember where Cara would be on this day of the week. She wished she had not waited, waited. When a car nearly hit her as she slanted across a street near the Campo dei Fiori, she made herself slow down. In the narrow streets of the old Jewish ghetto, she ran again until she reached the corner and twisting alley where their most recent haven had been.

She stepped quickly into a doorway across the street from theirs. A white Mercedes was parked outside. A man on the sidewalk stood close to the backseat door. The driver clutched the steering wheel in both hands and stared forward through the windshield. The door to the building opened, and a stout man with a kerchief around his neck leaned out, looking up and down the street. Then two other men came through, pulling along someone they held firmly by the arms, almost lifting him because his legs wobbled loosely. When his face lifted, Olivia knew it was Piero only by the shape of his head, the bald spot that had shown when he came into the light. His face was dark with blood, features leveled to a broken surface of torn flesh. The back door was opened, he was pushed in, and the other men jumped into the front and back, slamming the doors as the car left the curb.

For a moment she held still, her hand clutched against her belly as if a sharp pain were about to double her over. She walked away, face turned to the walls, and began running again until she came to the taxi stand near Largo Argentina. As she approached the ruins, she looked carefully at the three passports, put two of them back in her pocket, and dropped the third into the sunken area of temples. She could not help him now, and she should not have his picture on her.

She made the driver wait outside the school grounds.

"She's always late," she said to him. "The teachers never remember to read carefully the excuse I send with her."

Yes, the man agreed. The nuns gave good education, but sometimes they did not understand how the world did not always run on their time.

A bell rang. The door swung open and a nun in a blue habit stepped out. Behind and around her, the girls in their smocks spilled onto the yard beyond the fence. Cara came near the end, by herself, and the nun said something to her as she passed, but Cara did not seem to take any notice of her.

"One moment," Olivia said, stepping from the cab.

Cara's back was turned when she reached her. She clutched the girl's arm.

"Come. Quickly," she said in a whisper so the child nearby would not hear.

Cara frowned at her for a moment but did not pull away from Olivia's hand.

"Where? Are you coming to take me away? Where's Bruno?"

"Excuse me," the nun was calling from the top of the stairs, gesturing toward them.

"The taxi. Quickly or it will be too late."

Cara glanced at the nun and began walking with Olivia.

"Caterina? Where are you going?"

Olivia kept Cara ahead of her. At the gate she turned. The nun was beginning to come down the stairs. She was calling, "Wait, wait!" when Olivia slammed the door of the cab.

"She wants something?" the driver asked.

"Nothing important. She thinks Cara needs her coat."

He pulled away before the nun could reach the curb. "They are worse mothers than our own mothers." He was glancing at them in the rearview mirror. "Where?"

"Da Vinci airport."

He frowned. "You didn't tell me. I can get out there and not snag a fare for hours."

"We'll miss our flight if we don't hurry. I can't stop to find another cab. I'll pay you double."

He nodded. "It's worth it then. Sorry. You know how it is. If I don't make a certain amount each day, I'm in trouble."

Cara watched them both carefully, then she stared at her mother. When she began to speak, Olivia pressed her hand tightly.

"Later," she whispered. "I'll explain later."

Had Bruno and Anna trained her for this? Or had she imagined it for a long time? Cara stared forward, moving her hand so that it was no longer in contact with Olivia's.

When they were going up the ramp to the terminal, she said

quietly, "When you tell me will you let me decide? Will you do that?"

Olivia stared at the profile, the jaw tensed, neck held stiff and straight.

"Yes. But you will have to decide quickly."

Police were patrolling the sidewalks, some leaning into cars. The driver laughed once.

"Fools. Do they think Moro's killers would come here to be caught?" He pointed one finger at his temple. "They have nothing here, signora. Even trained monkeys could do better."

She clutched Cara's hand, and they were not stopped. In the lobby she made for the ticket counter of TWA, and as they walked she said, "We're going to America, Cara. We have to leave quickly or they will find me. They might even now. I want you with me. I want you to stay with me."

"Where is my father? Where is Piero?"

"He can't come now."

"Have you told Bruno?"

"There wasn't any time."

They stood in line, and Olivia stooped so that they could talk as quietly as possible. How could she say all she needed to say with people around them?

"What if you have to leave me there, when we're in America? How do I know you won't give me away again?"

"I won't. I promise."

"Why should I trust you?"

The man behind them touched Olivia on the shoulder. The line had moved forward. When she stooped again, Olivia stared at Cara's face. She took the child's chin gently in her fingers and turned the face toward her. At first the eyes looked only at Olivia's forehead.

"Look at me, Cara. Please. It's important."

She did, but the gesture was still stubborn, and she kept her eyes unfocused.

"No. At me, Cara. Please. Look at me."

The eyes were staring at her, wide but no longer vague.

"I love you, Cara."

For a moment the child did not answer. "Will I ever come to Rome again? Will I ever see Bruno and Anna?"

"I don't know. I'm trying to tell the truth to you. I hope so."

"You know I don't know if I love you. I love Bruno and Anna."

Olivia stiffened. Was Cara going to weep? Was it all too much? What if she lost control and in her weeping blurted out things that the people around could hear? But she only nodded, her eyes filling with tears.

"I'll go with you."

At the counter Olivia produced her credit card, accepted the flight for New York that would be leaving in one hour. There had been a cancellation. *Your lucky day,* the ticket agent kept saying. *No luggage?* No, they had some carry-on stuff they had left by their seats in the lobby. *Shouldn't do that,* she reprimanded. *Better get back to them quickly.* She asked for the passports. Olivia watched her flip through Cara's, then turn to the other. She looked from the picture to Olivia and then back again.

"You've changed your hairstyle," she said absentmindedly as she punched Olivia's fictitious name into the computer.

Olivia reached down. She took hold of Cara's hand but did not look at her. She held it very tightly as if the child had some magical power that could surge through her own hand and then out to the computer and ticket agent. But the woman stuffed the tickets into envelopes and handed the stack with passports back to Olivia.

"It's started to board already. Gate 29."

Cara closed her hand tightly on Olivia's as they walked through the terminal to the gate, and when they were standing in line, she pressed her side against her mother. Olivia did not look at her, afraid the child might pull away. The touch of that body against her own seemed strangely miraculous, as if the weight and compact length of the infant who had stretched sleeping in her arms could not have grown so much that her body could touch Olivia's along her arm, her hip, her calf. She thought of Piero, not as she had seen him last but when she had been leaving the room that morning. He had been standing near the window, his hands in his pockets, staring at the slit of sky above the buildings. *Don't be long*, he had said.

Then they were striding through the tunnel, being greeted by a stewardess and directed to their seats near the wing. A man was already sitting by the window reading a magazine. Cara sat in the middle, Olivia on the aisle. Just before time to depart, two *carabinieri* came in, passing slowly down the aisle on the other side of the plane. Olivia stared at her lap. She waited for the touch on her shoulder, some question maybe, or a simple command. She could hear their footsteps, then from the corner of her eyes she saw the dark cloth with its bright, red stripe, and it was not moving. Cara put down the magazine she had been trying to read in English. Olivia watched her look up. She smiled.

"*Buon giorno,*" she said. "Are you going to America too?"

The man laughed. "Would you like us to come?"

"Yes." Cara's voice was piping, clear, but Olivia could hear it was not the voice she usually spoke with. "Then we would be safe. My mother says it isn't very safe in Italy now. We're going to visit my uncle."

Olivia knew she had to look up. She shrugged, trying to smile. The officer was grinning at them.

"Well, when you come home, soon, everyone will be very safe."

They walked on, and then they were gone and the doors slammed shut and the captain was talking over the intercom.

Olivia reached over to take Cara's hand. Was it because the plane was accelerating down the runway, lumbering and tossing with speed as if it would never be able to rid itself of the earth, that Cara did not pull away? Olivia wanted to say thank you, but the noise of the jet engines was too loud, and then the earth was falling away from them and dwindling, and soon they were looking down on sea and ragged shoreline.

Olivia thought that maybe Cara had fallen asleep. Her eyes were closed, and she had folded her hands in her lap, but while she was staring at the child's face, the eyes opened.

"Can I be Cara in America?"

"I think so."

"In America can I always tell the truth?"

Olivia paused. The man sitting next to them was reading a book now, in English.

"Yes."

"Don't you speak the truth in Italy?" he said in Italian that was correct but marred by the use of American vowel sounds.

Cara stared at him for a moment. "Not always to the nuns."

He seemed to find that very funny. "Would you like to sit by the window? You can see more clouds that way."

Cara nodded, but the stewardess was bringing drinks so they postponed their switch.

"What do you do in America?" Cara asked him.

"I'm a lawyer. I work for a large company that does business with a large Italian company. I'm trying to learn Italian. Am I doing OK?"

"You talk a little funny, but I can understand. Not like the Yugoslavian boy in my school."

The man leaned forward to see around her, smiling at Olivia, who was sorry she had not closed her eyes and pretended to be asleep. She did not feel like talking.

"And what does your mother do?"

Cara was silent but stared for a moment at Olivia. As if making up her mind, she said, "My mother is a terrorist."

The man was trying very hard not to laugh. "And do you want to be a terrorist too when you grow up?"

Cara lowered her head and frowned. "I don't think so. I don't think it would be a very good life."

living the revolution

The last time Melissa and I talked she came to my apartment in New York to tell me off, to let me know again what a failure I was to humanity, society, her. Her, primarily, but by then she was so securely locked into boxes of abstractions and principles that she did not believe she had a specific individuality. After a few years of constant criticism/self-criticism sessions with her cell, she was convinced she had purged herself of all the characteristics of bourgeois personality—attachments to others, the need for privacy, cleanliness, politeness, tolerance, humor. The situation of the world was much too serious for such frivolous traits.

She had walked directly to my apartment after she was released from jail. It was mid-morning and I was correcting some bad papers from my tenth-grade class. They were supposed to have read Robert Hayden's "Those Sunday Mornings," but what they were discussing had no resemblance to the poem I'd read. Melissa stood in the doorway in her boots, the baggy black pants, T-shirt with some faded slogan zig-zagging across it like lightning and obviously no bra beneath. Her hair, as it had been for a few years now, was hacked short with no attempt to cut it evenly, and her face, once so capable of moving quickly from laughter to a pout or irritation, was as fixed and pale as a death mask. I could get dizzy looking at her and trying to find the adopted sister I had known, the one whom I always thought of as a kid because I was thirteen when they brought her into our house, a one-year-old whose birthday was so close to mine that I never again had one entirely my own, at least until it didn't matter. Now, when we talked, I tried to stare to one side of her face, listening, responding cautiously, talking as if my real sister were hovering somewhere just beyond this Melissa who was determined to make herself into a stranger.

"Don't just stand there, Mel. Come in."

But she stood firmly on the threshold, legs slightly apart and arms folded. Was this the way a Hitler Youth might have planted herself after she had told the local Gestapo that her parents received messages through a radio they kept under the floorboards?

"Look, Sis. If what you've got on is all your worldly possessions now, you're welcome to stay with me. I won't argue with you. You can crash here, leave when you like. You already know I'm not a very good cook."

Her lips tightened, if that was possible.

"You paid the bail, didn't you?"

I nodded. "After my last visit. I didn't like the place."

She tossed her head, and I could have broken down right there. It was an old gesture, going back to the days before she'd left Sarah Lawrence and gotten sucked into the problems at Columbia University, when she had a long ponytail reaching to the small of her back and she would toss it with a jerk of her head like a horse swiping at flies. Maybe her own horse, like the one in Devon that our father bought for her. But I wasn't sure which way I would break—into tears or a rage that might have led me to grab those slim shoulders and shake until all the hard metal she'd forged to case herself in went flying apart.

She sidled a few steps into the room, keeping her face to me.

"I didn't want that. I have friends. They'd have gotten me out eventually."

"I'm more than a friend. Remember me? I'm a brother. Joe."

"I don't have family anymore." Then she made that sound that I'd learned in the past year stood for a laugh—a quick, high bleat without any modulation. "I never did. They gave me away and ran off. Then your parents picked me up at the baby farm. I've come to understand how lucky I was, though. Most of my friends have had a hard time purging themselves of family. It was easy for me."

"I can see that. You look real easygoing, Mel. Relaxed."

"I don't want to be. It's not time to be. We need to be ready, vigilant."

"How about a vigilant beer?"

"I came to tell you something."

"Can we sit?"

"You sit."

She walked, no, strode to the window. She was always slim, but now she was walking bone with some sinew and skin. She had that starved, pulled-tight look that made her eyes far more sunken than they ever had been. If I hadn't seen her changing over a few years, I would not have been able to pick her out of a lineup—which I suspected someone was going to be doing before long. Weathermen went looking for trouble and had found it, and her recent arrest was not the first. So I sat on the couch and waited until she turned her back to the window and drab view of the opposite brownstone and a pewter sky.

"Tell me."

"You might never get that money back. I might skip bail."

"Might? Or are you afraid to tell me you will?"

"I haven't decided."

"It's a lot of money."

"I didn't ask you for it."

"True. I'm tempted to try the ploy, but I didn't intend to use it as a way to keep you in town or get you into a trial where at least I'd know where you were."

"It's none of your business where I am."

I slipped my hand into the crack between the sofa cushions and curled it into a fist so she couldn't see where I was putting the frustration.

"Better in court than in a town house like Kathy Boutin."

"That was dumb. Someone goofed. Bad training."

"Maybe. I'm just saying I'm glad you weren't there."

"They'll be remembered, though. More of us will have to die before it's over."

"You didn't say if you wanted that beer."

The light was dim from the window, a cloudy day, so I was annoyed that she stood with her back to it. For just a moment I thought I saw the posture sag slightly. I wanted to know if the features could soften.

"I'm hungry."

I stood quickly. The voice was lower. She turned and leaned on the windowsill, propped on stiffened arms. I knew better than to move too close, so I went to the kitchen.

"Some eggs? Toast? Or a bagel?"

"Anything."

So I cooked, keeping my back to her, letting her breathe the air in my apartment, hoping she might take in something from the ambience that could work on her like a magic potion—dragging her back to the time when that twelve-year-old could run me down as we played touch football in Fairfield Park. When I brought the plate out to put it on the table that was my desk as well, she was standing with her hands in her pockets, staring at the picture of all of us—Mom, Dad, her, myself—in front of the tiger cages at the zoo.

"Who took it?" she said, the quiet voice still there.

"You don't remember?"

"Jesus, I must have been nine."

"Eight. The nurse from the first aid station just across the path took it. After you put your finger in the rabbit cage and the rabbit bit you."

She didn't laugh, but she also didn't turn away.

"They look so old now."

"When was the last time you saw them? It's Dad's heart, you know. They can't do much about it."

"He'll die soon."

I could tell she was trying to keep it tough. Parents come, parents go. In a world in which kinship is a shameful relationship, necessary but something to be rid of as soon as possible, death is just a thing that happens.

"Probably. It's aged her also."

She turned then, but she walked by me without looking into my face. She sat and began tucking away the eggs, gnawing at the chunk of bread and butter, either as if she hadn't eaten for days or she thought it was shameful to admit her body had to be fed.

"You didn't answer me. When did you see them last?"

"A week ago. Just before I came back and was picked up for the action at Rockaway."

"Would he talk to you? Or was it just Mother again?"

"I said I saw them. They didn't see me."

She stared at her empty coffee cup. I filled it and had some myself. I had to keep pulling myself back, leaving that space I knew she wanted between us. But she was breathing slowly now, and the words weren't muffled by a clamped jaw.

"Tell me."

We had used that phrase often when we were younger. I'd come back to town and surprise her by being outside her high school, or I'd appear at her dorm at Sarah Lawrence and take her to some restaurant she liked, where she could eat every-thing on the menu if she wanted, and I'd pick at something and drink a whole bottle of good wine. She didn't like wine, just Coke and sometimes root beer. The words would be what she waited for, as if she trusted my instinct that this was the time to lean back and tell each other our stories, whatever we'd seen and done during the months, sometimes even a year, since we'd last seen each other. We never wrote. She seemed to know I'd always come back. *Tell me,* I'd say, and a little later I'd trade a story of mine for hers. I liked hers better—until they started losing specificity, lapsed slowly into political rant—too often the parroted clichés I was hearing everywhere on the news—SDS, the Black Panthers, and finally Weathermen. I was a fool, though. I just stopped seeing her, telling myself that was what she wanted anyway. All we did was wrangle, and too often I ended up telling her I thought she had a better mind, her own mind, and she didn't need to turn it over to people who couldn't say much more than "Up the pigs," and "Kill the honky dogs," and snap their fingers, *Like man, you know.* And I didn't have to ask her about drugs, given the way her eyes would snap around in her head in the restaurant while she lit a cigarette, forgetting she already had one going and resting on the table edge beside her.

"I didn't want to talk to them. It didn't work last time."

She looked up and stared into my eyes then, maybe wanting me to say our father had changed his mind, said something to me. Or maybe it was only defiance again, a look that was meant to say, "I'm just as glad he called me a disgrace to the family and told me to get out and told me he wasn't responsible for my genes, just my bills, and he wasn't paying them anymore."

"He was too upset to make sense the last time you talked to him. No. He was scared."

"Scared into saying what he meant." She shrugged. "He

thought he owned me, maybe. He paid the bills for years. He loved me until I became someone he didn't want to love. He could kick me out. Anyway, he might have had a heart attack if he saw me or something. I wouldn't want to kill him."

"So? What do you mean you saw them?"

"Have you got a cigarette?"

"I don't smoke anymore."

"I didn't ask about that. I said, 'Do you have a cigarette?'"

I went into my bedroom, opened the bottom drawer, found the box, took the key out of the bathroom closet, and came back with the unopened pack. It was my way of making it hard. Usually by the time I got to the closet, I'd shamed myself out of it. She lit it and dragged in deeply.

"I needed to. I don't know where it's all going now. I mean after the town house. I don't think all of us have been identified yet. They would have treated me differently this last time if they'd known I was with Weathermen. We're going underground. Deep under, I mean. And then we'll strike back. Hard. It's time."

I didn't want to get into all that. I didn't want to know. Christ, I didn't want to be seeing her name on a list of casualties, seeing her added to some grim statistics, having my fellow teachers stop me in the hall to commiserate.

"What did you need, Mel? Tell me."

She glanced to see if I was being sarcastic. I didn't mean it that way. She was always good at reading my expressions.

"I mean I just wanted to look at them. Again."

"What did you see?"

"Two old people. Who probably have too much money. Who don't look well for their ages."

"That's it?"

"I don't owe them anything. I didn't ask them to be my parents. They went out and got me."

"And gave you love, among other things."

"They did what they were supposed to do. What we're all conditioned to do."

I waited a minute. She ground out her cigarette. She was breathing more quickly. I had too much to say, so much that it had turned into a gray lump of wordless matter sticking in my craw.

"No, Christ. I don't know why I wanted to see them." She stood abruptly but sat down again, reached for the pack of cigarettes, but threw it back onto the table without taking one. "I don't know what I felt. Not what I just said. It was hunger. Something in my gut like hunger. I could have killed them or run over and thrown my arms around them. Him. Especially him. He looked so fucking old. He shouldn't have. Shit, Joe, all I've wanted is to live, live, live."

I couldn't sit that one out. I stood this time and leaned at her. I think I was shouting. "Then why the hell do you and your friends act as though you only want to kill, kill, kill? Even if you're not doing it to the rest of the world, and already some of you have, you're doing it to yourself."

But she was pulling back. Her hand was trembling slightly when she slid out the cigarette, but it was steady by the time she struck the match.

"It was just a weak moment, that's all. You asked me to tell. I did. I also told the group in our last self-criticism session. They went through me for two hours. I got it straightened out."

"I'm sorry, Mel. You don't need more shouting from me. Your friends give you enough of that."

"I came to tell you I didn't need your money. But I didn't want to feel like I'd stolen it either. You'll lose it probably. Bad bet."

"Easy come, easy go for us capitalist entrepreneurs, right?"

"You said it. I didn't."

I really did want her to go then. Maybe I was enough of a bourgeois schmuck to care about five thousand bucks, but I think it was the weariness of playing her game, always her game. I couldn't get through. But she didn't hang around.

"Where are you going?"

"Tonight, back to the group. Afterward, wherever the weather takes us."

She opened the door but turned, letting her eyes rest fully on mine.

"Thanks, Joe. You're trying and I know it must be hard."

But she couldn't hold it. Condescension just wasn't natural to her.

"It isn't easy for me either," she said, the voice trembling, and when she saw my hand reaching toward her she put the door between us. I watched her from the window, walking down the sidewalk toward the river and never looking back. I tried to imagine the ponytail swinging with her, but the chopped hair wouldn't let me. I turned my back. The panic I felt was that I might lose the image of her childhood self forever, and if I did, I didn't know where I'd find my own, the one I had even before she was adopted.

I could hear again my father's rising voice on one of those bitter evenings before Melissa stopped coming home, a meal arranged with high hopes by my mother who would say to me, "Joe, please, try to help them talk about nice things, can you? Can't we have a dinner like we used to when Melissa was younger and you weren't so busy? Remember how we used to laugh?" But not even well into the first course Melissa and my father would be arguing about the dangers of socialism or the need to abandon monogamy as a failed system of relationship between men and women, and he would finally lash out, saying, "I was right when I said you should never have gone to that Sarah Lawrence place. It's full of crackpot Jewish professors who've never taken their noses out of books. You should have gone to Penn and stayed home." I asked him once if he really believed that, and he said quietly, "Only when I'm angry."

Melissa and her horses. She loved horses, and our father loved giving one to her, although he didn't want to live in the posh, Anglo-Saxon suburbs of Main Line, Philadelphia. We could have afforded to, after the business went well. But his, and my mother's, was the Italian community of Philadelphia, people sitting on their stoops on humid July nights or on seats in the bleachers of Shibe Park. He supported Melissa's love of horses that began with looking at magazines and movies, ended in a thoroughbred kept in a stable in Devon, riding lessons, shows, and riding competitions. She would catch the Paoli Local to Devon almost every afternoon when school was over. On Saturdays he would drive out to watch her take the jumps, sitting in the stands with a pocket flask of grappa and a stinking Parodi that Mother always made him smoke outside. "So much money for a creature that couldn't even haul a plow," he would say to tease Melissa, and in those days she seemed to understand, knew that he had to show his love by chiding.

Melissa the young horsewoman, Melissa who had just won at a show in Devon, her first blue ribbon, although she never collected very many. When I can choose, she's the Melissa I remember. She was good but not consistently good, and her competition were young women who had riding deep in their genes, third-generation debs whose mothers and grandmothers had liked nothing better than the smell of liniment and horse sweat and the straw-riddled dung of stalls. Even from where I was sitting I could tell she was so scared that she had turned herself to steel when she stepped forward to take the ribbon and the silver cup on which they would inscribe her name, the year, then ensconce it forever in the clubhouse display case. Her hair was tightly pulled back, and she was trying very hard to have no expression on her face. But I had seen her throw her arms around the neck of her horse, rub her face along his long jaw before she let a handler take him off to the stable. As we were walking through the iron gate to our house she paused, clutched my elbow and said, "Joe, you tell him first, please? If I do he won't believe me, or he'll kid me, and I won't want him to do that." So I did, but my father went into the hallway and put his arms around her and hugged, lifting her off the floor, saying, "Hey, that's my kid, my kid the winner," and the only thing he was angry about was the fact he hadn't been able to be there because an important client was in town.

And one day, long afterward, when Melissa was God knows where and my father was saying he didn't want her to come home anyway till she was herself again, I found him standing in the living room looking out the window to the back yard, hands in pockets, and he said, once he knew I had come in, "All right. I'll tell you where I was today, Joe. I took a drive."

"I thought you weren't supposed to."

It was just after his second heart attack. They didn't want him driving in case he had another. He waved a hand as if brushing off my mother.

"I went to Devon. I went into the clubhouse and looked at the trophies. I made them open the case and let me hold that one with her name on it."

"Why?"

"I wanted to know it was true. Not that she'd won, but that there was a Melissa Mangione like the one I think there was then."

"There still is."

"Where, Joe?" He hadn't turned from the window. He shook

his head. "No. She's only here." And he put his finger to his temple as if it were a gun.

So I wasn't too happy that April weekend when I came home because my mother called and said she wanted me to be there.

"She's bringing her friend home with her. Your father's not going to like him. When Melissa called she said they were already living together and she expected both of them to stay in her room." When she paused I pushed the receiver hard against my ear. I wanted to hear some muffled laughing, some indication that this was going to be one of those future family stories that involved my father's anger and our transgressions. But she wasn't laughing.

Melissa was spending most of her time at Columbia, where the cauldron was simmering, ready to boil over in another year, and she wasn't there to attend classes. But many of the players were already assuming their parts, and she hung close to the fringes, sitting in on any radical meetings she could go to, gathering in the coffeehouses to hear the rant, share whatever natural or manufactured mind-enhancer was being passed around. Since it was my city then too, I'd dropped in on some of these scenes, although, purely by chance, never the same ones Melissa attended. I found them boringly repetitive, and I'd drop out, taking refuge in a distant bar where the worst I could expect would be getting rolled in the alley when I left. She hadn't cropped her hair yet, and despite her new alliances still looked very Seven Sisterish, although she had begun to put on some weight and her eyes would move around my face as she talked, but not onto my eyes, almost as if she wasn't secure enough to back up some of the things she said with whatever self was developing. She was like a butterfly just out of the chrysalis, beating its damp wings but not daring to trust them to flight. At this point I loved her all the more for it. Perhaps like my mother I still believed that what she was trying on she would not finally wear. Better to keep our senses of humor, my mother and I would say while my father raged. But after all he was a father, she a daughter.

I don't even remember his name. Call him Doug. Their relationship did not last, although they were part of the same group from time to time as segments broke off and reformed like fragments of mercury rolling around freely on a wobbly surface. By the time she mentioned him to me again, probably two years later, she could fix me with a hard stare and say, "Of course we get together and fuck from time to time, if that's what you mean. We don't believe in permanent attachments. We don't have to parcel out our love." But when she said it, I remembered the way he had said almost the same thing at the dinner table that weekend when my father had inserted into some pause in the acrimonious discussion Melissa had started by describing "the group's" view of monogamy, "I hope your present living conditions will either come to an end soon or express a more responsible way of treating each other."

Doug grinned. He had curly, blond hair, a very boyish face, and wire-rimmed glasses. There was something puckish and disarming in the smile, the eyes that seemed always happy-go-lucky, even the way he would hunch his shoulders quickly from time to time as he spoke, as if he just wanted to get up and twirl around the room. But his conversation was full of the vapid jargon of the time, the light quality of his gestures totally undercut by the doctrinaire approach to any subject, whether it was the veal ("I suppose you know what they do to them to make this delicious dinner?") or the cigar my father offered him, a gesture whose gravity Doug could never have understood ("Do you know why you can't get Cuban cigars anymore? Because we want to starve the Cubans into being like us.") So my father's question was only a setup.

"Man, we're free of all that stuff. We don't need your permission to ball whenever we want. We didn't ask to be born, and we're not going to get locked in like you guys are." He flicked a hand at my mother and father.

My father stared at his plate and the chocolate cake decorated with my mother's home-cured cherries, a special recipe from the Abruzzi, his favorite. He looked at it as if she had used some Betty Crocker cake mix. Then he looked at each one of us, excluding Doug. He must have seen something in Melissa's posture, some twitch crossing her face that I couldn't see that restrained him. He had listened to Doug on the nature of imperialist America's history since the Second World War with only a few surly responses ("I wish you could have joined me at Monte Cassino," at which point I am certain he was thinking of a German pillbox after a haphazard bomb had hit it squarely), Doug on the repressive nature of pig America's treatment of the revolutionary young, Doug on the valueless and grasping nature of middle-class America's conversion of all principles into cash. He had managed a few phrases like "You've got some living to do, I see" or "Maybe when you have to do something more than sit around and talk, you'll change your mind." Now he finally settled his eyes on Melissa's face. She was staring at her cake as he had been, but when she looked up she did not do so to meet her father's eyes. She looked at Doug as if waiting for him to signal her that it was OK to deal with the old man, OK to go along with him for now. When she turned to my father, he had already stood, was placing his napkin carefully in the ring that was always by his fork. He put it down firmly. He looked very pale to me, a complexion I saw only when he was angry. It made the dark stubble of his face stand out as if he had not shaved for days.

"Excuse me," he said in a toneless voice, "but I don't feel well."

For the rest of the dinner my mother and I tried to hold on, and his wedge of untouched cake was a mute accusation of our own lack of courage. But Melissa was ebullient. She chattered around the fringes of Doug's next exposé—I think he was taking on the Supreme Court.

That night I looked down from the window of my room, the same one I'd had as a kid even before Melissa was brought into the house. I never came back to it without the vague sense that I was an imposter, as if I'd betrayed the boy who grew up in it by keeping so much of my life unknown to my parents that the connection between that kid and myself was too disjunct to be acknowledged. They didn't know about two near-marriages, had never met the women involved, even though my mother often chided me and listed old school chums who already had children. Was I really the orphan, I'd ask myself then? Or was it that when Melissa was folded into the family, she became the natural child and I was the adopted son? It wasn't jealousy—it was a slight geological shift, but one that never completely realigned.

I could hear my father and mother discussing loudly in their own bedroom, not the words, but the tones of my father's disgust, my mother's dismay. They could both speak Italian, but rarely did—and when they did it was with the strange American twist of vowels learned in the streets of Philadelphia's Little Italy. I thought they might be doing that now, especially since their room was closer to Melissa's than mine—even though my father had hung tough and relegated Doug to the guest room, which he'd gracefully accepted by saying, "OK, man. Whatever turns you on." I wondered if Doug would even be allowed to get through this one night under the roof with my father or whether they would meet in the hallway and my father would tell him to pack up and go leech off some other capitalist.

Then I saw Melissa and Doug come out from the porch

beneath me and wander onto the lawn. The sky was suffused with the lights of the city; there might have been a moon but certainly not full, and they were just two shadowy figures that seemed to be strolling like all lovers would on a warm night, tucked close to each other, pausing from time to time to kiss, motionless so they wouldn't jar their teeth together. In fact, it seemed so stereotypical that I had to think that what their minds were doing at dinner was just emptying themselves of all the garbage they'd packed in during the past months. Patience, I wanted to say to my father. I'm somewhere between them and you. But I'm out of it. They will be too.

But when I saw what they were going about doing in the next few minutes, I knew they were further along than I had been. They had taken off their clothes and were spreading them on the lawn. There was no danger of neighbors or strollers seeing them. We had high hedges to protect that little square of property, and the nearest house had a blank wall turned to ours. They could have done what they were doing in the basement, in Doug's room, in hers, or even in the living room if they had waited until my parents' voices died down. But they went into the middle of the lawn where their silver bodies stood twined for a moment and then were writhing on the dark grass. I felt no anger, no Oedipal rage, not even a twinge of undiscovered lust. I felt a terrible loneliness for Melissa. She didn't know she was not really there.

I wonder sometimes what might have happened if I had been a few years younger, like a protective brother who would have stepped onto some playground to keep an idiot from pawing her in junior high. Maybe that was part of what she wanted, not letting herself know it, as she moaned on the damp lawn, although I am sure he wanted her parents to come to their window and deal with his statement. And often I've imagined what her view must have been—my darkened window, the windows of my parents' room, where probably the shades were drawn—the eyes of the home she had grown up in staring down at her and her lover, the stars blinking dimly through the city's corona. He didn't deserve the woman he played some small part in helping to destroy. But when I turned to lie fully clothed on my bed and wait for dawn to release me so that I could leave my note and drive away, I might as well have been colluding with Doug, or whatever his name was.

Criticism/self-criticism. It was in those sessions that Melissa received her training, worked on stripping away the "bourgeois constraints" of family, friendship, close attachments to individuals, whatever values could work against the melding of the autonomous being with the group and its ideals. It was hard work, brutal, a destruction that often left young men and women so debilitated that when the group dispersed or rejected them, the pieces never came together again. Although witnessing only one session did not explain to me why Melissa was there or would want to stay there, I at least knew more fully *how* she had become the stranger I would encounter at the end.

She took me to the meeting defiantly. She was at the height of her own power with the group who lived in a warehouse apartment on Canal Street—a group that was sometimes as large as ten people, often as few as four. She had her dominance by being one of the few who had been an early participant with SDS, even if only on the fringes, had been to Chicago in '68, been truncheoned into a bad concussion during that failed gathering called the Days of Rage in 1969, when hundreds of thousands of young people were supposed to gather and begin the final leap to revolution but numbered only in the hundreds at most and ended in skirmishes with overarmed, overprepared authorities. Now she was with the increasingly radical and violent Weathermen, about to go underground, not accepting the fact that the very gesture of having to do so represented the failure of all these movements. They had to go underground because they had no support beyond their own converted few—no masses to join them, no sustaining political factions to rescue them. They were slipping from the position of igniting the revolution to making it—from scratch.

"Who's he?" the dark-haired boy had asked. He was dressed as anonymously as most of the rest of them in their imitation Maoist pajamas. He sat in the loft's window so that I could not make out the expression on his face.

"My brother."

"Family or comrade? Is he with us?"

"Family. He's here to visit."

"Shit, Mel." Someone rose out of a sofa that had lost its legs and squatted against one wall. I thought it was a man, but when she came closer I saw the round and smooth face, the pendulous breasts of a very stout woman. Her voice rose as she continued. "You know you can't have observers at sessions. You're in it or you're not."

"Well?" Melissa said, hand on one hip. I knew that slight smile but had not seen it since we were younger, when she might have trapped me in some silly lie or evasion I was making to excuse a disappointment I'd given her. She was daring me but also knew I had too much curiosity to leave.

"I'm here," I said.

"What does he do?"

"I'm a teacher. My name is Joe, not 'he.'"

"Do you care? We might all be 'he' or 'she' for all we care. You didn't give yourself that name, did you?" She was not about to go back to lolling on the couch until she had established some dominance. I was reminded of the pack behavior of dogs when a strange mutt is brought in—the sniffing, nipping, circling to see if the newcomer will assume low ranking in order to be accepted. I didn't care where I was in their order. I was certain I'd never come again.

"Call me 'he' if you like. I've gotten used to 'Joe.'"

The dark one jumped down from his windowsill. "That's just the problem, isn't it? Stick around. We'll help you get rid of everything you're used to. You don't need it. It took Melissa awhile."

Two other people were in the room, a very lanky, scruffy-faced young man with a band around his forehead who was sucking furiously on the remnant of a joint as if his thumb and fingertip held the last essential breath on earth, and a woman who was the only one dressed in clothes that would have passed inspection as a receptionist's costume—blouse, dangling necklace, tight wool skirt, and high-heeled shoes. I learned later that she was the one for the time being who was holding down a job in order to supply them with food, money for the rent. They took turns, unless someone appeared with a bank account to contribute. I had learned that for a while Melissa worked at a bar pouring drinks, and then she did some stints as a topless dancer. "As long as they like my tits," she had said to me, watching my face for any twitches, "I'll survive." Later, of course, they would settle into routine shoplifting, then occasional bank robberies, moving out further and further into areas they dignified with the term "guerilla actions."

For a while they "helped" Mindy with her problem, a husband and infant she had left in San Francisco and occasionally had yearnings for. I watched Melissa. For all the time I was there, I watched Melissa. I was certain that the only person in the room who was not watching her, because even her gestures seemed significant to them, was the young man who had been sitting in the window and seemed to be named Carl.

251

And she was watching him, taking cues from his glances and gestures, even speaking at times, I thought, as if she were speaking for him. Ventriloquism.

"It's time, isn't it?" Carl said quietly.

Tom, the lanky one who had been twitching in his chair, rolling his eyes, interjecting the usual phrases from time to time, his legs spread wide, hands occasionally groping the air as if trying to catch a bat, said, "Yeah, man."

I don't know what time he thought it was. Time for another joint to drop into his lap? Time to get up and "Kill the pigs" as he had blurted when Mindy was talking about her son's first attempts at walking, or attack all "running dogs," who seemed to be any number of groups opposed to their own plans?

"Time for what?" Fran leaned over her knees toward Carl, her face sweating from the effort.

"I think we need to talk about Melissa."

They stared at her. Even I could sense this was some sort of signal. Everything else had been prologue. They had known when they entered the room that the brunt of concentration would be on one of them, not this unfocused outpouring. To give them all credit, I think it could have been Carl as much as anyone else. The feeling in that room was that anyone could be it, and only after their "vibes" had been let loose for a while would they instinctively know whom it should be. Did her cockiness bring the focus on her that night? Or was she hoping to be the focus so that I would have to see and hear it all? Or did they all want to get to me through her? That was what began it.

"I want to hear from Melissa why she thinks bringing her brother to see us is so important, why she is so afraid of us that she has to have him come."

"Afraid? Just the opposite. I wanted him to see where we're at. I wanted him to know what his future looks like."

It didn't hold up. Not for me either, I must admit. I knew Melissa couldn't have expected me to alter in any way in this setting. The problem was that I began at that moment to enter into the session as a participant, not a satirical observer. I wanted to know the answer to Carl's question as much as he did, even if for very different reasons.

But if the meeting changed it was not only because my attention was attached now in ways that it was not before, but also because more people joined us, slipping in quietly, sitting attentively in a circle. Six, seven? I could not stop to count because I was watching Melissa, Carl, the others as they hurled questions at Melissa. Why was she so proud? So standoffish? Why did she think she was so superior just because she had been in the movement longer? What did a brother mean to her if she had really gone beyond caring about her family, as she said she had? And Mindy added to that, asking how could Melissa possibly criticize Mindy's pain at leaving a son when Melissa clearly could not even step away from a sibling? And some of the new people chimed in too, as if they had known Melissa for some time, maybe had been waiting for this moment. They brought me into it from time to time, pointing at me, accusing me, asking for my commentary, finding I was able only to give phrases that gave them too little to hold onto, or silence. They didn't need me anyway. Melissa was the quarry. They were glad to have me there as the excuse to concentrate on her.

What restrained me? I did not want to see her punished. I waited for some signal I would have known from childhood, some flick of the eyebrows, a turn of the mouth, her hand lifting and falling like a shot bird, to tell me they had reached her in some way that I should deal with. I could have said something to bring them back, baying at me. Whatever pain they could cause me would be only for the brief time I was there. I've thought often of this since, worrying that what I sensed about her involvement was an excuse I made to protect myself. But the more they criticized her, the more she seemed to want it.

She pushed back at them—or at times said, "Yes, that's true. You're right," all in such a way that whatever protective instincts rose in me were stifled by her. Still, I flinched, I knew that even if they did not know, they were scoring. You could not take some of the things they said and walk away unchanged. But that was the purpose, wasn't it? Permanent change. I understood by the end of the evening. It was cauterizing. Keep burning the nerve ends. They will become insensitive. We will not care. She reached a triumphant moment when she stood and began leaning toward Carl, then put her hands in the back pockets of her jeans and walked around the seated figures, her head twisting and turning as she spoke, and she was making the speech she must have held ready for this, if that is what the plotting unconscious does.

"Me? You make me laugh," she was saying. "Do you understand something? I have no father or mother. I have no brother. I washed up on the shore and someone brought me to a house. They bought me. They gave me a name. They tried to buy me for all the years I was with them."

A hand was flung into the air and swept over their heads like a scimitar.

"*Adopted* means *abandoned*. *Abandoned* means *freedom*. I have no one to leave. I was left. Even when I bring home money from letting every crotch-itching man in the borough look at my tits, I am not owned. You don't know what freedom is. Look at Mindy. She still does not understand that what she is offering that baby by leaving him is what was given to me. Freedom. Now."

"You have no parents?" I pushed off of the couch. "If you

brought me here to listen to that crap again, it doesn't work here any better than in my apartment or yours or over lunch. Your father is my father, your mother is mine. We're talking about love."

But I'd only fueled the fires. They went on from there. I didn't. I went out on the landing. I could hear the voices continuing but not the words. I leaned over the railing to look down a long ramp. I couldn't figure what the building had been used for. But I could imagine crates and loaders and sawdust on the floors, men heaving and piling—the dignity of work, not gassy verbiage. I waited maybe fifteen minutes. I wasn't going to rescue her or participate. I'd served their purposes, I think. Melissa's too? Mine? That was much more problematical. Neither of us knew what they were. I walked out, walked all the way uptown to clear my head. But I couldn't.

She called the next afternoon. She wanted to meet, talk the evening over. I tried to gauge her tone. I couldn't get past the seeming indifference. But when I met her and we drank coffee together for the last time until she came to excoriate me for paying her bail, I knew she was out of my reach for a while.

"Wasn't it wonderful?" she said, her hand trembling as she lifted the cup. "Don't you see? It's hard to become, to change, to find your real self. I wish you'd stayed. You see, unlike everyone else now, we understand, Joe, we understand."

We finished our coffee. We stood outside in a wind too cold for April before she walked away, turning abruptly without the peck on my cheek that a teenaged Melissa would give me when I had come home and was about to leave again. She only gave me a "See you later." My own soul was becoming as hardened as hers. It was saying, "Not for a while. Not till you've really come back." That night I woke from a terrifying dream in which I heard her crying in another room, but they were the hungry cries of a one-year-old who had come into a house where I had been the only infant and did not know why another human being would make such noise in the night. Sustenance was all she wanted then. I turned on the light and waited for dawn.

I sometimes imagined kidnapping Melissa, deprogramming her with a canoe trip to the northern woods or fishing on some lake in Alaska where we'd have to be dropped off and abandoned for a few weeks. But instead of my making a call to her, a call came to me when I was in Washington chaperoning a senior class trip. It was from the family lawyer.

"Joe. It's Anselmo. This may be bad news. Can you get to New Orleans?"

"I can get there. Do I want to go there?"

"It's Melissa. Maybe."

"I will get there. What about her?"

I didn't like the silence. Anselmo had been a friend of my father's, fifteen years younger, but someone Giuliano had helped along the way because his father had been a friend of my father's father. Those habits did not change in America. After my father's death, and then my mother's soon after, he had continued to manage the family assets that came from the sale of the business.

"It's an identification, Joseph."

"What kind?" I knew what he meant. I wanted it to be a police lineup, a young woman (or was she that young anymore?) in a cell, a woman like the one I'd bailed out. I was hoping money could do it again.

"It's a body. They're not sure. A wallet was in the room she rented. A note."

I told Bonnie Smith, the other chaperon, staying with the girls, that I had to go. "Family emergency," I muttered, and left her with the problem of ten hormonally charged teenaged boys. The flight was a journey into the landscape of my nightmares. All of it was familiar—the waiting room lights and music at the airport trying to say "all is well," the passengers leaning into their books and slumping in chairs because each of us should have been in bed, the announcements by voices we have heard again and again because they train themselves to be stereotypically businesslike and cheery, the baby squalling ferociously somewhere but always too near. I'd done it often, but never toward an ending that made every gesture seem like the last, every voice too sane to be true.

They opened the drawer and pulled back the plastic covering and I looked at my sister, nodded, then said, "Yes," because they insisted on words first, signatures later. Her face might have been untouched in the sense of unmutilated, but not unchanged. No expression. This was not even the expressionless face I had come to know, because there was no longer any will in it. When she had cropped her hair and frozen her body into the postures of her political beliefs, a person was still there, even if it tried to be a mannequin. But I could find the flicker of fire behind the eyes, the stuttered consonant on the tip of the tongue that showed me where the princess was sleeping. I could never have kissed her awake, but if she had given herself a little longer, life would have. Life does not permit us to live in stone forever. It chips away. The same force behind the tides that wash away the shores and then arbitrarily restore them will not let us merely pretend to be alive.

On hot and humid evenings in Philadelphia when we were not trapping fireflies before she had to go to bed and I had to return to my homework, we would play "statues," flinging each other around in a dizzy circle with our hands clasped, then calling out "Freeze!" when we let go, bound by the terms of the game to assume whatever posture our far-flung bodies were in. This was her parody of that game. I looked down on her utterly colorless face, more pinched and desiccated than it had ever been, the hair now not only chopped but lusterless, the bare shoulders and their bones thrust upward against the fallen skin and flesh. Not my Melissa. Melissa's body, which was all right for a corpse to be if necessary, but not necessary for me to believe in. She was gone and had left a footprint, a vague resemblance that I could point to in the presence of other men and say, "Yes, my sister passed by here."

She left a note. It was so incoherent, so scrawled, that I couldn't do much better than the handwriting experts who analyzed it. What had to be established was whether this was suicide or something that needed further investigation. For authorities, I learned quickly, suicide is the easiest alternative. We doped out enough words to establish the kind of message needed, and she had enough pills in her gut to fulfill the medical requirements. I helped by indicating I would not be surprised to know she had taken her own life. I could read my name in an incoherent sentence, and Giuliano's also. Not our mother's. I found nothing that resembled that. At one moment I felt I was sitting in front of the Rosetta Stone. Melissa's Rosetta Stone. If only there were a parallel text, not an indecipherable scrawl that would go with her into darkness. I have kept it. The authorities kept a copy. Once we had decided there was no "foul play," they did not need evidence. Just another tortured soul. Just a life.

My name is there. One of the few decipherable phrases is, *I can't find what's left of myself.* The rest of the message might be saying something to me I wouldn't have known otherwise, but I doubt it. If we did not freeze at the moment of command, we toppled onto the lawn, laughing, having lost because we were not in a position to maintain balance. She lost and fell. I was still there to play but had no one to clasp hands with and circle until gravity made our blood retreat and confused our minds, and part of me is frozen into the posture of whatever our lives gave us before she called an end to the game.

I have her last words. My students and I worked with words. I know how they rise from incoherence, trail back into their origins. My name is on that paper, and it could not have been inscribed without love, because love is naming, the lifting from silence into meaning before we let go.

I had her cremated. I tried to find any friends, acquaintances. The place where she had been staying was a rooming house where the woman who ran it locked herself every night into a room with wire meshing on the windows and doors. "I don't know who stays here, don't care," she said to me suspiciously, not willing to come out of her room into the hall. The room where they found Melissa was large enough for sleeping, not for living. The woman who worked in a nearby convenience store said, "Yessir. Seen her, I think, every few days. I give her a quart of milk on days when she couldn't pay. Usually she paid it back. Don't tell the boss, though, OK?" I told her I wouldn't, gave her twenty bucks. I took Melissa's ashes to the river. I watched them wash downstream in the slow current. For as long as I could see them, they didn't sink.

I quit my job at the school before the superintendent called me in to fire me. Two of the boys had sneaked out and been robbed, were lucky still to be alive. I couldn't blame Bonnie. I'm not sure I could have kept tabs on them either. I took my money out of savings, sold everything in the apartment that I couldn't fit in two suitcases, and bought a one-way ticket to Athens. There, I bought passage on a boat to Santorini. I'd had a roommate in college who couldn't stop talking about the place. He was right. But he didn't know about a woman named Cathy who ran a small restaurant there. Her husband had died two years earlier, an Italian who liked cooking as much as she did. I'm not much of a cook, but I like to eat and I like to wait on good people and then sit and talk with them over some ouzo.

Sometimes there is too much light on this island and I have

to leave. I like Rome especially. London also. I don't go back to the States unless Anselmo needs me to do something important with the funds left to me through my father's estate. Sometimes Cathy travels alone also, needing to push away from me when an island can be too small. But the restaurant is doing well, successful with the tourists, but the locals like it too, mostly because of Cathy, I think—Cathy's laugh is worth going all the way around the world and back just to hear. I'm very happy to proceed one glass of wine at a time. Enjoy the company when it's there.

I don't expect to know more about Melissa than I do. What I know is enough, and more and more the person who comes to me in dreams or the flashes of memory is Melissa as a child, a young teenager, Melissa riding straight-backed and proud on her horse. The rest can go to hell with all those rotten times she and the world around her went through. Sometimes when Cathy and I are sitting together to watch the sun become a blood orange sinking into the darkening sea, I imagine my own voice speaking, Melissa listening. I am telling her how in this moment I could never have anticipated, I am finding what is left of myself.

a tour of the islands

When he first saw the couple, Marshall was leaning on a railing of the ferry boat and looking down onto the dock at Brindisi. The man was arguing with an official at the bottom of the gangplank, but the clatter of vans and cars driving up the nearby ramp blanked out his words. The woman stood very straight, nodding her head emphatically. Behind the couple other passengers were backed up into a line that spread into a fan. The official kept shrugging and spreading his hands, palms up, until the man began waving his tickets and jabbing at them with the forefinger of his other hand as if hoping to impale them.

Someone in the crowd shouted. The official stood on tiptoes and peered over the couple. Then he looked toward the sky, bunched his fingers, grabbed the man's tickets, tore, and brusquely motioned them forward. As they passed up the gangplank beneath Marshall, he could hear the man's voice, high and penetrating. The woman glanced up and her eyes met Marshall's, almost as if she were appealing for agreement.

His previous trips on boats had destroyed any illusions for Marshall that he might be a good sailor. He took Dramamine, always at least an hour or two before embarking. It relaxed him, and watching the couple he had been able to remain amused and aloof. Now he straightened up slowly, one hand still on the rail, and gazed toward the town and its rim of lights along the bay.

He was of medium height and stocky build, a man who had been obliged all his life to fight against a tendency to gain weight easily. In the ten years since his wife, Winifred, had died he had lost the battle. He was not obese, but his features were blurred, his belly pressed forward against the rail, and before leaving home he had needed to alter most of his summer clothes. He had been nearly bald for more than twenty years, but when he was slimmer that had not seemed to age him. Now he looked at least his sixty-five years. He tended to walk slowly, hands behind his back, easing himself in and out of chairs as if his knees and hips were not accustomed to the new weight they carried.

Marshall strolled to the large room where passengers who had not bought cabin berths would sit and doze on the overnight passage to Corfu or Patras. He had already staked out his claim to one long seat by arranging his suitcases to look as if two persons would occupy the space. On the bench facing his were the man and woman he had observed.

They nodded to him as Marshall stepped carefully to take his seat by the window.

"Typical," the man was saying. "I should have mistrusted the agent when I saw it was not an official office of CIT."

"You should have. What if we'd been stuck here all night?"

"So you buy the tickets next time. Anyway, I suppose the jerk at the gangplank would have done anything if I'd slipped him a thousand. It's all fraud, fraud, fraud."

He was a small man with peppered spikes of hair and a wiry mustache. The deep circles under his eyes gave him a permanently weary expression, and the irritable, petulant tone of his voice added to the impression that he slept poorly. His companion was large-boned and taller, and despite the fact that her face was fleshy, it was mobile and expressive. At this moment it showed dour disapproval that reminded Marshall of a schoolteacher he had suffered under who always accused him of mischief he had not done.

Marshall leaned into the window, cupping his hands to see out. The boat had left the dock, and the lights of the town were receding into the black heap of landscape.

"Oh, well. On to Greece," the man was saying, and Marshall sensed the words were spoken loudly enough to include him.

"I gather you had a problem out there."

The woman rolled her eyes back and waved a hand.

The man said, "Agent in Rome cheated us. We thought we were paying for a cabin. Wasn't till we were on the train that we noticed he'd given us coach tickets. No way we could prove how much we'd really paid, of course."

"They all do it," she added. "They seem to find any little place where you might be off-guard, and then your money's gone."

"Abel Dworkin." He stuck out his hand. "And this is my wife, Monica."

"Marshall Littlefield. Have you been in Italy long?"

Two days later, as he sat in his hotel room in Delphi, Marshall found time to make some entries in his journal.

> Pleasant enough on the surface but somehow bitter and vain underneath. Or perhaps insecure? Often testy with his wife, but she seemed used to it, maybe even needled him on purpose. I've never understood people like that: the way they need to rub each other the wrong way to be sure the other person is there. Always sensed he might be judging me harshly. A writer. Asked him titles of his books so I could look them up when home. He launched into

a long explanation of how many stories and poems he'd written, but didn't have any friends in high places. Lack of books seemed to be everyone else's fault. She was looking at the dark window all this time. Heard it all often before? Her hand constantly tugged her skirt over her knees as if afraid it was riding up. I changed topic as soon as I could. Talked about how rough it could be between Brindisi and Corfu. They never asked about me.

Perhaps it was having that couple on the seat opposite me, or the simple fact that the trip to Greece was the most vivid part of our journey, but I spent much of the night recalling when I did this with Winnie. Remembered how I'd never felt so sick in my life. February, and very rough. After a while I couldn't even make it to the rail. Just sat against the cabin wall on deck. Let the waves and rain soak me. Cold as hell. Endless dry heaves. Thought at one time I'd just throw myself over. I was sure it would go on forever. Winnie helping me. Not sick at all. Then those three days we stopped over in Corfu and I had a terrible cold. Exposure? Dear Winnie. On our way to Patras and when the ferry was passing Ithaca she said quite seriously, "That? That's Ithaca? No wonder Odysseus avoided going home."

Everyone looking haggard at dawn. Dworkin pretended to be reading a book, but his eyes were not moving across the page. She stared out the window at the dawn, elbow propped on the windowsill, hand holding up her chin. She and I talked a bit. She started to tell me about the death of her mother the year before—how she had spent most of the winter in Massachusetts helping to care for her while Abel was in Duluth. Suddenly he spoke from behind his book. "No reason strangers would be interested in all that." Her only response was to turn and stare at him, but he kept reading. Gave me an excuse to take a stroll on deck.

Very bracing wind, but mild. I sensed Winnie somewhere to my right, slightly behind, like they say you still feel a limb after an amputation. I wonder if this trip is a wise thing to do. Decided I wouldn't get off at Corfu.

Ship docking when I went back to my seat. She was peeling an orange. He sat with hands folded in his lap, head back. Told them I was staying on till Patras, had already been to Corfu some years ago. When they left, she waved from the doorway hesitantly, as if I might already have forgotten them. Very odd man. Glad not to be bumping into them on some little island like Corfu.

I need to buy a hat.

He found a suitable imitation Panama with a wide, black band, and it amused him to see his jaunty reflection in storefront windows as he strolled along the docks before leaving for Delphi. There, in the evening he sat on the terrace of his small hotel, the setting sun in his face, the Bay of Corinth a sparkling sheet of water, and he sipped his glass of ouzo. Some tree was flowering nearby, shocking in the intensity of its sweetness. The sun lowered to the point where he could stare at its rim, and the water faded from bronze to aquamarine and finally to a shimmering silver. The carefully spaced groves of olives in the plains below absorbed the last pale light and then turned black. That night he slept so deeply that he could not recall a single dream.

With guidebook in hand and a boxed lunch in the small pack he had brought for such occasions, he spent the day clambering in the ruins, pausing often in the shade of almond or wild fig trees to read entries in his overly detailed guide. He ate sitting on a stone at one end of the stadium, uncorking the half-bottle of retsinated wine he had bought in Itea, watching the busloads of tourists be hustled through.

Climbed as high as I could on the lower slopes of Parnassus after lunch. Dry gorse, loose stones, my ticker telling me to slow down from time to time. Topped a small ridge and could see an upper slope. Thought it was white rock, but binoculars told me it was snow. Wonder if it stays all summer?

Sat for an hour there. Amazing view of bay, ruins below. Read about how they used to hurl the sacrilegious from the east rock face. Actually felt queasy for a few minutes. Had that feeling you get in a high tower or on the edge of a cliff when your mind suddenly thinks of jumping or being pushed. Could see a small figure (me?) tumbling past the jags and ravines. Watched the eagles rising in slow, wide circles.

Walked down. Not slowly enough. Turned my ankle just above the theater. OK, but will be sore for some days. Suspect Dr. Simpson is right. I've put on a bit too much weight lately. Made a vow before dinner to try to lose a few pounds. But lovely pastries with fig filling did in my resolve.

Dreamed last night of being flung from great heights, praying to sprout wings like the eagles. Do I accuse myself of betraying our memories, our past, by being in Greece alone? Since we never went to Delphi, I did not expect any tensions here, but there is no way to avoid a simple loneliness as when I woke in the middle of the night. Coming to a new place like this might be harder than Corfu. Know how much she would have loved Delphi—the regret complicated—not just that she isn't here, but that we had not included it in our trip when she could have been. Not grief through memory but greed for the future we lost when she died.

Athens. Thursday. Should have known it would happen, of course. Two things you can always expect when traveling in Europe. Bound to run into an acquaintance from home, and if you've chatted with someone earlier in the trip, you'll meet again later. I was in one of those shops just below the entrance to the Acropolis, trying to decide which kind of worry beads I wanted to buy.

"The green ones," a voice by my shoulder said.

Monica Dworkin. Her husband was at the counter haggling over a small marble replica of the Parthenon. Evidently he had not seen me yet. I should have recognized his sharp voice, though, which had been jabbing at my consciousness for a few minutes.

He joined us. "I hate this junk, but the kids will expect me to bring something home."

He held up the plastic bag, probably carrying a few Parthenons. Looked almost annoyed to have been discovered being a typical tourist.

"These." I selected the green ones.

"Well, this is where we part," Abel said.

Thought he had to be talking to me. I started to say good-bye again when I saw he was talking to his wife.

"That place in the Plaka. At one?" she said.

"I've seen the Acropolis too many times," he said to me as if I had asked him for justification.

She and I decided to go together. She had never been there. Abel, she explained as we strolled up the ramps and broken steps, had an appointment to meet with some famous elderly Greek poet. Not his first visit to Greece, as I might have gathered from his casual relationship to the ruins. He had lived in Athens for half a year before she knew him.

"How many children?" I asked. Two, but neither were hers. She's his third wife.

"I think I could find my way around here blindfolded," she said. "I've even had dreams take place here. I studied it for years."

They chatted for the first time as friendly strangers might, she talking about her attempt to finish a Ph.D. in art history, he about his years as a teacher of American history before retiring. When they stood before the last stretch of uneven stones, the columns and architrave looming above them into a pale blue sky enameled under a layer of mother-of-pearl, she tried to say something, but her voice was choked.

"Sorry. It's just too beautiful."

He almost put an arm around her shoulder, pulling her close as he imagined he would if she were his middle-aged daughter.

"Let's sit a moment." He guided her to a block of tilted marble.

They faced the oblique view of the Parthenon and the city below strewn to the horizon. She remained silent for a while, drawing her feet up onto the stone, tucking her wide skirt around her. She leaned her chin on her knees. Marshall pretended to be consulting his guidebook, but he did not focus on the words.

They were suddenly surrounded by a group of teenaged boys and girls jabbering in some Scandinavian tongue, paying no attention to a thin man with thick-lensed glasses who was speaking at the top of his voice and sweeping his hand back and forth as if trying to polish a distant lintel of the temple. A girl in a green smock stumbled into Marshall, said some syllables that must have been asking pardon, and then hunched her shoulders and giggled into her hand when the girls around her laughed. Their leader strode on, beckoning the herd to follow.

Monica shook her head. "I suppose if a child is yours, you see her differently. One parent's darling is a stranger's brat. I think about that because of Abel's children. I do like them, but I'm glad they aren't mine. I would have been a very possessive mother. Do you have any?"

"We wanted them. It just never happened."

"I don't think Abel would even if I wanted. He says he can't stand a child's first four or five years. But I'm not sure how much of his kids he really saw at those ages anyway."

Marshall began to say something about his sister's children, but the words stuck. He did not want to continue a casual conversation about children, but the shift in his mood puzzled him.

"I'll be late for lunch." She was looking at her watch. "I'd suggest we meet for dinner tonight, but--"

"I shouldn't anyway. I've bought a ticket for a tour of the Cyclades. Boat leaves early in the morning, I'm afraid."

"Then it isn't good-bye at all."

"You too?"

She nodded, laughing. "Are you following us?"

When she left, she walked quickly across the stones and around the groups, her long skirt swaying and rippling like the draped folds of a dancing maenad. He turned and walked slowly around the Parthenon, but he was not really seeing the structure. He was tired, even depressed. Why did she and Abel have that effect on him? He thought of canceling his trip. He stood for a while on the edge of the Acropolis staring across the haze and smog of the city. Ridiculous. Other people would be on the boat. He had loved those islands the first time. Just tired, hungry. Tourist's malaise. He decided to have something to eat and then go back to his hotel for a nap.

Chartres. That's where it was. Cloudy day, but still the windows were glowing, colors dark but rich. Winnie sat on a bench, I kept wandering, peering into the chapels. Remember returning to Winnie from the other direction, her back to me. At first didn't recognize her, thought she was someone worshiping, head bowed, shoulders moving slightly as if she might be telling her beads. Reached her, saw she was weeping, stifling the sounds. Just stood there for a few moments utterly shocked. Couldn't understand why. She saw me and stopped crying. I sat beside her, kept saying, "What's the matter?" She only shook her head. Finally she said it was because the place was so beautiful she was overcome, but she was looking away from me. She wouldn't say more. I did not believe her.

I remember thinking that night when I heard her sleeping beside me that I hardly knew her after all the years. And me. Did she know me? Everything fine the next day. We talked about how disorienting it is to be in unfamiliar places. Knew we were just patching it over. Until Monica this morning, I hadn't thought of that for years, especially how I finally doped out what had been troubling her, what it meant for her that her period had begun. George Schattner once said casually to me that he did not think a couple ever really knew each other until they had children. Then he was embarrassed and apologized to me as if afraid I thought he was lording it over me. So much for the Parthenon. What a crooked thing the mind is.

"Strabo the historian says that there were so many bald men on this island that 'Mykonian' became synonymous with baldness," Abel said as he separated the flesh of his snapper from its fine bones in the restaurant on Mykonos where the three of them went the first evening of their trip.

"Then I claim citizenship." Marshall swiped his hand across the top of his head.

Abel was frowning as he tended to when pursuing a topic. "Interesting example of a genetic pool, I suspect. Isolated population, gradually increasing prevalence of the gene for baldness."

"You said you've been here before?" Monica asked. She had ordered shrimp, but agreed to share with Marshall if he ordered squid since neither of them wanted to take the risk alone.

"The same trip I mentioned earlier. I thought I'd recall some things more quickly, but it's all coming in a very spotty way. I do remember Delos well."

She reached her fork to jab at a tentacle. "You're not having enough shrimp. Please."

"Memory," Abel said, refilling all their glasses with the white Demestica, "is never at one's command. At least the area of memory I suspect you are hoping for."

"Oh, I'm not sure I'm exactly hoping."

But Abel did not seem to hear. "Recall is more likely when it concerns dates, names, factual material—if you've a propensity for that. Sensuous memory, that seems to be triggered more unconsciously. They often don't mix well. But you're a historian. I'm sure you know what I'm talking about."

"I think they're rather closely connected."

Abel paused to work a small bone to the front of his mouth, nip it between his teeth, and extract it with his fingers. He waved a fork.

"Mmm, mmm. Take my father. He was a professor, too."

"Really? Of—?"

"Classics. Greek. Hellenistic period, mostly. Interested in what happened to the outposts of Alexander's conquests. But anyway, he had one of those minds perfectly adjusted to the field, or a mind that was fortunate enough to find its right field. Never forgot names, dates. Could recite poems he'd learned in grade school fifty years earlier. Daunted me entirely." He lifted his glass, took a large quaff of the wine, swallowed quickly in his urgency to keep talking. His eyes were looking between Monica and Marshall as if his father were hovering in that middle distance. "What I came to see in my twenties was that actually if I'd had that kind of memory, I'd never get a damn thing written. You see, I forget everything."

Monica laughed. "It's true."

He frowned as if she had been the one to say it and had meant it critically. "I say it's really all there—all I've lived— just as much for me as for my father. But my facts are usable, not tied down to time and space in literal ways that would make it impossible for me to transform them without feeling some guilt. Seems to me my father was burdened. He could never make a story out of what he knew. When I was younger and would show him something coming out of personal experience, he'd say, 'But look, your Uncle Morris wasn't even married then.' Made me angry. It was the story I cared about, not what had 'really' happened. Lying was never a problem for me."

His eyes snapped into place on Marshall, he waited a second, then returned his concentration to the waiting fish.

"I agree with Marshall. Most of us," Monica said, leaning to refill her own glass and pour some for Marshall too, since Abel's latest trip to the bottle had included only himself, "just live in a confusion of both memories—getting all tangled up with what's true, what's a lie."

Abel shrugged impatiently, placing his knife and fork over the last shreds of fish to indicate he had finished. "I didn't mean that, of course. We all do that. Another bottle, please."

The waiter grabbed the empty bottle by its neck. Dessert followed, some pastries that Abel found too sweet for his taste. He pushed aside his plate and concentrated on the wine. Marshall found his attention wandering as Abel's monologue continued, something about the nature of language and the burden of its past that he had been discussing with the Greek poet in Athens.

Together they strolled back to the dock where the boat was

moored, but just as they were about to walk up the awninged gangplank, Abel stopped.

"I'm going to walk off my fidgets. Not sleepy. You coming?"

Monica shook her head. She had walked beside him till then, one hand on his elbow almost as if guiding a blind man. She let go. Abel strode away, turning along the harbor seawall.

In his cabin Marshall washed his face in the tepid water, took off his clothes, and stood naked for a few minutes in the dark, gazing through a small porthole toward the open sea. The mild breeze, salty and flavored by a backdraft from land with some kitchen's burning charcoal, cooled his face and the hand he rested near the opening. For a moment he was a small boy who had dreamed he would one day stand at the porthole of a pirate ship watching an island filled with treasure rising from the sea. He decided Abel knew nothing about memory at all. His rants were either mere self-justification or he was too young.

> The day began as a bright, choppy morning, the boat at dock even tugging and bumping a bit at its moorings. Were warned that we might not be able to make the crossing to Delos if it kept up. But things had calmed a little by nine, and off we went, although the spray when we were broadside to the wind did wet all of us down some.
>
> I couldn't keep up with the group on the island. The guide, our Mrs. Stavropoulos from the boat, flitted ahead of us like a wren, and everyone else seemed willing to try to keep up with her. Irritates me that I seem to be the oldest one here. I can't get acquainted with the others, so I'm constantly thrown back on the Dworkins.
>
> The knee was bothering me again. No trouble with it since last winter and I'd thought maybe it was only a cold weather malady, but it gave a twinge as we

started up to the first level, and I decided to sit a while as the group went on. Monica came back briefly, wondered if I was all right. Told her most certainly yes, just wanted to take my own time looking at things. They were out of sight soon, and when I did start on again, I must have taken a different turn, because soon I was rising beyond the major ruins, up higher onto the slope. Wanted that, though. When I turned and sat down again, I could see them: small bodies straggling along through the boxes of some walls and columns.

"The breast of the sea," the Greeks called it, I suppose because the island rises out of the sea like the breast of a woman lying down, the rest of her just under the water. I could see back to Mykonos, over to the small island of Rheneia. I slowly began to have the sense that someone was sitting beside me. I even felt a slight pressure along my arm and hip as if a person were leaning or had touched me in shifting position. I did not say her name. I thought it. Then it was gone and I was embarrassed, as if I had been overheard by someone when I called out in a dream. I actually checked my pulse, wondered if I had suffered a small stroke. Nothing. I could see the group was not coming so high, and I walked down to join them.

I came around a broken wall to find Abel and Monica alone and leaning at each other in mid-argument—not the shouting kind, but when two people stand close as if one of them has just drawn a line in the sand that they are staring across— fists clenched and necks straining, whatever words getting out of the tight throat sounding more like guttural moans. In fact before I saw them, when the wall was still between us, I thought some couple was making love. I have no idea what it was all about. I tried to retreat, but my foot scraped on the loose gravel, they looked over. Her face pale and expressionless, his lips drawn back.

"Oh, hell," he said when he saw me, then strode by, spitting out, "can't you leave us alone even for a minute?"

She stared at his retreating figure, and her voice did not tremble when she said, "I'm sorry. He didn't mean that. When Abel's angry he flails." Her eyes were half-lidded, as if she had just woken up.

"I understand." I started to leave.

"Wait. Let's walk down together."

I was trapped again. Didn't want her to feel I was hurt by the weird man's outburst, but I certainly wanted to be elsewhere. Unfortunately we had plenty of time. We were not due to take the boat back to Mykonos for a few hours.

"You mustn't take his moods seriously. He's such a child. It may seem a little odd after what just happened, but we were about to go looking for you. Abel's hired a caique for the afternoon. He wants to cross over to Rheneia, that larger island over there. Says he's seen all he wants of Delos before. Would you like to join us?"

I looked to see how genuine all that was. Thought she might be trying to patch up after what Abel had said. Part of me wanted to say, "Not if you're that sick of me." I hadn't asked to be thrown with them so often. I was wondering if she had begun to include me out of pity—the lonely old man, should help him along, etc. But I began to feel a little stubborn, even perverse.

"All right."

We strolled down slowly.

"I don't want you to think our arguments are because I'm about to become another former Mrs. Dworkin. We argue a lot."

"Angry?" was all I could think to say.

"Abel's always angry these days. Sometimes at me. Edgy even when he's not. I was hoping the trip would help. His work just hasn't gone well lately."

"I gather the trip isn't helping."

But she seemed to misunderstand me, and in a quite distant tone she said, "I don't really need any help."

Didn't want to hear more anyway. Am I getting too old to want to be bothered with other people's troubles? I don't know why I could not sympathize with her even though I am beginning to dislike Abel immensely. It's hard to see her as a victim when she seems so thoroughly under her own control.

Abel sat facing Monica and me in the small boat. I thought he was going to ignore the whole scene the three of us had been through in the ruins. But he leaned at me, tapped me on the knee, and said something that began with "Sorry about" and was torn into nonsense syllables by a rise in the engine's rattle. I nodded as if to a deaf-mute, mouthing, "All right, perfectly all right." They ate their lunches as we crossed. I had forgotten mine but was not hungry anyway.

Rheneia. A very small dock, no other boats tied up, a desolate shore and landscape with little indication of ruins. As we walked along the shore, Abel explained: place where the Athenians had exiled the pregnant and aged citizens of Delos when they seized it and decided no one should live on the island because it was too sacred. After we had trudged along a treacherously uneven path, we came to ruins of houses for the women and midwives clustered near circular tombs of a necropolis.

He began reciting in Greek in a mock-serious tone, flailing a stiff arm with histrionic gestures, Monica fanning herself with her hat. I stood close to her to pick up some breeze, afraid to take my own hat off.

The heat pressed down flat as a palm in the limestone depression. Then I heard my own voice at a great distance saying very matter-of-factly, "Feeling sort of faint, I think."

I found myself stretched out in a cleft where the breeze was coming in off the sea. Alone. Utterly disoriented. No question I was awake, but might as well have been dreaming. Had no idea where I was for a few seconds—minutes?—some timeless interval that at first had no panic in it because my life was suspended. My hat and glasses were in my lap, I was propped at an angle so that I could not slip to right or left, and what I saw was the distant merging of various blues—ocean, sky, even some scattered islands tinted blue.

All of it, the landscape, the eyes I looked through, the heart I began to feel surging with slow regularity in the arteries of my neck, the breeze that made small hisses in the rocks as if paper were being shredded, was Winnie's presence. She was everywhere. Then I began to find myself again in a place of mere sea and rocks, playing out the comedy of an old man's inability to take the heat.

Abel came into my alcove but I did not move. I may have been whispering the word "Winnie," but perhaps that was an echo in my head. I must have looked in dire condition—eyes wide open, probably unblinking, body lax. For the first time since I had known him, the mask-like quality of Abel's face was not there, no defensive pose of irony or indignation. He knelt toward me. I tried to sit up, but he pressed a hand on my shoulder and kept me down. Already I had begun to feel better, but embarrassed.

His voice was quiet and uncertain. "I was afraid. It was like my father, his first stroke."

"No, no. Just the heat. I shouldn't have skipped lunch."

I wish I had been more accepting of his concern. But this unexpected intimacy of expression from him aroused my own reticence. His mouth pursed, eyes narrowed slightly into his more habitual expression.

"True. We're into the heat of the day. Monica's gone down to the boat to get some water, a cloth."

She came around the jutting rock bearing a bottle and Abel's handkerchief soaked with sea water. I drank the tepid juice left over from their lunch. Monica knelt and began to swab my brow but I took over.

"I'm not a lightweight. Hope you didn't have to lug the guts far. I don't recall a thing."

Abel was looking nervously at his watch as I stood. My head was perfectly clear, and standing in the stiffening breeze brought me around completely. When we reached the dock on Delos, the others were all waiting for us. Stav circled us like a sheepdog, barking us into the boats. I did not see either of them later since I went to my cabin and did not come up for dinner. Tired, but with that weariness that will not allow easy sleep, and I kept entering a half-waking state most of the night, floating in the jetsam of that confused day. Boats, ruins, a couple in clenched debate, and a landscape that was not rock and sea and sky but my woman, my love. I hope I am not losing my mind.

Sailed from Mykonos into a storm. Steady but violent winds, unusual for this time of year, they say. Nothing visible from the windows or porthole of my cabin but shades of gray—water and sky indistinguishable but for the white spray and foam along the crests of waves. Very few people on their feet by lunch, even some of the waiters looking queasy. Luckily my Dramamine took hold. Captain made the rounds of the tables chatting with the few of us who ate. He invited me up to the bridge to have some coffee with him and see the storm from a different perspective. We sat looking through the wide window toward the prow. Wind-driven water from sky and sea, momentary rifts that showed the racked, flung clouds. I felt as if we were traveling through the full cascade of a huge waterfall.

At one point he said, "Paros. There. When the clouds break again."

The first glimpse was a vague shape I would never have thought to be land. A grayish hump like cloud and water. Then a wide rift opened and the island was very clear, even some clusters of houses distinguishable from the rock and patches of gorse. Quickly gone. Did not reappear. That was Paros.

Dark came sooner than usual. Tried to read. Undressed, turned out the lights, and lay on my bunk listening to the clangs and tremors of metal, the nagging complaint of the propeller meeting varied resistances. No sleep waiting for me. Rose to sit at the small writing table, and this.

I know it was the worst argument we had on the trip. But I can't even begin to remember what it was about. Probably that's why it was so bad. Must have been one of those disagreements over something small that deepens and gathers fury because it is only the mechanism to release stored-up differences between two lives. I can see the restaurant close to the harbor in the town of Paros. Brightly white-washed exterior, inside also white with blue-tiled floor. I remember wondering if we would finish the dinner without making a public scene. Some self-justifying anger was high in me, a voice saying, "It's about time you put your foot down and made it clear this sort of behavior will not be accepted."

How goading Winnie could be when angry—those lips becoming drawn and prim, the eyes never looking at mine, skin stretched tight across the brow as if someone were pulling her hair from behind. Always made me want to grab her head in both hands, hold it tightly, make her look directly at me—like I think I would have treated a child.

Made it through dinner. We were walking back to the hotel when the whole harbor went dark. Bright stars and a moon rising, but the town, docks, streetlamps extinguished. A few voices yelled out. Then flickerings of candles appeared, the wandering fireflies of flashlights. We made it back to the hotel, were given two candles in sconces and some matches.

We would have enjoyed all that if we had not already fallen into our separate pits. I think that made me even angrier or at least more petulant, as if the fact that she was ruining a possible pleasure through her stubbornness justified my cause even more fully. I vowed to say nothing unless she did. We undressed in silence, lay down in silence, stayed as close as possible to our respective edges of the bed, and sent no messages to the enemy.

In the middle of the night power was restored and all the lights in the room, left on when we went to dinner, flared, startling both of us out of sleep. We rose blinking, collided while groping to turn off the glare like insects scrambling when a stone is turned over, looked at each other before the dark was reestablished as if the evening had been a bad dream, then let it become reality again as we went back to our separate portions of the bed. All done in pantomime.

I remember the knocking on our door, the usual tray of breads and thick coffee and a chunk of feta, bright sun and a spritzy ocean breeze washing over us when I swung back the latticed blinds. We said only enough to each other to be certain we were going to stay with our plan—a trip into the hills to visit some of the ancient marble quarries. She showered and dressed and combed her hair. I shaved and

showered and dressed. Like hieratic statues of a pha-
raoh and his wife we strode side by side, fists
clenched.

We were in a small bus with some other tourists.
We wound up into some hills, through sparse patches
of green, some very bony sheep. In the quarries
Winnie and I stood on opposite sides of the little
group whenever we could. We spoke to our companions as amiably as possible to prove to each other
that the argument was not really getting to us, thank
you.

The end was so simple. We were squeezing through
a small doorway to exit from one of the quarries.
Our hips touched. Then our hands. We passed into
the glare of sunlight, facing the path to the next cav-
ern. She turned away from the group, along a rut to
the left that climbed through some abandoned
chunks toward a green cleft. Her hand did not let
go, pulling me with her.

The path and its cleft twisted, opened out into a
small plateau with some bushes, a stunted fig tree—
God knows how ancient—and a view from its far
edge down the rocky steps of hillside to the glitter of
sea and Naoussa's harbor.

She turned so suddenly to burrow her face against
my chest that the wind was knocked out of me. I
flinched. Her shoulders were shaking. She was laughing at our usual awkwardness—both of us so damned
ungainly that we often bumped in the night and
made unintentional bruises.

She moved us toward the fig tree and its circle of
shade. We sat down. We had never made love in the
open air. We did not then, but almost did. Oh,
Winnie. Those broken stems of wild thyme I still
found tangled in your hair that night in our room—
the wide splotches of shade from the fig leaves on
the ground around us, your breath against my neck.

They were all waiting in the bus, hot and angry with us. We smiled and told them about the lovely view. If there is a judgment day and resurrection, I'll hope for a forgiving decision on a life of sins more to be described as ones of omission than commission, but I already know what the resurrection will be like. I have been there. There can be no better— a cool breeze slipping through the window of a clattering bus, the sea rising slowly toward us, her thigh against mine, head resting on my shoulder.

Now I will try sleep again, if only to see if I have succeeded in teaching my dreams where to go.

He woke to a world of bright sun, calm sea, and the circlet of Thira's lagoon. The first impression was so buoyantly magical that Marshall did not even pause to shave but dressed and walked up to the deck to lean and gaze down into the layers of blue isinglass or out to the steep cliffs and town perched above them.

Because this would be the longest stopover, the passengers were all staying in a hotel, but he decided to see if he could cut himself free of the Dworkins for the next days. He was weary of being berated by Abel, and he had begun to find that to be near Monica was inevitably to worry about her emotional state. Her cool silences were draining, perhaps even more demanding than Abel's abrasiveness, since at least the man could be dismissed as a crank when he ranted.

He dragged his baggage to the hotel's van and bought his ticket for the trip by donkey. He concentrated on adjusting his body to the motions of the beast, whose legs seemed mismatched—nothing else could explain the way that he was jostled up and down and sideways at each step the donkey took on the loosely graveled path. Slowly the sea and harbor fell away from him, the sky fanned out in limitless blues, and the glare of whitewash from walls and domes below made him shield his eyes with one hand. The higher they rose, the more he was drawn to look down. The old volcano's crater, long filled with water to form the lagoon, gave such a concentric clarity to the view that the downward pull toward some core made him lean away, into the wall of rock.

He took no tours that day and avoided the hotel as much as possible. He wanted to be alone with the town and its busy people, to wander the small streets, in and out of shops and churches, never quite focusing on wall or window or alleyway as if by blurring his vision he would enter the source of light. Objects seemed to have been constructed simply to display the light in all its levels of intensity—from flat and blinding white to a dying, purplish tint in the twist of some long corridor. And Marshall never lost the slight tension in his calves and thighs as if he were walking a narrow ridge between two immense pits, even though at times he could not see the ocean or any edge.

He found it hard to believe that this was the light arriving on his earth from the same sun he knew elsewhere. It emanated from below and from all sides, was trapped and glowing in the air itself, or passed through everything it touched to glow from the other side. He wondered if the light could be the long, unfading afterglow of that huge explosion of the volcano. Perhaps what he saw was the melding of two violent and molten sources—the sun and the earth's core.

By late afternoon he was exhausted. He looked about in a small square and found a stone bench tucked against a shadowed wall. He leaned his head and shoulders back and closed his eyes. His pulse was racing as if he had been swimming underwater and had just broken to the surface. He breathed deeply. His heartbeat slowed. Sounds of children kicking a ball on the other side of the square returned to him, some women gabbling brightly as they walked by. A breeze played about his ankles but reached no higher, as if his feet were resting in the current of a passing brook.

Would this island also have a special darkness? When light left Thira would the air be like the center of congealed lava or layers of pumice and ash? Marshall placed his palms flat on the bench on each side of himself. His eyelids were translucent and veined with scarlet threads. He was light and giddy and floating. He whispered his own name slowly. Then Winnie's. They were only syllables, and he was reminded of his childhood when he could not sleep but wanted to, and he would take any word that entered his mind and say it over and over again until it became the broken syllables of some ancient language that had no key. He would sink to sleep in a world that had become nonsense.

He opened his eyes. The children were still kicking up spurts of dust when they missed the ball, a man was leading a weary donkey loaded with sacks. The shadows were lengthening. The ball with its black and white checks rolled into the middle of the square, slowed, stopped. For a moment no one came to retrieve it.

The ball sat on the dividing line of shade and open sunlight. For the first time all day the walls and cobblestones and window frames and nearby tower were solid and fixed, coalesced from a background of light. Those two worlds came together for him—the flowing, insubstantial light, the fixed and unyielding matter in that stream—and he was at peace.

> At dinner I saw Monica and Abel a few tables away—they had been concealed by another party near me. She must have been waiting to catch my glance. She smiled—that somewhat tired or maybe only hooded expression—then waved her fingers at

me. Abel frowned as he cracked the claw of a lobster, his neck bibbed. Then he waved the claw, his face breaking into his usual contradictory scowl and quick smile. I waved and returned to my lemon soup. They finished first and paused at my table on their way out. Abel had not managed to protect himself despite the bib, and his shirt front was spattered with drippings of butter. He was picking at his teeth with a toothpick. Had I enjoyed my day, Monica asked me. I was so eager to keep our meeting brief that I said as little as possible.

My day's exertions, the half bottle of wine with dinner, the comforting sense that the journey was only a few days away from ending made me so drowsy that I barely had time to undress, turn out the lights, and admire the night sky. I vowed to save enough energy the next day to take a stroll after dinner. Even from my tiny balcony I could see how the constellations were barely traceable because of the massed layers of stars. I left the windows open to a very gentle sea breeze and distant rumors of the port far below.

But I woke to grunts, words not clear, and a pounding as if someone were being repeatedly thrown against my door. I opened it and Monica nearly fell against me, would have except Abel had the front of her blouse clutched in his fist.

"You bitch," he was hissing at her.

A number of other doors along the corridor were opened, faces peering out. I found myself staring over her shoulder and directly into Abel's snarl. But he did not seem to recognize me, and not once in the incident that followed did they say anything to me. They were totally absorbed in each other.

She lifted her knee hard. Abel's face paled and contorted, but he did not let go. He lashed out with the back of his other hand and struck her full across the face. Her head was thrown hard against me, and I tasted blood on my lips.

"Stop this!" I yelled.

She tried to knee him again, then managed to rake one hand across his cheek. When he swung, she ducked, and this time his hand caught me across the temple. I staggered back. She tore herself loose, her blouse ripped open, breasts bared since she had been wearing nothing beneath it. They stood panting, slightly stooped, like wrestlers about to leap into a new hold. Someone down the corridor was yelling, "Police, police!"

The blow had dizzied me, and my own breath was coming too short to let me say anything. Abel's lips were drawn back, and he blinked against the sweat in his eyes. His cheek was bleeding where she had raked him.

Would they have gone back to their brawling? For the few seconds left I thought they were on the verge of falling together into an embrace. Her eyes were wide, mouth slightly open—a look of ecstasy that I've seen on statues of dancing maenads. His arms were lifting from his sides as if to reach for her. But the police arrived, grabbed them, hustled them off to the office below. Of course, an officer came from room to room asking us for details, but I'm not sure he understood English well enough to follow my ramble, and he seemed to be performing a mere duty in the most perfunctory manner. His demeanor expressed a mild contempt for all foreigners, as if I too might be capable of doing something equally inconvenient. But he was helpful in arranging medical assistance for the cut on my lip.

I have no idea what happened to the Dworkins. I am sure they were only slapped on the wrist and told to behave themselves. Perhaps because they had not spoken to me during it, the scene in the corridor is a dream fragment for me, one of those dreams in which we create an image for the nature of a whole relationship.

But I had no desire to know more about their lives in any way. In fact, I found them so repugnant that I arranged to charter a flight back to Athens in a small plane. The idea of being cooped up on a boat with them on the return trip, of having to eat in the same hall, even pass them on deck, was so disagreeable that I would have stayed on Thira and waited for the next boat if necessary.

Am finishing off this journal at home now. Despite its unfortunate conclusion, the trip left me with some interesting matters of history and culture to pursue. The study of Greece and Greek art has become a pleasant hobby. But a peculiar simplification has also occurred in memory. I hold two places in mind.

One is the view from my window that I woke to on the flight home. I lift the shade and am momentarily blinded by a dazzling but cold sky. The air makes a steely hiss around me. I look down on the surface of my planet where a long spit of land is thrust into a sea that is almost black. It is a place that belies its name. Greenland. The indifferent ice sheds a hard glare of light. This is no place to live.

And there is also a space where Winnie and I can sit—a square on an island filled with light. We are there.

the burden of light

At length, the dead man, 'mid that beauteous scene
Of trees and hills and water, bolt upright
Rose with his ghastly face . . .
—Wordsworth, "The Prelude"

When Jonathan Holmes decided to go to England again, his wife, Gloria, had been dead for seven years. For seven years he filled every waking moment with matters so trivial and obsessive that they even entered most of his dreams and blocked her presence there. He took every substitute teaching job in local schools that was offered to him, some even as far as fifty miles away. Students groaned when told he would be their teacher because they knew he would assign two or three papers a week and would ask them to have conferences with him after school, but none of them knew he did this so that he would have stacks of work for evenings when he arrived home late and while he finished his daily bottle of red wine. If he worked intensely enough he might drop onto his bed and into a sleep that sometimes lasted till the first pale wash of dawn.

Gloria was always with him, a low hum vibrating in the back of his head. Sometimes he also saw her in the faces of people around him who had known her and could not meet him without thinking Gloria is dead. This subliminally transmitted message would make him realize that friends would never be able to see him without calling up his "other self." Well, he had to admit, he also liked them for that. He would not have wanted them to forget her. His paralysis since Gloria's death was like a black hole in his private galaxy, sucking in his weeks and months so that even the brightest days were only a glaze concealing the blank space, and shadows were rifts showing the darkness beyond. Gloria's arrival in his life, and her willingness to stay there, were the central miracle and mystery of his existence. Deep sleep was the only place where he found some peace and comfort.

Whenever Jon thought of traveling, he considered a trip to the Lake Country in England. He had been there twice with Gloria, once by himself. Since childhood he had loved the poetry of Wordsworth and often taught it in classes when the students were either bright or patient enough to endure his rambling discussions of various poems. But if he went, would he only be plunging himself into intense memories that would make her loss even worse? Whenever he looked up the phone numbers of travel agencies, he would close the book, sit down, and concentrate on practical excuses. Finally one evening he stood just outside the closet where some of her belongings were still packed away in boxes, his face to the door. This was the center of Bluebeard's Castle, even if he had only one wife hanging up in there. If he went to Coniston Water, he would certainly find her in ways not even the closet could contain. He could list everything in the closet because he had packed all the boxes and hung the clothes in bags. In a place where he and Gloria had been for only two weeks at a time but had been there happily, he would find her in unexpected locations and smells. He imagined her in Coniston Water itself, very deep and dark in places. How far would he have to dive to bring her to the surface there, if he wanted to?

Which, he decided, was what he actually did want. Enough of her diffuse and constant presence, the low hum. A resurrection in Coniston. Time to bring Gloria to the surface. He called the travel agent with the largest ad in the phone book, opened his evening bottle of Chianti, and cooked some pasta over which he poured the heated contents of a can of tomato sauce. When he was sipping the last glass of wine, standing naked in the dark beside his empty bed and in the silence of his house, he toasted Gloria, then his father, finally even his mother—all of whom were dead—as if to exorcise his ghosts. The next morning he wondered if that was the excessive glass that gave him the meanest headache he had suffered in years.

The first time Gloria and Jon had gone to England, her illness had not become apparent. By the second visit, she seemed nearly recovered. She had been diagnosed as suffering from either bipolar or unipolar affective disorder. The terms were confusing, and their doctor's attempt to describe the effects of either one was not clarifying. The consultation immediately flung Gloria into a depression deeper than any Jon had seen her enter in the two years since her state of mind had begun to show itself overtly. For the first time, as he sat in their bedroom all afternoon, reading while she lay on her side and stared at the dresser that hunched against one wall, unwilling to let her out of his sight because even his very brief reading in the library that morning had indicated that some sort of self-destructive gesture was possible, he was frightened.

In the beginning they never stopped talking about it, except in those worst moments, which could stretch into hours and days before the right drugs were found to keep at least the swings of her moods in check, although not providing a cure. They searched for causes. Jon began, like anyone living closely with someone undergoing such a profound change, by blaming himself, trying to probe Gloria for things he might have done or not done.

"Don't," she said to him two weeks after they had visited Dr. Salter and she was about to go to the hospital for more tests. "There's no point in all this talking." She had lost weight. It showed in the way her cheekbones had become more prominent, the way her slacks hung loose and her belt had to be cinched in, making pleats where they were not intended to be. She blinked, her hands clenched tightly in her lap. "It got worse. Maybe it will go away."

He did not answer. He was becoming more and more tongue-tied after the initial flurry of verbalizing that they had gone through.

"I can't explain this well since you might not believe me. I hate it but it doesn't frighten me like it does you. It's part of me and always has been. You just haven't known me."

That was when Jon understood what all of his palaver up to then was trying to cover up. What she was saying was true, and he was being confronted with the fact that this person he thought he knew so well after some years of marriage was a stranger in a profound way. He came back to this moment at times over the years, especially after the longer intervals in which her problem was so well controlled that he was lulled into forgetting it until something would initiate one of those deep withdrawals—perhaps forgetting to take the pills, or taking them in the wrong sequence, or times when the doctors altered dosage and new drugs were administered. When she died, he was forced to remember those words vividly: *You just haven't known me.*

The wall, he came to see, was always there between the one who was living the pain and the one who offered solace. The deepest pain was totally private, even when shared with others who knew it. Gloria tried attending some group sessions with persons who suffered various kinds of depressive states, listening and sharing and occasionally returning home with a sense of relief that never seemed to last beyond that night's sleep. Therapy never took with her. She found some comfort in knowing other people suffered from the same condition and were surviving, but she was not about to describe her own relationship to it or babble on about her difficult childhood and adolescence. Even in their own relationship, Jon and Gloria had taken years to tell some of those stories to each other.

Jon and Gloria met in Colombus State College's Evening Division when he was teaching a basic course in the writing of expository prose. He was teaching it in addition to his daytime schedule in schools because he wanted to make a hefty down payment on a new car since his ancient Ford was so rusted that he could see the road beneath if he lifted the patch on the floor of the passenger's side. She was taking the course because the advisor in her allied health program suggested it would make her a better technician. She wanted not only to write up her reports with greater clarity but also to be able to express herself more fully in any form of writing. He did not tell her or the other students that this was the one course he had vowed, if he ever had the power to choose, never again to teach. Nuts and bolts—distinguishing the Allen wrench from the monkey wrench, the ball peen hammer from the claw hammer—was the nature of the course as designed by the committee that oversaw it, and to bring a piece of literature into that setting was regarded as heretical. The students were not there because of any propensity for the elegant sentence, the rhythms of words. They wanted to know how to lay one cinder block on top of the other and then give it all an inexpensive facing of bricks.

Three weeks into the course she came up to his desk after class and waited out two other students who wanted to complain about the way a quiz on various types of sentences had been graded. He had enjoyed talking to Gloria before, about her reasons for being in the course, about her concern for dangling modifiers and how to better identify them. "They always get me in trouble," she had said. He found that letting his eyes wander to wherever she was sitting, letting his gaze pass over without lingering too obviously on her golden hair or the attentive, always expressive face, was a strong antidote for having to explain the proper punctuation in bibliographical citations. While he dealt with the complainers, she had been packing her books neatly in a blue canvas bag she always brought with her. When they left, he began stacking his books and did not try to conceal the very deep breath he took, a way to banish the need to scream furious obscenities down the hallway at the departing dolts who would never be able to distinguish a compound from a periodic sentence and would furthermore take pride in that.

"You really hate this course, don't you?" she asked.

"I'm trying to make a down payment on a car."

She did not seem shocked or upset. She nodded slightly as if she had already figured that out.

"What do you like to teach?"

"The Romantic Poets. Chaucer. Shakespeare. Donne. Milton. Spenser."

When he paused to gather breath, she said simply, "Literature."

"Yes. Anything but these bloody, naked parts of speech."

"Are you English?"

He began to sense that he was in the presence of a "hopper," as he called persons who jumped from one moving thought to the next, some of them going in the opposite direction.

"What do you mean?"

"Just the way you used 'bloody.'"

"Occupational hazard. I spend too much time reading through the heads of Englishmen. And women. I haven't been to England often. I hope to do so soon, though. After I get the car."

She smiled. "Will you do this course again? To go to England?"

"I decided last night, and tonight confirms it, that I will go into debt before I teach this course again. Ever."

"Are you going to make it through till December?"

"Miss Donnelly, I will. Please don't desert me."

"I won't. I'm getting just what I signed up for and what I expected. I understand much more about how to write the kind of dull and utterly ephemeral documents I have to write." She smiled again. "Is that cynical?"

"No. Accurate. Bless you anyway."

"I have a suggestion."

"Shoot."

"Do you like that expression? I wish people wouldn't use it. I don't like to think I'm shooting someone when I say something."

"You're right. Don't use me for target practice. I'm listening."

"Why don't you just teach the course using the things you love? Why don't you bring in some poems and give them to us? Surely we can learn things about writing from them or thinking about them."

"That's subversive, Miss Donnelly."

"Gloria, please. My parents used to call me that when they were scolding me."

"Gloria."

"Then be subversive. You say you don't want to teach the course again. If you do it your way, they'll never let you."

"But you said you liked the course. You're learning from it."

She was listening again, and he began to understand it was to an inner voice, testing the words before she said them, which was an odd contradiction to the way she followed the leaps in her thoughts so spontaneously.

"I am. But I think I'd learn more if you were teaching something you loved. And frankly, I can't bear watching you go through such misery. I find it painful."

She lifted her bag, he lifted his stack, and they both walked down the hall and out to the lot where their cars were parked.

They made some casual conversation on the way and then said they were both looking forward to Friday and the last class of the week. From that evening until the end of the semester they entered into a conspiracy together that brought Wordsworth and Keats and Coleridge and then Donne, Marvell, Herrick, Shakespeare, and many others tumbling into the room where they cavorted and sang in front of the bewildered faces of students still trying to distinguish the head of a screw from the head of a nail. He did not care if they saw the slot or not. Gloria listened and read and then wrote papers about the poems he loved in ways that allowed him to see them differently from how he ever had before. Which continued for all the days they lived together, unmarried or married—she helping Jon to see many things in ways he never had before.

After her death, one of his most tortured recurrent dreams was to find himself in the classroom again, seeing Gloria as he first knew her. She would be, as she usually was, leaning forward, her face concentrating intently, pen held ready to take a note but never moving as she followed some thought she would tell him later, her golden hair released in an absentminded moment. When he had finished the class, he would wait until all the other students filed out of the room. He would gather his books and papers, then sit for a few moments to stare at a blackboard scattered with equations from a math class, incomprehensible numbers and letters leading to an equal sign that in turn led to more symbols, undoubtedly the elegant resolution of a problem. One last time he would breathe deeply without regret the odor of chalk and veneered wood scratched with the graffiti of names and messages. Then he would stand, and she would stand too, and they would walk out of that place slowly, hand in hand.

On the evening before his departure for England, he sat in

the living room and untied his running shoes, deciding he would not take his usual run. A calf muscle had tightened two days before and was not stretching out. Maybe he would take a walk after packing. So he gathered the few guidebooks he and Gloria had collected, especially the *Blue Guide to the Lake Country*, and took them upstairs to his empty suitcase. The book fell as he stooped, and a note slipped out—two sheets of folded paper, written in neat and tightly packed lines. Gloria's handwriting. At first he assumed it was a letter she had been composing on their last trip and had forgotten to send. But it was addressed to him.

Dear Jon,

Please do not take this note as a cowardly act. The gesture that follows it may be, at least in the eyes of many people. Of course, I don't think of it that way, and I am hoping that since you have lived through all of this with me, you won't either. We have discussed the possibility often, and you have put up good arguments against it. I guess I am counting on you to remember those conversations and to read this brief summary of reasons, and then to understand. It's all too compelling, and I can't continue in this way any longer.

I am putting this in the *Blue Guide to the Lake Country* because I know you will be going there soon if you do what I hope will happen: continue into your life, especially finding solace in the places where you have found it before, your books and landscapes you enjoy. But none of this should be suggested by me. I am not trying to control your future life. I am only explaining why the note is in this place.

It is horrible for me to imagine that you will find me, and in my milder versions, I have one of the neighbors look into the garage and discover that the car is running and someone is in the car. But realistically this is much too fortuitous. It will be you. And then there will be the usual business of ambulance, police, investigations, etc., that must accompany any death and must especially be attached to a suicide since the act is so abhorred by our culture. Like other people who have come to my "conclusion," I consider the act to be inalienably mine and a gesture, finally, of freedom.

But I will come back to that. What I am trying to provide for you is some of the privacy I know you treasure so much. My act is private, its effects are very much private, and our relationship is no one else's business. I am almost as grieved at the thought of what I am putting you through in societal terms as I am by our loss of each other. You, the house, our lives will be swarmed over briefly, and all of our friends and acquaintances will conjecture, will commiserate with you but hope for clues and explanations, will make you feel invaded. Not for long, dear Jon, I hope. May they leave you alone soon. But a suicide note is a public document, and this note is intended for no one but you. It's our last conversation, which I, unfairly, have turned into a monologue. I know what you are thinking, maybe even saying aloud, and I accept the scolding. Maybe if I'd taken the risk of saying all this to you again, you would have dissuaded me. Maybe I'm not giving you that chance because I'm afraid of that possibility. We're not noble Romans and Stoics. You would not be able to walk with me to the garage, give me a final kiss, and close the doors yourself. But even imagining that provides me with comfort. As I go about doing this, I may well conjure that up as a final image to hold onto—you closing my eyes with kisses four, as if I were weary from a long day in the lab, and you, about to work later into the evening, have come to pull the blankets higher around me and wish me good night.

I am doing this because I am unwilling to continue the eternal damnation of the up and down, the pattern that no drugs have totally eradicated, and above all, the threat of it, which is almost as fearful as the hours when I am trapped in the whirlpool. Even when the pills are working, even when life for me assumes the kind of even-toned and monotonously leveled sequence of days that most people can experience (I'm not saying other people are dull, nor am I excluding the passions that can jerk us around from day to day—but we live with them and can cope or learn to cope, and what I live with is not directly under my control, hence almost not mine, alien, an invasion), I am aware of the fact that this is an illusory state. The real one lies just below the surface, the huge and undulating coils of some water serpent that will drag me to depths further and further down each time I go.

But now I will tell you a terrible paradox. Although I say this monstrous condition is almost alien, it and the struggle I have with it are more mine than anything else in my life. What is clear to me now is that whatever I know of truth and understanding is located in those darkest moments. I mean dark beyond all light, dark like being closed up in the core of a granite mountain. What I find there is the fearful center of the universe, not just my own dread and horror. I have never wanted to be there. I never chose to be there. I love light. But now I enter that place with a sense of knowledge. Or has the knowledge passed into the realm of wisdom? That darkness is me and all that is not me. Not to enter it forever and as soon as possible is only to delay the inevitable. Instead of having it be alien, something that seizes me, I will seize it and welcome it and become one with it. I have only been fighting my own fate for all these years. Science and medicine have blunted my understanding of this. If only I could tell you how clearly what I am about to do is to me an act of affirmation, acceptance, unity, the highest act of a free will.

My beloved Jonathan. I'm not asking for forgiveness. I am still too stubborn for that. Perhaps I am desperately wrong, perhaps this is all just chemistry gone berserk and what I think I see and know are delusions. Then tear this up and think of it in whatever way you must. I would never want to take away from you all that we have had by taking myself away. I hope all of what we had together, good and bad, will continue to live with you. I could never have come this far without you, and coming into your presence has given me all the light anyone could ask for.

Love,
Gloria

Jon sat on the windowseat and stared at the distant mountains across Lake Champlain. For a while he felt nothing at all. The letter had been placed correctly in terms of the Jonathan Holmes she knew. But it had taken him seven years to go looking for her or to risk the trip she anticipated he would take much sooner. She was right in one way: he would not have been able to give her that last, imagined gift of kissing her to sleep. Who could live with that afterward?

For some minutes he had been seeing a very concrete image, the one that came to him often, when he let himself remember that terrible afternoon: the chair in the den where she kept her computer, the chair she sat in while working on a report she might have brought home or writing letters. It had fallen over and was lying on its back, the legs pointing forward, the cushion flopped against the backrest. When he walked into the house that afternoon and, as usual, called her name, but received no answer, he wandered through the rooms, unbuttoning his shirt, expecting to see her concentrating on something so hard that she had not heard him. He entered the den last and did not find her there, but the chair was on its back, pointing toward him. In that moment he had no reason to suspect what was waiting for him in the garage, but he felt apprehensive, as if the fallen chair were a mute image of violence.

He righted it, then took a shower and changed his clothes, something he always did when returning from the stuffy room of a high school, its air reeking of old tennis shoes and decades of chalk dust and uncleaned lunch boxes. The ritual ablution passed him over from the outside world and its stench to the inner sanctuary of home: cooking a meal, the evening in which they would putter about the house or read or occasionally watch some television, always aware that the other person was there by the small sounds in another room, a cough, maybe a laugh at something read that would have to be shared. Often he would hear her voice speaking to someone on the phone, and he would not listen to the words, would go on about reading his book or magazine, and all that he would listen for were the tones telling him if the conversation was making her angry or annoyed or happy. And always he would find some way during the evening of reassuring himself that her medications were working, never by asking direct questions, but by concentrating briefly on her gestures, expressions, responses to something he might casually say. He did not think she was aware of this. He tried very hard to keep it as cloaked as possible because he knew it only made her feel her condition even more fully, and he did not want to seem to be questioning her ability to cope.

He picked up the morning paper, which he had been too hurried to read during breakfast, and he sat in the living room waiting for her to come home. By five-thirty she was not back yet and he had not even read the editorial page. He checked the kitchen table where they sometimes left each other messages. Nothing. But the dinner he had planned was more complicated than usual, requiring him to roll out some homemade pasta and then prepare a sauce with Gorgonzola and some finely chopped prosciutto. He set to work, running the strips of pasta through the hand-cranked machine, then hanging them to dry on a rack. The double boiler began to steam and he started on the sauce. He would go as far as he could, then wait for her, and short of actually boiling the pasta, everything could be ready. It was unusual for her to be late, but not rare. Sometimes a patient would come for an appointment at the end of the day and would need immediate lab work so that one of the doctors could make a decision. She liked the doctors, liked being reminded that what she was doing could be crucial even if most of the time it was as routine as emptying bedpans.

He took the double boiler off the heat when the sauce was done. The kitchen quieted down. He had not yet started to boil the water for the pasta. He went to the windows looking out on the driveway and detached garage, watching the birdfeeder. The chickadees were making quick flights to grab a sunflower seed and retreat to the branch of the nearby spruce where they would peck it open and discard the hull. A cardinal settled onto the rail to do his work without carrying seeds away. Jon admired his bright red chest and the buff female when she joined her mate. As he watched them peck and eat and jerk their heads around in pert watchfulness, he began to hear the low, continuous hum of a car engine and realized that he had been hearing it for some time, a drone just beneath the level of consciousness. He was going to walk to the front of the house to see if someone could be parked out in the street when his gaze focused beyond the birds to the door of the garage, and he saw the faint line of gray fumes exuding from its base.

He had no doubt what it was—the car engine running, the garage full of exhaust, the dim figure of Gloria lying back against the seat. But the door was locked and he had to rush to the bedroom, retrieve his key, grope it into the lock with shaking hand, fling up the door. He held his breath like a diver who must descend ninety feet and rise again to the surface without breathing. The car door was locked also. She was on the passenger side, legs drawn up under her and cheek nestled to the seatback, as she often rode when they were going on long trips together and she wanted to nap. Head pounding, chest clenched against the need to breathe, he managed to half carry, half drag her out to the driveway where he covered her mouth with his and blew into her again and again, pausing for any sign of her own lungs trying to fill themselves without his help. But she was still and cold and nothing moved, not even the eyelids, closed in such a relaxed and peaceful manner that he was not willing to believe this was death.

He yelled once or twice, hoping one of the neighbors would look out a window and help by calling an ambulance. But no one heard him, and he knew soon that he was doing no good. He went inside and picked up the phone. From where he was standing, he could see her lying on her back, legs bent and drawn up slightly, one arm flung wide as if she had been swinging from something and fallen. Later he remembered how he had wondered what he would do with the pasta and its sauce.

Some insensitive minor investigator felt obliged to berate him for moving her, but he was reprimanded in Jon's presence, and various officials kept making him go through the sequence of events. For five days he lived in a peculiar state of denial in which he knew he was being irrational but needed to cling to anything that would block the relentless image he had of Gloria walking to the garage, closing the door and locking it to give herself that extra time should one of the neighbors understand what was going on and try to rescue her. Gloria starting the engine, moving to the passenger side, making herself comfortable for the long voyage, and then staring unmoving at the window, the steering wheel, perhaps the dim contents of the messy garage. Surely the process had taken time. The fumes would have to gather for a while before concentrating enough to begin to work. But he knew her patience and determination once she had decided something. She might almost have waited with the curiosity of a fine medical technician. Would the first signs be a slowing of the pulse, a gradual drifting of consciousness as it is when sitting in a comfortable chair with a book and beginning to nod, losing the sense of which line of print to focus on, starting to insert a daydream into the text? Would at least one of those moments have been a sudden regret, a struggle to change her mind and escape? But her pose was too relentlessly relaxed. Then darkness. The darkness she was seeking. Home, as he learned she regarded it from the note in the guidebook he read seven years later.

He concentrated on the overturned chair. He took the officers into the den and pointed to where it had lain, his voice trembling with rage. He insisted she had not done this to herself. Someone had been involved. This was a crime of violence, even if it looked like a suicide. Where was the note, if it was suicide? His wife would not have done this without leaving a message. They listened to him carefully. He wondered if one of the detectives on the case might even have been conjecturing that this might be some kind of quirky confession from a deranged man who had killed his wife. They had not had the advantage of seeing her position in the car. Perhaps the detective imagined her thrown onto the back seat after being made unconscious in some manner, then dragged out when enough time had passed. Jon pushed the man's suspicions, willing to be considered the murderer of his wife rather than be left in limbo, because he was hurt, baffled, deeply violated by the fact that she had left him no explanation. Only her body. Only what she had already told him over the years. "The chair," he said, as the detective stared at him impassively, and he tilted it over into the position it had occupied when he found it. "We don't go around our house knocking over chairs and leaving them that way. Something awful happened in this room."

An autopsy was performed. The room was carefully screened. The car doors were dusted for fingerprints. Neighbors were questioned. The police did everything they should have, and within a few days they had no doubts and left Jon none either. No signs of violence anywhere on her body. No traces of chemicals other than her medications. No other poisons in her body than carbon monoxide. Death self-inflicted. He sat down and wrote a brief letter to the officer who was heading the investigation. He thanked him for his patience under the pressure of tirades. He hoped he would accept the fact that Jon was too bewildered to be rational. The man did not write back. He telephoned and let Jon know that he had not been the least bit put out by his behavior. Very understandable. He had seen much worse. He hoped Jon understood how very sorry he and his colleagues were, and if anyone could help, to please let them know. Jon thanked him. He tried to sound as though he had returned to his more normal behavior. He even tried to reassure the detective that Gloria's death was "not unexpected, you know, given the long struggle with her disability." He made it sound like the first stage of his recovery. He wanted them to leave him alone.

But it *was* unexpected. Yes, he had imagined it often, but that afternoon when he made pasta and watched the chickadees finish off their day with sunflower seeds, he was not expecting her to die. Her death would always be unexpected because otherwise it would become acceptable. And no, he did not accept Gloria's death. Some part of him would always be furious at her. He was willing to continue the argument until he found his own way into the center of that stone—or perhaps into greater light than he had ever known.

Whatever her letter had brought to mind was not new. No totally forgotten or ignored memories were released. But the ragged intensity, the randomness with which they returned buffeted him all evening. He had never been able to explain the overturned chair. Finally he had settled on the assumption that one of the animals was responsible, most likely the cat, who sometimes, when climbing a chair to be closer to a fly batting against the ceiling, would topple it. He had to let it go at that. The chair was overturned. It was a fact that would always be simply a fact. Like the statement "Gloria has killed herself."

No funeral. No service of any kind. Some friends sent flowers to Jon. Many wrote or called. To any who asked, he said no, he had decided Gloria would have preferred only the simple message he wrote for the obituaries in the local paper. Donations to the charity of your choice. He was moved by a few letters he received from patients in the medical practice where she had worked. They remembered how cheerful and calm she had been when doing their lab work, how she always knew their names and recalled even the names of children they had talked about. He took the time to write each of them a note. He told them how that human contact was what she valued most about her job—not the hours working up the results. Her body was cremated and he kept the ashes, placing them in the back of a closet. After a few years he managed to store enough objects in front of the box containing the urn that he could not see it. He could never decide on a suitable place for scattering the ashes, but he was certain that someday he would know.

He could find no consolation in her letter, other than the fact that he now could be certain that she had considered the effect of her action on him, which he had, in his worst moments, sometimes doubted when no note was found. But for one of the few times in his life, he simply did not want to know. He almost preferred the ignorance he had lived with before opening the guidebook. He did not want to have the letter's words constantly coming back to him in phrases like the fragment of some song that would not leave consciousness. He did not want her way of seeing her death to come between her dying and what it meant to him. But he knew he was being unfair. Part of the problem in all this was the timing, and the fact that he had not discovered the letter relatively soon after her death was his own fault, not hers. He was not sure what it would have meant to him to have it a few months, even a year afterward rather than seven years later. Now, when he was reaching the point in his life where he could look through the bleak moments—her depressions, her death, his grief—and discover more and more what came to mind were their happier times, he was being forced back into another layer of mourning.

He picked up the guidebooks to England and held them, staring at the titles on their spines. Perhaps he would go no further than London, a city he had always liked but never stayed in long enough. For a moment he sensed his life stretching ahead of him interminably—twenty, maybe thirty years more—and he wondered whether he could invent a life to fill those years. But sometimes recently the days had a fullness even if he did not see what they contained. A certain fall light shining through the maple branches and in the window of the living room would either call a particular memory up or more likely some overlay that was her presence, and he would feel calm, glad that what they had found stayed with him. But what he was beginning to feel now was very simple: a stubbornness that made him place the books carefully in the center of his half-packed suitcase.

He leaned against the alcove wall as the light lengthened. No matter how dense Gloria thought the darkness was that she had entered, she was light to him and nothing would change that. One winter they went in pursuit of sunlight, doing something unusual for them since they did not like resorts and preferred to save their money to enrich their lives in more lasting ways—trips to England, books, concerts, some piece of furniture that she would find in an antique store that was just right for a corner of the house that had stood blank and waiting for it for years. The winter had been long and very cold. If it stopped snowing and the temperature climbed, the sky would turn gray again and this time the hard earth would be glazed with freezing rain. When the ground was bare, the temperature plummeted and the cold edged in from every corner of the house, working its way even through wool, flesh, deep to the bone. The medical practice had given everyone a substantial bonus at Christmas, and Gloria had set it aside for an oriental rug she thought would do well in the dining room, but the price was still too high and she was waiting for it to come down. By mid-February the price was not lower, spring seemed impossibly far away, and even her medications could do nothing with the form of depression that settled around them. She went to the store determined to buy the rug even if she did not have enough to pay, willing to take interest charges on her card for the right to assert her will against the icy winds, the intractably gray sky. But the rug had been sold.

Jon came home that afternoon to find her hunched on the couch weeping. He sat beside her and asked what was wrong. Had she taken her pills? Yes, yes, it wasn't that sort of thing. Then, sobbing so hard that her words came in gasps, she told him about the rug and how it was just right and she had waited too long and it was gone, gone, and nothing was right about this shitty winter and her idiot head and the stupid cups filled with everyone's piss and why didn't it just all go away? He held onto her tightly while she lapsed into wordless heaves, her breath hot against his collarbone. He was almost relieved to see her grieving in this way. This was not the silent staring at a wall or vacant window, the pit she could fall into so deeply that all she could do was make mute gestures to Jon from a distance—a nod of her head, a shrug. She was mourning like a child would who has been told she could not go to the circus because the show had been cancelled.

"Let's go somewhere. Let's get on an airplane and go looking for the sun."

She held still. "We can't do that. How can we do that? You teach, I have to work—go where?"

She turned her face sideways so that she was not speaking into his chest. He kept running his hand through her hair, along her wet cheek.

"I'll talk to Jerry about that place in the Virgin Islands he and Bonnie went to last spring. This sub job I have ends next week. You have some vacation days."

"You can do that? You never do that, just walking out on the next job."

"I'll tell the agency it's a family emergency."

In an hour she was defiant. She would fling the rug money in the face of the fickle weather. She asked him to call Jerry right away. She wanted to know that it was going to happen. In the middle of dinner she stood and closed the drapes. Stand-

308

ing a few feet away from him she slowly stripped off her clothes, and when she was done she leaned down and put her arms around his neck and said, "Dear heart, how like you this?" quoting one of their favorite poems, the one she had written her best paper on. He liked it so much that he carried her upstairs and they let dinner get cold, and before they came down again to heat it up and enjoy the rest of the wine, they made love slowly and talked for a while about how lovely it was going to be to lie on warm sand and close their eyes and listen to the ocean.

They did all that, although for the first two days they were plunged into another form of let-down that neither of them could discuss because they were too disappointed and the prospect of failure was too bleak. The weather seemed to follow them down the coast. Coldest February they'd ever had, the desk clerk told them, and it looked as if only Gloria and Jon had not known this. The hotel was almost empty, and nothing was more depressing than the dining room with only a few guests, an overabundance of waiters falling all over each other and their table just to have something to do, silence in the lobby that made their footsteps seem invasive, gray beyond every window that even turned the palm trees to pewter. They woke early, ate without appetite, took desultory walks along a beach clutching their arms tightly to themselves because they had each brought only one sweater. Even the seashells they tried to collect, tried to hold up and admire, had lost all color.

One evening darkness came much too early. From the window of their room they saw the strokes of lightning far out to sea, but each one coming closer. The storm crashed over them and hovered there for much of the night—waves of storms like the pounding surf that they could hear between each heave—and they slept fitfully, waking to a room made strange by its sudden coming and going in the flicker and blast. Just before dawn, the wind ceased, the rain no longer pulsed against the windows, and they slept deeply, as if being rocked in the slow, steady rhythm of the waves.

They woke to sunshine unlike any they had known, unrelated to the brilliant, edgy light of the north that etched patterns of shadow and pierced the cracks in granite. This was mellow, encompassing, something that made the air both billowy and ripe. They stood on the balcony, and Jon told Gloria that the sun looked plump and she laughed. It did. Everything did. Light made everything fleshy; sand was satiny with warmth. They did not waste much time with food that day. They slathered themselves with protective oils and wore as little as they could. They walked as far as they could along the sloping beach and sometimes ran and veered into the wide, tumbling waves, touching each other, always touching each other so that when they flung themselves apart to enter the water or scamper along the reach of a wave, it was only to create an excuse to be close again, and when Jon thought of snow and ice, he could not believe they existed anymore.

When evening came they walked to the most deserted part of the beach and took off what little they were wearing and swam far out into the calm lift and fall of the sea until, floating side by side, they could look back to the distant white walls of the hotel, the line of dark green palms above the strand, and he smoothed his hand along her side, the lift of her hips, her slowly moving thigh and wished they could be borne up by the sea like dolphins joining, rolling together into the depths and rising again to the oncoming velvet night. They swam back, and he reached shore first, standing unsteadily on sand again as if using legs for the first time and unwilling to accept the return of gravity's laws.

Jon stared back into the blood-orange sun that hovered just

above the water, spilling its final light over the ragged horizon of waves. For a moment, he was terrified. He could not see her anywhere. The sun full in his face, he could see only the bloody surface and she was not part of it. Had she gone under, drowned, been pulled down without a cry? He staggered toward the water again.

"Gloria?"

She stood, curved body rising from the water, sun turning her hair molten, and for a moment she did not move, his Venus emerging from the sea, his Gloria holding out her arms and waiting for him to join her.